INTO THE LIGHT

OTHER TITLES BY ALEATHA ROMIG

The Infidelity Series

Betrayal

Cunning

Deception

Entrapment

Fidelity

The Consequences Series

Consequences

Truth

Convicted

Revealed

Beyond the Consequences

and companions

Behind His Eyes: Consequences

Behind His Eyes: Truth

Tales from the Dark Side

Insidious

INTO THE LIGHT

Book One of The Light Series

ALEATHA ROMIG

THOMAS & MERCER

Published by Thomas & Mercer, Seattle

www.apub.com

Amazon, the Amazon logo, and Thomas & Mercer are trademarks of Amazon.com, Inc., or its affiliates.

ISBN-13: 9781503935150
ISBN-10: 1503935159

Cover design by Shasti O'Leary-Soudant

Printed in the United States of America

To parents near and far. The lessons you bestow may seem to go unheard, but each word is buried deep in the hearts of children. With time, those memories provide the foundation to carry us through to another day.

God gave us memory so that we may have roses in December.

—*J. M. Barrie*

PROLOGUE

An impenetrable fog cloaked the woman's thoughts, seeping into her being, binding and erasing everything she'd ever known. Before was gone. The only thing that mattered, with increasing urgency, was the present.

Desperately she tried to see past the darkness.

Nothing but black.

She winced with every turn, razor-sharp metal slicing her hands as she fought to escape the mangled cage. With only the howling wind as her guide, she searched for freedom, persisting until her bloodied fingers slid upon the vehicle's slick exterior.

As she lifted her face to the wind, sleet pelted her cheeks and frigid air contracted her lungs. Each breath was more painful than the last. Her heart raced and adrenaline surged while a low hiss and an overpowering stench of gasoline assaulted her senses. With a final shove, she freed herself from the wreckage, falling onto the wet, hard ground.

Still unable to see, she created visions in her mind. The offending odor of fuel wafting through the icy air became a monster's putrid breath, that of a dragon from a fairy tale capable of exhaling fire. Her imagination sounded an alarm that was both a nightmare and a beacon.

I need to get away.

As her other senses heightened, she moved to her hands and knees and began to crawl.

Right, left, then right again.

Without warning the dragon's fiery breath bellowed and heat rolled in waves around her, thawing the frozen air and knocking her flat. Thanking God that she'd awakened and gotten out of the vehicle in time, she hoarsely screamed to the darkness.

The darkness didn't reply.

She righted herself again and—inch by inch, foot by foot—crawled away from the dragon's heat, her confidence and speed building with each yard.

Then, suddenly, her head collided with an unseen force that struck her left cheek. Before she could process what had happened, a deep, commanding voice shattered her isolation.

"Don't!"

The single word echoed around her as pain, surpassing anything she'd ever felt, struck her lower leg. Crumbling, she collapsed to the icy ground.

"No! Stop!" she begged, unsure of what was happening.

With no sympathy for her pleas, the assault continued. Air left her lungs as her midsection sustained blow after blow. Turning into herself, she shielded her face and pulled her good leg to her chest.

"Stop!" the voice demanded.

Paralyzed by fear, she lay still, tears freezing upon her cheeks and her chest heaving with great, ragged breaths. Footsteps shuffled nearby before a new excruciating pain shot through her. She cried out as strong, masculine arms lifted her from the ground.

The clouding fog returned, settling upon her like a heavy blanket and lessening her pain with each of the man's steps. The scent of leather and musk replaced the odor of gasoline as the simplest question came to her mind.

Who am I?

Unable to find the answer, the woman settled her cheek against the man's chest. Her unseeing eyes closed, and she surrendered to the fog and the dark.

CHAPTER 1
Sara

In a place without light, I began to heal. Wrapped in protective noth-ingness, cold and pain no longer existed, concerns and deadlines were things of the past. I welcomed the dark, relishing its armor as it buffered me from the outside world. Slowly small recollections returned, flickers that made my body tense until I physically trembled. I recalled intense agony and an explosion of heat, yet my cocoon of blackness smothered the impending fire, keeping its flames at bay.

My mind sent signals that my body didn't obey. Helpless, my hands, feet, and even the lids of my eyes sat heavy and immobile. Occasionally actual voices penetrated my cocoon and infiltrated my darkness. With rep-etition they became familiar. They wanted me and, finally, I wanted them.

"Sara, can you hear me?" the strong, deep voice called from beyond the darkness.

"Keep talking, Brother. We aren't sure what a person hears while unconscious."

"Sara . . ." Warmth enveloped my hand as it was lifted from my side. "I'm here. It's Jacob. I'm not leaving you. You aren't leaving me." His voice cracked with emotion. "Come back."

Sara . . . Sara . . . the name echoed in my mind.

Brother? Is he talking to me? Am I Sara? Who is Jacob?

The obvious emotion in each syllable of his request impelled me to answer him, to ease his distress, but I couldn't. My mind and my body were still at odds.

The cocoon's layers that had been my refuge now swallowed my will. No longer did they protect—they strangled and suffocated, muting my ability to speak. The warmth of Jacob's hand and even the sound of his voice slipped away as I once again surrendered to the nothingness.

~

Smidgens of life scratched and tore at my darkened world. Slowly sounds returned, not only to register, but to linger—particularly one steady voice that called out over and over, repeating the name Sara.

The name ricocheted through my consciousness, and I searched for more, for more names, for faces. There were none. My only memory, the smallest semblance of recognition, was of piercing blue eyes. I couldn't remember the entirety of the face, but blue eyes filled the voids when the voices stilled and my world quieted to the steady rhythm of mechanical beeps. I longed for the familiarity of that gaze.

~

With time I grew stronger, until finally I was fully cognizant of the world beyond me. As if a switch had been flipped, my battered body was suddenly present. I was no longer floating in nothingness—now there was a bed below me and a blanket upon my chest. The beeps that had been the backdrop of my unconsciousness became clearer. A clean, sterile scent permeated the stagnant air painfully filling my lungs. Exhaling slowly, I opened my eyes.

Adrenaline flooded my system, accelerating my heartbeat and sense of panic.

I can't see.

Lifting my too-heavy arm and reaching for my eyes, I heard a voice. The voice that had stayed with me through the darkness splintered the stillness with a welcome sound.

"Sara? Are you finally awake?"

A spark of recollection flickered in my dark world. Jacob. I'd heard the name repeatedly in my unconscious state. Instead of reaching for my eyes, I reached toward the hoarse voice, toward *his* face. At the first contact, I flinched; even the tips of my fingers were tender. Trying again, I connected with his scruffy cheek and traced his strong, defined jaw. With each caress I tried to imagine what I couldn't see, but my mind's canvas remained blank.

"I'm here. Thank The Light, Sara. I knew you'd come back. I knew you didn't want to leave me."

"I-I . . ." Squeaks like fingernails on a chalkboard came forth as I tried to form words. "C-can't." Beads of perspiration dotted my skin. I closed my cracked lips and wished away the dryness of my mouth.

"No, Sara," he reprimanded. "Don't talk. Your neck was hurt, damaging your vocal cords. Just listen."

I wanted to tell him that I couldn't see, but he was right about my neck. My throat ached. Sucking my lower lip between my teeth, I snagged its crusted surface. When I touched my neck, the skin was tender.

"Here." A cool, damp cloth touched my lips.

Instinctively I sucked the moisture from the rag.

"I need to confirm that you're allowed to drink. We'll find out soon."

He took the rag away, but I wanted more. "P-please, more."

A touch to my lips muted more of my request.

"Sara . . ." His words slowed. "I said no talking. Don't make me repeat myself." He lowered his voice to a whisper and brought his lips close to my ear. "Obeying isn't optional. Remember that."

Goose bumps materialized on my skin at his rebuke.

"They'll be in here soon to question you. Don't embarrass me."

Embarrass him? My pulse quickened as I struggled to understand. What the hell was he saying? This wasn't right.

"They've told me," he continued, "that after all that happened, your injuries could've been worse."

Wordlessly I asked the question I couldn't speak. Lifting my hand, I found a soft material covering my eyes.

Whatever it was, I wanted it gone; however, before I could remove the covering, Jacob stopped my hand.

"Your eyes were also injured in the accident. You hit your head. They say a nerve or something was damaged—there was an explosion." He moved my hand away from the material. "Don't touch the bandages. They need to stay in place and allow your eyes to rest."

An involuntary shudder raced through me as I recalled an explosion . . . and heat . . . and pain. Understanding that the bandages served a purpose, I nodded my unspoken comprehension. Simultaneously a groan escaped my lips and pain stampeded through my body. The simple bob of my head had caused my temples to throb, drowning out Jacob's words, leaving only a sickening internal buzz that echoed and twisted my empty stomach.

I pursed my lips and slowly exhaled in an attempt to calm the bubbling nausea. As it began to subside, the bed beneath me unexpectedly moved. I was being raised to a sitting position. Trying to hide the pain the movement inflicted, I pressed my lips together and willed my tears to stay behind the bandages.

The bed stopped, leaving me sitting up. I had so many questions. If only my throat weren't hurt and I could speak.

Jacob's gentle touch erased a renegade tear from my cheek. "I'm going to take you home, Sara. We'll get through this, together." His mellowed tone, as well as his vow, broke through my inner turmoil, endearing this man I couldn't recall to me. As I took in his promise, warm lips brushed my forehead.

A cloud of leather and musk enveloped me—his scent. I again searched for recognition but found none. Any memories I'd had of Jacob or of my past were gone. He obviously knew me—not only knew me, but expected me to know him, to trust him. To obey him.

I'm not a dog.

One moment he'd reprimand me like a child and the next offer kindness and support. His tone when he'd reminded me to be silent scared me, yet the fleeting kiss upon my forehead left me wanting. The pendulum swing was too much and too new. Releasing the breath I'd held, I smiled toward his warmth.

Then I heard his footsteps walk away, and my panic returned.

From farther away he said, "Sara, I'll be right back. They need to know you're finally awake. Do not speak to anyone." With a sigh he added, "We don't want you hurting your vocal cords."

They? Who needs to know? Doctors and nurses?

I was obviously in a hospital bed. Once I heard the click of the closing door, I sat and listened to the room around me. Confident that I was indeed alone, I reached again for the soft bandage securely covering my eyes. Following it with my fingers, I found that the softness went all the way around my head and that under the material were hard domes covering both eyes.

My eyes could already be healed. How could someone else know if I could see? As the instinct to remove the bandages grew stronger, the word *obey* sounded in my head and I lowered my hands. Jacob had said my vocal cords and eyes had been injured in an accident. As I shifted, the pain told me he was right about the accident. I was probably more injured than he'd said. I took a mental inventory: my side hurt the worst, but my left leg came second. Reaching below the blanket, I found the edge of something hard, a cast.

I sighed and allowed my head to sink into the pillow. Each discovery was too much. Nothing seemed familiar. Nothing seemed right.

My cracked lips as well as the stale, dry taste in my mouth reminded me of the damp washcloth Jacob had offered me earlier. Fumbling for what I couldn't see, I reached beyond the bed rails. When I did, I realized there was something attached to my right arm. An IV? Beyond that I found only air. My shoulders slumped, and I tucked my suddenly cold hands under the warm blanket and rubbed my still-sore fingertips.

Beneath the blanket I reached for the fourth finger of my left hand and found a ring. As I slowly turned it, the smooth surface remained the same. I was wearing a wedding band. I was married. How could I be married and not remember? Was I married to Jacob?

Questions continued to come fast and furious, each one without an answer, each one more unsettling than the one before.

While I searched for memories, the sound of the opening door brought me back to the present. Footsteps shuffled about the room while multiple people spoke at once. Though none of them spoke directly to me, I seemed to be the topic of conversation. Struggling to understand the ongoing discussions, I listened for Jacob's deep voice. Finally the roar faded to a low murmur and then to silence as anticipation filled the room.

"Sara," Jacob said, breaking the tension.

With a sense of relief, I inclined my face ever so slightly toward his familiar voice. His warm breath grazed my skin.

"The Commission," he continued, "confirmed that you can't speak, not yet, but they have questions. Right now they need to know that you're hearing and understanding. So"—he picked up my hand—"I want you to respond by squeezing my hand."

I tried to keep up, but I had no point of reference. Who or what was the Commission? Why did it have a say in my care? Unable to voice my concerns, I waited as Jacob's fingers intertwined with mine.

"When a question is asked," Jacob directed, "squeeze my hand once for yes and twice for no. Do you understand?"

I squeezed my answer, ignoring my tender fingertips.

"Brother Timothy is here to ask you some questions."

Brother? Is he my brother? Do I have a brother?

I'd expected to see my doctor, or rather expected that he or she would see me. My mind spun. Brother Timothy was perhaps a part of the Commission. As Jacob's grip tightened, I sensed that he was genuinely worried about what was about to happen. This must be the situation he'd been thinking of when he warned me not to embarrass him. I wanted to comply, but I also wished he'd given me more prompting, more background. Then again, I hadn't spoken. There was no way he could know that I didn't remember anything.

"First," Jacob began, "the Commission wants confirmation that you remember me, your husband. You do remember me, don't you?"

I hesitated, wanting to squeeze his hand only once, to give him something for his dedication and support. After all, I recalled him in recent memories—he'd been by my bedside while I slept in the darkness. But I couldn't lie. Unless . . . unless he was the man with the blue eyes. I latched on to that glimmer of hope. If he was my blue-eyed vision, then I did remember him.

"Sara, stay with us. Tell everyone that you remember me." His plea swelled with emotion, not only in his voice, but flowing in waves from his hand to mine.

In this unknown world, he'd been my one constant. Apprehensively I squeezed. The room seemed to hold its collective breath as I deliberated the second squeeze. Finally I relaxed my grip.

Jacob sighed, leaned closer, and brushed my hair away from my forehead. This still felt wrong. Nevertheless I needed time to make sense of everything. During that time, I didn't want to fight the darkness alone. I took strength from his warm breath and adoration.

An unfamiliar voice spoke from near the end of my bed. "Sister Sara, I hope you recognize the seriousness of this situation."

Why did they all talk strangely? I couldn't understand why he called me *sister*, but by the way the small hairs on the back of my neck stood at attention, I recognized that whatever was happening was serious.

"Sara," Jacob reminded me. "Brother Timothy needs you to respond."

I squeezed Jacob's hand once to indicate I understood.

"She understands," Jacob said.

"If you could speak," Brother Timothy continued, "I'd ask you for a full account of the incident. I'd ask you to describe in detail your role and the aftermath. Since you're unable to talk, we'll begin with questions. Once I have your answers, I'll take what I find informative back to the rest of the Commission. We'll decide what should be passed on to Father Gabriel. Of course, the final decree regarding this transgression lies solely with him. The two of you will abide by Father Gabriel's decision."

My tired mind spun. *What decree? Who is Father Gabriel? And by "the two of you," does he mean Jacob and me? What have we done?*

The throbbing returned to my temples as Jacob's fingers unlaced from mine and both of his hands encased my one. I tried, again, to recall the accident, but incomplete memories of dragon-sharp teeth and fiery breath created an unfinished mosaic.

Before my mind was able to fill in the blanks or I could respond, Jacob verbally agreed to everything that Brother Timothy had just said.

"Sara, do you remember why you took Jacob's truck the day of the incident?"

I had no recollection of having taken a truck. If Jacob and I were married, wouldn't it be my truck too? I lowered my chin to my chest and squeezed Jacob's hand twice.

"She said yes, Brother. She remembers."

My face snapped toward Jacob's voice, sending pain surging through my head. I hadn't indicated yes—I'd squeezed twice, which meant no.

Brother Timothy continued, "Did you have your husband's permission to drive his truck?"

"I told you that she—"

Brother Timothy interrupted Jacob's reply. "We're here to get answers from Sister Sara. If you're not willing to wait for your wife's responses, we can have Lilith hold her hand. Sister Sara, yes or no?"

I now understood why Jacob had completely covered my hand with both of his. He was going to answer the questions the way he chose, regardless of how I replied. I squeezed twice—no—and waited.

"She said yes, she had my permission. Which I believe is the same answer I gave the Commission."

Brother Timothy went on with his questions, asking if I remembered where I'd been going, if I knew that what I'd done had been beyond my approved scope.

My approved scope?

My heart thundered in my chest with each question and each answer that Jacob gave on my behalf. In a short time, I learned details about the accident that I couldn't recall. Apparently I had been driving Jacob's truck to pick up supplies he needed. Since I'd been following my husband's instructions, I hadn't realized that driving alone outside the community was forbidden.

"Do you remember who was responsible for your incident?"

The room waited for my answer. It didn't matter that I didn't know who was responsible or recall anything relating to the accident; I wouldn't be the one to answer. As the silence grew, I fidgeted against the mattress. My leg and ribs ached and even swallowing hurt. I squeezed Jacob's hand twice.

"Yes, Brother, she remembers."

As the voices murmured among themselves at this response, a chill passed through me, then the temperature of the room seemed to rise. I wanted to scream. Perspiration beaded on my chest and dripped uncomfortably between my breasts. Jacob's grip tightened and I flinched as someone touched my neck.

Brother Timothy raised his voice above the din. "Sister Sara, your current physical suffering is a sign of the correction you deserve for your actions. God taught us, saying, 'I will punish the world for its evil and the wicked for their iniquity.' God doesn't punish the righteous. Therefore your suffering is evidence of your evil intent."

"Brother," Jacob replied, my hand still in his. "She just respectfully indicated that her intent wasn't evil. She did what I demanded. Her intent was to obey her husband. With the icy roads I should have considered her lack of driving experience before sending her to complete my errand."

"When Sara is able to speak, you'll both be brought before the Commission. It'll be up to Father Gabriel to determine if correction is complete."

"As her husband, I take responsibility for her actions. I guarantee that my wife didn't willfully disobey the laws of The Light. If she had, I'd see to her correction myself."

I fell back to my pillow, unable to comprehend the discussion around me. *Why is this happening? Why are they discussing me, without me?*

Mute as I was, with my eyes covered and my hand encased in Jacob's, no one but my husband noticed my lack of participation. I remained still as he continued to relay my nonexistent responses, leaving me a bystander to my own story and unable to affect its outcome.

Maybe this wasn't real, maybe it was a bad dream and the scene would soon fade. My stomach twisted as their exchange continued and they discussed my insubordination and correction. Each time Brother Timothy condemned, Jacob reminded him that my transgressions were alleged, not proven. It was as if suddenly I were on trial in my hospital room instead of in a court of law.

It wasn't until I heard the word *banishment* that their conversation again registered. Whatever had been said had apparently been the parting word. Murmurs floated above the sound of various sets of feet exiting, then finally there was silence. When the door clicked closed I released my breath.

Turning toward my husband, I waited for an explanation. Nothing. I was about to pull my hand away when I felt a tug on my right arm and a woman spoke.

"Brother Jacob, Dr. Newton would like to examine Sister Sara now." So many brothers and sisters. So unfamiliar.

"Are you giving her more medicine?" Jacob asked.

"After the doctor comes. He'd like her to be awake."

"Tell him he'll need to wait until morning. She's had enough commotion for her first day. Bring her medicine, something to drink, and let her sleep."

I pressed my lips together in protest. Not that anyone noticed. They were doing it again. Discussing me while I was right there. *Why does no one else find this wrong?*

"I'm sorry," the woman, who I assumed was a nurse, said. "The Commission hasn't approved her intake of fluids. Refusal of nutrients is an approved decree."

Jacob's grip tensed. "I'm quite aware of the Commission's approved decrees."

"I'm sorry, Brother. I didn't mean to . . ."

"It's been over a week. She needs more than what she's getting from that needle."

"I believe they'll discuss it in the morning since Brother Timothy was able to see and talk to her. They should have a revised decision by tomorrow. I can't go against . . ."

Jacob sighed and his grip remained tight. "I understand," he conceded. "Then bring me ice chips. If we hurry before they melt, they'll be solids and not liquids. That won't violate the Commission's authority."

"Brother?"

"Bring me ice."

CHAPTER 2
Stella

It was past three in the afternoon when I finished chasing leads—ones that seemed to go nowhere—and dragged my tired self back to the TV station. I plugged in my dead cell phone and collapsed at my desk. As I laid my head on my arm, I realized, only slightly ashamed, that I was wearing the same blouse and slacks I'd worn the day before. When I'd been out in the field, it hadn't occurred to me, but here, I was suddenly self-conscious.

I must've bumped my mouse, because a light brighter than the Michigan summer sun filled my cubicle, and my monitor roared to life. The number flashing at the top of my screen mocked my exhaustion, alerting me to the hundreds of e-mails all in desperate need of immediate response. That's what happened when I spent my entire day out of the office. Sighing, I scooted my chair closer and began to scroll.

Rarely did true leads pop up in my inbox. Most of them came on the street or from reliable sources. Many times they came from people who preferred to remain anonymous. It wasn't until the really damning evidence was discovered that names and sources were needed. Even then, thanks to the First Amendment, most sources could remain undisclosed.

Today I'd spent hours with the border patrol. It was a stimulating way to spend a day, watching cars pass from the United States to

Canada and vice versa for hours on end. The US Border Patrol wasn't keen on allowing reporters or investigative journalists open access, but thankfully, I had a friend who had a friend, which was the way most of this worked. Unfortunately, today it hadn't done me much good.

As I finished reading the second page of e-mails, my cell phone rang, its melody alerting me to my caller.

"Hello, Bernard."

"Stella, where are you?"

"About thirty feet away," I replied with a tired laugh.

"In my office."

The phone went silent.

I lifted my brow and stared at the screen. Dylan, the man I'd left early this morning in his warm bed, was right; Barney, as Dylan called him, was a pompous ass. The civilized world used salutations: *hello* and *good-bye*. Shrugging away my annoyance, I pulled myself to my feet and walked to my boss's office. Before I reached his door, he stood, walked toward me, and motioned to the chairs facing his desk. As I sat, he closed the door.

"I didn't realize you were back," he said, as he sat behind his desk. "How are you?"

I eyed him suspiciously. In the nearly a year I'd worked for him, I'd replied to every one of his requests for discussion. I'd dragged myself to this office, to coffee shops, bars, restaurants, and a million other places at all hours of the day and night. Never once had he stood as I approached. Never once had he greeted me with more than a shrug before beginning his rant. This new, unfamiliar adherence to etiquette frightened me more than his normal pompous behavior.

"What did you learn?"

I shook my head. "Nothing. I spent half the day at the border. Around eleven I followed up on some leads at the shipyard. I talked to some people, but honestly, nothing stuck out."

His eyes fell to his desk. Despite nearing retirement, Bernard was still a handsome man—tall, tan, fit. The only suggestions of his age were his salt-and-pepper hair and the fine lines around his eyes. Currently his hair was slicked back, his face was made up for the cameras, and he was dressed in a nice suit. Though the news wouldn't be starting for another hour or so, judging by his attire, he'd been filming one of his stories. That meant he would be needed back on the set to introduce the story during the five and six o'clock news. As I waited for him to look back up, it hit me. I'd never known him to look away. It was one of his things, one of his one-upmanship tendencies.

Is he going to move me off this story, or fire me?

I sat forward on the edge of the seat, my nerves electrified, waking my body with a surge of adrenaline. "I'll keep looking. You don't need to worry. If there's as big of a drug operation out there as they say, someone's going to talk. I've got feelers all over. Don't take me off this. I'll get the story."

His dark eyes peered upward, but I couldn't read his expression.

"No one's moving you off the story. This isn't about the drugs."

"But you just asked—"

"I don't do touchy-feely shit, but it's no secret how much we all cared about Mindy . . ."

My stomach sank. "Oh, God, h-have they, have they found her?"

"The medical examiner called for you, over an hour ago. She said she tried your cell. I tried your cell—"

"The damn battery died. I plugged it in at my desk as soon as I got here."

"She's not sure if it's Mindy. She only said it's a female meeting Mindy's description."

"Where did they find her?" I asked, afraid of the answer. "Was this body found in the river too?"

Bernard shook his head. "No. This one was found in an abandoned building in Highland Heights."

"Highland Heights?" I sucked my lower lip between my teeth and fought the bubbling nausea. "Mindy wouldn't go to Highland Heights." It was one of the worst parts of Detroit, riddled with gangs, crime, drugs, and poverty.

"I know," he said. "It doesn't make sense." He leaned forward. "Listen, I'm due on the set in a few. If you wait, Foster can go with you. You shouldn't go to the morgue alone. I know how hard it was last time."

"No, thanks, Bernard. I can handle it. I need to do it for Mindy and for Mr. and Mrs. Rosemont. I promised them I would."

"Are you sure you can drive? It's almost rush hour and . . ."

I lifted my hand. "Please, just let me go. I've already wasted time. The sooner I go, the sooner we'll know."

"Call me and let me know what you learn. Don't worry about coming back here tonight. There's nothing that can't wait, but call me."

Nodding, I stood and rushed to my cubicle. Turning off my computer, I grabbed my partially charged cell phone and purse and headed out, all the while avoiding my coworkers' eyes. I hoped it looked as if I were heading out to chase another lead, not to possibly identify the body of my missing best friend.

Skipping the elevator, I hurried down the back steps to the garage and got in my car. As I drove toward the Office of the Wayne County Medical Examiner, my mind filled with memories of Mindy. It was almost the end of July, and she'd been missing for nearly two weeks. I did what I'd done a thousand times since the morning she hadn't shown up for work—I remembered.

My mind flashed back to our freshman year of college nearly ten years before. She'd been sitting across the aisle from me in a journalism seminar. As I thought back, I believed that one reason I'd noticed her was that we looked alike: blonde hair and similar build. I remembered her chewing on the cap of her pen, reading our assignment, and I'd thought I had her beat. I'd already read it. That was still my approach to everything, always sizing up my competition.

Little had I known, Mindy had already read our assignment. She was rereading, because that was who she was. It turned out we were made to be best friends. Fate paired us for our first group project and sheer determination kept us together. During the next five years we were roommates, classmates in college and a master's program, friends, enemies, and everything in between. Though we'd do anything for each other—and had, many times—it was our competitive spirit that continually pushed us through the long hours of classes and studying, and on to our internships. Together we celebrated success and mourned loss. No matter what life threw at us—asshole professors, scumbag boyfriends, dreaded hangovers—we knew that the one constant was each other. Of course, that closeness never stopped our siblinglike rivalry, the one that drove us to be the best. We vied for the top GPA, and through it all, neither one of us backed down.

After graduate school we went our separate ways to follow our dreams. It wasn't until Mindy landed her job at the WCJB TV station that we found our way back together. At the time I was working for a big law firm in downtown Detroit as an investigator. I'd had an internship in a crime lab as an undergraduate student and one with Homeland Security during graduate school. Those experiences had taught me how to delve into people's personal business and spot inconsistencies. At our firm a client's innocence or lack thereof was never at issue—finding the evidence to substantiate their innocence was my job. In only a short time, I became one of the people on whom the partners depended to find answers.

Then, when Mindy introduced me to the people at WCJB, our friendship opened the door to my current position working for Bernard Cooper, the lead investigative journalist at WCJB. Not only did Bernard work for the top TV station in Detroit, but he also was well known in the industry. His stories were often picked up for national broadcasts.

The mere mention of his name inspired fear and respect. Because of him politicians unexpectedly withdrew from elections and corporations faced millions of dollars in fines. Corruption on any level was his to expose. Whether it was a scandal involving mob bosses, gangs, or the dangers of contaminated lemons at a local restaurant chain, no story was above or beneath him. Stories were everywhere—we just had to find them.

Since Mindy's parents lived in California, they'd authorized me to make visual confirmation should her body be found. Of course, they'd come here after her disappearance, but there was no sense summoning them each time a body matching Mindy's description surfaced.

My reminiscing ended as I entered the county government building and took a deep breath. I'd been here only a week before, asked to identify a bloated body that, thankfully, hadn't turned out to be Mindy. However, memories of the stench-filled examination room and the unnatural color of the body's stretched skin brought back a rush of nausea. Swallowing the rising bile, I steadied my steps and willed my investigative mask of indifference in place.

As I descended through the winding catacombs on my way to the ME's office, my mind spun with possibilities. While the number of homicides in Detroit had decreased since the early 1990s, so had the population. Detroit still had the dubious distinction of one of the highest violent crime rates in the nation. The city where I lived and my best friend had disappeared was dangerous, and I was about to witness another of its casualties. I'd encountered death in the course of my job—often. But that was different. That was work. This was personal.

As I rounded the final corner, I stopped and my eyes locked on the compassionate but piercing stare of Dylan Richards.

"Why are you here?" I asked.

His confident swagger disappeared as he moved silently toward me. Each step measured the time I stood rooted to the tile.

"I didn't want you to do this alone," he said, reaching for my hands. His warmth enveloped my fingers, making me suddenly aware of the coolness of my own body.

"How did you know to come here? Do you know that this is her?" My anxiety rose with each question, as did the pitch of my voice. "Have you seen her?"

He shook his head. "I haven't seen her, and I don't know. I was at the police station and heard the buzz. I tried to reach you, but your phone went to voice mail. I sent you a couple of texts. When you didn't answer, I took a chance and called Barney. He told me that he'd just told you about this." Dylan squeezed my hand again. "Like I said, I didn't want you to do this alone."

CHAPTER 3
Sara

The moment the nurse left, Jacob wordlessly released my hand, scooted his chair across the floor, and began pacing, his footsteps sounding from near the foot of my bed. I didn't need to see him to know his mood—his irritation was evident in each stomp. I waited for him to say something about what had just happened. I wanted him to explain who Brother Timothy and Father Gabriel were and what power they possessed. I wanted to know how these men had the right to withhold water from me or anyone else. I wanted to understand the allegations that Brother Timothy mentioned. I needed answers.

Though it seemed as if Jacob had defended me and my behavior, he'd also lied and answered each question without regard for my response. I wanted to understand why he'd done that. With each strike of his hard-soled shoes that drummed a staccato beat across the tile floor, I sensed his unease as mine grew.

The rhythm of Jacob's pacing monopolized my thoughts, playing in a loop with a four-four count: four strides to cross the width of the room, the fourth step containing a scuff—his turn—then four strides back again.

My mind swirled with theories. Maybe we'd argued before the accident. Maybe he hadn't sent me out on the icy roads. Each thought increased my anxiety, causing it to rise degree by degree until it neared the boiling point. I imagined the man who continued to pace. The vision I created had blue eyes and a scruffy jaw. I wasn't sure if that image was my memory returning or an imagined portrait based on the feel of his hands and face.

Suddenly my heart stilled as a loud knock echoed throughout the room. Pressing my lips together, I cringed at the thought of someone from the Commission returning.

"I have the ice chips," the nurse said, with the opening of the door. "Would you like me to feed Sara?"

Internally I groaned. Again I wasn't being addressed, only spoken about. After all, I *was* Sara. *Maybe someone can ask me?*

Before I had time to dwell on my lack of autonomy, Jacob replied, "No, give me the cup. I'll take care of it."

"It's my assignment—"

"Sister, if we hurry before the ice melts, it won't violate the Commission's authority. But if the Commission decides that ice is a fluid, it'll be my responsibility, not yours. I asked for ice and you brought it to *me*, not Sara."

"Thank you," she replied. "I won't mention it."

"But if it's mentioned," he said with authority, "you gave the ice to *me*."

"Yes, Brother. Do you need anything else?"

"Sara's medication. Dr. Newton said her body heals best while she sleeps."

"I'll get it, but first I'll give you some time with your ice. The sleep medication works very fast."

Seconds later the door clicked shut and, judging by the silence, I believed the nurse had left. Suddenly everything I'd wanted to say and learn dissolved under my growing need for the moisture of the ice chips. Unconsciously my tongue darted to my chapped, cracked lips as I waited for the cool wetness Jacob controlled.

Finally I heard Jacob scoot the chair beside my bed closer. In my mind I'd created images of my tiny world. In those images the cushion of the chair where Jacob sat was covered in plastic or vinyl. I didn't know the color but had determined the material by the hiss it made as he lowered his weight.

Jacob brushed my cheek, wiping away a tear that I hadn't realized I'd shed. I turned away from his touch. This wasn't right. I couldn't put my finger on my reasoning, but deep down I didn't believe I was someone who cried or allowed others to control my every move. Jacob pulled my chin back toward him. I waited for his words of support and encouragement. They didn't come. Instead he simply demanded, "Open your mouth."

The bristling of my spine told me to fight, but if I did, I wouldn't get the moisture my body craved. After only a moment's hesitation, I did as he instructed. My reward for obeying came in the form of a tiny sliver of ice. It wasn't much, but the cold moisture felt like rain on the dry cracked earth. Closing my lips, I savored the clean, fresh goodness sliding down my throat.

"Again."

I did as he said, wanting more: more ice, more water, more of his deep voice. I was tired of the silence, and judging by Jacob's earlier pacing, he had things he wanted to say. I waited, but other than the sound of his directives, the stillness lingered. Over and over, I opened my mouth, and each time he fed me chips of ice. Soon we fell into a rhythm, and even his directives disappeared. Each time, I'd swallow and then immediately open my lips, unashamedly greedy for the next piece of heavenly coolness. As my throat numbed, I wondered if I'd ever enjoyed frozen water as much as I did at this moment. My new obsession with devouring the entire cup superseded my wish to hear him speak. My concerns temporarily disappeared into a calming fog as his fingers brushed my lips and I contentedly took what he gave.

Suddenly the door opened and our forged connection shattered. I quickly closed my mouth as Jacob's chair moved. In those few seconds, my heart skipped a beat, and I feared the sound of Brother Timothy's voice. Instead I heard Jacob speak to the nurse, calling her by name, Sister Raquel.

As they discussed my medications and she tugged on my IV, I tried to recall all the things I'd wanted to say. I wanted to tell Jacob that I didn't remember the accident, the Commission, The Light, or even him. I wanted answers, to know more about us, who we were, and why we'd come to be somewhere that felt so wrong.

My questions were on the tip of my tongue, yet I couldn't ask them. It wasn't only because he'd told me not to talk; it was as if their urgency was fading. It took all my might to hold on to them. Fatigue hit me like a freight train, causing Jacob's and Sister Raquel's words to slur and my limbs to grow increasingly heavy. In no time at all, my tiny, unfamiliar world floated away.

~

As I woke slowly from a deep sleep, my mind lingered in that space where the world was both a dream and a reality. It wasn't until I tried to open my eyes and found only darkness that everything came rushing back. *Everything* . . . that word normally encompassed so much. But now, to me, it meant only recalling what had happened the day before.

My name is Sara. My husband's name is Jacob. According to him, our last name is Adams. I've been in an accident and am in a hospital.

No matter how I tried, I couldn't remember anything before the previous day. *Have I blocked it all out? Why? And why do my recent memories seem wrong, like they belong to someone else?*

I lay still and a smile graced my lips as I recalled the previous night's ice chips. I couldn't recall Jacob, yet his protectiveness filled me with an unfamiliar sense of warmth. Then the sound of the door brushing over the tile brought me back to the present.

"Brother Jacob?" a female voice whispered.

I waited, wondering if it was a nurse who was speaking. A few seconds later, when the woman repeated Jacob's name, the chair moved against the floor and my bed creaked. Jacob must have been sleeping with his head on the mattress.

"Sister Lilith, why are you here?"

Lilith? The name sounded familiar to me.

"The Assembly will convene soon. I was sent to stay with Sara."

"Why?"

"You've been summoned."

"Summoned now? Surely they understand I need to stay here."

Summoned? That sounded so ominous.

"I'm sure they'll discuss it with you. Each one of us has a job that must be completed. If one person doesn't fulfill their assignment, it affects the entire community. Not only has Sara's job gone undone for the last week, but so has yours. I'm sure you can guess whose job the Commission views as the most crucial. It was one thing while she lay unconscious, but now she's—"

"Now she's injured, unable to speak or get up. Dr. Newton hasn't been in since she woke. Instead her energy was used up on your husband's visit."

Husband? That was why her name sounded familiar—Brother Timothy had mentioned Lilith when he was here . . . had it been the day before? *She must've been in that crowd of people.*

Jacob continued, "I understand the importance of my job, but I've been in touch with Brother Micah. No delivery or pickup has gone undone . . ."

His determination increased with each sentence as he continued his defense. Sister Lilith spoke firmly but Jacob held his own. I rolled my shoulders and straightened my neck. With the volume of their conversation, there was no way I would've stayed asleep, not without medication. The last thing I gleaned from their conversation was something Jacob said about me eating. I pressed my lips together and waited for her response.

"Father Gabriel"—Sister Lilith's voice softened—"knows what's best. We must trust him, even when we don't understand his ways. Only he knows the plans and what's best for the community. If Sister Sara purposely chose to disobey—"

Jacob interrupted, "She didn't. I've testified. You were here yesterday. You heard Sara's responses to Timothy's questions."

"*Brother* Timothy and we heard your responses," she replied. "We've yet to hear hers. They're expecting you at Assembly. I'm not privy to know the thoughts of the Commission, but I'd assume that after Assembly your petition for Sara's nutrients will be heard. I'm confident that without your presence, it won't. Truly, as with all things, the decision is yours."

Jacob was part of this, part of some assembly. *What does that mean? And how can she threaten me but say that the decision is his?*

For the first time since the room cleared the night before, Jacob gathered my hand in his. "Sara, can you hear me?"

I squeezed his hand once.

"You won't be alone. Sister Lilith is here. I'll contact Dr. Newton and tell him not to examine you until I return. Do you understand?"

I squeezed his hand.

"I'm also going to call Brother Luke. I believe he'll allow Sister Elizabeth to come and sit with you. Above all, you must rest your vocal cords." His tone turned more empathic. "No matter what *anyone* says, it's important that you don't speak. It doesn't matter who it is. As your husband, I forbid speaking. Is that clear?"

Though his demand seemed archaic, there was something more in Jacob's voice than a dictatorial directive. Strategically hidden between the words was a warning, one I planned to heed. He wasn't so much restricting my speech as he was talking about whom I could trust. Could this be the reason for my accident? Were these people dangerous? My questions continued as I squeezed his hand.

"I'll be back as soon as I can, and then we'll learn what Dr. Newton has to say."

I had the distinct feeling that there was no love lost between Sister Lilith and my husband. I didn't know why, but I didn't care much for her either. Yet, for some reason, I felt differently about the Elizabeth he'd mentioned. There was something about her name that felt warm.

With a cursory squeeze of my hand, Jacob was gone.

As Sister Lilith moved across the room, the click of her shoes was different from Jacob's or even Sister Raquel's. After hearing her take a few more steps, I decided she was wearing high heels. Resting quietly against the pillow, I hoped again that this was just some long nightmare; however, it wasn't. With each passing moment it became more obvious why I'd blocked my memories of this life. It was simply too bizarre.

Sister Lilith's footsteps stopped as someone new entered the room.

"Good morning, Sister Sara."

I recognized Raquel's voice, and my cheeks rose. Finally I was being addressed directly.

While Sister Raquel moved the bedsheets, she spoke with Sister Lilith. The more I listened, the more I liked Raquel. She was respectful of whatever power Brother Timothy's wife held, yet at the same time she was efficient with her job, explaining her duties and what we'd be doing for the next thirty or so minutes. According to the conversations I'd overheard, I'd been unconscious for nearly a week. With my second day of consciousness, I wanted to move—but mostly I was thrilled to learn I'd be able to shower. Politely, Sister Raquel asked Sister Lilith to step into the hall. The awkward silence that followed had me picturing some sort of standoff. I don't know if that really happened, but thankfully, the door finally opened and closed and Raquel sighed.

Every part of my body ached from my injuries, inactivity, and lack of nutrients. Sister Raquel's voice reassured me as she talked me through each task. Before I could leave the bed, there were tubes to be removed. I had no idea what they were giving me through the IV. Jacob said it fed me, but I suspected it was delivering medication too. Once I was unattached, Sister Raquel urged me to the edge of the bed. Even sitting on my own took effort.

"Don't put any weight on your bad leg. Eventually you'll have a walking cast. This isn't it. We'll use a wheelchair to get you around for now."

She directed me to move from the bed to the chair and then rolled me to what I assumed was a bathroom. Without strength or sight, I was totally at her mercy. Throughout her instructions, she asked if I was all right or comfortable. Remembering Jacob's warning, I only moved my head. The first time I did, I expected the throbbing from the day before, but it didn't return. Maybe I was healing.

Now if only my memories would come back.

Sister Raquel removed something that felt like tape from my side, explaining that I had at least one broken rib. Then she fashioned some kind of covering for my cast that fastened tightly on my upper thigh. As she secured the material, I envisioned plastic wrap surrounding my leg. To prevent my leg from bearing weight, she directed my hand to a handle above my head. I guessed it was suspended from the ceiling. Holding tight, I was supposed to navigate on my one good leg; however, my underused muscles rebelled, cramping with each exhausting step.

I began to wonder if it was worth the effort until I sat on a plastic bench, she turned on the shower, and warm water rained upon my skin and hair. The clean scent of soap and shampoo filled my senses, washing away the musty remains of the hospital bed and tubes. Without thinking about the consequences, I opened my lips, filling my mouth with the water that continued to rain.

"Not too much, Sara; it wouldn't be good for you," Sister Raquel whispered, reminding me of the Commission's decree.

After I rinsed off, she helped me out of the shower and dried my skin. She wrapped me in a soft robe as droplets of water continued to fall from my hair, and she said, "Your hair is quite pretty."

I contemplated her comment and realized I couldn't picture my own hair. By the way it clung to my back, I knew it was long, but no matter how hard I tried, I couldn't envision the color.

Would I even know my own reflection? I was lost in thoughts of other things I'd forgotten when Raquel helped me into the wheelchair, handed me a toothbrush, and directed my hand toward a cup of water. Unsure what to do with the water, I hesitated, not knowing if it was a test, or if she wanted me to drink.

"If you're all right in here, I'm going to leave you alone for a moment while you brush your teeth. I need to go back in your room and change your sheets. When I come back, I'll bring a fresh nightgown."

I nodded. The little bit of water I'd consumed in the shower had merely whetted my thirst. I wanted more. As soon as I sensed that Raquel was gone, I drained the cup and hastily refilled it. At the rush of the running water, a cold chill tingled down my spine. I remembered Sister Lilith and felt sure that if she heard, she wouldn't hesitate to reprimand me for my blatant disregard of the Commission's decree. Nevertheless my thirst prevailed as I drank another cup of water before brushing my teeth.

Sister Raquel returned and whispered, "Elizabeth just arrived. I'm pretty sure Sister Lilith is ready to go, but she won't leave until she sees you again."

My tired muscles tensed and the water in my stomach churned at the mere mention of her name.

"Don't worry," Raquel continued, "They're both still in the hallway. We're the only ones in here. Before I take you back out, I want to get you dressed and comb your hair, and I need to replace the bandages on your eyes. It's not good for them to stay wet."

I sucked my lip between my freshly brushed teeth to keep from speaking. She was going to remove the bandage around my head. *What if I can see? What if my eyes aren't damaged? Then again, what if they are?*

Raquel slipped a fresh nightgown over my head. Taking in the soft material, I felt long sleeves and buttons that ran down its entire front.

Whether from exhaustion or from being disconnected from the medicine, my fingers shook badly as I tried to fasten the buttons. The water I'd managed to drink sloshed violently in my otherwise empty stomach.

"Are you all right?" Sister Raquel asked as she reached out to stop me from falling forward.

I shook my head, perspiration coating my freshly washed skin.

"I was going to change your bandage and braid your hair, but let's get you back to bed." Concern laced each word. "I don't want to be the one explaining to Father Gabriel why you collapsed in the bathroom."

Father Gabriel? Wouldn't she tell Jacob?

I heard the opening of the door and footsteps as Raquel wheeled me toward the bed. Though the footsteps sounded similar, they were different, letting me know that more than one person had entered my room. When my chair stopped, another set of hands helped me stand. I turned my covered eyes in that person's direction.

"Sara, I've missed you," the person said. It wasn't Sister Lilith, which meant it must be Sister Elizabeth. "I'm so glad Brother Jacob called so I could come to see you." From the location of her voice, she was taller than me, and by the way she held my hand and referred to me without the awkward title *Sister*, I got the feeling we were friends.

"I'll inform the Commission that *she's* doing better."

Our reunion stilled at the sound of Sister Lilith's voice coming from near the door. The way she referred to me made the hair on the back of my neck stand on end.

"Thank you, Sister Lilith, for staying until I could arrive." Though it was polite, ice rolled from Elizabeth's response. It seemed we all felt the same about Sister Lilith.

Sister Lilith didn't respond, but I heard the door open and, eventually, the click-clack of her heels disappeared into the distance.

My nausea calmed a bit as I exhaled and settled on the clean sheets. Elizabeth adjusted my cast, putting pillows under my leg, while Raquel, on my right, reconnected my IV. The way they chatted felt familiar and safe. For the first time since I'd awoken from my accident, the atmosphere didn't feel wrong.

Was Elizabeth my friend or, perhaps, a sister? *Do I have family, other than a husband? Do I have children? Are Jacob and I parents? How old are we?* My hand flew to my lips to stop me from speaking. I had so many questions.

As I rested against the pillow, their soft voices filled the once-frightening room with a feeling of friendship. My earlier bout of nausea had passed but the perspiration left me chilled. As if reading my thoughts, Elizabeth pulled the blankets over my shivering body. I managed a tired smile as the warmth enveloped me. Though I wanted to hear everything they said, in no time at all, their voices drifted away and sleep stole my first real chance for answers.

CHAPTER 4
Sara

A heated conversation infiltrated my dream, harsh words seeping unwontedly into the blissful scene before me. I tuned out the voices and inhaled the sweet scent of lavender. Step by step, I traveled across a purple-dotted meadow as tall grass brushed my bare legs. As I paused under the sun's rays, my toes sank into the soft, cool ground and my skin radiated warmth. On the horizon, pink and purple clouds swirled together like paint upon a canvas. The brilliant sky was like a pair of blue eyes, shining with happiness.

The voice's clatter wafted in ripples, small at first and only a word or two. But then it crashed like waves upon a beach destined to bear a hurricane's wrath, each burst larger and louder than the one before.

I scanned the horizon in search of peace. The colorful clouds turned dark and ominous, bubbling and swirling above, changing the crystal-clear hues to varying shades of gray. I stood in awe of the building storm, while the wind howled and long hair whipped violently about my face.

The louder the wind roared, the more acutely aware I became of my impending doom. Panic swelled as strands of blonde tingled with electricity. Scanning in all directions, I sought shelter from the storm and then the harsh voices awoke me.

"I'll need confirmation," an unfamiliar voice boomed.

"You have it, from me," Jacob growled. "Have you forgotten that I'm a member of the Assembly?"

"The Assembly is under the Commission. The decree came from the Commission."

"Then call them. Ask! I stood before them and talked for nearly an hour. Father Gabriel himself gave the approval. I want food in here before she wakes. She hasn't eaten anything in nearly a week. I'm not waiting any longer."

"Calm down. You're going to wake her."

"I'm past calm. Tell me what she can eat."

"If—"

"Not if," Jacob interjected. "*What* can her body tolerate?"

"When I receive word that the decree has been lifted, we'll need to start her with a bland diet: Jell-O, soup, rice. She could have some bread, but not too much."

"Then go. Have it prepared. I told you the decree's been removed. If you don't believe me, call them."

"I can't question the Commission. It's up to them to notify me." The unfamiliar voice gasped, then pleaded, "No, don't call . . ."

"This has gone on long enough," Jacob said. His voice remained fierce but sounded more in control. "Hello, Brother Daniel. I'm with Dr. Newton. Apparently he hasn't received the message regarding my wife . . . Yes, he's here . . . I told him . . . Yes, let me hand him the phone."

Jacob was arguing with my doctor? What kind of doctor was this? Surely there had to be more doctors in this hospital, people not under the control of the Commission.

"Hello, Brother Daniel?" Dr. Newton's greeting came out more like a question. "Yes, I realize he is . . . Yes, I understand that the Assembly is a governing party and as a member his word is true. I wanted to be . . . Right away. Good-bye." There was a pause, then Dr. Newton continued, "Brother Jacob, I'll have Sister Deborah bring in food."

Jacob exhaled.

The doctor's tone became commanding as he moved closer to my bed. "You should wake her and take her to the bathroom. She's no longer catheterized and can't get out of the bed alone. That cast isn't for walking." There was a tug on my IV. "She'll have one that she can walk on once I receive approval. I'll return after she's eaten. It's past time for my exam."

"Thank you." Though the thunder was gone from Jacob's voice, the storm was still present. "You should understand my insistence. I'm not losing her to starvation, not after all she's been through."

"I do, but you know that we all have rules. My oath is to help people, but I too have a family. Following decrees isn't optional. We all know that."

"Yes, we do," Jacob said defiantly. "That won't happen this time. I won't allow it."

The doctor's words brought my reality back with a vengeance. I was at the mercy of these people, people I couldn't see or remember. People with frightening tones, rules, and decrees. I clenched my teeth and searched my memories for anything. Anything to confirm that I belonged here, or anything to confirm that I didn't.

Jacob approached, brushing my hair away from my forehead, and spoke. "I'm sure you're awake. I don't think even you could sleep through that."

Even me? What does he mean?

I nodded. As his large hand lingered on my hair, I remembered part of my dream and wondered if my hair was blonde.

"Sara, the nurse will bring you some food. Dr. Newton wants me to help you get up before she comes."

I reached up to my eyes. Though I felt the dampness of my hair, the bandages were dry.

"Sister Raquel replaced your bandages." His fingers raked my hair. "But she couldn't brush or braid your hair with you asleep."

A lump formed in my chest. She'd changed my bandages and I'd missed it.

"I'm going to lift you from the bed."

The blankets moved and cool air permeated my warm haven, but before the chill registered, Jacob's arms cradled my back and legs. I winced as he lifted me. Pain emanated from my side. Sucking in a breath, I braced for him to set me in the wheelchair, but he didn't. Instead he held me close and stepped effortlessly away from the bed. Reaching toward him, my hands spanned the breadth of his shoulders and came to rest upon his chest. Laying my cheek against his soft shirt, I inhaled the scent of leather and musk. With each step his scruffy chin brushed the top of my head. For only a second, something triggered a memory, but just as quickly it was gone.

We had apparently crossed the room, since Jacob said, "We're in the bathroom. Raquel said you did well this morning, though I'm not sure how much of this you can do on your own."

I reached up and pointed, hoping he'd see the handle that I'd used earlier. He must have, because he gently placed my good foot on the floor and directed my hand to the handle. At the thought of what I needed to do, blood rushed to my cheeks. I quickly lowered my chin, not wanting Jacob to sense my embarrassment. After all, he didn't know that to me he was a stranger. To him we were married. He'd no doubt seen me naked many times.

His large hands framed my cheeks and lifted my face toward his. Though I couldn't see him, we were very close. His warm breath tickled my nose, and his words were soft and reassuring. "I'd leave you alone for privacy, but the way you're shaking, I'm afraid you might fall."

I blindly lifted my face toward the handle. The apparatuses that held it in place clinked with my movements. I hadn't realized how badly my hands and legs were trembling.

"Let me help you," he offered as he released my face.

My trembling eased at his tone. It was as if he was asking instead of telling. Nodding my approval, I released the handle and placed my hands on his chest. Slowly he moved his hands to the hem of my nightgown. As he moved my gown slowly upward, his pulse beneath my hands quickened. Once the nightgown was above my waist, I felt his body stiffen.

I lowered my chin, unsure of what my expression revealed. There were too many thoughts trying to take root. Bewilderment and uncertainty swirled with embarrassment, yet they all seemed just beyond my reach. Taking a deep breath, I concentrated on the task at hand. Jacob and I worked together in silence. He spoke only to alert me of our movements, which I appreciated. Each one, no matter how gentle he tried to make it, aggravated my tender side. With his alert, I'd bite my lower lip and hold my breath. It didn't stop the pain, but at least I avoided wincing. By the time he placed me back in my bed, the telltale copper taste let me know that I'd punctured the inside of my lower lip.

Heavy silence loomed around us as we waited for my food. By the sound of Jacob's footsteps and occasional sighs I sensed that he too was fighting a whirlwind of thoughts, though I doubted we were thinking the same things. With each passing moment, I contemplated my options. I wanted food, but I wanted more than that. I needed more than that. I needed to understand what had happened with my accident as well as what was happening now.

The questions weren't only in my mind. They filled the room, swirling around us, taunting me. Like the faceless shadows in my dreams, they mocked me with the knowledge they refused to share. As time passed, I felt increasingly trapped—claustrophobic—as if I needed air.

What do I normally do for an outlet?

The answer washed over me with a cleansing release.

I run.

A strange sense of relief filled me as I closed my eyes and imagined paths and trails. It was so real. I not only saw the sun's long beams dancing through the tall trees, I felt the warmth as I passed through the shafts of light and my feet pounded the ground. I pushed my body, exercising its limits. No longer suffocating in an unknown world, I was moderating my breathing, keeping my pulse steady as I gained the strength to continue. I never doubted my ability to keep going. The motion came naturally. Peering beyond the woods, I spotted the open meadow where a cool morning mist had settled near the ground. Inhaling the fresh air, I smiled at the dew glistening like diamonds in the early light.

I audibly gasped at the intense memory. My body tensed. I wasn't there, I was here. However, what I'd imagined couldn't have been a dream. The terrain was familiar, more so than anything around me. I tensed as Jacob once again touched my hair.

"Sara, are you all right? What happened?"

I nodded with newfound strength. I was all right. I would be. I had a memory, a real memory. Since I couldn't tell him what had happened, I smiled and moved my head from side to side. I wanted to say that nothing was wrong. For the first time since I'd awakened in this unfamiliar world, something seemed right.

I concentrated on the images I'd created. Just like physically running, the thoughts relaxed me, easing the blanket of doubt and worry.

"I should look for your brush. Do you think you can brush your hair?" Jacob asked. "It's unlike you for it to be like this." With each sentence his fingers smoothed and caressed my long unruly tresses. Before I noticed he'd left, he was back. Placing a handle in my hand, he said, "You're much better at this than I."

Careful not to snag the bandages, I pulled the bristles through my hair. As I did, the floral scent of shampoo reminded me of the lavender flowers in my dream. I imagined the long blonde hair blowing in the wind and wondered if that was what I was brushing.

The length seemed right. It was the color that eluded me. Once silkiness replaced the tangles, I began to braid. The rote motion came without effort and resulted in a loose braid, beginning on my left and lying upon my right shoulder. As my fingers neared the end, Jacob placed a hair tie in my hand.

It was silly, only a braid, but my chest no longer ached. It was the first thing I'd done on my own. My hands remembered what to do just as my mind recalled running. It was only a start, but I clung to it.

When the door opened, my hunger woke with a vengeance.

"Place it over here," Jacob directed.

Where's "here"?

Tension returned to my shoulders as I pressed my lips together, suppressing the comments I instinctively knew wouldn't be welcomed. This macho-man routine was getting old. After the door opened and closed, wheels moved against the floor. With this new sound, I envisioned a table, one that could move in front of me and over my bed. I reached out.

"No, Sara. You didn't forget about blessing the food, did you?"

I had. It hadn't occurred to me. Consuming it was my only thought.

I bowed my head as Jacob's deep voice filled the room. He thanked Father Gabriel and the Commission for my food. *Really?* He asked God to use its nutrients to help me heal. *OK.* When he paused, I began to move, but then he spoke again: "Let this food be a reminder that privileges given can be taken away. Thank you for correcting my wife and reminding me of my role. We won't fail you again, for we trust you and Father Gabriel in all things. Amen."

I didn't move. My hunger suddenly waned.

What does all of that mean? What correction? Is Jacob agreeing with Brother Timothy that my suffering is because I sinned?

"Sara," he said, lifting my chin. "You need to eat."

He was right. I needed to eat, get strong, and get away. This wasn't right. Everything about this wasn't right. In my heart I knew I didn't belong here. I reached again for the tray. This time, wordlessly, Jacob captured my hands and placed them upon my lap. Apparently, just as with the ice chips the night before, Jacob planned to feed me.

"Open."

At that first command, my teeth clenched. I understood why he'd helped me last night, I'd been weak, but now I was relatively certain I could lift a spoon and find my mouth. Nevertheless, with just one word, he'd made it clear: food was coming, but only through him. Unable to argue, I could still refuse.

Though I entertained the thought, when the spoon touched my lip, I did as he'd said and opened my mouth. Bite by bite, my anger faded as my stomach filled. The soup—more like broth—was my favorite. I may have even hummed after the first bite. Each time it hit my tongue I savored the warmth and flavor. Even with Jacob's careful feeding, the salty chicken broth occasionally dribbled down my chin. The first time it happened, Jacob laughed. It wasn't loud, barely a scoff, but it made me smile. I couldn't remember my husband's laugh. Since I'd awakened, I'd mostly heard his anger and commands. Surely there was more to our marriage than that. It wasn't until the soup and Jell-O were finished that he placed a small roll into my hands.

"Here's a little bread. You can probably handle this on your own."

I nodded, rolling the bread between my hands, assessing the size. Lifting it to my nose, I inhaled the scent. When I placed it between my teeth, the hard outer crust gave way to a soft warm center. Each bite melted in my mouth as I sparingly nibbled. I didn't want it to end, but as it did, I realized that it was the chewing I enjoyed as much as the roll. Deprivation formed the strangest needs. All too soon the roll was gone, and a straw appeared at my lips.

"Dr. Newton said to go easy on liquids, but here's some water."

I pursed my lips and sucked. The cool water reminded me that my throat felt better, even better than it had the day before. At the sound of his name, I remembered the doctor's promise to return. Just as the thought occurred, I heard the door open.

"Doctor," Jacob said, perhaps to inform me of who'd entered.

"I assume you're ready for me?"

I nodded, forgetting that rarely did anyone speak to me.

"Yes," Jacob replied. "Sara's finished her meal. Assuming her body handles it, I want her to have a larger portion for dinner."

Dinner? I guess I just ate lunch?

I had no way to judge time. Hearing that the day was only half-over filled my mind with a mixture of thoughts. While the promise of more food excited me, the idea of spending more time in this dark, unfamiliar life made me uneasy. Silently I longed for the familiarity of my dreams.

"We'll need to assess . . ."

Jacob reached for my hand. "She's lost entirely too much weight. I'm not sure of the amount, but she's skin and bones."

"Sister Sara," Dr. Newton began. "I need to complete your examination. Then we'll discuss your injuries. Do you understand?"

I nodded, feeling Jacob's reassuring squeeze. With the slightest shift, his callused fingers caressed my knuckles, and I wondered what Jacob did for a living. From his hand I guessed that he worked hard physically, and when he'd carried me to the bathroom, I'd sensed how much bigger he was than I.

What did my accident do to his work? What about me? What do I do?

As my bed reclined for my examination, I realized the man holding my hand had argued for me, supported and assisted me, yet I didn't know him.

Do I love him? Does he love me?

No matter how hard I searched the recesses of my mind, the answers mocked me, willfully staying beyond my reach.

CHAPTER 5
Jacob

I wanted to see her eyes. Over thirty years of studying people, reading them, and somehow I'd forgotten that eyes were key. Without them I had only secondary and insignificant clues.

I understood why she wasn't allowed to see, at least not yet. Just because the psychology made sense didn't mean I approved. Taking a wife had been my duty, responsibility, and obligation to The Light. I'd seen and agreed with the process in the past—but that had been in theory and from a distance. This was up close and personal.

I'd known that eventually my time would come. I'd hoped it wouldn't, that I could avoid it, but refusing a wife when she was presented wasn't an option. Taking on this responsibility cemented my bond to The Light and solidified my standing in the community. My compliance and cooperation assured Father Gabriel, the Commission, and the Assembly of my faithfulness.

My gaze darted to Sara's face. Her hand had just clamped into a tight ball within my grasp. Though I couldn't see her eyes, her lower lip blanched from the tight hold of her teeth. Damn, she'd bite clean through it if she didn't stop putting it in that vise grip. I'd seen the drops of blood earlier today when I'd returned her to her bed. At least this time, I wasn't the cause of her lip-biting. This reaction was caused by the movement of the bed as Dr. Newton reclined it. I guessed it was the damn broken rib or ribs. Why Raquel hadn't rewrapped it after Sara's shower, I didn't know. I would say something, but then she'd probably be corrected. They might even decide to replace her as Sara's main caregiver. I didn't want that.

What I wanted was for that horrible dark bruise, those shades of purple and green, to go away. Seeing it when I'd lifted her nightgown had been like experiencing the kick all over again. The reverberations had sent shock waves through both of us. Maybe I didn't want to see her eyes. The pain she felt, when the bed reclined or when I lifted her, seeped from her pores and filled the room with its stench.

Doesn't Dr. Newton realize what he's doing?

I glanced up, but he wasn't looking at me.

He was looking at her.

My teeth rattled as I clamped them tight and assessed his expression. He was the community's sole physician, and I expected to see compassion and the desire to heal in his face. Instead images of Dr. Mengele popped into my thoughts.

What kind of doctor participates in the things Dr. Newton does without reservation?

I might not have signed up for this mission, but, damn it, Sara was now my wife.

Who the hell am I kidding?

I was as responsible as Dr. Newton, if not more. Not for all the other women who'd come to the community in this same way, but for Sara. When the Commission explained what needed to be done, I didn't question. Orders were orders. I obeyed them as well as gave them. That's how I'd advanced as fast as I had within the community—I understood rules and procedures. The Light wasn't that different from the military. My training there served me well, and my experience in the army created the perfect history for a faithful follower.

Dr. Newton spoke, refocusing my attention. "I'm going to unbutton your gown to better see your injuries."

Though she nodded, I reapplied the pressure to my poor teeth. I'd be lucky if they weren't splinters of enamel by the time this was done. Dr. Newton started at the top button of her nightgown, near the neckline, and worked his way down. He'd managed to unfasten a few buttons when I let go of her hand and pushed his away. I'd seen under her gown and knew she wasn't wearing a bra.

Her breasts may have been smaller than I preferred, but they were pleasantly round and firm. Earlier, in the bathroom, probably due to the temperature, I'd noticed how her nipples hardened and how the pink around them darkened.

It didn't matter if they were small or large: they were mine. I also knew damn well that they hadn't been injured during her accident, and Newton knew that too. He'd examined her before. There was no reason for him to see her breasts again. Loosening my clenched jaw, I said, "Her injuries are lower. I'll help you." I wanted to say more, but Sara didn't need to listen to a pissing contest above her exposed body.

The good doctor's hands went up willingly in surrender, but the smirk on his face once again made my jaw go rigid. *The arrogant ass.* There was no way in hell he would ever examine her without me present. I wouldn't allow it. If I had to petition the Commission, I would. They wanted me to take having a wife seriously, and I was.

Taking a deep breath, I refastened the gown's top buttons and undid the ones starting at the bottom. Sara's exposed skin dotted with goose bumps as I laid the fabric of her nightgown aside. With the blankets down, she was now visible from her toes to past her navel. All the right parts were covered. No doubt *in the dark*, the world outside The Light, she'd worn less on a beach than what she wore now as panties. That didn't matter. When she'd been in the dark she hadn't been my wife. Now she was, and having Newton's eyes on her pissed me off.

I held my tongue and concentrated on her cast. The damn thing went halfway up her left thigh. Since only her tibia was broken, the cast could easily have stopped below her knee. It was one more piece of the psychological warfare, part of the plan to wear her down, take away her abilities, and make her dependent. The more physical limitations she endured, the easier it was to instill psychological limitations.

The Light had a job, a calling. Its original followers had been predominantly male. Father Gabriel's teachings originated from fundamentalist roots. Women were appreciated for the strength through which they fulfilled their duties—and because men had needs. According to Father Gabriel's teachings, those needs were best served by wives. While some women found their way to The Light of their own volition, others—like Sara—were acquired. The acquisition and indoctrination process was in a continual state of revision. Each case was gauged by its success or failure. Though the entire community participated in the acquisition, ultimately it was the participants in each acquisition who were responsible for the outcome. In our case that would be Sara and me. Because I was her husband, my role was infinitely important. The only road to my continued success within The Light was through her.

I took Sara's hand again in mine. *We will not fail.* The mantra repeated like a chant in the recesses of my mind. I'd witnessed failure, and I'd labored too long to allow that to be my end. Though Sara's hand trembled, I refused to let emotion cloud my objective. We would succeed.

"Squeeze your husband's hand when I touch a place that hurts."

The asshole went for the epicenter, directly above the broken ribs. As he did, Sara moaned and squeezed with all her might, before clamping her lips tightly together.

"There," I said, looking up to the doctor's raised brows.

"You broke at least one rib in your accident," he explained.

Her lip was back between her teeth as she nodded her understanding.

"There isn't much that can be done. We'll have to wait. They'll heal in time. Now what about here?" The doctor continued his exercise until he'd discussed her broken ribs, broken leg, and possible concussion. He explained that her cheek had hit the steering wheel of the truck. If she could have seen herself in a mirror, she'd have known that wasn't the case, but she seemed to take the doctor at his word. Touching her tender throat, he asked again if she had pain. Her squeeze was softer than before.

"Does that mean that it doesn't hurt there as much as before?" I asked.

She nodded.

"I believe you'll be able to talk within a day or two," Dr. Newton said. "Tomorrow or Friday we'll remove this cast and set a new one that'll allow you to walk. Your bone was broken, but luckily not severely. It didn't break the skin. That'll help with your recovery."

"What about food and drink?" I asked.

"How are you feeling now?" he asked her. "Did you handle the lunch OK?"

She nodded.

"Another day of bland and then we'll reevaluate."

"I want to take her home." I'd agreed to accept the Commission's and Father Gabriel's power, but I didn't like Newton's. I'd seen too many things over the past three years that I'd been at the Northern Light. In my opinion even the Commission didn't fully trust him—if they did, he'd be part of the Assembly.

"We'll need to watch how she adapts to the walking cast and alert the Commission. Where she goes from here is ultimately their decision."

By the way she flinched at his last statement, the process was working. She was beginning to understand how much the Commission ultimately controlled. Tomorrow at Assembly they'd ask, and I'd be honest. I'm sure they'd be quite proud of themselves—the recent refinements with the indoctrination process were proving effective. The old ways produced slower results. As a member of the Assembly, I normally would've been pleased too, but this time was different. I wasn't only an Assemblyman—I was her husband. The tighter Sara clung to my hand, the less content with the process I became.

Freeing my hand, I began closing the buttons of her nightgown. As I did, Sara raised her arm and pointed to her eyes. Father Gabriel's teachings instructed me to reprimand her, to remind her of a rule she'd never heard, that females answered questions—they didn't question. Instead I inwardly smirked at her ingenuity. The only rule she'd been told was not to speak, and while she obeyed, she'd found a way to communicate.

My wife was smart and resourceful. She'd learn quickly and we would succeed.

Newton's beady eyes widened and met mine.

I squared my shoulders and relayed her question. "When will you be able to remove the bandages from her eyes?"

His lips pursed. He'd probably report this to anyone who'd listen. Surely Lilith and Timothy were champing at the bit for me to fail. The way I saw it, Sara had a simple question. It wasn't as if she demanded equality; she simply wanted to know when she might regain sight.

"Brother," Dr. Newton began, effectively removing her from the discussion. "As we've discussed, the concussion likely affected her optic nerve. Unfortunately that wasn't the only injury to her eyes. When your truck exploded, the intense light and heat damaged her retinas. Both injuries require rest and time. I don't foresee the bandages being removed anytime in the near future. It could easily be weeks."

"Thank you, Doctor. If there's nothing else, I believe my wife needs rest."

I supported The Light and Father Gabriel, but as I pulled the blankets over Sara's closed gown, I vowed to do what I could to make this easier on her. She was a person who'd lost the right to choose her future. It was now my responsibility, and I intended to do anything necessary for our survival. The stakes were too high.

"One last thing," Dr. Newton said. "I was informed that Sara's schedule will be set as of tomorrow."

"Her schedule?"

"Yes. She needs to be awake, dressed, and have breakfast eaten by the time you leave for Assembly."

My body tensed as I consciously loosened my grip on Sara's hand. Modulating my voice, I asked, "Who informed you of this?"

"Sister Lilith."

This time Sara's grasp shuddered. She was a quick study.

"Because . . . ," I coaxed.

"I don't remember," Dr. Newton replied flippantly, his lips sliding into a sleazy grin. Shrugging, he added, "It was something about training."

Training?

I released Sara's hand and stepped toward the door, hoping that Newton would get the hint that I wanted him out. I wanted them all out. "Thank you, I'll be sure she's ready in the morning. As long as you believe she's healthy enough." Being the only physician, Dr. Newton could provide her with a valid reason to avoid Lilith's training, at least for a few more days.

"From what I could tell—with my limited examination—yes, your wife is healthy enough to begin training."

Asshole!

I shook my head. Clearly this was Newton's plan. If I wouldn't allow him full access to Sara, he'd throw her to the wolves.

Hell no. I'd fight it.

I opened the door and watched it shut behind the doctor, wishing it had a lock.

In four steps I crossed the room. This small space felt like a damn cage, but I refused to leave Sara's side. The soles of my boots created a rhythm as I paced back and forth, a habit I'd started as a teen. I processed thoughts better when I moved. I'd rather be moving in one direction, but living in this godforsaken region of Alaska, in a walled community, didn't offer many opportunities for running. It was better in the summer, but now, with the sunlight waning, it was freezing cold.

I had to hand it to Father Gabriel, though. There was nothing like being isolated in the middle of nowhere to bring people together and help form a cohesive group.

The rush for Sara's training didn't make sense. *Are they trying for another failure?*

From the corner of my eye, I noticed the movement of her hand and my steps stilled.

Shit. She'd just wiped away a tear.

What the hell am I supposed to do?

CHAPTER 6
Stella

Standing outside the door to the Wayne County Morgue, I gave Dylan a strained smile.

"Really?" I asked, shaking my head.

"Really. I haven't been in. If they knew for sure it was her, they wouldn't need you. After last time I thought it might help if you weren't alone."

I feigned a smile. I appreciated his help; however, having him here, holding my hand, set fire to my emotions, causing them to bubble to the top instead of remaining hidden behind a mask of indifference.

"Thank you, Dylan. But I need to walk in there as a journalist, not a friend. I'm not sure I can take seeing my friend laid out on a large stainless table."

He tilted his head. "But Stella Montgomery, sleuth investigator, can?"

"No, not really, but *sleuth investigator*"—I couldn't help but smile, releasing a bit of the tension at his description—"can keep it together until she's alone."

"How about you don't have to be alone?" Holding my hand and stepping back, Dylan looked deep into my eyes, and his gaze narrowed. I knew that look. His police wheels were spinning. "You know," he said curiously, "I raced down here as soon as Barney told me you'd left. WCJB is closer than the precinct. How did I get here before you?"

I shrugged. "My mind's a blur. I missed my exit and . . ." I let my voice fade to a whisper. "I found myself headed north."

"Tell me you didn't go to Highland Heights."

I straightened my neck and set my shoulders back defensively. "Don't. Don't play macho policeman. If that's Mindy in there, then they found her in that neighborhood in an abandoned house. If it's her, I needed to see it. I need to find out who did this. That's what I do."

"*If*, Stella. *If* is the imperative word. You're putting the cart before the horse." His mussed, dark-blond hair failed to hide his furrowed brow as he repeated his question, slower this time. "Did you go to Highland Heights alone, without telling anyone?"

I knew that telling someone where you're going—leaving a trail— was rule number one, but rules were meant to be broken. Sometimes moving on instinct didn't allow for time to check in. Not appreciating his interrogation, I shook off his grip. "I just drove around, all right? I didn't get out."

"Christ, are you trying to turn up missing too?"

I'd never, in all my adult life, answered to anyone. This relation-ship—or whatever it was—with Dylan was still in its infancy. We were still working on our boundaries, and he'd just crossed one of mine. With heat rising to my face and my jaw clenched, I replied, "I'm not having this conversation with you in the hallway outside of the morgue. Why are you here, anyway? To lecture me on safety? Because right now I'm safe, but whoever the hell is on that table isn't."

Dylan's gaze softened. "No, I didn't come here to lecture you. I came because last time you did this alone. I didn't want you to do that again. I know how upsetting it was for you. I hope to God this isn't Mindy, but if it is . . ."

I sighed. "I appreciate that, I do. I just don't need lectures right now." I let out another long breath. "Seeing dead bodies never gets easier, at least not to me."

"No, it doesn't. Each one, no matter what they did or what happened to them, was a person, someone's kid."

Or sister, or brother, or best friend.

Dylan once again grasped my hand. "Let's get this over with. They're ready for us."

I held back my tears, steeled my resolve, and nodded. Together we walked through the doors and entered the cold room, cold both in temperature and personality. The buzz of the lights combined with the offending odor threw my nerves into overdrive. Dylan's hand became a vise as I took in the surroundings. It was the same as it'd been a week earlier, with cement walls, tile floors, and tables and countertops made of a shiny, disinfected metal.

A young, thin woman entered from the other side of the room at the same time that we came in. I barely noticed her as I concentrated on the body, lying on a table near the far end of the room, a silhouette covered with a white sheet.

"Thank you for coming. I'll skip all the formalities and make this as quick as possible," the young technician said.

Biting my lip, I nodded.

"We only need for you to give us your impression. You don't need to look any longer than necessary."

I nodded again, fearful that if I spoke I'd taste the strange aroma hanging in the air.

"It's not too late," she continued. "If you'd like to go to another room, we can do this via closed-circuit cameras. You don't have to be in here."

Though bile bubbled in my throat, I released Dylan's hand and straightened my stance. "I assure you, if this is Mindy, I do need to be here. Please continue."

The young woman grabbed the edge of the sheet with her blue-gloved hands and slowly lowered it. Panic ran through me when I saw blonde hair, blonde like Mindy's, like mine. Next I saw eyes, their lids partially closed, hiding their color. Did this body have the same pale eyes that Mindy and I shared? The cheeks were bruised in various shades. And then the tech lowered the sheet past the nose and mouth and I knew. I knew.

"It's not her. It's not her." Relief crashed down as I leaned against Dylan's tall frame, grasping his bicep to keep myself from falling. The worry that had propelled me toward the body had evaporated, leaving me physically weak.

The body before us was now uncovered to just above her breasts, with her arms visible, giving us a full view of the plethora of injuries marking her skin. Whoever she was, she'd lived through hell and died there. The relief that washed through me left a sickening trail of remorse. I was thrilled that this wasn't Mindy, but, as Dylan had said, it was still a person, someone who might or might not have had a family. Someone who might or might not be missed.

How did she get to this table, to the house where she was found? What is her story?

And what about Mindy?

The theory that my friend's disappearance was voluntary was ridiculous. An intelligent, successful twenty-nine-year-old woman didn't decide one day to disappear. Even if she had, with GPS, traffic cameras, surveillance, it wouldn't be easy, not without help. Mindy had no reason to walk away from her life. She wouldn't have. She had every reason to stay.

Standing beside the table, I found myself back to more questions than answers, back to imagining scenarios that made my stomach turn. I'd researched the number of female disappearances nationwide. The numbers were staggering and, looking at the woman before me, I knew that numbers were only a part of the story. Each report was a life.

What I saw in this woman's injuries took my imagination to dark places. Her bruises were an array of colors, indicating a pattern of abuse. Yellow and green peppered her exposed arms and cheekbone. I knew enough from my time in the crime lab to determine that she'd gotten those over a week ago. There was also a purple crescent under her left eye and a dark bluish-purple band surrounding her throat. Something besides hands had made the mark around her neck. The first finger and thumb were the strongest and usually left definitive marks. The customary differentiation of fingers was missing. This bruise on this body's throat was a consistent dark color, indicating that whatever had been around her neck, had been in place for a long time. She also had lacerations. There was a partially healed wound visible on her chest above the edge of the sheet.

Now that I knew this wasn't Mindy, my investigative side took over. I longed to remove the sheet and meet this woman, understand her, and learn her story. However, it was more than that. The vile taste in my mouth, the way the tiny hairs on my arms rose, told me that part of me feared that Mindy could be experiencing, at this very moment, the same terror that this woman had known.

I needed answers, for Mindy, for this woman, and for any other women who had disappeared from their lives to awaken in a nightmare.

"Miss Montgomery?"

The technician's voice pulled me back to the cold room.

"Yes?"

"If you need to sit down, you may go into one of our rooms for a few minutes before you leave. We realize this is difficult. I'm sorry we've brought you in here twice. I hope you know that we wouldn't do that if we didn't think there was a possibility . . ."

I straightened my shoulders. "No, I don't need to sit down, and I want you to call me. If there's even a chance that you have Mindy, call me again. I'll be here." I looked up toward Dylan, then back to the young lady. "Thank you. What about this woman?"

"We'll run some more tests to see if we can find any markers. Since the tips of her fingers have been burned, our only means of identification are DNA and dental records. Those are both long shots unless she matches a missing-persons list or a national registry."

My gaze dropped to the woman's hands. The way they lay next to her still body, I hadn't noticed anything about them, but now I saw that the skin on the tips of her fingers was ghostly white.

"Burned?" I asked. "With what?"

"We're not exactly sure. As you can see, it wasn't fire. We're assuming acid."

"When?" My voice came out softer than I liked.

Dylan reached for my wrist, pulling me gently toward the door. I didn't move. I steadied my feet and turned back to the technician. I couldn't help it. The questions came fast and furious. "What the hell happened to this woman? Do you think someone put her fingers in acid before she died?"

"I really can't—"

"Stella, let's go," Dylan said. "This isn't your story."

I turned to face him. "Whose story or case will it be? Who'll give a shit about her or what she suffered?"

"It's an open investigation," the technician volunteered. "The police are working on it."

"If someone were to use an acid strong enough to take away her fingerprints, wouldn't there be more damage to her skin?" I asked.

The young woman nodded. "If it were done all at once. However, if it's done over time, each application takes away a little more. Then it scars, making the final result more effective. Some terrorist groups willingly do this to lose their previous identities." She looked down. "I really shouldn't say any more."

"Stella, we need to go." Dylan placed his hand on my shoulder.

I nodded as I scanned the features of the woman on the table. Briefly I wondered what she had looked like before she was hurt, killed, and left for rat food in an abandoned house. That was what some ass-hole had done. If drugged-out kids hadn't gone into the house to shoot up or hook up in the middle of a Detroit summer, this woman would've been consumed by rodents, greatly reducing any hope of identification.

Shaking my head, I looked back at the technician. That's when I saw it, a look in her eyes that seemed to plead for my help, asking me to use the resources at my discretion to do something.

I tested the waters. "Thank you for your help. What's your name? I apologize for not asking sooner."

"Tracy, Dr. Tracy Howell, assistant forensic pathologist."

I stood straighter. "Doctor. Again, I apologize. I just assumed you were a technician."

Dr. Howell smiled. "I'm used to it. It's all right. When people enter our labs, they aren't in the best place. I'm sorry, Miss Montgomery, that your friend is still missing. Thank you for stopping by." Her eyes shifted to Dylan, then back to me. I got the feeling that Dr. Howell didn't want to talk with others around.

"Call me Stella, please. Thank you again, Doctor."

As Dylan and I walked through the door to the hallway, I took one last look over my shoulder and saw Dr. Howell cover the blonde woman's head with the sheet. The vision of the woman settled into the back of my mind: her yellow hair combed away from her battered face; her eyes partially opened, irises hidden by the veiled lids; her fingers curved slightly, their distinguishing marks burned away.

And something else.

One of the earlobes, the one on the right, was split, as if an earring had been ripped from the ear. My feet stopped. We'd made it to the security gate but I'd suddenly forgotten how to move.

"What is it?" Dylan asked in a low voice.

I barely heard his question as I tried to make sense of the injury. *Should I go back and confirm what I saw?*

Mindy's ears weren't pierced. That was one of the things I'd specifically told the medical examiner.

Why did Dr. Howell call me down here if she knew it wasn't Mindy?

Perhaps there was a simple explanation. With all the injuries the woman had, her ear could have gone unnoticed.

"You're scaring me. Are you going into shock? What's the matter?"

I shook my head. "I was just thinking about Mindy."

Mindy and I used to joke about getting tattoos. Neither of us had actually wanted one, but we were curious. We'd wondered what the fascination was, why people continued to get them. The subject didn't come up every day, usually only when we'd had a little too much to drink. Regardless, it always ended the same way, with Mindy biting her lip and recounting her fear of needles, telling how she'd reacted when her mom took her to a store in the mall to have her ears pierced.

She'd begged and pleaded with her mother for weeks. All her friends had pierced ears and she'd wanted them too, until she was there, sitting on the stool, watching the clerk pick up the silver gun. She'd usually start to laugh as she recalled how she'd been struck by an overwhelming wave of panic. How she'd screamed at the top of her lungs, completely out of control. She'd even fallen from the stool. Needless to say, she never had her ears pierced, and after we saw *The Girl with the Dragon Tattoo*, we never again even joked about getting a tattoo.

Dylan's warm hand rubbed a circle on the small of my back. "Why don't I take you home? I'm sure if you call Barney he'll understand. This is too hard on you. I don't like that they keep calling. I think they should call me. If I'm not sure, then I'll have you come down and confirm. That woman obviously wasn't Mindy."

I shook my head. "Thank you, but I want to be the one they call, and I can't go home. I still have work that needs to be done at the station. Besides, I don't think sitting in my apartment with only memories and a vivid imagination is a good idea."

Dylan took my hand and walked me through the building. By the time we made it to the parking lot, I'd tucked Mindy away, to a safe place. "Where's your car?"

Pointing to the left, he said, "It's right over there."

I turned and spotted his unmarked Charger.

"How about when you're done with work, you come back to my place, instead of going home to that empty apartment?" Dylan leaned closer. "You left in a hurry this morning and besides, I'd like to learn more about that vivid imagination of yours."

I blushed, liking how he'd twisted my comment. "I'd like that too, but I didn't go home yesterday, and I don't have any clean clothes. Oh, and then there's Fred. I need to check on him."

Dylan's eyes sparkled in the warm Detroit summer sunshine. "Fred's a fish. I think he'll make it. As for clothes, I have this amazing new technology. It's called a washing machine. I bought one because I'd heard they were all the rage. I can cook some dinner; you can experiment with the new technology?"

I tilted my head and sighed. "You're terrible. If I used that *amazing new technology*, what would I possibly wear? I mean, I need *all* my clothes clean."

"Oh! That's the fun part. That's where your vivid imagination comes in. If you need help"—he pulled me close, circling my waist—"I'm sure I can come up with a few ideas that don't require clothes."

I reached for his shoulders, stood up on my toes, and kissed his cheek. "Thank you for being here. I appreciate it. But I think I'll take a rain check. The same outfit at work for three days, even if it's clean, will get people talking, and seriously, you don't know Fred. He mopes if I'm not there. It's really sad to see his little blue betta fins all drooped. Bye."

As I walked away, my phone buzzed, and I opened the text message:

Dylan: FRESH SALMON?

He definitely wasn't playing fair. Cooking wasn't my thing.

I started my car and looked in my rearview mirror. Dylan hadn't pulled away. He hadn't even gotten into his car. Instead he was leaning against the Charger, his long, jean-covered legs crossed at the ankles, his black, short-sleeved shirt looking too damn good stretched over his chest. I backed my car out and drove toward him. His face lit up, glowing triumphantly from his sparkling eyes to his shiny white teeth.

I came to a stop and rolled down my window. "You're not playing fair! You know how I am about your cooking."

He laughed. "You know how I feel about yours. That's why I offered. I'll cook some salmon on the grill, with some asparagus, a few cold beers . . ." He pouted. "But if you'd rather hang out with Barney."

I shook my head. "Give me an hour and I'll call you. No promises."

He winked. "I'll be waiting."

I rolled up my window, cranked the air conditioning, and headed back to the station.

Even the thought of his cooking made my stomach rumble and growl, but no, I couldn't go back to his house tonight. It wasn't that Bernard needed me, though I needed to call him to tell him the body wasn't Mindy's. What I wanted to do had nothing to do with work or with the drug distribution happening at the port. What I wanted was to call Dr. Tracy Howell and find out why she'd called me down to the morgue twice, and what she was really trying to tell me.

I reached for my phone to call Bernard and saw my wrinkled slacks. I definitely needed to go home. Turning my car toward my apartment, I decided to call Bernard and do more research from home.

CHAPTER 7
Sara

After I heard Jacob walk Dr. Newton to the door, I expected him to explain what the doctor meant about my training.

Will I be left alone with Sister Lilith? Will Raquel or Elizabeth be there? For some reason, I suspected that this was a women-only thing. *Do I remember that or do I just suspect it?*

Instead of talking to me, however, Jacob resumed his pacing. Back and forth, four steps. Though he was still taking big strides, his shoes didn't pound the floor with the force and intensity they had last night.

One, two, three, four—turn, one, two, three, four—turn . . .

I lay back and searched for my memories, hoping for something, a clue, a crumb . . . anything. I couldn't understand how I'd willingly come to this place, a place where shadows of perversion lingered outside my reach. I also wondered why I'd want to do training and if I'd done it before. *Does everyone do it? If I did, why am I doing it again?* I tried to clear my mind, to think about nothing, in the hope that something would come. Nothing did.

It didn't make sense. Everyone here knew me. Everyone knew my past . . . except me. I wasn't ready to face the reality that the problem must be me.

Time passed as tears slid silently from beneath the bandages and down my cheeks. Even that felt wrong. I wasn't a crier. Then again, maybe I was.

I didn't try to stop the tears. They were my wordless appeal to my husband, my unspoken request for support. I needed more than him fighting for me while others were present. I needed him to help me when we were alone, to explain why this all felt wrong. Mindlessly I wiped away the tears that I'd vowed to let rain free. The longer they fell, the more I understood: my tears didn't matter. Nothing mattered.

"Sara."

Lost in my own thoughts, I startled at Jacob's voice beside me. I hadn't heard his pacing cease. I didn't move or turn in his direction. It was too late. I didn't care anymore. If showing weakness was what it took to get his attention, then I didn't want him or his support.

Instead what I wanted was to get away . . . away to a place where I wasn't powerless, where I had a voice, where I belonged. I didn't know where that was. All I knew with increasing certainty was that it wasn't here. Here, I was trapped.

My dampened face fell toward my chest as my tears morphed into sobs, each one deeper than the one before. The cries didn't come from my throat but from my soul, consuming me. Each sob thrust deep into my heart, splitting it open, crying out for my stolen sense of self.

Under this onslaught, my heart was unable to beat at its normal rhythm, instead thudding in my chest, a dull repeating sound echoing in my ears. Without its steady rhythm I'd cease to exist. Then I realized . . . it had already happened. I no longer existed.

Whoever I really am is gone.

I gasped, but air wouldn't inflate my lungs. My heart, my lungs . . . internally I was disappearing.

The bed rail beside me lowered. Jacob lifted my hand, but I couldn't feel his touch. Even his words were gone. I heard only the sound of my cries. The bed shifted, but where our bodies connected there was no warmth. Mine no longer belonged to me. Jacob held someone else's hand, his leg pressed against someone else's thigh. The wails grew louder and louder.

Who was this desperate person?

Sara.

Jacob spoke to her, to Sara. He called her by name as he tried to calm her. His words were there, but I didn't listen. His tone was comforting, but I was beyond calming. It didn't matter, because he wasn't talking to me. He was talking to the woman on the edge of panic, the woman who willingly lived a life of subservience. A woman who could exist in this strange and terrible place.

That's not me! I didn't want any of this. I wasn't that person. There'd been a mistake, a terrible mistake. Sara and I were two different people, and somehow I had to make him understand. I didn't know who I was, but without a doubt, I wasn't Sara.

With a fleeting gasp, air finally came, finding its way to my lungs. The deep breath momentarily stilled the sobs, though the ringing in my ears continued. My inhalation brought the sharp pain back to my side. It was the hurt that Brother Timothy said was mine to bear for sins I'd committed.

Anger sparked a fire that had nearly died. *I didn't commit any sins.* Perhaps Sara had, I didn't know nor did I care. The only sin I recalled was allowing others to determine my future, to dominate my life and body. A cold chill went through me and a sour taste filled my mouth as I remembered Dr. Newton's recent examination. I hadn't been able to see their faces, but they had been there, both he and Jacob standing, touching and viewing my exposed body. It felt wrong, almost immoral. These people preached against sin, accused me of transgressions, yet expected me to submit to their violations.

Another jolt of pain in my side reinforced my newfound determination. Whoever I truly was, wasn't gone, not yet. I needed to fight. But I couldn't do it alone. Mentally I reached for Sara and she and I united.

I wasn't her, but I needed her body to save me. I couldn't stay trapped any longer. I wouldn't.

"Sara, that's enough." Jacob's caring tone was gone. He grabbed my chin.

I pulled away from his grip.

My freedom was short-lived as Jacob recaptured my chin, his hold stronger than before. "I'm your husband. You'll show me the respect—"

Shaking my head violently, I broke free. If I had been thinking clearly, I would have realized the futility of my protest, but I wasn't thinking clearly. I was done living someone else's life.

"Don't touch me!" I screamed, blindly pushing against his unmoving chest with a new jolt of strength. Speaking came so effortlessly that I didn't think about his warning or the consequences. The words spewed forth, louder and louder. "Stop! I'm not Sara! I'm not your wife! I don't know you!" Each statement lifted the weight of helplessness from my chest. "I don't belong here! You've all made a mis—"

My right cheek stung with the force of his slap.

Stunned back into silence, I covered my cheek and turned away. The hurt faded as I waited for Jacob's next move. My earlier misjudgment was suddenly clear. No matter who I was, in my current condition, I was at his mercy—their mercy. With my lower lip tightly held between my teeth, new tears flowed, burning my eyes and leaving a trail of shame. For the first time, I welcomed the bandages that covered my eyes. I'd use them to my advantage, hide behind them and block out the world around me. I'd try to block him out.

But I couldn't. I felt his strong hold, pinching my chin, pulling my face back to his. The lunch I'd eaten earlier solidified in my stomach.

"You. Are. Sara. Adams." Jacob spoke each word staccato, as if saying them slowly made them true. He continued to hold my face painfully close to his as he took a deep breath. His exhalation skirted across my dampened cheeks. "Your speaking restrictions will resume, but first, since you apparently are capable of talking, repeat after me"—*What the hell?*—"'My name is Sara Adams,'" he continued.

The stone my lunch had become in my stomach moved to my throat. I didn't speak, keeping my lip securely between my teeth. His grasp on my chin moved behind my head, forcing my tender neck forward.

His tone morphed into a menacing whisper as he spoke through clenched jaws. "'My. Name. Is. Sara. Adams.' Don't make me repeat your instructions."

My teeth released their captive and my breathing stuttered. "M-my name is Sara Adams."

Though his hand remained, the pressure eased.

"'I am the wife of Jacob Adams.'"

I swallowed my tears, tasting the salty liquid. I'd say his words; that didn't mean I believed them. "I am the wife of Jacob Adams."

He released my neck, and he moved to brush away my tears. Though his intent may have been gentle, I flinched at the contact.

"Sara, do *not* pull away from me. I don't want to punish you. Hurting you has never been my goal."

I stilled, holding my breath and concentrating on remaining motionless as he wiped my tears.

"Our roles are clear. As your husband, I'm the head of our household. With that title comes responsibility. You're my responsibility. Your behavior reflects on me. How do you think it looks when a man can't control his own wife? When we said our vows, you promised to honor and obey."

Though I didn't mean to respond, involuntarily my head moved ever so slightly from side to side. Had he not been holding my cheek, he might not have noticed, but he was and he did. With increased volume, Jacob said, "Sara? You've already disobeyed me by speaking. Explain why you're shaking your head."

"It's nothing," I said, my voice barely a whisper.

"Nothing?"

"I didn't mean to shake my head," I lied. I didn't remember vows, and if I'd said them, I couldn't imagine having said those. *Do people really still say* obey?

"But you did. You meant to shake your head, and now you're lying. You realize that lying is a sin, don't you?"

Oh my God! I nodded, not wanting to have this conversation. Suddenly I didn't want any conversation. I wanted to go back to not talking, to both of us not talking.

"No, Sara." He was again speaking slowly and calmly. "Right now we're talking. You may respond verbally." When I hesitated, he added, "You *will* respond verbally."

Is he serious?

"I'm very tired. I think maybe that when I hit my head in the accident it affected my memory. Things are fuzzy." I lowered my chin again. "Please, let me go back to sleep." I needed to use the restroom, but I wasn't about to ask for his help. Maybe Raquel or Elizabeth would return, or the nurse who'd brought my lunch. Deborah.

"Not yet. You didn't answer my question."

"Your question?" I couldn't remember his question.

"Lying. You remember what lying is, don't you?"

"Yes, I know lying is a sin."

"What happens to sinners?"

"They go to hell?"

"Was that a question?" He took my hand. "If it was, yes, when sinners die they go to hell. I'm talking about before that. I'm talking about what happens when sinners are still alive. As my wife, it's my responsibility to keep you from sin. How do I do that, Sara?"

The dryness of my mouth made speaking difficult. I truly didn't know what he wanted, but at this point I'd say whatever it was to make him go away. "Jacob, I'm sorry. I won't sin."

"That's a big promise. One that isn't your burden to bear. It's mine. It's my job to see that you live a virtuous life. It's my job to correct you when you fail. That's why I slapped you. It was punishment, punishment for disobeying, correction for your outburst." He again caressed my cheek. "It's up to you, Sara. It always has been. If you obey my rules and those of Father Gabriel, there's no need for correction. The rules keep you from sin. You don't want to be a sinner, do you?"

I shook my head, not understanding why his words affected me. "No, I don't."

Jacob lifted the end of my braid and his tone lightened. "We have a lot to discuss, and you said you're tired, but first." He paused. "It's nearly three in the afternoon. Do you need to use the restroom again?"

Damn. I hated that I needed him or anyone for such basic things. I nodded.

"Sara? We're speaking, so speak."

"Yes, I do."

The bed shifted as Jacob released my hand and stood. His footsteps moved to the right side of my bed. By the tugging, I figured that he was fumbling with my IV.

"I've watched them hook and unhook this many times," he said. "But I'm not sure how they did it." Things clanked. "This pole is on wheels. I think I can carry you and move it at the same time."

I considered offering to hold on to it, but I didn't know how the speech restriction worked. Would he tell me when it had been reinstated? Instead of talking, I waited until he pulled back the blankets. The cool air reminded me of Dr. Newton and his exam, and I shuddered.

"Jacob?"

"Yes?"

"May I tell you something?"

He smoothed my hair away from my forehead. The repetitive motion was beginning to remind me of someone petting a dog or a cat. "You've always been able to be honest with me."

Always? How long has that been? I raked my lower lip between my teeth.

"Why are you doing that? Were you not planning on being honest?"

"No, I was. It's that it's about Dr. Newton, and I don't know if I should say anything."

"You asked to speak. There must be something you want to say."

I contemplated my words. Finally I replied, "I don't remember him. That's all. Should I?" My pulse raced. I *didn't* remember Dr. Newton or anyone else, but that wasn't what I'd wanted to say. I'd wanted to say that Dr. Newton gave me the creeps, that I didn't like him, or Brother Timothy, or Sister Lilith, but could I? Could I be that honest?

His arms moved behind my back and under my legs. "I'm going to lift you."

I started to nod, but changed my mind and replied, "I'm ready."

As he lifted, I inhaled, clenching my teeth. By the time I exhaled through the pain from my rib, Jacob was speaking, his chest vibrating with his deep voice. I'd missed some of what he'd said.

". . . for years. I'm not sure why you wouldn't remember him. What other things don't you remember?"

He lowered me to the floor, and directed my hand to the handle. I'd learned before that the handle slid across the room, supporting me from the shower, to the sink, to the toilet.

"May I have some privacy?"

"No."

What the hell? My shoulders tensed as I searched for an appropriate response. Oh, I had a response—I just didn't think my husband would appreciate it. The words on the tip of my tongue were probably a sin too.

"Sara, you're not strong enough to move on your own. I told you that it's never been my goal to hurt you and that I'm responsible for you. Do you remember me saying that?"

"Yes."

"Very good. See, your memory's improving." *Asshole, you said that a few minutes ago.* "I'm sure you'll remember more with time. For now you need my help. I wouldn't want you to fall, or be injured. Now let me help you."

I released the handle and held his shoulders as he lifted my gown and lowered my panties. My good leg stiffened and heat flooded my cheeks. If he noticed, he didn't say anything.

"Go ahead," he continued, "hold on to my neck and you can sit."

This is so embarrassing. I did as he said. With my left leg straight in the cast, I wasn't comfortable, but I was where I needed to be. Modestly I pulled my nightgown over my knees.

"You do remember that we're married, right?" The small amount of amusement in his voice brought a shy grin to my lips. *Maybe this is progress.*

I nodded. It was a lie, but right now my whole life was a lie. I needed to get stronger before I could fight it.

"I'll step back to the room, but I'm leaving the door open. When you need me, you may speak."

I may? So much for progress. I waited until his footsteps moved away. When I was confident he was gone, I shook my head. I wasn't sure why I did. Maybe I was rattling my brain in an effort to get everything to fall into place, to try to understand how I'd come to live this life.

The recent events went through my mind. The smile at his amusement disappeared with the thumping of my temples. He'd slapped me. My husband had actually slapped me. He'd claimed it was justifiable. He'd called it *correction.*

My temples entered a full throb, beating in time with my heart. I lifted my fingertips to my right cheek. It was tender, but not as tender as my left, and that had been hurt in the accident . . . how long ago?

I was glad I'd distracted Jacob from his question about what I didn't remember. I was afraid to answer honestly. After all, when I told him the truth, it earned me correction. As I thought about it, I supposed it could've been the way I said it, or more accurately, screamed it. Regardless, I didn't know if I wanted to risk it again. I believed that deep down I was a fighter; however, I wasn't stupid. I'd play this role until I figured it out.

After I finished, I called out, and Jacob helped me to the sink. When I turned the knob on the sink, my throat clenched. I'd had a drink with my lunch, but I wanted another. As I blindly fumbled around the sink, Jacob directed my hands to the dispenser of soap. Though that wasn't what I sought, I washed my hands. Once I was done, I searched again.

"What are you doing?" he asked.

Why do his questions make me uncomfortable? "I'm searching for the cup. There was one earlier when I brushed my teeth. I thought since I was here, I'd get a drink."

Handing me a towel, he replied, "If you want a drink, you need to ask."

"Well, that won't do me much good if I'm not allowed to speak." My pulse quickened as the atmosphere of the room changed. I immediately knew that I shouldn't have replied and braced myself for more correction.

Instead Jacob said, "Hold on to my neck, I'm going to take you back to bed."

I did as he said and reached for the pole attached to my IV.

"If your speech is restricted, you won't ask. You'll wait until I offer. That goes for anything, not only a drink."

As he carried me back to bed with the pole following close behind, I contemplated his answer. *Why would I need to ask for everything? I don't remember my age, but I'm an adult.*

Settling back onto my bed, I took a deep breath and did as he'd said. "May I have a drink?"

He didn't respond as I heard him maneuver the IV pole back to the other side of my bed and felt him straighten my blankets. Just as

I debated asking again, a straw touched my lips. I sucked, wanting to reach out and hold the cup, but cautious that I'd be corrected. Unsure when I'd have another opportunity, I continued drinking as long as he offered. It wasn't until air filled the straw that he took it away.

"Thank you."

"We do have more to discuss, but you haven't officially been cleared to speak."

I nodded, waiting for more.

"For right now, you may speak only to me and only when we're alone. Is that understood?"

"Yes."

"Sara, it doesn't matter what anyone else says. No one has the authority to override my rules. No one except Father Gabriel. Remember that."

I nodded.

"This is of the utmost importance." He lifted my hand and intertwined our fingers. "Who is your husband?"

"You."

"And who makes your rules?"

Heaviness filled my chest. Though I didn't like the answer I was about to utter, I'd learned my lesson—or Sara's lesson—and didn't hesitate. "You do."

"What will happen if you disobey me?" His warm hand tensed as he waited for my answer.

"You'll correct me." I hated the words the second they left my mouth, but by the way his lips brushed my forehead, it was the right answer, or at least the one he wanted. "May I please rest?" I didn't want to talk anymore.

He petted my hair. "I'll put the bed back a little so you can sleep." As it began to recline, he said, "Sara, I want what's best for you. The responsibility that Father Gabriel and God bestowed upon me as your husband is great. A component of that responsibility is your correction. It's only one part of the overall picture, but it's a part I've always taken seriously. We don't want another incident like the one that got you in this bed. To help you, I won't hesitate to reinforce your obedience. Remember that."

The bed stopped, and my thoughts drifted to the ache in my cheek. Obviously he wouldn't hesitate.

"As long as you behave appropriately," he continued, "you have nothing to fear. Father Gabriel often says that this arrangement is a blessing for wives. As a wife you don't question. By doing as you're told, you're relieved of the responsibility of decisions. Correction is at my discretion, and once it is delivered, the transgression is over. For example, today's outburst, your disobedience with speaking—you've been punished and it's done. Once the correction is complete, you no longer need to feel guilty. It's as if it never happened. It's a blessing. Don't you agree?"

Though I was sleepy, his explanation ricocheted around my brain. I didn't agree. I wasn't a child or a pet. Nevertheless I saw the appeal of putting things behind us and moving on. Then I remembered what Brother Timothy had said, that only Father Gabriel could decide if my punishment was complete. The anticipation of what was yet to come was unnerving. Instead of answering I asked, "Are corrections always corporal?"

"See what I mean? Isn't it better to not worry about that and move on?"

I was fading into sleepiness. I wasn't sure if the answer I was about to utter was mine or Sara's, but either way, it felt like the easiest way to end this discussion and allow me to rest. "Yes, thank you."

"You're welcome. Now get some sleep."

I nodded against the pillow. I didn't want to think about the people with the strange familial titles or about governing bodies that held unknown power. As much as I hated myself for condoning any part of Jacob's correction, I was thankful that my outburst was behind us. For my sanity I needed to fall asleep thinking about the man who'd defended and helped me, not the husband I couldn't remember who claimed to be my disciplinarian.

Is that what Sara did? Is that how she survived?

CHAPTER 8
Sara

I can do this . . .

To survive I needed to convince myself that I could reclaim my life. No matter how hard I wished, my current situation wasn't a dream or even a nightmare—if it were, I could wake and it would be over. So far three days and nights had passed and I was still here, in Sara's life.

During the last night, I had awakened to the sound of Jacob's steady breathing. Knowing he was asleep, I lay awake thinking about everything. I thought about the things that people took for granted and vowed to myself that in the future, I'd value the mundane knowledge that most people never questioned. I would, because I now knew what it was like to have it outside my reach. Simple, basic facts were gone. I couldn't recall my own reflection, the color of my eyes or hair, or the shape of my face. My birthday and even my age were mysteries. I didn't know if I had family, other than Jacob, though I assumed that if we had children he would've mentioned them, especially during some part of his *responsibility* discussion.

Sadly, I didn't know me.

Yet there were some aspects of this life that had felt clear. Like Raquel and Elizabeth. With them everything seemed right, as if I were safe. The opposite was true about the strange people with titles that seemed unfamiliar. Merely the mention of their names and the *brother* and *sister* references caused my chest to tighten and pulse to quicken. Though I couldn't recall my past, the anxiety those people and their power instilled in me was palpably real.

Jacob remained unclear. As I had listened to his breathing, knowing that he was once again sleeping with his head upon my bed, I'd found myself conflicted by his dichotomy. His presence, even in sleep, gave me a sense of protection from the outside world. With him near, I didn't fear the Commission, Dr. Newton, or even the apparently all-powerful Father Gabriel. Jacob was my husband and my protector. And yet a sense of uncertainty also nagged at my soul. Yes, he kept me safe from everything outside our bubble—it was inside our bubble that concerned me.

Due to my injuries my options were limited, but they did exist. Jacob had made that clear. I could obey his and Father Gabriel's rules or disobey them—it was up to me. In my darkened world, I decided to do my best to obey. I definitely had issues with what I was obeying, with how my husband believed he had the right to exercise complete domination at his discretion. I didn't understand how I'd gotten to this point or why I'd agreed to this in the past. However, the large gaps— really, gaping caverns—in my memory gave me hope. I must've had a reason. Apparently at one time I'd willingly chosen him and this life. I must have seen more to my husband. Maybe if I learned to think like Sara, I could figure out how to survive.

Following Dr. Newton's examination, I'd admittedly been overwhelmed. I had been rendered powerless to communicate, my emotions too jumbled to articulate. At that time, my body began to surrender, but as I drifted toward nothingness, my mind fought back. During my outburst I'd learned something about myself. I'd learned that I was a survivor, not a quitter, and I wouldn't quit fighting.

My verbal tirade had come from the depths of panic. If I wanted to win my fight—if I wanted not only to survive, but to recover and remember—I needed to battle smarter.

My first goal was to get stronger. And as I did, I needed to understand my battlefield. Lashing out in the darkness wasn't, and wouldn't be, successful. I needed to size up my opponents, distinguish my allies from my enemies, and learn the rules of my new war.

Jacob believed I already knew his and Father Gabriel's rules, and he expected me to follow them. I'd obey as long as those rules helped me heal and gain strength. Plus, admittedly, I didn't want to fight alone. I needed allies in this strange world. It seemed clear that my battle would be better fought with Jacob than against him.

I'd heard his determination when he answered Brother Timothy and Sister Lilith's questions, and when he argued with Dr. Newton. I'd also felt his slap—his correction.

Jacob stood strong for what he believed, and he believed that I was his wife, Sara. He was willing to fight for that. I was going to fight to discover myself. If I truly was Sara, then we were striving for the same thing.

Since my eyes were covered and my speaking was restricted, my battle plan was to concentrate on surveillance. I'd spend my days as a sponge, absorbing everything around me. In many ways sight blinded people to the truth, and in my current condition I wasn't preoccupied by appearances or visual distractions. The bandages allowed me to go beyond the surface and hear the true intentions of those around me.

"Sara," Jacob said, pulling me from my thoughts and back to the present.

He held a straw to my lips. As I sipped, the water moistened my throat, helping me wash down the oatmeal he'd been feeding me. I'd obediently accepted each spoonful but I hadn't liked it. It was warm and slightly sweet, but it was also thick, too thick to drink and yet not thick enough to chew. Thankfully, it hadn't been my only food. I'd also had a banana and toast and had even been allowed to hold them and feed myself. As I continued sipping the water, he spoke.

"I'm going to need to leave soon for Assembly. I wanted to talk to Sister Lilith, to remind her that you're still not cleared to speak. I'll talk with Raquel, and she can relay my message. I don't want her trying to . . . well, even if she tells you that you're cleared to speak, remember that I said no."

I had no intention of speaking with Sister Lilith, though I was becoming increasingly curious about what she planned to say. Since Jacob and I were still alone, I whispered, "I promise, I won't speak." I got the feeling that this training made him as uncomfortable as it did me. If we were fighting on the same side, I wanted to reassure him that my compliance wasn't in question. "I've given everything you've told me a lot of thought. You can trust me to do as you've said." I reached to find his hand. Once I found it, I added, "I hope you already do . . . trust me, I mean. After all, we're married. You trusted me enough to ask me to be your wife, didn't you?" I was fishing for more about our past.

He cleared his throat. "Um, yes."

I didn't know what his answer meant, but I tried for more. "May I continue?"

"Sara, we have rules, not just my rules—the community's rules, The Light's rules. I'm sure reminding you of some of those will be part of Sister Lilith's plan."

"OK."

"Tell me you remember them. After all, we've lived and abided by The Light for a while now."

How long is a while? I pressed my lips together and lowered my chin. "I'm sorry, I don't. I want to." I did. I wanted to understand the world around me.

"That's why it's better to listen when Sister Lilith is here. Be cautious of what you agree to or disagree with. She and Brother Timothy have been very suspicious of what preceded your accident. I don't want her interpreting your lack of memory as guilt."

A sheen of perspiration coated my freshly washed skin. "B-but," I stuttered, "I really don't remember. Please." I squeezed his hand. "You answered their questions before. What you said, that's all I know. Tell me what happened."

"I will, but not yet."

"Why?"

Jacob sighed. "One strictly enforced rule was put into place by Father Gabriel to teach patience. That's one of the reasons so many of us follow him. He has answers, reasons behind each decree. He didn't create the rules for The Light arbitrarily; each one has meaning and purpose. As I said, this rule teaches that patience is a virtue. God's word instructs men to marry virtuous women. Therefore all women of The Light, such as yourself, are forbidden from questioning men, including your husband. This teaches you, and all the women, patience. Answers will be revealed in God's time, not yours."

I tried to understand. "You're saying that I can't ask you what happened? I'm supposed to wait until you tell me?"

"Yes," he said with a laugh. Kissing the top of my head, he added, "You do realize that was a question, yes?"

The corners of my lips moved upward. "No, I mean, now I do." I let go of his hand as my smile faded. "Does that mean you're going to . . . correct me?"

He reached for my hand. "I wish we had more time to discuss this right now." His thumb slowly moved in a circle, caressing my knuckles. "We originally learned all of this together. That was easier than explaining it now. It feels like I'm introducing you to a whole new way of life when in truth we chose this path together. Do you remember yesterday when I told you that I'd accepted responsibility for you?"

I nodded, trying unsuccessfully to stop my slight trembling.

"Part of that responsibility," he continued, "includes recognizing that not all violations are equal." He leaned closer and his body warmed my side. When he lifted my hand to his lips, my shaking stilled. Instead of correction, he was delivering gentle kisses to the tops of my knuckles. "Sara, whether you recall the particulars or not, we have a good marriage. You're not abused; you're disciplined. Correction is never done in anger. Father Gabriel teaches that men must lead. It's our job, how we were created. Taking responsibility for you is required, but you and I love one another and I accepted that challenge willingly. I do what I need to do to help you and make your life easier. Correction defines your boundaries, giving you the freedom to feel safe. Since the delivery of the correction, as well as the mode, is up to me, I can also decide when there are exceptions, times when correction isn't necessary. Part of my responsibility is to decipher intent." He lifted my chin. "I don't think that a moment ago you *intended* to question again, did you?"

I shook my head. "No, I didn't."

"I believe you. Your honesty is part of this equation. Sara, we've always been honest with one another. Don't let this problem with your memory change that."

I still didn't like the premise, but his explanation and absolution eased a bit of my apprehension. "Thank you for explaining. I'm sorry that I don't remember all of the rules. I'll try." I wanted to remember. I also liked this Jacob, the one who explained things. I wanted him on my side.

"I know you will. I'll be back as soon as I can. Sara." His tone changed when he said my name, clearly meaning that whatever he was about to say was beyond question. "No more talking, and be cognizant of your nonverbal responses to Sister Lilith's questions."

I nodded.

"Very good," Jacob said, petting my hair as he stood. The bed shifted and the warmth of his body against mine vanished. The tangible void sent a chill through me, reminding me that soon I'd be left alone—alone with Sister Lilith.

"Brother Jacob?"

Warmth returned as I grinned toward the sound of Raquel's now familiar voice from the doorway. It wasn't the first time she'd entered my room today. She'd been in earlier to help with my shower. Well, not really *with* my shower. Jacob had done that. She'd helped by putting whatever she used over my cast to keep it dry. Jacob was the one who'd washed my body. I'd expected to remember his touch, but I hadn't. It didn't feel wrong—it felt foreign, but then again, so did everything else.

Just now, when he'd kissed my hand, the sensation was different, unexpected—soft and affectionate. I liked that side of my husband. That was the side that made me feel safe and loved. I blushed at the memory of his using that word, saying that we *loved* one another. Even if I didn't remember, I was loved.

Lost in my thoughts, I'd forgotten my plan to be a sponge and missed part of Raquel and Jacob's conversation.

". . . I want that made perfectly clear." I didn't need to hear Jacob's entire speech. I knew what he was emphasizing.

"I will," Raquel replied. "I'd be happy to stay with Sara, to make this easier for her on her first day. Sister Lilith can't deny my presence, if you authorize it."

My heart leaped. I wanted it, but she wasn't asking me. Actually, she wasn't asking Jacob either—she was offering. Sucking my lower lip between my teeth, I made a mental note to think about semantics later and waited for his response. There was definitely a trick to being a . . . what did he call it? . . . *a woman of The Light.*

"Thank you." He sighed with relief. "By the smile on my wife's face, if she'd stop biting that lip, I think she'd be happy to have you." He tugged my lip free. "Remember my rules."

I nodded, grinning over his answer.

"I'll be back as soon as I can." His lips brushed the top of my head, then the door opened and he was gone.

"Sara," Raquel said once we were alone. "Are you nervous about this? You've done it before; we all have. It's pretty standard for one of the Commission wives to do a review after an incident. Father Gabriel believes that it helps all of us stay focused on his teachings. After something as traumatic as your accident, evil thoughts could try to confuse your mind. If you didn't go through a review, others in the community could question your commitment, and that could lead to dissent. The Light practices a single mind-set of enlightenment, all working as one, doing God's work, and fulfilling Father Gabriel's teaching." She giggled lightheartedly. "Oh, listen to me going on. I know you know all of that. Feel free to reach out and push me if I talk too much."

I wanted to tell her I didn't know, or at least I didn't remember. Either way, I appreciated her talking. I was also relieved to learn that this wasn't specifically about me. It was common protocol.

Hoping she was watching, I mouthed, *Thank you.*

"Oh, you say that now," she answered, as if I'd spoken. "After a few hours of listening to her read Father Gabriel's word and preaching at you, you won't be thanking me." She pulled the blankets back and moved the wheelchair close. "Brother Jacob must have brought you some more nightgowns. I meant to say something earlier. That's a great color on you."

Really? What color is it?

I reached over to my braid.

"You're good at that. Or did Brother Jacob do it?"

I shook my head with an amused grin.

"I wasn't sure, but it's pretty. I'm better at helping other people braid than doing it myself. I guess that's why this is my calling, helping others. If I had to braid my own hair, well, it'd look awful. That's why I usually wear mine in a bun, or a messy bun, or sometimes . . ."

Sister Raquel filled every moment after Jacob's departure with talk and the entire time, though I never said a word, I was part of the conversation. Soon I was back in bed and completely relaxed. I laughed at some of her stories and also practiced my sponging, learning things by listening to her friendly voice. I also learned more about my training. She joked that I'd undoubtedly already heard all the lessons and sermons that Sister Lilith would recite, and if I promised not to snore, I could probably catch a catnap under my bandages and still be able to answer all her questions.

When Sister Raquel mentioned her husband, Benjamin, her voice filled with adoration. I got the sense that their relationship was similar to what Jacob had described, one where she put her full trust in Benjamin and he assumed full responsibility for her. Her obvious contentment with her marriage gave me hope for my own. The only time she sounded sad was at the mention of children, sharing that she and Benjamin didn't have any. Even then, she quickly said that she believed God would provide them in His time. She confessed in a whisper that she needed to work on her patience.

I realized that if she and Benjamin were trying to have children, Father Gabriel must not preach against sex. For some reason that made me smile. I couldn't remember having been with Jacob in that way, but he said we had a good marriage and loved one another. The idea of being intimate didn't scare me as much as the thought of his correction. As a matter of fact, as my thoughts lingered on his washing and drying me, parts of my body woke from their sleep. I pondered who my husband was in the bedroom. *Is he the protector with a reassuring tone or the disciplinarian who demands obedience?*

I wouldn't be finding out as long as my leg and rib were in their current conditions, but with the way my insides tingled, I suspected that whoever he was, I liked him.

Raquel's conversation reassured me. Instead of facing Sister Lilith alone, I would have her by my side. Therefore when the door opened and Sister Lilith's high-heeled shoes entered, I was confident that I was ready to begin.

"Sister Sara," she began, "It's Sister Lilith. I'm happy to see you're ready to start this review of your training."

I nodded.

Raquel sat beside me on the bed where Jacob had been as she spoke. "I'm sorry if you weren't notified, Sister Lilith. Brother Jacob asked me to stay, at least for today. You see, Sara can't get to and from her bed to the bathroom by herself. Brother Jacob didn't want to burden you with the task." Though I'd zoned out through part of Jacob and Raquel's conversation, I didn't think Jacob had gone into that much detail.

"Well, yes," Sister Lilith replied. "We could always call for you . . ."

"Sister, I would go"—Sister Raquel's shoulder rubbed mine as it shrugged with her casual reply—"but I'm confident that Benjamin would punish me if I disobeyed Brother Jacob. And I wouldn't want Brother Timothy to learn that you suggested my disobedience."

"Of course not," she responded quickly. "Sister Raquel, we'll make do with all three of us today. I wasn't suggesting disobedience. We'll just forget that we even discussed it."

Oh, that is definitely a conversation I'm glad I sponged. I liked Raquel.

"Sister Raquel?" Sister Lilith asked. "Before we begin, do you know Dr. Newton's plans for Sister Sara's cast? I believe I heard she'll be receiving a walking cast soon." From the sound of the chair over the tile, I could tell she'd brought it from beside my bed toward the foot.

"I don't. He'll be here later. I'll let him know you're curious."

"Thank you. I'm just thinking it'll make our future review sessions easier for Sister Sara."

"Yes, I understand."

"Now, Sister Sara, since you're unable to respond, once I've read Father Gabriel's declaration of faith for The Light, I'll ask you basic yes-and-no questions. Your answers will help me determine where we'll go from there. Do you understand?"

I nodded.

Pages fluttered. "We the members of The Light believe in Father Gabriel and the enlightenment . . ."

CHAPTER 9
Jacob

Father Gabriel began each morning at Assembly with prayer. Only the members of the Assembly and the Commission were worthy to meet daily with our leader, though that privilege didn't always mean meeting in person.

Our campus in Alaska was one of three campuses of The Light. Ours, the Northern Light, was the largest and the most productive, but Father Gabriel's leadership was needed at all campuses. Because of this he often traveled. Though all the communities lived modestly, The Light possessed the latest technology. With protected webinars and tele-conferencing, and because of different time zones, it didn't matter where Father Gabriel was on any given day. He was always able to attend the morning Assembly of each campus.

Whether he was with us, or somewhere else, his aura of authority filled the room.

There were four commissioners at each campus, making up Father Gabriel's circle of twelve disciples. These were Father Gabriel's inner sanctum, the men he most trusted. Under the Commissioners there were twelve Assemblymen at each campus. The Assemblymen shared the Commissioners' burdens and were fully accountable to them. These sixteen men and their wives were *the chosen* of each campus. The system Father

Gabriel put into place worked well to govern The Light and was especially efficient when he was away and as the campuses continued to grow.

At last census the Northern Light had over 450 followers who all lived, worshipped, and worked for Father Gabriel and The Light. The Western Light had nearly three hundred, and the Eastern Light, the first campus, had over one hundred. The Eastern Light purposely remained small due to its urban location. It had neither the space nor the isolation of the Northern and Western Light communities. The Eastern Light served primarily as the point of entry for many of the followers. Once they were tested and found acceptable, they were assigned to one of the larger campuses. Assignment was usually based on the follower's abilities as well as the needs of each campus.

As Father Gabriel's voice transcended the miles and his prayer wished blessings on our souls, my thoughts returned to Sara, to Sister Lilith's intentions, and Sara's healing.

This is wrong. My body and mind should be focused on Father Gabriel.

Internal conflict was one reason I'd resisted the assignment of a wife. Another reason was my desire to succeed. Throughout my life, no matter the endeavor—from the military to The Light—my goal had always been success. With the addition of a wife, everything changed. For the first time, success wasn't contingent only upon me, but also upon Sara.

Before the Commission assigned a follower a wife, especially one in need of indoctrination, the husband-to-be received training. As a member of the Assembly, I'd been involved with many trainings. I knew the strict protocol and what was expected.

Since my assignment to the Assembly nearly a year ago, I'd listened to followers who claimed to be having difficulty with the indoctrination protocol. From my lofty position, I'd piously remind those followers that they were but a part of Father Gabriel's body of believers, as were their new wives, and all parts of the body must work together. I'd said, "We've been taught that if something causes us to lose our way, we must remove it. It's written that if your eye causes you to stumble, gouge it out. It's better to enter the kingdom of Light with only one eye than to be cast out." Then I'd ask, "Is your new wife causing you to lose your way, to forget Father Gabriel's teachings, or will you be able to control her and help her become a productive member of the body?"

Though everyone claimed they'd succeed, there were failures. Insubordinate members of the body were banished and removed— the ultimate penalty, paid with the ultimate price. My head knew the answers. Hell, I'd said the answers. I also knew the consequences.

However, now, for the first time in my memory, I felt conflicted. I was supposed to train and rule Sara, yet in a very short time, even without her eyes and with a limited ability to speak, she'd developed a power over me. When she'd asked me about my asking her to marry me, I was taken aback, and when her hands trembled at the mere thought of my correction, my stomach turned. Kissing her hand was a reflex. I didn't consider the penalties. I knew the prescribed timetable. At this point my affection was to be limited and nonsexual. The touching of her hair and even platonic kisses to her head were acceptable, but not affection or comfort, not yet.

As Father Gabriel concluded the opening prayer, guilt tugged at my conscience, and I contemplated confessing my affectionate behavior. The only thing stopping me was concern regarding punishment. I didn't worry about myself; I never had. I was a firm believer that if I did wrong, I deserved correction. I'd never expected less of myself than I did of my subordinates. Everyone was accountable.

Now was different. Though I hadn't planned on it, nor wanted it, now I cared. I cared about someone other than myself. I knew what Sara had endured and what was still to come.

". . . blessed by me, Father Gabriel, The Light of our God. Amen."

"Amen," came resoundingly from all sixteen men around the large conference table. I scanned the eyes around me.

Do they also have these conflicting thoughts or is it just me?

As soon as my gaze was met by Brother Timothy's, I knew that I wouldn't confess my show of affection. I couldn't risk it, not as long as

Sara was vulnerable. With Brother Timothy's eyes on me, I refused to show or admit to weakness.

I'd never understood the animosity that glowed in his eyes. When I'd first arrived at the Northern Light nearly three years before, he and Sister Lilith were the only unwelcoming followers. With time I'd learned to ignore them. Their enmity didn't affect my goal. Even after being appointed to the Assembly, I was able to ignore them.

Suddenly the thought crossed my mind: the Commission had assigned Sara to me.

Was I assigned Sara to fail? Does Brother Timothy dislike me so much as to capitalize on this unfamiliar assignment? Will Sara undo my success?

I forced myself to concentrate on the words spoken around me. The Assemblymen had begun reading their daily reports. We each had a specific topic, and since each topic was approached daily, the reports were often quick. It was a good way to keep the Assembly, the Commission, and Father Gabriel current on the overall status of the community.

My primary job for The Light was as one of the pilots. I transported Father Gabriel from campus to campus and flew supplies to the Northern Light. My military training had been significant in preparing me for The Light. Most importantly, I'd flown a C-12A in and out of Iraq, and also, I thrived under the regimented life. Taking and giving orders, as well as following and implementing rules, were my forte.

As an Assemblyman I was to oversee and settle disputes. Father Gabriel required cohesive living on all his campuses. Everyone's behavior was continually monitored. Any disobedience was brought to me. If I believed the behavior warranted correction, I took the offense to the Commission. If the Commission forwarded it to Father Gabriel, the usual course of action was public correction. Banishment was the ultimate punishment. Simply the knowledge that such punishments were possible served as a powerful deterrent.

Brother Raphael, the longest-standing Commissioner, conducted the morning meetings. At the Northern Light he was second in reverence only to Father Gabriel. His deep voice reverberated through the conference room. "Brother Jacob, please share your report."

I stood and addressed the Commission and Assembly. After my report was complete, he asked Brother Luke about some new followers. Luke and his wife Elizabeth were responsible for all new followers at the Northern Light.

Luke went on, talking about a husband and wife who'd come to The Light, how they were progressing well with their training and would soon be granted an apartment. Brother Raphael went on to ask the Assemblyman in charge of housing how soon an apartment would be ready. As they discussed the possible housing and job assignments for this new couple, the temperature of the room seemed to rise and my palms moistened. Though I knew Sara was the next topic of conversation, I tried to think of anything else. The way Brother Raphael had retained his Boston accent through all the years. The way Luke's back straightened with pride as he spoke about the new followers' success.

My eyes met Brother Timothy's and his cold glare interrupted my thoughts. Purposely I moved my gaze to Brother Daniel's face and took in its approving shine. As my overseer, Brother Daniel had repeatedly put his trust in me and my abilities.

Damn, I have to do this. I won't fail him or add fuel to Brother Timothy's dislike.

"Brother Jacob," Brother Raphael said. "I could ask Brother Luke, but let's skip ahead. Your new wife is awake. Please tell us how things are progressing at the clinic, and if you believe we have any problems or glitches with her progress."

I stood again and inhaled, my usual confidence waning. If I didn't say something about my unease, I feared it'd be noticed. I needed to tackle the subject head on. "I apologize for my less-than-stellar presentation. I've spent the last ten nights sleeping in a chair, my head on the end of Sara's bed." I shrugged my shoulders. "It's less than conducive to a good night's sleep. If my demeanor seems off, I plead matrimonial insomnia."

Benjamin laughed, breaking my mounting tension and coming to my rescue. "No, Brother Jacob, in another month we can rib you about matrimonial insomnia; now you're just exhausted. At least in a month you'll have a smile." Laughter came from all around the table before Benjamin continued, "Raquel told me about your wife. It sounds as though she's coming along."

I nodded, eternally grateful for the change in formality. "Being in this position is considerably different from training someone for it. Currently Sister Lilith"—I turned toward my nemesis—"thank you, Brother Timothy, currently Sister Lilith is beginning Sara's training."

"Why?" Brother Raphael spoke sharply.

"I was told—"

Brother Timothy interrupted. "You see, Sara seemed to be doing well, very well, and she isn't coming to us as a mere follower. She'll be filling the role of a wife of an Assemblyman, part of the chosen. Her success is paramount and, after what has happened in the past . . . we believed it was better to jump ahead and begin Sara's training. Father Gabriel teaches that an idle mind is the devil's playground. Keeping Sara occupied, engaged, and learning is—"

"Brother Jacob?" The entire room stopped—moving, breathing, everything—at the rare sound of Father Gabriel's voice. He was often more of an observer of our meetings than a participant.

"Yes, Father Gabriel." I turned respectfully toward the screen.

"I want to hear the particulars, not about what others are doing. Sara was given to you. You've been absent from us since her arrival and accident over a week ago until yesterday. Yesterday you pleaded the case for her nutrients. I see what's happening. I want to hear it from you."

He sees what's happening? What does that mean?

My pulse quickened. "Father, what particulars?"

"Taking on a wife is a big responsibility. The Lord chose the church as his bride, and now your bride has arrived. It's your responsibility to acclimate her. Tell us, how is it progressing?"

"I believe it's progressing well. So far she doesn't seem to have memories of her life in the dark. She's nervous and scared, which is normal. The loss of sight, as well as her injuries, are keeping her dependent. I'm doing what I've told others to do, teaching her the rules, her role as my wife, and the restrictions she can expect, all the while convincing her this was, and has been, her life." I took a breath. "Speaking of restrictions, I know her sight must be restricted until some of her injuries heal. However, I'd like to have the cast on her leg changed to one that would allow her to wa—"

"It's not time!" Brother Timothy interjected.

"Brother Timothy." Father Gabriel's voice transcended the miles. "It wasn't time for Sister Lilith to begin training either. Let Brother Jacob continue. And let me make myself clear: I don't want history to repeat itself. The Eastern Light usually weeds out failures. Sara is at the Northern Light. We must all work toward her success."

"Yes, Father," Brother Timothy replied.

"Brother Jacob, tell us if there have been any problems."

"Only one." I swallowed. "Though Sara was forbidden to speak, yesterday she did."

Murmurs came from around the table.

"What was your response?" Father Gabriel asked.

"I corrected her. I take my responsibility seriously. The Commission is ultimately responsible, but it's my duty to teach, correct, and bring her into The Light."

The room waited as Father Gabriel sat quietly, his fingers steepled before him, thinking and watching. His customary shirt and tie, without a suit coat, were a stark contrast to the cherry-paneled wall behind him.

"Yes," Father Gabriel finally said. "Brother Timothy was right—most new followers don't come into The Light as chosen. Sister Sara has already achieved a status most women never will. While this is unusual, thankfully, Brother Jacob, you have a better understanding of the acclimation protocol than the average follower. I'm pleased to learn that you're compliant and capable of handling situations as they occur. I'm certain you're aware of the consequences not only to Sara but to you should this indoctrination fail?"

"Yes, Father, I am," I answered, steadfast.

"Brother Luke," Father Gabriel continued. "Sister Sara's continued treatment is under your supervision. You and Dr. Newton decide when it's time for her cast to be changed. However, I have a few more questions for Brother Jacob."

"Yes, Father?"

"Tell us how your wife responded when she learned of your control over her necessities: eating, using the restroom, sleeping, drinking, and hygiene."

"She hasn't fought my control. She's acquiesced."

"And when you corrected her? What did you do? How did she respond?"

I looked toward Brother Daniel. His expression instructed me to answer honestly. The lump in my throat grew, but I continued. "When she spoke, without permission, I utilized corporal punishment. I slapped her. It was a swift carriage of correction."

"Acceptable," Father Gabriel replied. "Go on."

"I then required her to repeat her name and that we were wed." Before anyone could speak, I added, "And she did. That was yesterday. This morning I discussed it with her further. Though she seems confused, I believe she's a quick learner and is adapting."

I wasn't completely forthcoming—I didn't tell them about her trembling or my affection—but I'd answered truthfully.

"Brother Jacob?" Brother Timothy's voice dominated the room.

"Yes?"

"We know what happened during the incident. Tell the Commission what happened yesterday during Dr. Newton's examination."

I stood taller and clenched my teeth. Timothy's question meant one thing: Newton had talked to him.

"Was there a problem?" Luke asked.

"I take the responsibility you've entrusted to me very seriously," I began. "That goes for all my responsibilities, from my quest to follow The Light to my assignment on the Assembly. One day Sara will be mine in all ways. I've helped her with things that by The Light's decree aren't to be shared by those not bound by marriage. Father, you speak of modesty for our women. Therefore I demanded to be present during Dr. Newton's examination, and only allowed him access to Sara's injuries." I took a deep breath and turned back to Brother Daniel. I wouldn't mention her questioning her eyes unless it was brought up.

"Brother Timothy?" Brother Daniel asked. "Is there something I missed? Are you aware of anything else that happened during Sister Sara's examination that wasn't acceptable?"

I held my breath as Timothy glared in my direction.

"Dr. Newton doesn't believe he was allowed full access to his patient."

"Brother Timothy?"

We all turned toward Father Gabriel's voice.

"Yes, Father?" Timothy responded.

"Perhaps you've forgotten what it's like to have a new wife. I believe Brother Jacob's protectiveness is supported by my doctrine. Do you see a problem with that? If so, please, Brother, enlighten us."

I bit my tongue, wanting to interject, but happy with Father Gabriel's input.

"No, not at all." Brother Timothy sat taller. "However, I'm concerned that we won't be able to get a good assessment of Sister Sara until Dr. Newton and my wife are able to spend significant time with her."

"Fine. Brother Jacob." Father Gabriel changed the subject. "Have you continued Sister Sara's speech restriction? Since she's spoken, she obviously knows she can do so without damage to her vocal cords?"

"Yes, Father. I'm only allowing her to speak with me."

"And?"

"And she's obeyed. I realize that speaking now is sooner than the protocol recommends. For that reason, Father, I request your permission to allow her to only speak to me, for the next few days. As we all know, this early stage of indoctrination is extremely formative. If you agree, I'd continue to allow Sister Lilith's training and Sister Raquel's assistance. Of course Dr. Newton can treat her, with me present, but I request that for now she only be questioned in a yes-no format by anyone other than me." This was a rare opportunity to bypass the Commission, and I presented my case. "She's still confused, as is standard. Even if she's allowed to get the walking cast, with her other injuries she won't be able to move without pain. I understand this important stage. I've seen what can happen. For Sara, myself, and our future family, I ask that I be allowed to be the one who walks my wife into The Light."

My request was brazen and unusual, but then again, Brother Timothy was right, most women were given to followers who needed the guidance of the Assembly. As a member of the Assembly, I was exercising my right, or so I hoped.

"Brother, after Assembly, I'll meet with the Commission. Brother Daniel will contact you later with my answer. Shall we carry on?"

"Thank you, Father," I said, resuming my seat and avoiding Brother Timothy's glare.

"Now," Brother Raphael said. "It's time for our report regarding the powerhouse. With the colder-than-normal November temperatures, tell us about the turbines. Is there any fear of them freezing?"

∾

Two and a half hours after I'd left Sara, I returned to the clinic. Though parts of it resembled a hospital, only Dr. Newton had a medical degree. The others who staffed the clinic were there on assignment based on their attributes. Most of the support staff's skills were acquired here at the Northern Light, unless they came willingly with prior knowledge. Either way, the dedication and commitment of the followers made them excellent learners. As I approached Sara's room, one of the only single rooms—the primary one used for acclimation of acquired followers—I listened.

Hearing only silence, I assumed Lilith had left. Though I considered looking for Raquel to learn more about the training, I chose instead to open the door. I was right: Sara was alone. With the head of her bed reclined, I saw only the back of her head, her golden braid loose from lying against the pillow. I waited for her to turn, wondering if she was awake or asleep, and then I heard the sniffles and saw her shoulders shudder. She was awake—and was crying.

Clenching my teeth, sure that this was Lilith's doing, I moved cautiously to the side of her bed and continued my assignment.

"Sara?"

At the sound of my voice, her shoulders sagged. Slowly she turned in my direction. Her cheeks were damp and blotchy. The bandages, with their solid domed patch over each eye, allowed her tears to escape. When she didn't speak, I moved closer. Raising the head of her bed and lowering the side rail, I sat beside her. Fear and sadness not only showed on her wet cheeks but settled around her like a cloud.

Screw the timetable and the rules. She won't make it through this in this shape.

With my leg against her wounded body, I grabbed a tissue and began to dry her cheeks.

Where the hell is Raquel, and most importantly, what did Lilith do?

My chest ached at Sara's labored breathing. Surely she had things to say, but she was obeying my last command and remaining silent. When her breathing finally settled, I said, "No one else is here, you may speak. What is it? Why are you crying?"

CHAPTER 10
Stella

Detroit in July might as well be Miami. The humidity and heat were as intense without the benefit of the Atlantic Ocean. The Detroit River was definitely not as spectacular. Stepping into the cool air conditioning of Jumbo's, I eyed a table near the back, next to a pool table. Thankfully, it was still too early for the players to be out. Come ten o'clock, this place would be rocking.

Though I'd been thinking about that cold beer Dylan had mentioned before I left him in the parking lot, I ordered lemonade and sat down to wait for Dr. Howell.

I kept remembering the pierced ear of the woman on the table—well, more accurately, the injured ear. Maybe it wasn't a piercing injury. Maybe I'd read too much into the expression I thought I saw when Tracy Howell looked at me.

When I looked up, I smiled, seeing the doctor walking toward me. She'd looked young at the morgue, but now, with a maxi-skirt, T-shirt, and flip-flops, and her long, dark hair flowing loosely down her back, she looked more like a high school student than a forensic pathologist.

Dr. Howell didn't return my smile as she settled in the seat across from me. Glancing from side to side, she did little to hide her nerves. "Stella," she began. "Once again, I apologize for calling you in today.

The blonde hair and the body type, both similar to Mindy's . . . I just had to be sure."

"Doctor, how many unidentified bodies—female bodies—do you see?"

She shrugged. "Too many."

I tilted my head. "I've been called down twice in two weeks, for blonde females. Is that par for the course?"

Dr. Howell's let her eyes fall to the table, suddenly interested in a sticky substance left by patrons before us. "I'd be happy to talk about Mindy Rosemont."

"That's the thing, I think we are. I think you're trying to tell me something." With my hair secured in a low ponytail, my exposed brow rose questioningly. "Is there any chance that I'm on to something?"

She sighed and leaned forward. "I can't be quoted."

"You won't be. I'm not sure if this will become a story. I don't even know if this will help me find Mindy or at least find out what happened to her, but please, tell me what you know. If I'm totally off base then we can get a beer, rack some balls, and call it a night."

Dr. Howell looked at me contemplatively. For a moment I expected her to stand and walk to the cue box, but then she sat back and sighed. "Let's start by you calling me Tracy. I'm not sure what I know. I've only been with the Wayne County ME for about five months, but from what I've seen, something is going on. We see a lot of gang and gun violence, and historically, the profile of our unclaimed bodies tends to be young males. Ethnicity varies. It used to be more African-Americans and Latinos, but not anymore. White males are dying as fast as everyone else. Those deaths are sad, but they make sense. There are multiple causes: fights, shootings, knives, and of course drugs. With drug deaths we see women too, many of those are prostitutes. The thing that's different about the more recent female bodies is that many don't have illegal drugs in their systems. Some, like the one today, are beaten up, but not all. As you've heard, we have a backlog on rape kits. But the ones that have been completed often don't show sexual activity. Many of them have varying degrees of that burned-off fingerprint thing."

"Are they all blondes?"

"No, their hair color doesn't seem to matter. They range in age from about eighteen to about thirty." She slapped the table and firmed her shoulders. "Do you see the problem?"

My eyes widened. "Besides the obvious issue of women dying all around us?"

"I'm talking about the lack of consistency. I've taken my concerns to my bosses and been told that it is what it is. We report our findings to the National Center for Health Statistics and they compile statistical data. If there's an unusual occurrence in their findings, they'll notify the police and Wayne County. But I don't think there will be a statistically significant occurrence. The victims vary just enough. While men go missing, it's the women that I'm the most concerned about. The ones I've seen, or learned about while going back in the records, also vary in ethnicity."

I sipped my lemonade and thought about all she'd just said. "You knew that the woman today wasn't Mindy, didn't you?"

"I want you to find your friend. I just thought . . ."

I reached out and covered her hand. "I can't promise anything. I won't even take any of this to Bernard until I have more, but I'll look around, ask some questions, do some research. If there's any chance that this information will help me find Mindy, I'll do it."

Tracy nodded. "I can't go on the record, but if there's any way I can help, if you need information, I can . . ." She reached into her purse and took out a flash drive. Handing it to me, she said, "Here. Just know that I'll deny that what's on there came from me."

I rolled the drive between my fingers. "What's on this?"

"Something that you don't want to view on a full stomach. I started going back through the records and looking into deaths of women in this specific age group who didn't fit the typical profile. It's really the only two matching criteria, age and sex. I only went back ten years. That drive contains names and pictures as well as victims who will forever be nameless. The examination results are there too, if an autopsy was done."

"Isn't there always an autopsy with suspicious deaths?"

She shrugged. "Not all the deaths were suspicious. In some cases the cause was obvious. I've been putting the data together and looking for a connection. I feel like it's there, but I just don't know what it is. I was hoping that maybe you could take a look. Maybe you'll see a pattern that I don't."

"I'll do it."

"I recognized the man with you today. I know he's a detective with the homicide and narcotics unit of DPD."

I nodded.

"I've seen him in the lab before. What I haven't seen before is Detective Richards holding someone's hand, supporting them. He's usually a hard-ass."

I sat up straight. "Detective Richards and I are dating."

"It's none of my business, but don't you see that as a conflict of interest?"

"You're right, it's not any of your business."

Tracy persisted. "Well, what I mean is that you're an investigative journalist and he works for the people who try to keep all of this shit covered up."

I sucked my lower lip between my teeth and contemplated my response. "Tracy, you work for Wayne County. Do you believe they handle cases differently than the Detroit Police Department?"

"Unfortunately, no. I don't blame you for thinking what I said was a dis on your boyfriend. It really wasn't. It's this whole city. No city wants to be known for its crime. The mayor, the chamber of commerce, they're constantly harping about revitalization. They're bidding on businesses, improved infrastructure, human capital, and social programs.

They don't want to acknowledge that we have a real problem, a new real problem."

"New? You said you have data going back ten years."

"I do," Tracy admitted. "But ten years is new, new for all the revitalization that's been happening."

She was right. It was. If we had some pattern of random women being kidnapped and killed, no company would want to invest in Detroit. "So you're saying that it's the system, or systems. No one in authority wants to admit this is happening."

"Yes. And I'd rather you don't say anything to Detective Richards. If you do, please don't say it was me that started you on this quest for answers."

"Don't worry. Dylan and I keep work out of our private lives. Professional courtesy," I added.

"Thank you, Stella. If I'm wasting your time, I'm sorry. I just feel like we have something significant occurring, and everyone is turning a blind eye."

∼

Hours later I turned away from the computer screen, wishing I could unsee what I'd seen. The information that Tracy had compiled was compelling and sickening. The women in Dr. Howell's files didn't seem to have one common denominator other than being dead. Even the injuries they'd sustained varied: some showed signs of only recent trauma, others patterns of ongoing abuse.

I rubbed my throbbing temples and forced myself to walk away from my computer. It was nearly midnight, and all I'd managed to do was scan the collection of pictures, autopsy results, and police reports. Just enough to turn my stomach. My goal had been to get an overview of what Tracy was trying to tell me. As a woman, I'd hoped that the crazy things on television or in books were fiction, only fiction. As an investigative journalist, I knew they weren't. Yet before tonight I'd never seen information compiled so succinctly about crimes against women taking place in my own city.

In an effort to clear my head, I wandered through my apartment and checked my phone. Dylan never texted me back after I let him know that I wouldn't be coming over. It didn't bother me. This relationship was relatively new. While I appreciated his having met me at the morgue, I needed space. I'd been on my own for too long to suddenly jump into anything serious. Staying at his house was nice—more than nice. But I wasn't ready to leave a change of clothes or a toothbrush.

It would take more than hot, steamy sex and salmon on the grill to prompt me to move Fred's fishbowl. Joint custody of a fish was more domesticated than I wanted to do right now. Besides, I had my own washing machine.

I needed to go to bed. It'd been a long day. Yet at the same time, I couldn't stop thinking about the last profile I'd read on Dr. Howell's memory drive. The picture the victim's parents had given to the police showed two daughters: two beautiful twenty-year-old coeds with their entire lives before them, smiling for the camera. Unfortunately, no one had realized how short a time *their entire lives* would be.

The victim named in the profile was twenty-year-old Elisa Ortiz. Even postmortem, her attractiveness was obvious. She was tall, five feet nine inches, and fit, 135 pounds, with vibrant red hair and striking green eyes. The image was permanently etched behind my lids.

I poured myself a glass of wine and contemplated her unusual case.

In some ways Elisa Ortiz could be considered a lucky one. She'd been identified. As I thought about the Rosemonts and Mindy, I knew in my heart that closure was important.

Collapsing on the couch, I sipped my wine. The thing nagging at me about the Elisa case was that she wasn't the only Ortiz daughter to have gone missing seven years ago. Elisa had an identical twin sister, Emma. Making the investigative leap, I pulled up the National Missing and Unidentified Persons System and learned that, even now, Emma Ortiz was considered missing.

According to the information in Dr. Howell's report, the two sisters had been close and lived together in a small apartment near the campus of Wayne State University. There was no evidence of risky or suspicious behavior in either of their background checks. According to testimonials, the two sisters were inseparable college students with good GPAs. Interviews with Wayne State professors and students unanimously produced stories of friendly, yet quiet, young women. No one recalled seeing either woman with a young man, much less partying. By all accounts the two spent most of their time at school, at the library, in the gym, or in their apartment. Their parents confirmed these descriptions and added that their daughters were never in trouble, never had serious boyfriends, and were actively involved in their church in their hometown.

Apparently the only thing Elisa and Emma Ortiz did, besides study, was work out. They did it often. That was their activity the night they went missing. The gym willingly surrendered a surveillance video showing both women arriving, working out, and leaving. The video also confirmed that neither woman made it to their car, even though it was parked right outside the gym. The case had stumped the DPD and was still considered open.

Taking another sip of wine, I thought about how the circumstances of this case defied Dylan's belief that there was safety in numbers. These two sisters had gone to the gym together. One theory was that they were taken at the same time. There was also speculation they'd left willingly.

Neither theory could be verified. Food in their refrigerator and a load of laundry in their dryer seemed to refute the theory of a planned exodus. Even their toothbrushes and bank cards were still in their apartment.

The gym, which had long since closed its doors for good, had time-lapse video of the parking lot. The older surveillance system consisted of a rotation of cameras: thirty seconds per camera with four cameras. The feed featuring the sisters and their car stopped recording as the women exited the gym's door. In the minute and a half it took to get back to that angle, they were gone. Nothing suspicious was found on any of the other feeds. There were no witnesses to their disappearance. It was as if the two women had literally vanished into thin air.

I shook my head and took another drink of wine.

Elisa Ortiz's body was found four days later, abandoned naked near the state fair grounds. According to the ME's report, her time of death was over thirty-six hours before her discovery. The examination revealed facial cranial injuries believed to have been caused by blunt force trauma: bruising around her left eye and cheek, as well as zygomatic and nasal fractures. Bruising was also evident around her neck, and on her arms, legs, and torso.

While working at the crime lab, I learned that the location of facial injuries was a surprisingly accurate indication of the mode of trauma. Muggings and domestic abuse—intimate partner violence—were most often associated with injuries like Elisa Ortiz's. Injuries to the upper third of the face usually indicated damage inflicted by another person. Those injuries, though typically not life-threatening, were often accompanied by tissue trauma and nerve damage, which could vary from paralysis of the facial muscles to damage to the optic nerve. In some cases the nerve damage led to temporary or permanent loss of feeling and/or sight.

In most cases, the more severe the trauma, the closer the victim and assailant were thought to have been. Crimes of passion could yield horrendous trauma. However, since there wasn't evidence that either Elisa or Emma were involved in an intimate relationship, and Elisa's examination showed no evidence of sexual assault, police theorized that her injuries were from a mugging or a random act of violence.

The second most common cause of facial injuries in both men and women was automobile accidents. Those injuries differed from perpetrator-inflicted injuries in their location—car accidents most often inflicted damage to the lower half of the face. When the victim's face collided with the steering wheel or dashboard, the typical injuries were fractured mandibles—broken jaws.

Elisa Ortiz's most severe injuries were to her torso. The postmortem photographs showed a large hematoma with midsection distention. The autopsy had discovered severe internal hemorrhaging caused by a ruptured spleen and lacerated liver. The cause of death had been ruled cardiac arrest due to internal bleeding.

I topped off my glass of wine and ran a new Internet search. My stomach twisted. Perhaps it was due to the alcohol on an empty stomach, but I chose to blame the information on my screen. From what I gleaned, the human body was constructed to protect its fragile organs, so for the kind of trauma that Elisa had experienced, extreme blunt force trauma was needed. When these organs were injured and left untreated, a slow and painful death occurred. Some injuries, like a ruptured aorta, result in death rather quickly, but Elisa hadn't been that fortunate. Her time of death had been estimated at ten to fifteen hours post-trauma.

Draining my glass, I backed up Tracy's memory drive on my laptop and turned off my computer.

Why had someone done this to this woman, and what the hell happened to Emma?

CHAPTER 11
Sara

I didn't need to hear Jacob's voice to know he was the one who entered my room. I knew his footsteps against the tile and the unique way he opened the door. If those clues weren't enough, after he entered, the faint scent of leather and musk, the manly aroma I'd learned to associate with him, broke through the antiseptic odor.

If I weren't so hysterical, I'd have found my ability to perceive without sight fascinating, but I was, for a lack of a better word, hysterical. I couldn't think or reason. I didn't know what he'd do or say or what I could possibly do in return. Somehow I'd done something terrible. I just couldn't remember.

Sister Lilith had spoken only a little about marriage. In that short time, she'd reinforced everything Jacob had said. Apparently it was the way we all lived in The Light. However, instead of going into detail regarding my role as a wife in The Light, she emphasized that I was the wife of an Assemblyman, and that because of that my behavior, meaning the incident, reflected poorly not only on Jacob but also on all the Assembly wives. She said that the other eleven women were appalled by my behavior, and the entire community was waiting for Father Gabriel's decree. Banishment was still an option. If that was chosen, it would include Jacob. She said that though Jacob had the right to and responsibility for my correction, when my behavior represented so many, for the cohesiveness of the community, the members of The Light needed to witness Father Gabriel's decree. Consequences were coming, not only from Jacob, but also from Father Gabriel. If God hadn't chosen to punish me with my injuries, the other correction would've already been delivered.

None of that was said in front of Raquel.

During most of the *training* I'd been lulled into a false sense of security, sitting beside Raquel and listening intently as she discussed Father Gabriel's teachings and the beliefs shared in The Light. I didn't remember the things she discussed and many seemed foreign, yet occasionally something seemed familiar.

I didn't nap, as Raquel had joked that I might. I paid attention and answered all Sister Lilith's questions with a nod or shake of my head. I didn't understand my motivation other than a new desire not to further embarrass Jacob.

When Raquel was called away to help with another patient, she asked Sister Lilith if she was about done. Sister Lilith said yes, but she wasn't. Like a snake in the grass, she was waiting.

In my current state, Sister Lilith's berating hit me hard. I didn't know how to respond. I didn't have enough information. Technically I wasn't supposed to say anything, but I didn't know how to react. What upset me was Sister Lilith's promise that correction was coming—correction for blatant insubordination. Then, as she was about to leave, she whispered her promise to return in the morning for more time alone.

I couldn't put my finger on it, but in the three days since I'd awoken, it seemed as though my true self had slipped further away. Each day, while I questioned my own identity, the answer became more clear. I was Sara Adams. Though I still wanted to understand the oddities of this strange world, more and more of me wanted to be the Sara Jacob expected me to be.

Maybe I was going crazy. I didn't care anymore about the color of my hair or features of my face. I wanted to know my state of mind. How had I become someone who could be reduced to tears twice in two days? Not just tears, not salty drops of water gently gliding down my cheeks. No, I was crying ugly sobs that ached in my chest as my eyes and nose leaked profusely, covering not only my face but my pillow too.

"Sara?"

I was so lost in Sister Lilith's words, I'd almost forgotten that Jacob was there. As the bed moved upward, I slowly turned his way. It wasn't bravery that gave me the strength to face him, even though, according to Lilith, I should be turning toward his wrath. It was a combination of shame and duty. I'd failed him, and as his wife, I needed to learn my fate.

My temples ached as I tried to reason. Could I speak and ask him what had happened?

No. I couldn't ask questions. I needed to wait for answers.

Oh, God! The wait was worse than knowing my fate.

Silently Jacob lifted my chin as the bed rail lowered. Sitting with his leg touching my arm, he gently wiped my face, cleaning away the evidence of my second meltdown in two days. I'd expected punishment, yet in mere moments his silent support gave me strength. Taking a ragged breath, I shuddered, trying to process his conflicting reactions.

Instead of discipline, his large hands delivered tenderness. Instead of a cold wrath, his body against mine provided warmth. Strong and reserved, his voice flowed with compassion. "No one else is here; you may speak. What is it? Why are you crying?"

I gasped for air to replace the sobs. With a firm grip on my chin, he continued to wipe away new tears as I evaluated his actions against Sister Lilith's words. They didn't match.

Though I understood that I was completely at his mercy, something spoke to my heart. From the internal chaos I heard a voice. Speaking softly, it whispered, *Believe in yourself. You are stronger than this. Always stay true.*

"Sara, don't make me repeat myself. You're upset. Part of my responsibility is helping you. I can't help you if you don't tell me what happened. Does this have to do with Sister Lilith?"

Stay true . . . I nodded.

"Let me hear you," he reprimanded. "The Commission knows you're speaking. I've asked for your speech to be restricted to only me for a while. I'll soon learn if my petition was granted." He paused. When I didn't respond, he repeated himself, the second time firmer than the one before. "Sara, speak now."

You are strong . . . "I'm so confused."

Jacob framed my cheeks and held my face close to his, allowing our noses to touch. He asked, "What happened? Why are you confused?"

"I don't understand what's happening. I don't remember what happened or what I did, but she said it was bad . . ." My voice faded.

Tilting my head forward, Jacob kissed my hair. "Listen to me."

Nodding, I tried to gauge his response, but his voice was soft and gentle.

"It's not Sister Lilith's place to say that to you. You're my responsibility. We'll get through this together."

"But because of the Assembly." My phrases were interrupted by feeble attempts to breathe. "I've jeopardized your position, and she said I shamed all the Assembly wives."

"She told you that?"

"Yes, and that we could be banished . . . I'm not even sure what that means, but all your hard work for the Assembly and Father Gabriel . . ." I gulped the oxygen that wouldn't stay in my lungs. "Gone."

"When she spoke, did you verbally respond to her?"

My head began moving from side to side as soon as his question began. "No. I haven't spoken to anyone, anyone but you."

"And she said all of this, in front of Raquel?"

"No, Raquel had to leave. Sister Lilith said it when we were alone."

The hands that still held my face tensed, yet his voice remained composed and reassuring. "Of course she did. She didn't know you were able to repeat it to me. Don't worry. I was just with the Assembly, Commission, and Father Gabriel. I can honestly say I don't think banishment is going to happen."

I covered his hand with mine. "You're upset. I feel it."

He kissed my hair again. "I am upset, but not at you. Do you remember Sister Raquel's husband?"

"I don't remember anyone, but she talked about him. His name is Benjamin."

"*Brother* Benjamin. All men deserve a title," he corrected. "And yes, if you don't remember him, you probably don't remember that he's also on the Assembly. Does Raquel seem ashamed of you?"

"No. No she doesn't, but why? Why would Sister Lilith say that?"

He released my cheeks, and his finger came to my lips. "No questions."

I lowered my face again and exhaled. "Jacob, I'm no good at this. I really can't remember why I was in your truck, or why I had an accident. I can't remember anything before three days ago. Except I feel like I'm not very good at following rules. I don't understand why you married me, why I'm here, in The Light . . . I'm not an Assemblyman's wife. You should just let them banish me before you end up losing all you've accomplished. I'm not who you think I am." The sobs were gone, but an occasional tear continued to flow.

Jacob lifted my hands and kissed the knuckles. A faint smile crossed my lips as I remembered him doing the same thing earlier this morning. Wrapping both of my hands within his grasp, he began, "Sara Adams, you're my wife." He wasn't saying it as he had when he wanted me to repeat after him. This time his tone made it more of a plea. "I married you and you married me. I'd do it again in a heartbeat. I'm honored to be on the Assembly, and I'm also honored to be your husband." He leaned down until our foreheads touched. "This road won't be easy, but never doubt where you belong or with whom. I don't know what I'd do without you, and I pray I never find out.

"We pledged our devotion to The Light and Father Gabriel, but before that, we pledged our love to one another. If I have to start from the beginning and recount our entire lives again to help you remember, I'll do it. I'd do whatever I needed to do to help you remember us. Sara, I'd marry you again." My chest ached with his declaration. "Sara, would you marry me?"

I couldn't speak as his words soaked deeper and deeper into my heart. My tears were dry. There probably weren't any left. However, the lump within my throat continued to grow, making my reply impossible. The man holding my hands and affirming his love overwhelmed me. Despite my shortcomings, he was declaring his devotion to me and our marriage. Finding myself lost in his grasp and surrounded by his masculine scent, I wondered if I deserved his steadfast love. I didn't know.

And then I remembered the voice: *believe in yourself.* I would believe, and even if I hadn't deserved Jacob's love in the past, I would in the future. Because for the first time, a part of me wanted it.

"Sara?"

I lifted my unseeing eyes, leaving only a whisper between our lips. "Yes, Jacob, I believe I'd marry you again."

With our hands still connected, our lips came together. His were firm and demanding, yet soft and accommodating. His kiss gave and took in equal portions, causing a firestorm to erupt deep within. My chest no longer cried from shame; instead my body screamed with desire. Without thinking, I willingly surrendered to the man with the fervent kiss. His kiss awakened me, my body, and my yearning. I had no doubt that this man filled my days and nights with earth-quaking passion. With only a kiss, I no longer wondered who my husband was in the bedroom; I knew. He was a man who conquered unapologetically and bestowed unsparingly.

When our lips parted, Jacob asked with a smile to his voice, "Are you better?"

"I am, thank you." Calm warmth settled over me as I thought about what he'd said when he found me crying. He'd said that part of his responsibility was helping me. I still couldn't wrap my head around all of it, but my life was becoming clearer. I was his. Yes, he'd correct me, but he'd also make things right and help me feel better. "Jacob?"

"Yes?"

"I don't remember anything from our past, and I won't lie to you and say I do. I get the feeling that isn't who we are. I don't think we lie to one another, do we?"

"Honesty is best."

"And there's something else," I said.

"Go on."

"I don't like the idea of being corrected, but I love how protective you are. I remember you saying I can't ask, so I won't, but I hope that you'll be patient with me." I allowed my grin to grow. "Because I'm anxious to be your wife again, in every way. Your kiss . . ." The blood rushed to my cheeks. "Well, since we're married, I hope I can say this. Your kiss makes me want more, makes me want to remember. I'm sorry for whatever happened. Thank you for standing by me."

"I'll always stand by you. I'll also be patient, but I will correct you, even while I'm being patient. I told you, correction isn't done out of anger, but for you. As a matter of fact, you just said something . . ."

I held my breath.

He went on, "You said you can't *ask*. That's not accurate. You may ask . . . actually, for many things you're required to ask. I told you that you can't *question*. There's a difference."

"I'm not sure I understand."

"You may ask for my patience, for things you need or desire. Remember, we spoke about you asking for a drink of water."

I remembered that.

"What you may not do is question. When I told you that I'd tell you what happened before the accident, but not now, you asked why. That's questioning my statement, my word. Those truths, the reasons behind decrees, decisions, and yes, even corrections, do not need to be explained to you. As a woman you must accept them, as faith that your husband or any man of The Light has the right answers. I promise, I'll never make a decision that will cause either of us harm."

"But you'll . . ." I purposely stopped, pressing my lips together, as my heart rate quickened.

"But I'll what?"

"I don't think I'm allowed to finish the sentence."

"But I'll . . . *correct you*?" he asked, properly completing my sentence.

I nodded.

"You're right. Normally you wouldn't be allowed to finish that sentence, or begin it, for that matter; however, to help you remember or at least understand, there'll need to be a few exceptions, and the answer is yes. Yes, I'll correct you when needed. Correction isn't harm. It may include pain, but it's not harm. Harm means physical or psychological damage. Why would I do that to my wife, the woman I've vowed to love and protect?"

I didn't know. There seemed to be a lot of things that I didn't know. Shrugging, I replied, "Thank you." I reached up to his face. With healing fingertips, I roamed the features of the man I longed to remember. "For loving me and protecting me. Thank you for the patience and exceptions. I know they're at your discretion, but knowing that you'll grant them makes me happy. I really am trying to understand. I want to be the wife you married, the one you want."

"I know you do. You always have."

Our lips reunited. Though only brief, the taste of his kiss combined with our connection rekindled the flicker of desire.

"Mrs. Adams," he said breathily, "you have a lot of healing to do before you can be my wife again in *every way*, to use your words, not mine. While we wait for that to happen, I hope you know, I want that too. I won't rush you, but just know I want it."

I sensed that Jacob had a way of getting what he wanted. As he stood, my cheeks filled with a healthy blush. The truth was I wanted it too.

"Hello?" Since I hadn't heard the door, I surmised that Jacob was talking on his phone. He continued, "Yes, that's great news. Thank you . . . Oh? What? . . . No, I haven't heard from him, but as long as I'm present, I have no issues . . . When? . . . Yes, we'll both be ready . . . Thank you, Brother Daniel."

After a few moments, he turned toward me. "Sara, it's about time to eat lunch, and Brother Daniel just informed me that you'll be receiving your walking cast this afternoon."

"OK." It wasn't as if I had any say in my treatment, but why would someone else be telling Jacob about my care? Shouldn't it be Dr. Newton making those decisions?

The covers moved from my legs, causing me to shiver at the cool air.

"It really will be good for you to start walking and rebuild your muscles again." His arms moved beneath me, and he said, "I'm going to lift you."

I nodded and prepared for my side to hurt.

"Why do you do that?" Jacob asked as he carried me toward the bathroom.

"Do what?"

"Bite your lip. It's not new. But now, without your eyes, I guess I've been watching your lips. The other day I thought you might put a hole through it."

I started to giggle, but sucked my lip between my teeth as he lowered my one good leg to the ground. Once I was standing, I released my lip and said, "I don't think about it, but maybe I do it to ease the pain from my ribs."

He smoothed my hair, tucking some behind my ear. "I don't want your ribs to hurt. I didn't want any of this."

Of course not. Who'd want their wife in an automobile accident?

"I know. It'll take time, but it'll heal."

He lifted my gown. "Even with your bruises, you're beautiful." He unexpectedly brushed his fingers over the side of one of my breasts, sending goose bumps up and down my skin and bringing a gasp from my lips. "I hope that healing doesn't take too much time."

Reaching for his shoulders, I stood perfectly still. Only the sound of breathing echoed throughout the bathroom. Reverently he lowered my panties. After what seemed like an eternity, he lifted one of my hands to the handle. "You'd better sit, and I'd better leave you alone."

I nodded, wondering if my desire was as obvious to his eyes as his was to my ears.

Once I was done, and as he carried me back to my bed, I asked, "Would it be asking or questioning to ask what you meant on the phone about you being present? I'm hoping it's about Sister Lilith." I added the last part hoping to take away from my question.

Jacob's chest expanded and contracted with a big breath. "That would be questioning. I know Lilith upset you. She won't be back today."

"She said she'd be back tomorrow, and we'd be alone again."

Jacob placed me on the bed. "Yes, she will and you will, but I'll make sure she doesn't discuss anything with you that she shouldn't. If I return tomorrow to a wife as upset as you were today, I'll have a talk with the Commission, and I guarantee that she'll be in worse shape." He tucked the blanket back around my cast and legs. "She may be a Commissioner's wife, but she's still a woman, and the Commission approved my petition. You may speak to me, but only to me."

"Thank you," I replied, nodding.

"Thank you?" Jacob asked. "You're all right with that?"

"Yes, although I'd love to talk to Raquel, if I can only speak to you, I can't talk to Sister Lilith, and she can only ask me yes-and-no questions. I really don't want to say more to her than that, and then there's Dr. Newton . . ."

"What about Dr. Newton?"

I exhaled and hoped that my honesty wouldn't get me in trouble. "I understand that he's a man and deserves respect, but I get a weird feeling from him." I sat very still, waiting for my correction.

Jacob brushed my cheek. "Sara, never be afraid to be honest with me. I need to know these things to protect you." He scoffed. "Perhaps God's time is now."

I didn't know what he meant, so I waited.

"Your question, about what I said on the phone about being present. It wasn't about Lilith. It was about Dr. Newton. I've forbidden him from being alone with you for any medical procedure. I must be present."

I smiled and reached for his hand. "It's always been like this, hasn't it? You protecting me?"

He touched my lips. "I am protecting you, but stop questioning. I can only be patient for so long."

His amused tone made me smile. As I settled quietly against the pillows waiting for my lunch, I decided that though this life still didn't feel right, it no longer felt wrong.

CHAPTER 12

Sara

I lifted my face toward the swish of the opening door. Even after almost two weeks, my body reacted to sounds as if I could see, but I couldn't, not yet. I hadn't even tried. My bandages were always changed in the bathroom with the door shut and the lights off. Raquel reassured me that the room could double as a darkroom if I ever wanted to develop film. I didn't, but it was good to know.

Dr. Newton explained that healing took time. He was especially concerned about the damage done by the flash of the explosion and warned that premature exposure to light could cause irreparable damage. Though I was curious, after he said that, I knew I'd wait.

"Hi, Sara."

Recognizing familiar voices was getting to be one of my specialties. Excited and somewhat wobbly, I stood. "Elizabeth! I didn't know you were coming to see me today."

She rushed my way and steadied my shoulders. "Should you be doing that? Standing, all by yourself?"

I grinned. "I can do more than that. I can walk. Watch," I said, taking one step and then another. "Jacob walked me around and around this room. I know every square inch. As long as no one moves the furniture on me, I'm pretty good. I'm not very fast, but I'm good."

"Well, look at you go! You'll be back to running before you know it."

I stopped and turned toward her voice. "Running?"

"Don't look so scared. You know what I mean."

"No, I mean, yes." My heart fluttered. "Oh, I remembered running. I did. It's something I used to do."

"You remembered it, like right now?"

Reaching through the air, I found my way to the chair and sat. As I ran my hands over the vinyl cushion, I smiled. I had been right about the material. "No, it wasn't right now. It was one of the first days after I woke. I don't remember exactly. It was before I was supposed to talk, and I was feeling stressed out. I didn't know where I was or even who I was. I felt like I was going to explode, but I couldn't. I didn't have a valve to release the pressure. Do you know what I mean?" I paused for her to respond. When she didn't, I giggled. "Hey, I'm not seeing head shakes, so I'd appreciate some verbal clues to know you're still there."

Elizabeth laughed. "Oh, sorry. I'm definitely here. So how did that make you remember running?"

I shrugged. "I don't know. I was thinking about ways to calm down, to release some stress, and it just came to me. I remembered running through a woods. There were tall trees and a meadow." I pressed my lips together, trying to recall. "I don't know. There was sunlight streaming down in beams through the leaves." I shrugged again. "That's about it."

"Wow, not a lot of sunlight this time of year. Must have been summer. So, did you remember anything else, anything before your accident?"

I shook my head.

"That's not fair; you didn't give me a verbal clue."

"No, I guess it isn't. But I'd take seeing over being able to shake my head any day."

"Hopefully, you'll be able to do both soon."

I sighed. "I hope so."

"So, any other memories?"

"Not really. The good news is that things are becoming more familiar." I smiled as big as I could. "And more comfortable. Like I recognized your voice and smiling doesn't hurt my face. My side still hurts, but the headaches aren't as frequent."

"That's wonderful, and you're walking!" Her tone became more serious. "If you do remember anything else, be sure to tell Brother Jacob. I'm sure he was happy you had one memory."

I found a string on my robe and tugged.

"Sara?"

I didn't respond.

"You did tell him about remembering running, didn't you?"

"No, um, I guess I'd forgotten about it, until you mentioned it. Besides, I'm sure he has other things to think about than a few random memories."

Elizabeth moved closer and touched my knee. Judging from the direction from which her voice came, she was bending or kneeling down on the floor. "A few random? You only said running."

"Yes, only running and the woods and sunshine. It's not that big of a deal."

"Are you taking your medicine?"

"Of course, I don't have much choice. I don't even know what I'm taking. Each morning either Jacob or Raquel hands me a cup with pills and I swallow them. I wanted to ask." I leaned back and sighed. "But I can't."

"No, you can't. You also can't keep secrets from Brother Jacob. If I didn't tell Luke something . . . well, let's just say I'd remember to tell him the next time."

My muscles tightened. "I wasn't hiding this from Jacob. I just forgot."

"Then tell him that. Since you weren't able to speak when you had the memory, he should go easy on you." She patted my knee. "Hey, enough about that. Have you been listening to the recordings?"

I nodded, still thinking about Jacob. Would he really be upset over something so trivial? Things were going well. I was doing better with not questioning, yet asking. It wasn't easy. I wasn't sure if at one time I had been naturally inquisitive or if it was because I was trying to remember so much. Either way, questioning came too easily. Usually, once I'd start to question, I'd catch myself.

I was petrified when he'd first told me I could speak to anyone who came to see me, but he'd reassured me it was safe. He'd allow only certain people to visit. Nevertheless I knew one of those people would be Sister Lilith. However, ever since the day she'd upset me, she never came alone. Sister Ruth, Brother Daniel's wife, came with her. I didn't know if that was Jacob's doing or not, but I liked Sister Ruth, and the extra company. She didn't say much. But she was a hugger and always smelled like vanilla. By the way she swallowed my shoulders in her embrace, I believed she was a bigger woman. I might not remember this life, and I'd figured out that women could be freer with their speech with one another than with men, but I knew asking about someone's weight or size wasn't appropriate. I didn't want to offend her. With her present, Sister Lilith never mentioned the accident or my impending punishment. She talked about my position as an Assembly wife and about the importance of my remembering Father Gabriel's teachings, and we studied.

At first I studied out of curiosity. I wanted to understand our world better. As time passed I found myself desiring to learn more.

"Sara?"

"Sorry. Yes, I've been listening to them, a lot. It's the only noise I have when I'm all alone. I like listening to Father Gabriel's voice. He's so knowledgeable. And listening to him and doing my training with Sister Lilith, well, it all makes sense. I guess."

"You guess?"

"I just wonder why I can't remember any of it. I mean, it's very interesting and some of it's pretty deep. It seems like something I shouldn't forget."

"You shouldn't!" Elizabeth said lightheartedly. "That's why you're listening and working with Sister Lilith, so you won't."

"Oh, Elizabeth, please tell me something, something about anything outside of this room. I'm going stir-crazy in here. Now that I can walk, I can't wait to get home."

"Well, this time of year, there isn't a lot outside, but the northern lights sure have been gorgeous."

"Northern lights?"

"You know, the colorful bands of light in the sky, the aurora borealis."

"Um, yes. I think so."

"Sara, they're beautiful. It's the best part of the dark season . . ."

I tried to picture what Elizabeth described as she went on about the colors. Apparently the lights are usually a brilliant yellow-green, but lately they'd been red, blue, and even purple. The excitement in her voice made them sound even more beautiful. Though I imagined their radiance, I longed for the time when I'd be able to truly see them.

If they're that visible, why don't I remember them?

"I thought you needed to be north to see those?" I asked when she paused.

"You do, silly. I don't think many people are farther north than us—"

The door opened and Elizabeth stood. My pulse quickened as she reached for my arm. Her hand trembled as she silently helped me stand. I was about to ask who was here, when he spoke.

"Sister Sara, Sister Elizabeth."

I gasped and grabbed Elizabeth's arm for support. For a moment I feared falling as my knees weakened. I knew the voice; I'd been listening to it for hours a day. Father Gabriel was in my room. As I tried to reason, I realized I was wearing only a nightgown and robe, mere feet from our leader. Bashfully I pulled the lapels closer together.

What am I supposed to do? Do I kneel or curtsy? I don't know.

"Father," Elizabeth replied.

"Sister Elizabeth, it's nice to see you helping your sister."

"Yes, Father."

"And Sister Sara, you're standing. Our God is good to help you heal." He reached for my hand and held it as he said, "I heard you were feeling better, and I wanted to see for myself."

"F-Father Gabriel, thank you."

"It's all right, Sister, you may sit. You're suddenly pale. Perhaps you're not well."

I felt back for the chair and replied, "Father, I'm just surprised."

"You knew me. You remembered my voice."

Oh! When Jacob gave me permission to talk to anyone who visited my room, I was certain he hadn't anticipated Father Gabriel. Yet I'd already spoken and I couldn't refuse Father Gabriel, could I?

"I've been listening to your sermons. I've been hearing your voice throughout my days."

"That's very good news. However, I'd hoped your memory was returning."

I lowered my chin and moved my head from side to side. "No, I'm sorry. I'm trying."

"That's what I've heard, Sister. That's all we can ask. I came today to personally invite you back to service. I know you've been working with Sisters Lilith and Ruth, but I miss seeing you seated with the Assembly wives. I think it's time that your seat is filled."

"Yes, Father."

"Very good. I'll see you tonight."

"Tonight?"

Someone else had entered my room with Father Gabriel, though whoever it was hadn't spoken, and I didn't know his identity. But by his sharp intake of breath, I knew it was a man.

Oh, shit. Did I just question Father Gabriel?

"Tonight," I repeated more confidently, "will be wonderful, with my husband's permission." The drumming of my heart echoed in my ears as I tried to decipher whether I'd saved myself, or made it worse.

Do I need my husband's permission, or does Father Gabriel's invitation supersede Jacob's orders?

"Very good, Sister. It seems as though Brother Jacob was correct, you're relearning the ways of The Light well. Sister Elizabeth, you may assist Sister Sara during this evening's service."

"Yes, Father," Elizabeth replied, "with my husband's permission, I'd be happy to."

When she reached down and squeezed my hand, I exhaled. I'd said that right.

"We'll leave you ladies to your devotions. Tonight."

"Thank you, Father," Elizabeth and I said in unison.

Neither of us spoke for a few moments after the shutting of the door. The silence continued to grow as my trepidation waned and shock grew. Finally I squeezed Elizabeth's hand one more time and whispered, "Holy shit!"

"Sara!" Elizabeth exclaimed with a giggle. "Don't let Brother Jacob or any other man hear you speak that way."

"But Father Gabriel was here! Oh, I need to tell Jacob." I stood and took a step toward my bed. "Elizabeth, I need clothes. Do I have clothes here? I can't go to service in a nightgown and robe." Falling back to the edge of the bed, I doubled forward and held my head. "Oh my gosh! Will I be punished for wearing this when he visited?"

"That's up to Brother Jacob, but you didn't have much choice. It wasn't like he announced he was coming." She was speaking from across the room, near my closet. "You have a skirt and sweater here, but I don't think you should change without . . ."

"I know, without Jacob's knowledge." My voice sounded defeated, even to me. "Be honest, please. Will Jacob be upset? Did I really question Father Gabriel?"

"I can't presume to answer for Brother Jacob, but you recovered beautifully." She sat beside me and gently elbowed my good side. "Father Gabriel even smiled at your response."

He smiled? Is that good?

"Who was the other person, and why didn't he announce himself? That's rude. It's obvious I can't see."

Elizabeth reached for my knee and lowered her voice. "Sara, I want to help you. I'm trying, but you need to be mindful. If we weren't friends, I could share this with Luke, and he'd tell Brother Jacob. The other person was Brother Timothy, and you should remember that a man doesn't owe us his words. He grants them. Your saying that he was rude makes you prideful. And the language you used makes you vulgar."

A tear escaped my bandages and slid down my cheek. "That's what I don't understand. I'm not good at this. I'm really not."

Elizabeth's arms wrapped around my shoulders and pulled me toward her. "You are. You were, and you'll get better again. I won't say anything, but you should."

"What?" I pulled away and sat straight.

"Our husbands can't be with us all the time. If we're honest about our transgressions when they're away, it shows them that we are trustworthy."

Prideful and vulgar?

More tears joined the stream. "No, I'm supposed to be at service tonight. I don't want Jacob upset with me. I need him. If I tell him, he'll be angry."

"He won't be upset. However, if he thinks your behavior warrants punishment, he'll handle it. Besides, other than walking you to your seat, he can't be with you at service."

"He can't?" I asked.

"No, he sits with the Assemblymen. As wives of the Assembly, we sit together just behind the Commission wives."

"So that's why Father Gabriel told you to assist me? You'll be with me?"

"With Luke's permission I will. So will Raquel. I believe Brother Benjamin will also approve."

I reached out and patted her leg. The material of her jeans made me think. "You're wearing jeans?"

"I am." She giggled. "That's a subject change."

"I guess it is. Why do I have a skirt?"

"Well, you have jeans too, if that's what you're asking. I've seen you wear them. I'd guess that Brother Jacob thought a skirt would be easier with your cast." *Oh, that makes sense.* "And we all wear dresses or skirts to service, even in this cold weather," she added. "Most of us are more casual for evening prayer. There're some who feel the need to always be dressed up. I'm sure you've noticed the high heels. I mean, we wear most everything we did in the dark, within reason. All the fashions in our store are approved first by the Commission. Our bodies are our temples, and we don't share that with anyone but our husbands."

She stood and continued, "With as cold as it's been, whether we're at evening prayer or our jobs, most women of The Light wear jeans and warm boots. Truthfully, modesty is dictated by Father Gabriel, but the particulars are up to our husbands. You wore jeans and warm boots before. I don't know why that would change."

I nodded. *Of course it is up to him. Everything seems to be up to my husband.*

"Sara, it's still early in the afternoon. Service isn't until seven. I'll speak with Luke about assisting you, and he'll talk to Jacob."

Suddenly the memory of what Sister Lilith had said about the Assembly wives came back. "Elizabeth?"

"What?"

"Are you appalled by me?"

"What? No!"

"Do the other wives of the Assembly hate me?"

"Of course not. Father Gabriel doesn't preach hate." She wrapped her arms around me and hugged. "We're all sisters."

I smiled a sad smile. "Thank you."

"As long as Luke approves, I won't leave your side. Who knows? Maybe you'll recognize the voices."

I nodded.

Maybe?

❧

As my afternoon progressed, my anxiety grew. Though I listened to Father Gabriel's recordings, I couldn't concentrate. The words *prideful* and *vulgar* kept repeating in my mind.

How is it that it was my friend who upset me—not Sister Lilith, not Jacob, but my friend?

Maybe it was because I cared what Elizabeth thought. I cared about her friendship.

Will she decide she doesn't want to be friends any longer if I can't remember the past, if I'm too different? What will happen if I do as she suggests and confess to Jacob? Don't we have enough happening, with going to service?

Remembering the running, I tried to pace the confines of my room. Though the cast made my left leg longer than my right, causing an uneven gait that aggravated my rib, I continued to move. Freedom was more important than the pain. After so long in my bed, I relished the ability to stand, walk, and sit of my own accord. Yet with each minute

I waited for Jacob, my apprehension of the unknown grew. I knew this room and was familiar with it. I'd counted the steps from my bed to the wall, my bed to the bathroom, and my bed to . . . anywhere within these four walls. I knew what was expected of me here.

What will happen out there, at service? What will happen when Jacob returns?

I rolled my head and shoulders, trying to relieve the tight muscles. My mind wanted to run, yet my body could hardly handle the pacing. Obviously my strength wasn't up to par. After a few laps, I'd sit, rest, and then try it again. During my walks I stopped at the closet multiple times to see my clothes. Of course I couldn't see. I could touch and feel. Elizabeth could be right, I might have jeans at home, but I didn't here. Mostly everything I touched was soft and long—nightgowns, I assumed. I found the skirt and sweater she'd mentioned. Now I wondered about a bra. I hadn't worn one since I'd awakened. It was one more thing to add to my stress.

If saying shit *is vulgar, what will happen if I go to service without a bra?*

Perhaps it was from my exercise, or maybe an escape mechanism, but as the hours passed, tiredness overcame me, and I decided to nap. That was where I was, in a dream world, when Jacob finally returned. Though his entering woke me, I didn't move. Remembering my transgressions, I lay still listening to his footsteps.

Is he upset or am I nervous and paranoid?

Panic pricked at my skin as I tried to decipher his mood. Each slap of his shoes against the tile echoed throughout the room, reverberating off the walls and accelerating my already too-rapid pulse. Slowly I turned, summoning what little bit of courage existed within me, and said, "Jacob?"

His steps lightened as he came closer and brushed my forehead with his lips. I didn't understand why we hadn't shared another kiss like the one over a week before. Maybe he knew I still needed to heal and didn't want one thing to lead to another. Right now I didn't know what I wanted. It was probably absolution.

"How was your afternoon?" he asked.

Shit! What does that mean? Do I have to tell him everything, or does he already know?

I wanted to ask, but I knew better. All I could do was answer. Moving my legs to the side of the bed, I sat, smoothed my hair, and replied, "Eventful."

"Really? Do tell."

The slight humor to his tone gave me strength. "Elizabeth came to see me."

"She did? That was nice. Did you have a nice chat?"

"Jacob, while Elizabeth was here . . ." My words trailed away.

"Did something happen?"

My face paled, my stomach twisted, and a sheen of perspiration coated my skin. Fighting the nausea, I went on. "Yes, actually. Do you remember . . ." *No, stupid, that's a question.* I rephrased. "I remembered that you said I could speak to anyone who came to my room."

"Yes. Of course you may speak to Elizabeth."

"Jacob, Father Gabriel came here this afternoon."

"Go on."

Shit! Shit! He's too calm.

"Sara, tell me about Father Gabriel's visit."

"Well, at first I was shocked. I knew his voice the moment he spoke. I've been listening to his recordings." The sentences ran together. "He was very nice and said that he wants me at service tonight, that he missed seeing me sitting with the Assembly wives, and that he was glad I was feeling better. Oh! And he told Elizabeth that she could assist me tonight, because I guess you have to sit with the Assembly." I took a breath.

"Then I guess we'd better both get ready for service tonight."

I nodded, swallowing the bile that had made its way from my stomach.

"Is that all?" he asked.

"All . . . that he said? Yes, I think."

He sat beside me and reached for my hand. "Perhaps you should think harder."

Tears trickled from my bandaged eyes. "I've told you before that I'm not good at this."

"You are. You were. You just need to be reminded." He cleared his throat. "I won't ask again."

I took a deep breath. "I may have questioned Father Gabriel."

"You *may have?*" He asked, still too calm. "You don't know?"

I stood and moved away from him. Holding on to the back of the chair for support, I replied, "I'd forgotten what day of the week it was. I mean, every day is the same. When he said he wanted me at service, I forgot it was Wednesday. I was shocked he meant *tonight.*"

"And what did you say?"

"I repeated *tonight*, and my tone may have sounded like a question, because Brother Timothy made a noise. As soon as he did, I realized what I'd done, and I said it again and told him that I'd be happy to be there. I added with your permission. I tried to make it seem like I didn't question"—my run-on sentence was interrupted only by muffled sobs—"but I did." I took a breath. "And after he left, I whispered a curse word to Elizabeth, which apparently makes me vulgar." I confessed the last part dejectedly.

"Oh! I didn't know about the swearing."

I nodded with a sigh.

"Is there anything else?"

"Yes," *I might as well admit everything.* "Brother Timothy never spoke while he was here. I didn't even know it was him with Father Gabriel until later when I asked Elizabeth. I said I thought it was rude of him to not announce his presence"—I shrugged—"since I can't see.

And, well, she reminded me that as women we aren't owed men's words, and thinking I was owed them made me prideful."

Jacob lifted my chin. "If I'm keeping count, we now have questioning, vulgarity, and pridefulness. You did have an eventful afternoon."

I shrugged, completely thrown off by his calm tone. "Will we still be going to service?"

"Yes."

Maybe that is all there is. Maybe I just need to confess?

"May I get ready?"

"Do you really think I can let this behavior pass?"

My heartbeat came back to my ears, echoing louder than before as my body began to tremble. What was he going to do? "I'm very sorry. I am trying."

"Yes, Sara, you are. While the vulgarity and pridefulness are new, we've been working on the questioning for some time now."

"And I'm getting bet—"

His finger touched my lips.

"There is still room for improvement. Don't you agree?"

With his finger still in place, I nodded.

"I believe it's time for a lesson in consequences, a punishment to help you remember."

Though his hand hadn't moved, I leaned slightly away. "Please, I promise—" This time he covered my mouth completely.

"Sara, do not make this worse. This is the way it is. You knew that there would be correction when you confessed, didn't you?"

I nodded. Though I'd hoped otherwise, I'd known.

"If we were home, we'd do this in our bedroom, but since we're here, go to the bathroom and prepare."

He released his hold, but I didn't move. I couldn't. Fear paralyzed my trembling body.

"Sara?"

"I-I don't know what you want me to do."

"Go into the bathroom, remove your clothes, and wait for me."

"But what about service?" My inner monologue screamed, calling me by name: *Sara, stop asking questions!* "I'm sorry." As I took a step toward the bathroom, a sob bubbled from my chest. "I told you everything. I was honest." I couldn't have hidden the defeat from my voice if I'd wanted.

I did as he said, entered the bathroom, removed my clothes, and waited. When he didn't come, I found my robe and put it over my shoulders. I didn't put my arms in the sleeves, but I didn't like being naked and alone. I wasn't sure how long he made me wait, but each minute was worse than the one before. When the door finally opened, I was sitting on the closed toilet, with my head down.

"Take my hand," he commanded.

I reached out to him. As our hands connected, I stood and my robe fell from my shoulders. Silently he moved me to the sink and turned me to face it.

"Put your hands on the edge of the vanity and don't let go of the counter, until I give you permission. Do you understand?"

"Yes," I replied, my trembling hands moist. When I gripped the edge, they slid upon the smooth surface. I gripped tighter.

"Move your legs back and apart. Brace yourself."

I continued to obey, still unsure of what was about to happen. It was then that I heard the distinct sound of his belt as he unbuckled it and pulled it from each loop.

No! This can't be happening!

My knees went weak. I bit my lip and fell forward onto the counter, still gripping the edge. The first contact wasn't his belt, but his hand. He ran it over my behind, rubbing and warming my skin.

"Sara, your honesty has earned you leniency. However, it's my job to watch over you and correct you." He continued caressing. "I need you to remember your place, especially now that we'll be out among more followers. I want you to remember the rules. I'm doing this to help you. Do you understand?"

"Yes, Jacob."

I sucked my lip back between my teeth. Though I'd replied appropriately, it wasn't what I wanted to say. I wanted to scream, to tell him he was crazy, tell him that I'd remember next time. I would. He didn't need to do this. I also wanted to tell him to just get on with it. Stop making me wait. But then the caress ended, and I changed my mind. I didn't want him to get on with it. I wanted to beg for it not to happen.

The still air filled with a whistle and then a crack.

It was a split second before the pain registered. In those milliseconds, I knew that I'd never forget this. I also knew that I'd never had this done to me. If I had, I'd remember, because I sure as hell wasn't ever going to forget this.

"Sara, you need to count. Next time I won't remind you."

Next time? No freakin' way! I am stronger than this.

"One."

Whistle. Crack!

"Two." Tears fell from my cheeks to the vanity below.

CHAPTER 13
Stella

"He works in narcotics and homicide, right?"

I stared incredulously at Bernard, hoping that maybe I'd misheard his innuendo, or that the chatter of the other patrons and clinking of the dishes had affected my hearing. "Umm, yes, *he* does, and I work for you. Would you like me sharing my research with him?"

Bernard's lips formed a tight line before he replied, "No. You know I wouldn't. I want to break this story, not DPD." He leaned across the small coffee shop table in Midtown where we'd met. "But Stella, you have a hell of a great resource at your disposal. I mean, I knew you two were friends, but I didn't realize how friendly you were until he called me. The guy was very determined to learn your location." He sighed and leaned back. Picking up his coffee cup, he asked, "What if you'd been out on assignment instead of going to the Wayne County Medical Examiner? Would he have expected me to tell him where you were then?" His brows rose. "I got the distinct impression that he doesn't often take no for an answer."

I shook my head. "Really? You're Bernard Cooper, since when do you worry about someone not taking no for an answer? I've never known you to even be fazed by the word. As a matter of fact, isn't that your calling card?"

"*I* don't take no for an answer, and yes, it is *my* calling card." His jaw clenched.

Unsure where this was going, I replied, "You lost me."

"I realize that this is overstepping my bounds, but, well, I have Mindy in the back of my brain, and I want to be sure you're all right. Does Detective Richards take no for an answer?"

Oh my God!

My neck stiffened. "I don't know if I should be flattered or offended. Let me tell you that yes, you've overstepped your bounds, but not just once. You've overstepped your bounds on two counts: First, Dylan and I do not talk work while we're together. We recognize the conflict of interest. So no, I won't ask him for information that could substantiate the rumors that something big is happening on the drug front. Second, my personal relationship is none of your business. While I appreciate your concern, I hope you know me well enough to know that I wouldn't be with a man who didn't take no for an answer. I'm not wired that way." I tilted my head to the side and took a drink of my coffee. When he didn't respond, I added, "After all, I love this job, and I'm damn good at it. But if I can tell my boss, *the great Bernard Cooper*, to mind his own damn business and take his suggestion to spy on my boyfriend and shove it up his ass, I think I can handle Dylan Richards. And since you've admitted to not taking no for an answer, should I be concerned about your wife?"

By the look on Bernard's face and the color of his neck and cheeks, I might have gone a little too far. Unfortunately, speaking my mind had never been something I was good at monitoring. In business I was usually pretty good at filtering, but not when it came to my personal life. My mouth would take on a mind of its own.

This was both business and personal. I should have filtered. I'd blame the fact that I hadn't on lack of sleep or worry over my friend. No matter the cause, I'd look for another job before I let Bernard Cooper or anyone else think that he or she could tell me what to do when it wasn't something I was comfortable doing.

The longer Bernard remained silent, the clearer my future became. Finally I nodded and threw my phone in my purse. As I began to scoot from the booth, Bernard said, "So you're walking away from this job you love because I'm concerned about you?"

I sat back down. "I assumed by your silence I was done."

His lips curled upward. "I like your fortitude. I really do. I don't know if Mindy would've reacted that determined. I just hope that you'll remember that inner strength as you keep doing your research and if and when you're called down to the ME's office, if it's not a false alarm." He lowered his voice. "I know I'm a hard-ass. It's who I am. At the same time, I like your determination. I have since I hired you. Keep it. Don't compromise it for anyone. In this business and many others it'll take you far." He grinned. "Hell, maybe I *should* fire you."

My eyes widened.

"Not because you're not good at your job, but because you're *too* good. If I keep you here, one day you'll probably have my job."

Wow, I wasn't expecting that.

"You've got a good gut," Bernard continued. "It's just that I've seen this kind of thing too many times." He lowered his eyes to the table, avoiding eye contact for the second time in recent memory. "Even with my own sister. It's not something I talk about, but it might be part of the reason I want to expose as many injustices as I can."

Who is this man?

"Remember," he went on. "You're stronger than you even know. Keep that gut instinct alive and stay true to yourself. Don't let Dylan Richards or anyone else stop your dream." He took a deep breath. "I wish I'd said that to my sister, or that someone else would have. You've got a bright future. Your reaction tells me that you believe that. You know you're talented. That's not conceit. It's believing in yourself.

"After you called to tell me it wasn't Mindy, I thought about Detective Richards's call, his determination to find you, and about Mindy's disappearance and how it was affecting everyone, especially you.

"Years ago my boss sat me down and gave me some great advice. He said that when the shit hits the fan, it's not time to turn away. It means the source of the manure is close and that means one thing: something is growing. Though it may stink, it's going to be big. Remember that, especially in our business, it means we're close. So put on your shitkickers and plow through. Believe in yourself"—he smiled as he looked deep into my moist eyes—"even if it means telling off your boss.

"And in case you didn't get it from that story, my wife's the one person who can emphatically tell me no."

I was suddenly rethinking every negative thought I'd ever had about Bernard. Maybe he could be a pompous ass, but perhaps that was his veneer and possibly underneath there was a real person. At nearly twenty years my senior he'd seen more than I had. He'd also been in this business for two-thirds of my life. Taking his advice suddenly seemed like a good idea.

"Thank you. I'll stay true. It's who I am, who my parents raised me to be. That's why I won't stop my search for Mindy. That doesn't mean I'll let my work for you or WCJB slip."

"I know you won't."

I sat taller. "I also won't use my personal relationship with Dylan to get a story, any more than he'd use my research to break a case."

Bernard nodded once, his expression undecipherable. "Then get your believing, true ass out there. I have the next three weeks of stories ready, and Foster has a few follow-ups I can always air. But I want more. I want to find out what's happening with the border patrol and if there's any connection between the drugs and the increase in missing persons."

I'd begun to stand when he told me to *get my ass out there*, but with his words I sat again. "What did you just say?"

His dark eyes sparkled. "You do listen well. That's one of your best attributes. For your information, I don't sit in my office all day and play solitaire, letting you and Foster have all the fun. I got where I am by doing my own research. You and Foster are good, very good. That's why you're my lead investigators. That doesn't mean I've forgotten how to get in the trenches. I still know my way around this town and have my share of connections. Those you made at that fancy law firm, Preston and Butler, aren't the only ones who can help with this."

"You've been talking drugs for three weeks. Now, you're suddenly throwing missing persons into the equation. Do you think they're connected?"

He shrugged.

I leaned forward and lowered my voice. "Don't shit with me. If you want me to break the damn story why wouldn't you share this with me, *one of your lead investigators?*"

"You've got great questions, now figure out the answers." His gaze narrowed. "Think about it."

I didn't look away. "You didn't expect me to agree to ask Dylan for information or spy on him, did you?"

His shoulder rose and lowered.

"It was a test," I confirmed.

He lifted his coffee cup toward me. "Congratulations, Stella, you passed."

Instead of clinking cups, I glared.

"Calm down. I only recently got the tip, and in light of Mindy, I think it deserves investigation. I needed to be sure that if I put you on it, you'd keep your head in the game and not let your personal life get in the way."

I inhaled and pressed my lips together.

"I don't only mean Detective Richards, though I don't want him knowing what you're doing, or, more accurately, the DPD knowing. I'm also talking about Mindy. This case could reveal nothing or it may shed light on everything. The only way to know is to do what I said, get your ass out there. Go check out what's happening on the border today, talk to your contacts, and come back to the station this afternoon. I'll share what I have then."

"Thanks, Bernard. I'll keep my phone charged. If I don't hear from you, I'll see you this afternoon."

"Be there by three, unless you get something else."

I threw a five on the table and with a wink said, "You've already overstepped enough bounds. I'll get my own coffee."

CHAPTER 14
Sara

The clank of the belt buckle hitting the floor alerted me to the end of my sentence. My whimpers and Jacob's labored breaths were the only sounds bouncing off the bathroom walls and rumbling through my head. The last spoken word had come from my lips—*five*. Though it was gone, the memory of it continued to echo in the distance.

Five. Five. Five.

My heart clenched, forgetting its normal rhythm, and seized in my chest as my bare breasts lay flat against the cool, smooth vanity top. Uncertainty paralyzed me, making me immobile while the counter's edge dug deeper into my hips, and my toes throbbed from supporting my weight. Not only couldn't I move, more importantly, I hadn't received permission to do so. By some miracle my hands were still where Jacob had placed them, their grip a vise, keeping me suspended and saving me from falling. Though my hands had done what he instructed, I hadn't been the one to keep them there.

I'd left. Not literally. No, literally, I was captive in a life I detested from the depths of my soul. I completely understood why I didn't remember: I didn't want to. I'd left metaphorically, in an out-of-body experience. However, my reprieve had been short-lived, and now I was back. Though the punishment was done, the pain went on. Each lash of Jacob's belt burned like fire through my nervous system. Synapse after synapse sparked with impulses until my entire body was consumed by flames.

"Sara, you may let go of the counter."

It took a moment before my brain and hands worked together. I heard his voice, yet the vise wouldn't loosen. When it finally did, my arms dropped to my sides. With my cheek still against the counter, I waited.

"Stand up and give me your hand."

The belt hadn't struck only my behind, but also the tops of my thighs. Transferring my weight brought back the intensity of each strike. Biting my lip, I tasted the copper of my blood. Maybe I had bitten a hole through it, as Jacob had predicted. I stood straighter, still facing the sink, lowered my chin to my chest, and lifted my hand.

Taking my hand, Jacob guided it toward my wounds. The tips of my fingers detected the raised skin. My fingertips flinched back, as if the evidence of his correction were actual fire, trails of hot coals waiting to cause more destruction.

"Do you feel the welts?"

I nodded.

"Sara, this punishment was done to help you remember. Do you need more help remembering to speak when I ask you a question?"

"No, I remember." My voice choked hoarsely. It wasn't that I'd cried out; I hadn't. I'd remained silent throughout the correction, except for speaking the numbers I'd been required to say. "Yes, I feel them."

"Your skin isn't broken. I told you I'd never cause irreparable damage." Once again he guided my hand to the welts. "If you could see, I'd have you look at them. They're red, raised, and angry markings on your pale skin."

I swallowed the sobs that shook my shoulders as I envisioned each welt.

"As you may or may not remember, five is the standard number of strikes per infraction. How many infractions did you commit?"

My heart raced to the point of making me faint. I couldn't take ten more. I couldn't. Turning my body toward his, I lifted my face and pleaded. Panic spilled from my voice. "Three. Please don't . . . I . . . c an't . . ."

He softly brushed my cheek. "Stop. I said your honesty earned you leniency. Five is all you'll get today."

I nodded as the relief of his clemency washed over me.

"Sara, I wanted you to touch the welts because they're your reminders not to question. Tonight when you walk or sit, each time you feel the pain, consider it a cue to think before you speak. Can you do that?"

"Yes."

He pulled a tissue from the box and wiped my cheeks. "It's up to you if more reminders will be necessary. I can't allow you to embarrass me in front of Father Gabriel or anyone else. Even your behavior in front of Elizabeth was unacceptable. I'll need to discuss it with Brother Luke. As I've said before, it's up to you. Only you can decide if today's correction will help you behave appropriately or if you'll need more assistance. Sara, will you need more reminders?"

I ran my fingers over the fiery raised skin again, suddenly intrigued by the sensations. "No, Jacob. I'm sorry I embarrassed you." I fought to catch my breath. "I'd like to avoid future reminders."

His lips brushed my forehead. "Very good. So would I."

The eerie calmness that had infiltrated his voice since he'd come back to my room this afternoon faded. As emotion returned to his tone, I found myself drawn to the man who had praised my answer.

"Now," Jacob continued, tucking a piece of my hair behind my ear. "That's done. Let's get us both ready for service."

"I . . . you . . . please, let me stay here."

"Nonsense. No one, not even the wife of an Assemblyman, can refuse a direct invitation from Father Gabriel; besides, I'm happy to have you at my side again as we enter the temple."

"But . . ."

"Sara, this is over. Remember what I said before? Correction works well, because the responsibility is transferred from you to me. You have your reminders to help you avoid future correction, but this infraction, as well as punishment, is done. It's history and now it's time to move on. We need to eat and change. We have service in an hour and a half, and as part of the Assembly, we must arrive in a timely manner."

As I contemplated the service with so many people I couldn't remember, the panic returned. Though I had five painful reasons reinforcing why I shouldn't, I leaned into Jacob's chest. The softness of his shirt brushed my cheek as his heartbeat drummed at my ear. Slowly his arms surrounded me, bringing warmth and security. I wrapped my arms around his trim waist, and for the first time that I could remember, really felt the firmness of his torso. My tears finally stopped, but I couldn't speak. Instead my naked body molded to his, silently saying what my lips couldn't admit.

I wasn't sure how to describe my whirlwind of emotions. I wasn't sure I could have if I'd been asked. The entire time I was bent over the vanity and the numbers came from my lips, I'd hated the man delivering the pain. It was an all-consuming hate, one that filled every cell of my body. In those minutes I'd understood why I'd blocked out the memories of my life: it was because they were too awful to remember. Red like the color Jacob described, as well as the blood that trickled from my lip, had filled my unseeing eyes. Hatred such as I couldn't recall had scratched like a wildcat to break free, to scream vulgarities and proclaim its presence.

And then it was over and now his voice was back.

CHAPTER 15
Jacob

Though my training told me to walk away and let Sara deal with the consequences of her correction alone, my body refused to cooperate. I tried to resist, but when she melted into me, with her body trembling, my arms took on a mind of their own. As I embraced her petite form, she stole another piece of my heart, a piece that was never meant to be shared. I'd carried her and helped her, but never had I truly held her, not like this. When she was engulfed in my hold, our size difference became suddenly apparent. I was wearing boots and she was completely nude, and I towered over her by nearly a head. With her face pressed against my chest my resolve shattered as my internal battle raged.

Sara had been found guilty of forgetting a rule she'd never known, and as her husband, I was responsible for delivering the punishment. I understood the principle of the correction, but *this* wasn't theory: it was reality.

I had held the leather belt in my hand and sensed the vibration as it crashed down upon her fragile body. Each strike had marred not only her but also me. As she'd spoken the numbers I demanded, I'd reminded myself that this was for her success and survival; nevertheless that reasoning hadn't appeased my self-loathing. She should hate me, not only for this, but for everything, yet here she was clinging to my shirt and waist as if she were holding on for dear life, afraid that if she let go, she might fly away, like dust in the wind. That wouldn't happen. I wouldn't let it. I couldn't.

I hadn't chosen Sara as my wife; then again, I hadn't refused her. That wasn't even possible. If I had, all that I'd accomplished and learned would have been lost. For me to succeed, she needed to as well. As we stood silent, apart from her occasional ragged breaths, for minutes upon minutes, she wrapped in my arms, I resolved that though the stakes were high, I was all in. She hadn't asked for this nor did she know how she'd complicated my mission, but she was here, and if this was what I needed to do for both of us to succeed, I would.

Sara's trembling finally calmed, yet her shoulders continued to quake with each broken gasp. Looking to the mirror, I saw the long unfettered ringlets of gold that flowed around her face and over my arms. No longer was her hair secured in the braid she'd woven this morning. Now it cascaded down her back, swaying slightly with each breath. I worked to keep my eyes on her hair and not look lower, but my gaze was pulled to the horror and evidence of my punishment—the reminders—I'd left behind. Five distinctively long, angry welts criss-crossed her firm round bottom and extended below onto her toned upper thighs. With the bathroom lighting, the redness glowed in stark contrast to the paleness of her complexion.

My chest continued to dampen as her tears soaked my shirt. Rubbing her bare back gently up and down, I stayed conscious of her skin and mindful to keep my large hand from straying to where it'd been marked. I'd caused her enough pain. In the three weeks since her arrival and incident, she'd begun to heal. My chest ached with the knowledge that her beautiful skin was once again spoiled, and this time I was responsible.

Each time I started to move, she burrowed closer, settling herself not only under my skin, but deeper into my heart. My body reacted as any man's would to the closeness of a naked woman, but I knew it wasn't time. Sara needed comfort, not sex. If we came together now, she'd forever associate sex with punishment, and when the time came, that wasn't what I wanted nor did I want it to be *sex*. When the time was right, I wanted to make love to the woman in my arms.

My belt lay curled on the tile floor by our feet, like a snake ready to strike. Its vile venom had hurt Sara, soaking into her flesh and causing her agony. If it had been a real snake, I'd have ripped its head from its long coiled body. Its fangs would no longer strike, and she'd be able to sleep soundly knowing the danger was gone. But that wouldn't happen. To her the danger was me. She didn't understand the levels and powers at work in our lives. She could never know the true danger that lurked around each corner. The only way to keep her safe was to stay on course. Her only objective was to embrace Sara and become Sara. Her conformity to The Light was the only means of saving her.

"Sara," I said, lifting her chin and seeing the blotches of red on her cheeks and neck. "We need to get ready. Raquel went home to prepare for service, so I'm going to cover your cast and put you in a warm shower." The way her body tensed, I knew what she was thinking. "The warm water will sting at first, but with time it'll make your welts feel better. I also have some ointment that you've said helped in the past."

My words were a grave. With each statement about the past we'd never shared I dug deeper and deeper.

She nodded against my shirt, and then, as if remembering to speak, she said, "If you say so."

I kissed her hair. "I do. I also think we should change your bandages around your eyes. Dr. Newton said it's not good to allow them to stay damp."

"All right." Her shoulders sagged while her voice carried a faraway tone, like a sad melody that had lost its zeal. I wanted obedience, not a lifeless zombie. Somehow I had to discover the way to help her find that place of contentment, the place where she was safe and happy and in accordance with Father Gabriel's Light.

I directed her to sit on the closed toilet. As she did, I remembered finding her there before . . . before I'd broken her. When her sore bottom connected with the cool seat, her lower lip disappeared between her teeth. It took every ounce of control I had not to fall to my knees and beg for her forgiveness. I couldn't. According to The Light this was her doing, not mine.

"I'm going to wrap your cast first," I said once she was settled.

"Does everyone go to service?"

I didn't know if she was trying to get her mind on other things, but if so, I'd gladly help. "Yes," I replied. "This is a big community. We all have jobs, but Sunday and Wednesday service are the only time that all jobs stop. Well, except for the powerhouse; that can't stop."

"Pow—" She stopped herself, then rephrased. "May I ask what that is?"

She is learning.

"It's what it sounds like. It's the place where hydropower turns turbines. They then work generators that supply power to our entire community."

"Like water?"

"Yes, though wind would work, it'd be more visible and less predictable. As long as the river flows, we have power."

"Will you tell me where we are, or is that something I need to wait to learn?"

I finished securing the plastic around her cast, reached for her hand, and helped her stand. Though it had to feel better to stand, she still grimaced with the movement. "Like I said before, we came here together, you and I. You knew where we were coming since before we arrived. You knew we were moving to the Northern Light, in Far North, Alaska."

As her head moved slowly from side to side her hair fell about her face. "I don't understand how it's all gone—my memory. It seems like I'd remember moving to Alaska or where we lived before."

"We don't have time to wash your hair," I said, changing the subject and removing the old hair tie dangling uselessly from a few strands of her hair. Once it was free, I raked my fingers down the length of blonde. "Besides, we washed it this morning and it still looks good. You'll need to redo your braid—it fell out."

"Do I have to keep it in a braid?"

The small fraction of emotion in her question made my cheeks rise. "Of course not. That's how you wore it most of the time in the past. That's why I mentioned it."

"Oh," she sighed. "Raquel mentioned a messy bun once. I think I'd like a messy bun for service." Her voice softened as she added, "If that's all right with you."

"As long as you remember how to secure it, it's fine. I can help with a lot, but you don't want me fixing your hair."

At the sound of my self-deprecating statement, she lifted her face toward mine, and her lips formed a stunning smile. In that grin she planted a glimmer of hope for our future. I felt the small seedling in my chest, its shell broken by roots that needed care, sunshine, and nutrients. I prayed a silent prayer to Father Gabriel that one day it would bloom.

"Here," I said as I handed her the hairbrush.

These weeks that she was required to spend without sight gave me the clear advantage. I could stare and study my wife without her being self-conscious. As she brushed her hair, I watched, admiring how truly beautiful she was, especially now that her cheeks were mostly clear. The earlier bruising and more recent red blotches were about gone, revealing her creamy soft skin. Though the purple of her throat had faded considerably, now merely a brown tint, it still needed to be covered. That was why Raquel had gotten Sara the turtleneck sweater.

Tonight would be Sara's first introduction to the followers. Everyone in the community understood the importance of making each follower feel welcomed. Newly acquired members were different. They didn't realize they were new. For that reason they were primarily surrounded by people who'd help with their acclimation. The entire Assembly and Commission, and their wives, were Sara's support group . . . well, with the exception of Brother Timothy and Sister Lilith. Since Brother Daniel was my overseer, he'd also become Sara's. That was why Sister Ruth had stepped in with her training. After Sara's breakdown, I'd gone to both of them privately and discussed my concern. I didn't ask for Sister Ruth's help, as that could have caused more problems with Lilith and Brother Timothy. However, I placed a bet on Sister Ruth's caring nature; my wager paid off.

As Lilith had explained to Sara, as an Assemblyman's wife, she held a special place of honor. For that, as well as other reasons, her transition into The Light was more difficult than that of a mere follower. Yet at the same time, the people in this inner circle of the chosen knew the way into The Light better than anyone, and would do their best to facilitate her success.

"There, that will work for my shower," she announced as she fastened the clip I'd recently handed her behind her head. I grinned at the blanched spot on her lip. She'd had it securely tucked between her teeth as she concentrated on her hair. With her announcement she'd released it, allowing the pink to return.

As the warm water assaulted her backside, her grip on my hand tightened. Insensitively I choked out the words I knew to say. "Will you remember not to question?"

"Yes, Jacob," she replied through gritted teeth.

It took a little time, but when her muscles relaxed, I knew she was finally more comfortable. Once she was out of the shower, I applied the ointment, explaining the whole time how it had helped her in the past. We turned off the light in the bathroom, and I replaced the bandages around her eyes. It wasn't until she was dressed and ready for service that she mentioned her punishment.

"I assume I'll be sitting at the service."

It was the first time I'd seen my wife, as my wife, in anything other than a nightgown. I couldn't help but stare at her splendor. She'd done as she'd asked to and secured her hair near the nape of her neck. Her turtleneck was black and ribbed, fitting snugly to her breasts, and disappeared at her small waist into the skirt that stopped about midcalf. The skirt was made of a blue-jean material. Over the turtleneck she wore a jacket that matched the skirt. The boot she wore on her right foot went almost to her knee and had a heel that nearly matched the height of the cast. With it on, she walked better than she had with slippers. Raquel had chosen her clothes, including the white bra and panties hidden beneath. Around Sara's neck I'd secured a necklace. Dangling from the chain was a silver cross. It was an exact duplicate of the one worn by all the Assembly and Commission wives.

There was something about Sara's presence and confidence, despite her punishment, that mesmerized me. As I stared at her, the only thing I could think, the only thing that registered, was that she was mine. All mine. Though my mind recognized the errors of our ways, in this world she was mine. Father Gabriel and The Light had given her to me, uniting us as husband and wife.

I tried to concentrate on her statement.

"Yes," I replied as she walked confidently toward me and the table that held our dinner.

Somewhat nervously she reached for her new necklace and slid the silver cross from side to side. Taking a deep breath, she dropped her chin a bit and asked, "May I please stand to eat?"

"Why, Sara?"

Yes, I am an ass.

"Because my reminders are still sore, and if you'll allow me, I'd like to let them rest."

She was more perfect than I'd ever imagined. It wasn't that in reality I needed this submission, but damn, it was hot. "What's the purpose of the pain?" I asked.

"It's to remind me to think before I speak and to not question."

"If I allow you to stand, will you continue to remember?"

As her lip quivered, twisting the knife in my heart, she replied, "Yes, I'll remember."

"You may stand."

"Thank you."

So insanely hot!

I readjusted myself, lessening the physical pressure of my obvious attraction.

We'd practiced walking about the room, but leaving the clinic was different. She had to completely trust me and allow me to lead her through a dark world. With her coat and gloves secured, we made our way out of her room, down the quiet halls, and out into the cold night. As she breathed the frigid air, I asked, "Are you all right? It's been a few weeks since you were out of the clinic."

With her petite hand wrapped in mine, she replied, "I am, as long as you're with me."

The thing was, I knew without a doubt that she meant it. In this warped world, I was her anchor. It was the plan from the beginning, but the fact that it had worked both elated and sickened me. She deserved a hell of a lot more than this.

Once we were in the temple, we were greeted by everyone. Though I'd given her only a brief synopsis on how to respond, she did so appropriately. To those she didn't know, she smiled and nodded, all the while holding tight to my hand. It wasn't until we met up with Brother Benjamin and Sister Raquel that we released our grip, and I placed her hand in Raquel's.

"Sara, I'll come and get you once service is over. Sister Raquel will take you to Sister Elizabeth. Sister Ruth is seated in front of your seat. They'll all be there for you and watch over you."

Raquel smiled in my direction as she squeezed Sara's hand.

"Thank you," Sara replied. "I'll be fine." She turned toward Raquel, understanding that she could speak to others who she knew. "Thank you too," she said.

Raquel nodded toward Brother Benjamin and me. "We'll be fine, I promise."

Murmurs filled the large room with the sound of normal preservice chatting as Benjamin and I made our way to the Assemblymen's seats. Once we were in our places, I glanced out to the congregation of followers. Sara and Raquel were making their way to the Assembly wives' seats, where Elizabeth was waiting. Though Sara tried to hide it, each time she sat or moved, her expression revealed her discomfort. After a while I watched as Sara's and Elizabeth's heads went together, and Elizabeth held Sara's hand. The two appeared to be speaking quietly between themselves. I wondered if Sara was confessing her punishment.

Just before service began, Brother Timothy leaned toward me. "I see Sister Sara made it here tonight."

"Yes, Brother, Father Gabriel invited her."

"Oh, I know. I just wasn't sure if she'd be able to walk, but it appears as though sitting is more her issue."

My body temperature rose. "Brother, she informed me of what occurred while you and Father Gabriel were in her room. I've taken care of my wife's impudence." I lifted my brow and settled my eyes on Lilith. "Perhaps you should follow suit."

Though I listened to Father Gabriel, my gaze never left my wife. Not being able to sit with her increased my anxiety. While I trusted Raquel and Elizabeth, they weren't me, and I was ultimately responsible. Nonetheless, as the evening progressed, my apprehension waned. If someone hadn't known the truth, they'd truly believe Sara Adams was back following her incident.

The word *incident* filled me with dread. Father Gabriel still hadn't pronounced his decree for Sara's perceived part. It was essential to the plan, the timetable, and the protocol, but that didn't mean I liked it or was comfortable with my wife suffering more correction. After closing prayer Brother Daniel came to me.

"Brother Jacob, I'm very pleased with Sister Sara's presence here tonight. You should be proud."

A little of the tension left my shoulders. "Thank you, Brother. I am."

"Father Gabriel would like to speak to us for a few minutes."

"Now?" I asked nervously, looking out toward the moving people. "Yes."

As he passed by, I reached for Benjamin's arm. "Brother, I need to speak with Father Gabriel. May I ask you—"

He didn't let me finish. "No need to ask. I'll get the ladies and escort them to the conservatory. We'll wait for you there."

Luke stepped closer. "Would you mind including Elizabeth? I'm part of this meeting we're about to have."

Benjamin nodded, unquestioning. "I've got your backs," he said with a grin as he walked toward our wives, still seated where they'd been.

Luke's elbow hit my ribs and he whispered, "You've got it bad."

"What?" My eyes opened wide. "Do you know something about this meeting?"

Laughter rumbled from his throat. "No, I don't know anything about the meeting. What I mean is that you've got it bad for your wife."

I shrugged. "Shouldn't I?"

"Eventually. Things are a little early. She could still . . ."

My heart stopped beating as I mentally finished his sentence. *She could still be banished.* Her probationary period wasn't complete. Truthfully, no one was ever completely without that threat. It didn't happen often to established members, but it could. Though I'd never been told, I had the feeling that had been the fate of the pilot I'd replaced.

Luke patted my shoulder. "Hey, forget I said that. Sara did great here tonight. I think you've got this covered."

I reached for his arm and stopped his steps before we neared Father Gabriel's office. "After this meeting I need to speak to you about something that happened earlier today."

The corner of Luke's mouth moved upward into a lopsided, knowing grin. "Elizabeth told me."

"Vulgarity? Prideful?" I asked, letting go of my grasp and repeating the words Sara had used earlier today.

He nodded. "New followers. It's my job. Elizabeth and I see and hear things like that often. It's not the end of the line for her, and besides, I watched Sara tonight. I believe you took care of it. Am I correct?"

"I did."

He patted my shoulder again. "Then we're good. It was dealt with, and according to The Light, it is as if it never happened."

I sighed with relief. "Wait a minute. Elizabeth told you? Were you planning on telling me?"

"I was. But Elizabeth said she encouraged Sara to tell you herself. We wanted to give her the chance. Again, we do this new-follower stuff all the time. Believe me when I say I only bring the bigger issues to the Assembly. We'd be there all day if I brought every detail. Of course I'll report this to your overseer, but I know Brother Daniel, and I bet he'll feel the same. The infraction happened. You took care of it. The issue has been resolved."

"Thanks."

"What about the memory she spoke of?" Luke asked.

"What memory?"

How much shit is going to be thrown at me tonight?

"Listen," Luke said, reaching for my arm. "You and Sara obviously had an eventful afternoon. As her husband, what you do is at your discretion. As the new-follower coordinator, can I offer some advice?"

I nodded.

"Sara mentioned to Elizabeth that she had a memory of recreational running. She said she had the memory one of the first days after the

incident. It happened before she was allowed to speak, and she'd forgotten all about it, until Elizabeth mentioned running."

His words echoed with the beat of my erratic heart. Surely Luke could see the way my chest pulsed.

What other memories has she had?

Luke went on. "Sara also said that she hasn't had any other memories and has been taking her medication. Elizabeth encouraged her to tell you if any more memories returned." He rested his hand on my shoulder. "Here's my advice, you had a lot to deal with this afternoon. It doesn't matter how many times we tell Sara that none of this is new, it is. The memory was probably not her biggest concern when you returned. She not only had her transgressions with Elizabeth but her one with Father Gabriel. Sara doesn't understand the significance of recalling a memory. If she's punished for not relaying that particular bit of information to you, she'll learn to fear memories; more accurately, she'll fear telling you. It's your choice, but remember that's why Brother Daniel and I are here. We'll be happy to give advice, and we want you both to succeed. The Light isn't a singular journey. You're not in this alone."

I sighed. "It's more difficult on this side than sitting on the Assembly."

Luke nodded. "I was there once. Well, Elizabeth wasn't acquired, but she still had to be indoctrinated. We're here for you, and for Sara. Now, let's see what's happening in there." He inclined his head toward Father Gabriel's office.

I nodded. Taking a deep breath, Luke and I entered the office.

From behind his desk, Father Gabriel looked up. Brother Daniel was already there, seated at one of the chairs facing him. Beside Brother Daniel were two empty chairs.

"Brothers," Father Gabriel greeted us. "Have a seat. Before we meet with the Assembly and Commission in the morning, I want to discuss my decree regarding Sara's retribution for the incident."

148

CHAPTER 16
Stella

Dylan's voice had that edge, the one that said he was serious. "No. I didn't call you to have you run to Highland Heights. I called to tell you to stay away."

"That doesn't make sense," I replied. Though I wasn't fazed by his tone, I was concerned about letting him know that I was already there. I'd been in Highland Heights most of the morning, not far off Woodward Avenue, sitting in my car parked in the lot of one of the few open businesses.

"What doesn't make sense is you wanting to come here. It's dangerous!" His voice was getting louder by the minute. "This is body number three in less than two weeks."

"Same house?" Sirens sounded from the phone and outside my open window. I quickly pushed the button to raise the window, hoping that Dylan would think the sounds were all occurring around him.

"No. I shouldn't even be telling you this. I need to get back to work."

My mind raced with questions as I turned from side to side, searching for the source of the sound. The sirens' roar grew louder and then softer, but they were nowhere to be seen.

How close is he?

"Where, Dylan? Is it near where the other two bodies were found? Is it a woman? A man? What's her age? Is she blonde?"

"Seriously?" he asked in disbelief. "Stay away from Highland Heights. The DPD will be covering the entire area today and tonight. If one patrolman, one detective, or hell, even a Highland Heights traffic cop tells me that he or she saw you or your car here, so help me . . ." His sentence trailed away.

My shoulders stiffened as my brows rose. The temperature inside my car wasn't going up only due to the closed windows. "Finish your threat, Detective Richards. I'd like to know exactly what you planned to say before I tell you to stick it up your—"

"It wasn't a threat." He exhaled. "Listen to me and I'll make you a deal."

"What kind of deal?"

"You stay away from here today, and in the morning, I'll escort you to the crime scene."

The opportunity sounded too good to be true. My curiosity was piqued. "Why? What are you hiding from me?" My hand moved to my suddenly racing heart. "Oh my God, do you think it's Mindy?"

"No. I know it isn't. Stella . . ."

I sighed. "Thank God. Then why? Why would you be willing to do that?"

More voices, growing louder, came through the phone, mingling with the sirens. "Listen, I've got to go. Just shut up." He paused.

Though my lips came together, and my rebuttal was on the tip of my tongue, I stayed silent since his time was obviously short.

Dylan continued hurriedly, "I'm offering because I know you. You're not going to listen to me unless you know you'll get to see this. Call me a controlling ass, I don't care. I don't want something to happen to you because you're in the wrong place. Just let the DPD handle it today. Tomorrow early, after dawn and before all the idiots hit the street, I'll bring you to both houses. That way you'll get a look at the crime scenes, satisfy your curiosity, and I'll know you're safe." He lowered his volume. "I'm hanging up. Tell me we have a deal."

Shit!

"OK, we have a deal."

"Good-bye."

"Bye—" I didn't have a chance to say it before the phone went dead. I shook my head. Turning on my ignition, I cranked the air conditioning and smoothed back my hair. Inhaling the cooled air, I lifted my ponytail from my neck and redirected the air-conditioning vent. Though it was past Labor Day and autumn was approaching, it hadn't stopped the heat. I'd lived in the area long enough to know that it could, any day. Seventy degrees one day and thirty the next. Welcome to autumn in Michigan.

I contemplated Dylan's warning. I drove a gray Ford Fusion, an inconspicuous car, for a reason. There had to be hundreds of them in the Detroit metropolitan area. Besides, it was only ten thirty in the morning.

If I leave this parking lot now, even to leave Highland Heights, will Dylan or one of the other officers see me? If they do, will they know it is me? How am I supposed to wait almost twenty-four hours before I learn more?

Waiting wasn't my thing, but then again, neither was surveillance, and I did it. Waiting was a big part of my job. The investigators on television had it easy. They parked their car and then boom, their suspect would walk right in front of them. That wasn't the way it worked in real life. I'd been sitting in this parking lot since before the sun came up, around six this morning, and my legs were beginning to feel it.

I grinned. Maybe it wasn't the surveillance my legs were feeling. Maybe it was the aftereffects of last night's activities. Dylan had made me an offer I couldn't refuse. Oh, I could have, but I hadn't wanted to.

At first I'd decided to cancel our evening plans. I was getting nowhere fast on my research, and I needed to jump in with both feet. Over the last two-plus weeks, I'd made it through all Dr. Howell's cases more than once. I'd even deciphered Bernard's sketchy information regarding drugs and missing persons. There were a few unsolved cases as well as people who crossed the border with increased regularity. That wasn't in itself a crime, but some of their information was questionable. Could that connect them to the drugs?

None of it made sense. There were dots to be connected; I just couldn't make out the picture they formed. Plus I'd promised the Rosemonts, once again, that I wouldn't stop. It was one thing to say it on the phone or in an e-mail, but the week before I'd said it while holding their hands. They'd been back to Detroit for the second time since Mindy's disappearance. I didn't blame them. Even though I'd promised to do everything at this end, they felt helpless in California and needed to feel involved. I didn't hold much hope that a solution would materialize from the flyers they'd put all over the city, but then again, who was I to fault them? I wasn't making progress either.

With that search for answers at the forefront of my mind, I'd made the decision to go straight home from work and forgo Dylan's house. Imagine my surprise when thirty minutes after I arrived home, he showed up at my door. Though I wanted to be mad, as soon as my gaze met his I knew I couldn't. It wasn't only the way he stood outside my door, his long legs barely covered by torn jeans, biceps bulging from his sleeves, and that smug sexy grin that turned my insides to jelly. It was what I saw as I scanned lower. My stomach growled as I saw the six-pack of beer in one hand and a pizza in the other. However, what sealed his fate was the package of time-release fish feeder blocks on top of the pizza box. Even now I had a difficult time keeping a smile from sneaking across my weary face. Shaking my head at the memory, I knew Detective Dylan Richards was getting to me.

I still wasn't sure if I was the relationship type. This was the first time I'd ever been with anyone as long as I had been with Dylan. That didn't mean I was ready to become more serious. However, it was becoming increasingly clear that if I didn't want it to go that way, I'd need distance and a Teflon coating for my heart.

It didn't bother me that others warned me about his hard-ass ways. The Dylan Richards I knew wasn't a tough detective. The one who was getting under my skin was the one who drove across the city to support me at the morgue and brought me fish food. Granted, the fish food was time-released, which allowed me to leave Fred on his own for a few days, but still, when I combined that with his sexier-than-hell grin and the bedroom-blue eyes, my pulse pitter-pattered and my insides tightened. The mere thought of him not only beside me, but inside me, had my mind replaying scenes that were probably illegal in some states.

I sighed and tried to concentrate on the task at hand.

The building I'd staked out all morning appeared as empty as it had when I'd arrived. Bernard's contact had shared the address, saying three different vehicles from there crossed the Canadian border almost every day. The vehicles were driven by different people, but all the passport information included this Gerald Street address. The obvious problem was that the address wasn't a home. It was some big abandoned building.

Over the past four hours, with the help of my hot spot, an Internet search, and my imagination, I'd constructed a story of a bustling neighborhood. In 1907 Henry Ford had built an automobile plant not far from where I sat. In the next thirteen years the population of this area had grown to over forty thousand. Five years later Chrysler was founded here. This area had thrived.

Then, during my lifetime, the latter decades of the twentieth century, Highland Heights experienced the same problems as Detroit and many other cities. Declining population led to loss of tax base. That, along with loss of employment opportunities, created increasing crime. At its peak this city within a city had boasted over fifty thousand residents. Today there were barely ten thousand.

Unfortunately, the exodus had left an excess of unused and abandoned buildings. Though the cities of Highland Heights and Detroit tried to keep the buildings boarded up or demolished, as long as they stood, they were magnets for illicit use. That the woman I'd seen at the morgue, as well as two more people, had been found dead inside one of them wasn't hard to believe.

I knew my imagination was running wild. Spending all my spare time dissecting Tracy Howell's "compilation theory" was getting to me. Every death and disappearance didn't have to be related. Though this neighborhood was a melting pot for crimes, so were other areas of the city. High-risk behaviors made areas like this good spots for deaths from self-inflicted causes, such as drug use. Unfortunately, they also made good dumping grounds. There were too many reasons for death among Dr. Howell's cases to assume that all, or even a large number, of them were related.

The area needed more places like the building I was sitting behind: a health clinic. Dr. Howell was right. New businesses wouldn't be willing to set up shop here if it was publicized that just down the street dead bodies kept surfacing.

The building I watched used to be a school, and the one next to it had once been a fire station. As I sat, I imagined what they were like in their heydays. Instead of being desolate, the area would've been filled with people. At one time children had run along the streets and played in the attached lots. Instead of dirt and debris, there had been grass, trees, and playground equipment. As I scanned the area, I knew that Dylan's concern was warranted. Going purely by the number of abandoned buildings in this neighborhood, it wasn't safe. However, the way I saw it, it was daylight, and I'd left my trail of bread crumbs. Bernard and Foster knew exactly where I was.

With each minute of nothing, I considered calling Bernard. His earlier suggestion to use Dylan as an informant might have been a test, but it had pissed me off. Now I wondered whether, if I told him about Dylan's offer, he'd think the sharing of information went both ways. Shrugging, I decided it could wait until after I received my tour tomorrow morning.

Therefore, instead of Bernard, I dialed Dr. Howell's cell phone. I was ready to leave a message when she finally answered on the fourth ring.

"Hi, Charlotte," she answered. "I'm surprised you're calling me at work."

Charlotte?

"OK," I replied, "I get it, you can't talk. Did you know another body's been found in Highland Heights?"

"Sure did." Tracy's upbeat tone combined with the morbid subject made me grin. She was obviously in the presence of someone she didn't want to include in our conversation.

"It was found in the same neighborhood as the woman from a week ago," I said softly, hoping my voice didn't transcend the phone and reach the unintended listener.

"Sounds about right. I'll call you after I get off work. I'm not sure if we can meet for a drink, but I'll let you know."

"Thanks, I'll be waiting for your call."

When the phone disconnected, I wondered who *Charlotte* was—I mean, besides me.

Unlike with my wasted morning, at least with that brief conversation I'd learned something. The ME's office had already received the call. Maybe I wouldn't have to wait until tomorrow for details. Maybe I'd get them this evening from Dr. Howell.

As I was about to give up on the abandoned building, a late-model black Suburban pulled up and around to the front. It stopped near the neighboring building, the one that looked like an old fire station. Though there were three large garage-type doors, the two men who got out of the SUV walked between the buildings.

I reached for my camera. While my phone took good pictures, my Nikon was capable of much more. With the two-hundred-millimeter-focal-length lens, the zooming abilities were superb. I pointed and snapped a rapid series of shots. The two men who walked between the buildings were white, average height, wearing dark jeans and white T-shirts. If I were to guess, I'd have put them roughly in their thirties. As I continued to take the photos, the word *nondescript* came to mind. The driver remained in the vehicle. Seeing him through the windshield, I couldn't get a great picture, but I saw that he was African-American and wearing a similar white T-shirt. From my angle, I couldn't make out much more.

Whatever the men did between the buildings didn't take long. In less than five minutes, they were out, and the Suburban pulled away, past me and toward Woodward. Ignoring Dylan's warning, I backed out of my space and pulled out of the parking lot, just in time to watch the Suburban turn right on Woodward. Justifying my decision—the SUV had turned in the direction in which I would need to go to get back to WCJB—I followed.

Since Woodward Avenue was a main thoroughfare, I wasn't concerned about the occupants of the SUV questioning my presence. That was, until we turned right onto Glendale Avenue. The hairs on the back of my neck tingled in warning. For a warm late-summer morning, the streets were very quiet. While I waited at a light at Second Avenue, the Suburban turned right. Once the stoplight changed, I followed. I turned just in time to see the black SUV pull into a parking lot behind a white brick building.

I continued to drive and circled the block.

Thankfully, wherever Dylan and the rest of the police were wasn't nearby. Approaching again from the front of the building, I slowed near the corner of Second and Glendale Avenues. During my circle I passed multiple buildings that weren't only abandoned, but charred remains of what had once been homes. As a matter of fact, I was currently across the street from one. An overgrowth of shrubbery near the intersection hid my location as I pulled to the side of the road.

Peering about, I didn't see a single person. Maybe it was the police presence somewhere in the vicinity, but for whatever reason, despite its being almost midday, the neighborhood was deadly still. I turned off the ignition, locked my car, and stepped onto the sidewalk. Weeds brushed my pant legs as I made my way through the debris littering the street and sidewalk.

Moving slowly around the overgrowth of bushes, I scanned the front of the building, the one where the SUV had parked. If I were to guess, it was or used to be an office building. Four stories tall, it had many windows in front, all covered interiorly by long white vertical blinds. This building's surroundings looked different from those of most buildings in the area. Unlike where I stood, there weren't any overgrown bushes or grass; even the sidewalk in front was clear of weeds and debris. A black chain-link fence surrounded the entire building, yet there didn't appear to be a lock of any kind on the front gate. Above the front entrance was a blue awning with white letters that simply read "The Light."

I snapped more pictures. Rotating from left to right I photographed the entire intersection. On the southwest corner, across Second Avenue from The Light, was a large limestone building surrounded by a rod iron fence. As I zoomed my camera, I made out the words *Public Schools of Highland Heights* etched in the stone. The trees and bushes as well as ground clutter indicated that, like many others, it was abandoned. Across from the old school was the skeleton of a house, decimated by fire, and on the corner where I stood was another building. The broken windows told me that it too was empty.

Getting back in my car, I watched the vertical blinds covering the windows on the front side of The Light. I didn't notice any movement. If the building held people, they were hidden. As I slowly drove toward the intersection, a group of three women walked from the back of The

Light, coming from near the parking lot. From that distance I couldn't make out distinguishing characteristics, but I could tell that they were women.

What are they doing?

I watched as they crossed Second Avenue toward the old school and disappeared behind an overgrowth of trees. Reaching for my camera, I waited for more people. When no one else emerged, I laid my camera down and drove forward, crossing the intersection. Driving slowly, I peered in the direction in which they had gone. The iron gate on the far side of the trees was closed. Beyond it was a door, but it had a "Do Not Trespass" sign attached and a chain laced through the handle from the outside.

Where did the women go?

They couldn't have entered that door. If they had, someone would have needed to chain it again from the outside. Even with my active imagination that seemed improbable; besides, the lock looked rusty and old. Stopping my car, I grabbed my camera. Quickly I took pictures of the side of the school. Looking back to The Light building, I noticed more windows, also covered from within. I snapped a few more pictures. The Suburban was still parked in the lot behind the building, along with a half-dozen other cars, none of which were new.

The wail of sirens in the distance propelled me to leave. Soon I was headed north and then east, back to Woodward Avenue.

Within ten minutes I was out of Highland Heights and safely into the North End of Detroit. I couldn't recall for sure, but I didn't remember having seen any police cars. Honestly, other than the patrons of the health clinic where I'd spent most of my morning, the men in my pictures, and the three women, I hadn't seen anyone. Hopefully, no one would report my whereabouts to my overprotective boyfriend.

I shrugged. If they did, he'd need to deal. Then again, I didn't want to lose my morning tour.

~

"Wake up, sleepyhead."

Dylan's raspy voice invaded my dream. I couldn't remember what I'd been seeing behind my closed eyes, but whatever it had been, I was confident the man above me was better. As I inhaled his musky scent, my lips formed a smile, only for it to morph into a pout.

"What if I don't want to?"

"Then I guess your lovely tour of downtown Highland Heights will need to wait."

My eyes sprang open and I started to sit. A laugh rumbled deep in Dylan's throat as he leaned over me, stopping my upward motion. The vibrations of his chest electrified my bare nipples, making them hard and tight, while my insides fluttered.

"I don't think I've gotten that quick of a reaction from you this early in the morning, ever. Not even when I was offering something a hell of a lot better than two rat-infested boarded-up houses."

This time I laughed. "I think it's the lovely description that has me enthralled. Who could pass up a tour of rat-infested boarded-up houses in lovely downtown Highland Heights?" I asked, mocking his words. "Besides, that other offer of yours, well . . ." I shrugged. "I've had that before."

Dylan rolled away, laying his head on the pillow and covering his eyes with his hard bicep. "You're seriously messing with my self-confidence."

I lifted my head and moved toward him. My long hair teased his skin. After a quick kiss on his cheek, I said, "I doubt that. I've never known a more—"

His finger touched my lips and his eyes sparkled. "Stop right there. Let me imagine the rest of the sentence, and just maybe, I might recover."

My grin blossomed into a full-out smile. "I'm so glad. I'd hate to be responsible for any of your nonexistent self-esteem issues."

Dylan captured my shoulders and pulled me close, flattening my breasts against his chest and sending my hair cascading around my face. We were two people in a tunnel of blonde. "I think," he teased, "we should skip the tour and work on my nonexistent issues."

I pulled away. "As I recall, we worked on your issues last night."

"But I have more."

Turning slightly, I peeked at the blankets and playfully shook my head at the way they now tented. Kissing his lips, I reminded him, "You're the one who told me we had to do this early, before . . . what did you say? The idiots came out?"

"That was me, wasn't it?"

"It was, and I want my tour."

Dylan looked at the clock, which read half past five. "Sunrise is a little after seven. We don't want to arrive before sunrise and surprise the rats."

My whole body quivered. "Yuck. It'd be all right with me if you quit mentioning those."

He poked my side, making me laugh. "You can always change your mind."

"Nope," I squeaked from the tickling. "Stop! You offered me a tour. I want it."

"OK. I was thinking that if we drove separately to WCJB, you could leave your car and ride with me to Highland Heights. Then I'll take you back to the station." He sighed. "Heck, we'll probably get you to work before Barney."

I slapped his shoulder. "*Bernard.* What about you?"

"What about me?"

"Last time I checked you needed to go to work too."

Dylan threw back the covers, stood, and stretched. Suddenly my eyes found it difficult to make their way up his sculpted body. It wasn't that I didn't enjoy his handsome face, I did. I also liked his shoulders, abs, and everything lower. "Hey," he said with a laugh. "My eyes are up here."

"Umm . . ." I sighed. Slowly I moved my gaze up to his blue smirk and winked.

"You, Miss Montgomery, happen to be dating a detective. Once I'm in the car, I can log on, and we're good. I'm officially on duty."

"If you get an exciting call, do I get to come along?"

"And have it end up on WCJB's evening news? No way."

"You're no fun," I said, jutting my lower lip out as far as it would go.

Dylan reached for my hand. "We've got a little time. How about you join me in the shower, and I show you how much fun I can be?"

I shrugged as I stood. "I guess, but I think a police chase would be more exciting."

Dylan slapped my behind, and the crack echoed through his bedroom.

"Ouch!"

His eyes sparkled. "Don't forget, I have issues."

Tracing my finger teasingly down his chest, I stepped close and kissed his neck. "Detective Richards, we all know that."

An hour later we were in Dylan's unmarked Charger on our way to Highland Heights. I pulled the black case I'd thrown in the backseat up to the front. I opened it, removed my Nikon, and began changing the lens. I wouldn't need the zooming power of yesterday. Well, unless there was a rat; then I'd be so far out of one of those houses, I would need the two-hundred-millimeter.

Dylan glanced my way. "Hey, what do you think you're doing?"

"It seems rather obvious, but if you're having problems, I'm changing the lens on my camera."

"No. You're not taking pictures. I'm taking you into a secured crime scene. I'm not losing my job."

"It's not like I'm going to take *your* picture," I replied. "Besides, it helps me remember everything. I can go home and study the pictures."

"No."

"They'll never end up on one of Bernard's broadcasts, I promise." I turned on the screen and scrolled through my pictures from yesterday.

Dylan looked in my direction and his knuckles blanched as his grip tightened on the steering wheel. "When did you take those?"

I looked up from the image of the white brick building with the blue awning.

Shit!

"Yesterday," I replied sheepishly.

"I thought we had a deal. I guess I should take you back to WCJB."

"We *do* have a deal," I pleaded. "The thing was, when you called, I was kind of already in Highland Heights. I left soon after our conversation."

"Jesus, Stella. Why?"

This time of the morning the traffic hadn't yet built. I watched the landmarks in New Center as we continued heading north on Woodward Avenue. If he wasn't turning around, I guessed I could answer him, at least partially. "I was staking out an abandoned building. It was an address from a source. I heard the sirens, but never saw the police cars. So, see, I wasn't really near you."

"Staking out *an abandoned building* doesn't exactly narrow down your location."

"Do you go to Highland Heights often?" I asked.

"The HHPD and DPD work together on some things. Usually Highland Heights takes care of its cases and we do ours. There's been some crossover lately."

"Why? What's changed?"

The morning sky was an array of reds and pinks as the sun brought light where dark had prevailed. Dylan turned right off Woodward, away from the sunrise, onto Cortland. This street was only two blocks south of Glendale, where I'd been yesterday. Dylan ran his fingers through his hair.

I started thinking about the body they'd found yesterday. This one was a man. No wonder Dylan had answered so fast that it wasn't Mindy. According to my talk with Tracy the night before, the guy was a typical gang member, one with the right tats and piercings. Even she didn't believe her compilation theory applied to him.

We had crossed Hamilton Avenue by the time Dylan finally spoke again.

"Do you recognize this area?"

"Not really. Why?"

"Because from the picture I saw, you weren't that fucking far from here *yesterday*." The way he emphasized the last word reminded me of Tracy saying how he was usually more of a hard-ass.

I reached out and covered his hand on the steering wheel, reminding him that I wasn't part of his work; I was his girlfriend. "Thank you for being concerned. I really wasn't here for Mindy or because of that other body. I was here for WCJB."

"What does Barney have you doing? The man's a lunatic sending you here. Why doesn't he send Foster? Or maybe he could man up and do it himself."

"You know I can't tell you what he has me doing."

The Charger stopped along the side of Cortland, in front of a house with plywood-covered windows and doors and bright-yellow police tape roped across the front porch.

Dylan put the car in park and turned my way. "Then show me the same courtesy. I'm bringing you here for one reason, so you won't come on your own. Fine, don't tell me what you're researching with that church. Just don't come back here alone, and don't ask me why DPD is working with HHPD."

Church?

There were so many questions I wanted to ask, but I didn't. He was right. If I wasn't willing to share, I shouldn't ask him to do it. I squeezed his hand, smiled my brightest smile, and nodded. "Agreed, Detective, now may I please have my tour?"

He took a deep breath and exhaled. Shaking his head, he said, "Yes, by all means. I believe we traded hot sex for this."

"Um, was the shower that forgettable?"

His grin showed me the return of the man I was falling for, not the hard-ass who liked to tell me where I could and could not go. "No," he said, "not forgettable, just quick. I hope that when we're done with this tour, you *don't* think it was a good trade."

CHAPTER 17
Sara

As Jacob slipped my nightgown over my head, my mind swirled with the happenings of the evening. I hadn't known what to expect at service, and it'd been all right, some parts even nice. With both Elizabeth and Raquel helping me, I'd made it through. My two friends alternated directing me, whispering when it was time to stand or time to sit. I tried to hide what had happened between Jacob and me—my correction—but apparently each time I sat down, the truth was evident. The strange thing, the part I struggled to understand, was that neither of my friends thought it was wrong. Elizabeth even told me she was proud of me for being honest. I thought maybe Raquel would respond differently; after all, she was my friend and my nurse. She'd seen my injuries from the accident and should understand that I didn't need more. Instead she squeezed my hand, told me she understood, and reminded me that when I prayed, I should thank God for a husband who loved me enough to correct me. Though it didn't make sense, I followed her advice.

Another part of the evening that left me uneasy came after service. I'd made it until the end, and as my reward, I wanted to be alone with my husband. However, that wasn't what happened. Instead Brother Benjamin came to us and announced that Brothers Luke and Jacob would be delayed, and then he and Raquel took Elizabeth and me with them to another room. The entire time my heart thudded with questions. It was Elizabeth's squeeze of my hand that told me what her words couldn't. Not only didn't we have a choice, we couldn't ask why. It wasn't until later, when I overheard Brother Benjamin speaking with another man, that I even knew our husbands were meeting with Father Gabriel. When I heard that, my stomach twisted, sure that their meeting had something to do with me, with what I'd done.

If it had, after Jacob retrieved me, he never mentioned a word. After all, he'd said my infraction had occurred, had been corrected, and was now done—his responsibility. Maybe he was right. It wasn't that he seemed upset; it was that he'd hardly spoken. I wanted to ask, to learn if I'd done all right at service and what had happened in his meeting, but the evidence of my earlier correction kept my questions at bay.

Jacob had been right when he'd said that the welts would serve as reminders. Without them I might have blurted out the thousand questions I had running through my head or the one invitation I wanted to bestow. Instead, as he helped me into bed and kissed my forehead, I took a deep breath, bit my lip, and silently scooted all the way to the right.

"Sara, if you're trying to get away from me, the bed isn't that big."

"I'm not trying to get away from you. I'm making room for you."

"What?" he asked.

"You've spent every night since I woke sleeping in that chair. I'm sure you'd be more comfortable in the bed." I held my breath.

He brushed my cheek.

"You don't . . ."

I reached for his hand.

"Please, don't punish me. You said I could ask for things I need, just not question. I'm not questioning why you've slept in the chair. I'm asking you to please sleep in the bed."

He exhaled. "I don't want to hurt you."

Though the irony of his statement wasn't lost on me, I heard more than his words; I heard his compassion. His sincerity pulled at my heartstrings and made me smile. "I know it's up to you, but *if* I could choose, I'd want you here"—I brushed the space beside me—"with me." The strong, brave front I'd tried to project while outside this room evaporated. "I . . ." My breathing stuttered. "I missed you during service." The bed moved as he sat.

"Brother Benjamin . . ."

I nodded. Brother Benjamin had told me of Jacob's delay. That didn't mean I liked it.

I scooted closer to the far edge of the bed, near the rail. As Jacob lay back against my pillow, he wrapped his arm around my shoulder and drew me close. Judging by the texture of his shirt, he was still wearing the clothes he'd worn to service. That probably meant he was only pacifying me; nevertheless I curled my body toward him and rested my head on his chest. His subtle scent reminded me of our body wash, fresh and clean; however, as I buried my cheek in the cotton, his signature leather-and-musk cloud filled my senses.

Though I'd hoped to learn more about his meeting, with the events of the day and the warmth of his silent embrace, in no time at all, I began to drift off to sleep. I was nearly there when Jacob moved. Rolling me to my back, he hovered close and smoothed my long hair away from my face.

"Are you still awake?" he asked, his minty breath blowing over me.

"Yes."

"I'm sorry . . ."

His simple apology had my full attention. I wasn't sure I remembered hearing those words from him.

". . . I meant to tell you how well you did at service."

I smiled. "Thank you. I was scared, but Raquel and Elizabeth were with me the entire time. And Brother Benjamin," I added, suddenly fearful of not acknowledging that a man had helped.

He continued to run his fingers through my hair. "I didn't want you to think that I'd been quiet because of anything you'd done. You were perfect."

It was difficult for me not to ask the questions running through my tired mind, but lying on my back helped me remember. "Thank you, Jacob. I want you to be proud. I'm sorry that I embarrassed you. I'm sure that's what Father Gabriel was speaking to you about."

His hand and breath stilled, as if he was considering his words carefully. "We're leaving the clinic tomorrow. However, instead of going to our apartment, we'll be staying at the pole barn for a while."

"I don't remember our apartment or the pole barn, but I'll go wherever you take me."

His lips brushed mine. The light touch ignited a spark that detonated flickers of yearning throughout my body. I lifted my lips to his, wanting more than the chaste endearment.

"Sara, I . . ." Jacob didn't complete his sentence; instead his hand slipped behind my head, pulling me toward him. His kiss, no longer apathetic, devoured. Zeal radiated from his lips, and soon his breaths were labored. Like magnets we were drawn toward one another, closer and closer. My body liquefied, becoming pliable to his touch, while conversely, his hardened, ready to claim what was already his.

As the heat of our passion washed over us, I forgot my punishment. My attention went elsewhere. A tug on my hair propelled my head to tilt, while the persistence of his minty tongue encouraged my lips to part. Whimpers and moans reverberated in my mouth and bubbled forth. They were wordless sounds declaring my body's approval.

The large, strong hands that had delivered pain now brought pleasure. I reached for his broad shoulders, opening my arms and willfully surrendering to his kisses. With a palpable hunger, his mouth moved from my lips to my neck and down to my collarbone. His actions sent shivers to my toes and tremors to my insides. Each kiss moved lower until he reached the neckline of my nightgown. The bra I'd worn to service was gone. My breaths quickened as each button came undone, leaving me bare and exposed to his desires.

The sound of my heart echoed in my ears as he praised my beauty and whispered admiration for what was his. When he wasn't speaking, his lips moved lower as his five o'clock shadow tantalized my sensitive skin. It was as his skilled fingers joined the assault, kneading my breasts and twisting my hardened nipples, that primal sounds came from in my throat. It wasn't that I feared speaking. It was that words weren't forming. Wanting what he could give, I reached for his head, wove my fingers through his hair, and pulled him closer.

Suddenly he stopped and pulled away, leaving me open to the cool air.

Dazed and chilled, I reached for my nightgown. Embarrassed and hurt, I began to button it. "Did I do something wrong?" The cool temperature of the room turned glacial as I realized my mistake. "Jacob, I'm sorry. I know not to question. It's just that . . ." The whirlwind of my emotions cycloned out of control. Though my nightgown wasn't completely buttoned, I rolled away, lost in my darkened world, as tears rained onto my pillow.

Reaching for my shoulder, Jacob turned me back toward him, wiped my tears, and kissed my nose. "You are so stubborn. You're going to be the death of us yet."

I didn't understand what had just happened.

How did we go from hot and steamy to frigid in record time?

My heart ached as the bed shifted and Jacob stood. Then seconds later it shifted again to his weight. This time when he pulled me to his chest, his shirt was soft. A T-shirt, I presumed. When I curled into him as I'd done before, my bare leg met his. The skin-to-skin contact brought a smile to my saddened lips. He'd gotten out of bed to remove his clothes, not to leave me. He was going to sleep with me.

He kissed the top of my head. "You didn't do anything wrong. We're in a hospital bed in the community clinic. It's not the most romantic place to make love to my wife."

I exhaled, thankful he'd explained his reasoning.

Gently rubbing my back, he continued, "Besides, like I said, I'm worried about your ribs. I weigh a lot more than you. I don't want to make them worse."

"I don't have to be on the bottom."

Oh, shit! I bit my lip. *Did I really just say that?*

The bed shook with the quake of his laughter. "Good night, Sara."

⁓

The next afternoon I burrowed my gloved hands deep inside my thick coat and sat silently as Jacob drove us away from the clinic. Judging from the height of the vehicle as he'd helped me into my seat, we were in a truck. I wanted to ask if it belonged to him.

After all, didn't I wreck his truck?

Instead I listened as the heater blew ferociously within and the wind howled outside. I was stuck in a battle of temperatures, and judging by my chattering teeth, the outside was winning. I tried to remember the time of year. Elizabeth had mentioned the *dark season*. Based on the temperature, it had to be winter. Then again, I didn't know if it ever got warm in Far North, Alaska.

Whatever time of year it was, I couldn't seem to get warm. On one foot I wore the boot from last night. On the other my cast was covered by a sort of sock. Under my long skirt I wore warm leggings, but despite it all, my body still shivered. The farther we drove, the more I thought about my friends. I'd recently told Elizabeth how anxious I was to leave my room. Now in less than twenty-four hours I'd done it twice, and this time we weren't returning, at least for a little while.

The new paradigm left me scared and lonely. As the reality of my circumstance settled in my consciousness, my desire to question slipped away. The acceptance of my life was a relief that allowed me to concentrate on what and who was around me. Outside the community I'd have Jacob, but I would also miss Raquel's constant presence and Elizabeth's visits. I even wondered about Sisters Lilith and Ruth. With Sister Ruth's presence, I'd come to enjoy my training. It was nice to have the women to talk to, people I could question, who could teach me the things I'd forgotten.

I tried to imagine a pole barn but had no frame of reference. I didn't even know what it was. The longer I thought about where we were going and how we were getting there, the more questions I had.

Can we live in a barn? Why do we want to?

It wasn't as if Jacob usually talked a lot, but ever since the previous night's service he had been quieter than normal. I believed it had something to do with his meeting, but what that something was I'd probably never know. If one day I learned, it would be in *God's time*. I reached for the door, to my right, and found a handle. My grip tightened as the tires bounced upon the uneven road.

"Are you all right?" Jacob asked, bringing my thoughts to the present.

Biting my lip, I nodded.

His gloved hand reached for my leg. "Sara," he said gently, "I can't help you if you're not honest with me. Don't try to hide your thoughts and feelings. I'll find out the truth."

"It's my ribs. The way the truck's bouncing . . . they hurt."

"There. Was that difficult? Is there more?" he asked.

When I covered his hand with mine, he turned his palm up and laced our fingers together. Taking a deep breath, I said, "I don't remember anything. I don't know where we're going other than what you've said. I don't even know what a pole barn is. Will"—I swallowed and rephrased—"I'm wondering if there'll be animals."

His laughter filled the truck, momentarily masking the wind and the squeak of the tires bouncing upon the uneven road. "I'm proud of you. You said all of that without questioning once." He squeezed my hand. "Very good. A pole barn is a type of building. No, there won't be any animals. One small section of the building has living quarters. Even without your sight, I believe you'll be able to navigate it well. There's a loft with a bedroom. The main level is one room with a kitchen and living area and a small separated bathroom. The rest is more of a hangar."

I turned in his direction and tried to imagine what he described. "The rest has an airplane." I tried to avoid any inflection that could make my words sound like a question.

"Airplanes, two." He sighed. "I keep forgetting that you don't remember. I'm a pilot. Father Gabriel needs me to get back to work. Now that you're doing better, I can. Last night he decided it would be better if you were with me out at the hangar, rather than leaving you in our apartment alone."

"I'll be alone while you're at Assembly *and* when you're working." My heartbeat quickened.

"You will, sometimes. Other times people will come to stay with you. All members of The Light pull their weight. We all work to fulfill Father Gabriel's dream. There's another pilot, Brother Micah, here at the Northern Light. For the last three weeks, since the accident, he's been handling everything alone. There's also another pilot who comes here who isn't a member of The Light, Xavier. He sometimes helps out by bringing supplies. Father Gabriel trusts him, so we do too."

I braced myself again as the terrain turned bumpier.

"We're almost there. Xavier is the reason the pole barn has living quarters. Sometimes when he brings supplies, he can't leave the same day. The Northern Light is located in a very remote part of the Far North region. This building is removed from the community so he has a place to stay."

"I know I can't say what I'm thinking without a question."

"If you ask, will it make you feel better?"

I shrugged. "I suppose. It depends on your answer, and if I have permission to ask."

The truck slowed to make another turn.

"Go ahead. You have my permission, but I can't promise I'll answer."

"You said you're a pilot and that sometimes Xavier needs to stay here overnight. Are you ever gone overnight?"

"I am."

I turned toward the window that I couldn't see and tried to quell the panic bubbling in my chest. I hated being so dependent on him, but I was.

"Father Gabriel won't ask me to do any overnight trips until you're fully recovered. And by the time I do, we'll be home in our apartment. You'll have the entire community. I'd never leave you alone out here for more than a few hours."

I nodded as the truck came to a stop. A mechanical sound—a garage door rising—came from outside, and then we slowly moved forward.

"Don't open your door," Jacob warned. "I'll help you out, but we need to wait for the door to close. This time of year, we need to be careful. The tall fences keep the polar bears out of the community, but out here you never know."

My face spun back toward him. "Oh my gosh, polar bears!"

He scoffed. "It's not like they're always outside our door. Technically we're only on the edge of the circumpolar north, but it's better to be safe. Don't you agree?"

"I do." I thought for a minute as the door descended. "But it's winter, they should be hibernating."

"We're not into meteorological winter yet, but I agree it feels like it; however, no, polar bears don't hibernate."

I sucked my lip between my teeth.

How could I forget I live with polar bears?

My door opened and Jacob reached for my chin. With his gloved hand he teased my lip free. "Don't worry. We're safe. Remember, I meant what I said. I promised to take care of you. I'd never do anything that caused you harm. That includes leaving you alone with polar bears."

I forced my cheeks to rise and reached for his hand. "Good."

"Now let's get inside the living quarters where it's warmer."

As I started to ease myself from the truck, Jacob said, "Hold on to my neck, I'll carry you."

"Oh, you don't have to do that. I can walk. It's actually easier with the boot on my other foot."

Undeterred, he wrapped me in his arms. "I've noticed that."

Shaking my head, I did as he said and reached for his neck. He effortlessly lifted me from my seat. After a few steps, I pulled his face toward mine and kissed his cheek.

"What was that for?"

"I was just thinking. Since I don't remember any of this, you carrying me like this, is like being carried over the threshold for the first time. It's like we're newlyweds."

"You did say you'd marry me again." His tone dropped. "But that was before—"

I interrupted him with another kiss, this time a light brush to his lips. "I still would," I assured him.

"Then by all means, Mrs. Adams, newlyweds we can be."

CHAPTER 18
Jacob

I pounded my palms against the steering wheel, trying with all my might to give the truck some of my frustration. At least when I struck it, the truck didn't cry or melt into my arms. I understood a truck, knew how it worked and how to fix it when it had problems. It was like our planes. Micah and I not only flew them, we knew how to fix them and service them—the mechanical part, not the technology. That shit was complicated. I grabbed a fistful of my hair and began my inner monologue.

Get yourself together, Jacob. You will do this.

I took one last glance at the door to the living quarters before I pushed the garage door button. I couldn't go back. If I did I wouldn't want to leave. Besides, I needed to be at Assembly in less than a half an hour.

Why does she want me with her? Why doesn't she hate me?

It wasn't that I wanted Sara to hate me, I didn't, but she should.

Backing out of the pole barn, I waited and watched the door fully close. Glancing at the clock on the dashboard, I saw it was almost half past eight on Friday morning and the sky was still dark. There had been a time in my life when that would've bothered me, or that it was still twilight at noon, or darkening by four, but right now I had too much happening to give it more than a fleeting thought.

Sara didn't even realize that this was her Commission-invoked retribution. I needed to inform her before she faced the Assembly, the Commission, or any of the wives—especially before she faced Father Gabriel.

As I drove toward the community, my mind drifted back to the meeting after Wednesday night's service. Father Gabriel had wasted no time on preliminaries, coming right to the point . . .

"Brothers, have a seat. Before we meet with the Assembly and Commission in the morning, I want to discuss my decree regarding Sara's retribution for the incident."

As I sat, I had tried to still the worry that ricocheted through my thoughts like an old-fashioned pinball.

"In similar cases I've pronounced an array of decrees. Your wife, as well as followers who're unaware, believe that Sara was your wife in the dark. While Sara believes she's lived here, the followers believe she was recently brought here. They all believe she took your truck and in the act of fleeing, she had an accident."

My back stiffened.

"Brother?"

"Father, I haven't discussed it with Sara. I told her I'd tell her when the time was right. All she knows is what I was told to say to Brother Timothy, the day she awoke."

"Which doesn't match, does it?"

"No. In that scenario, I was told to say that she took my truck for supplies with my permission."

Have I been set up?

Father Gabriel nodded. "I also believe you said that she remembered, but she doesn't."

"Yes."

"As a member of the Assembly, your word is to be true. What you said wasn't."

Well, hell, unless I'd said she didn't have an accident. Unless I'd said it was all staged with the right amount of drugs in her system and that a psycho Assemblyman beat the shit out of her before my eyes. That he would've done more, but I stopped him . . . unless I'd said that even after I stopped the assault, Sara received more injuries after she was given to Dr. Newton . . . unless I'd told Brother Timothy what he already knew—that the entire incident was all a deception—then I would've lied.

"Yes, Father."

"My judgment therefore must rectify both transgressions and placate the followers."

"Yes, Father."

"I've sought the advice of my Commission. Now that Sara is better, acclimating to the community and staking her claim as an Assemblyman's wife, her punishment needs to be public."

My gaze flashed toward Luke's. Though he didn't look my way, I saw the shock he was trying to hide. Sure that my heart had stopped beating, I almost doubled over with the pain of his verdict. I was in charge of disputes. I knew the meaning of public correction. Everything in me wanted to question, protest, and offer myself in her stead, but I knew it wouldn't help her cause. His decision was already made. The entire room stilled as everyone awaited my response.

Swallowing my objections, I said, "I'll honor your decision."

Brother Daniel exhaled. "Very good. I knew you had it in you." His cheeks stretched with the breadth of his smile.

Confused, I looked back to Father Gabriel.

"Brother Jacob, you truly are a man of The Light. I believe that once this is complete we'll be able to trust you with even more."

"Thank you . . . ?"

If Sara had used the same inflection, I probably would have reprimanded her. There was obviously a question mark hanging somewhere in the air.

Father Gabriel laughed. "Well, that wasn't as pronounced as your wife's question earlier today."

I shook my head. "I'm sorry. I'm still processing."

"Temporary banishment," he decreed.

Temporary?

I gripped the arms of the chair. My knuckles blanching from my hold. Fuck this! Banishment was death. No one could ever be permitted to leave The Light: not after they worked in the processing plant, not after they knew what we did here, especially not me. I knew about the other campuses.

"Brother, your self-control is impressive. Let me explain. Sara has been seen. She's developed relationships, not only with you, but also with Sisters Elizabeth and Raquel, as well as Sisters Lilith and Ruth. She's learning my teachings. Our goal is for her to desire our community and her husband. If I'm interpreting your clenched jaw, the heat in your brown eyes, and the grip you have on that chair, you've begun to feel protective of her?"

Consciously I released the chair's arms, relaxed my shoulders, and loosened my bite. Inhaling and exhaling, I admitted, "I have."

"Sexual attraction will come. I don't believe any man is impervious to it, not when he's been granted a virtuous wife, and she's been placed in his bed."

I nodded.

"Beginning tomorrow, Sara will be banished from the community."

I held my breath.

"For two weeks. During that time the two of you will live out at the hangar, in the living quarters. It's already been set up with supplies for your stay. The Northern Light needs you to return to your job. Micah hasn't complained, but we need you."

I gasped the air as it filled my lungs.

Two weeks. Thank The Light. Two weeks is doable.

"Of course, I'm more than willing."

"During the two weeks, she'll only see you, unless a member of the Commission or one of their wives receives permission to visit."

See?

"Father, she still isn't able to see anyone."

His lips pursed and his brow furrowed. With his elbows on his desk, Father Gabriel steepled his fingers. "After one week Dr. Newton will visit the pole barn and remove the bandages. Then, when she returns to the community, she'll be able to fully appreciate being back and begin a job."

"Do I understand that she'll be excluded from service during that time?"

"You both will."

I sat taller.

"Of course, we won't go into detail about this to anyone other than the Assembly and Commission, but the followers will draw their own conclusions. Once you return I'll personally welcome you both back. The correction will be done."

"As if it never occurred," Brother Daniel added. "However, Brother Jacob, you will continue to attend Assembly."

"And begin flights," Father Gabriel said.

"Sara will be left alone while I'm flying."

"Yes, it'll give her time to study my recordings and lament her transgression. Isolation is a powerful tool."

"Thank you for this correction. I'll work to bring Sara back to the community a fully active follower and the wife of an Assemblyman."

"We have no doubt you will," Brother Daniel said.

Father Gabriel stood. "Saturday, after Commission, you will fly me to the Western Light. I have some business to attend to."

I did the math in my head. If we left by eleven, by the time we flew there, he conducted his business, and I returned, it would be at least ten o'clock at night. In the Citation X, the flight alone would be three hours each way.

"I'll have the plane ready. Should I plan for overnight?"

I know the answer I want, but how isolated does he plan on making Sara?

"No. We won't leave Sara alone overnight, not until she's back to the community. This punishment is to help her want the community, not frighten her into hating us. I may stay there for a while. If that's the case, you and Brother Micah can pick up supplies and head back. I'll know more by Saturday."

I sighed. "Thank you."

Now as I drove through the final gate on Friday morning, I took a deep breath. In less than two weeks this would all be done: Sara and I would be part of the community. As a couple we'd be welcomed into The Light.

I smiled at the thought of how well she'd adapted to the pole barn. Yesterday, instead of lamenting her public correction, as Father Gabriel had said she would, she seemed to play house. I'd expected her to sit as she had in the clinic, but she hadn't. Of her own accord, Sara had used her hands and wandered around. Though I gave her a tour, with independent exploration she again found the bathroom and the kitchen, learned the location of each piece of furniture, and even went up and down the steps to the loft, careful to grip the banister. She also spent over an hour in the kitchen, opening drawers and cabinets, feeling the contents.

Each time she was sure of what she'd found, she'd announced it triumphantly. Father Gabriel had been wrong when he'd said the attraction *would come*. Sara was so damn cute with her discoveries, the attraction was there. She was also mastering the art of asking without questioning. Honestly, watching her curb her innate desire to question was sexy as hell.

The attraction was sometimes so *there*, it hurt.

After Sara mastered the contents of the kitchen, she asked to cook. Thankfully, the refrigerator was fully stocked with food that needed only to be warmed. After she had her sight, cooking would be her responsibility; however, since I was supposed to keep her safe, her wielding knives, maneuvering hot burners, and navigating the oven without sight was currently forbidden.

When I'd left the pole barn this morning, she was washing dishes, which seemed safe enough. Nevertheless I had visions of her breaking a glass, trying to clean it up, and bleeding out on the kitchen floor. Now, that may seem like extreme thinking, but that's what this whole thing had done to me. It had caused extra stress and sleepless nights. It was all beginning to take its toll.

Though I was the only member who needed to drive to Assembly, thankfully, I wasn't the last to arrive. As I found my way to my seat, Benjamin stopped me. "How is Sara?"

I shrugged. "Ignorance is bliss. She's doing better than me."

He nodded. "Raquel's worried. She knows better than to ask, but she's heard rumors. The wives talk."

His comment set my skin on fire as I thought about the wives gossiping about Sara. It was ridiculous. They all knew the truth. They all knew she wasn't really guilty, not of anything other than having been acquired.

"It's none of my business," he continued, "but you need to tell her. If Lilith or even Ruth show up and she's unaware that she's being punished, it could be worse."

I nodded. "Well, since they need their husbands to drive them outside of the community, I guess I'm safe through the Commission meeting."

Benjamin took a deep breath. "I'm going to share something with you. It happened before you came to The Light, but"—his face saddened—"Raquel was acquired."

I leaned back. "Wow, I didn't know. She's done great. It's difficult to tell which females came which way to The Light, once they're fully indoctrinated."

"I just wanted you to know, I understand what you're going through."

Aleatha Romig

"Were you on the Assembly?"

"No, you've got it rougher on that one. I was doing what I do now, working with Brother Raphael in the lab. While in the dark I was a pharmacist. I didn't have the chemistry and compound pharmacy experience—then," he added with a grin. "Anyway, I was working with Brother Raphael, and I have to say, he helped me get through it."

I looked around. "So, Sister Rebecca, Brother Raphael's wife was . . . acquired?"

He nodded. "You'd be surprised."

"Do you? Did you?" I ran my hand through my hair. "Have you ever been sorry?"

"No!" he whispered definitively. "It's the way of The Light. Brother Raphael helped me come to terms with that. God made Raquel for me. I wouldn't have known that if it weren't for Father Gabriel. We've been together over five years."

"Do you love her?"

I knew the answer by the way his eyes shone. "More than my own life."

"Thanks," I said, genuinely appreciative.

"When you go back out there, talk to her. Trust me. You don't want Lilith being the one to tell her."

I nodded. "You're right. I don't."

"Brothers, it's time to begin," Brother Raphael's voice, with his Boston accent, thundered over the chatter from about the room. "Father Gabriel's ready to pray."

CHAPTER 19
Sara

I ran my fingers along the surface of the bed, making sure that the blankets were straight and the pillows were in place. I wasn't sure if I'd always done these domesticated-type things, but I supposed I had. Jacob hadn't been the one to tell me I needed to do them, or that they were my responsibility. It had been Sister Lilith, during her training. I didn't mind. To be honest, on my first full day of freedom from my hospital room since my accident, I enjoyed doing anything. Besides, this place wasn't that big, so there wasn't too much I could do.

Since Jacob had left for Assembly, I'd washed our breakfast dishes, straightened the living room, and made the bed. I didn't know if he'd notice, but doing it made me feel as if I'd accomplished something.

As I sat on the edge of the freshly made bed, my thoughts went to unmaking it . . . with my husband. So far all I could remember was actually sleeping with him, his arm around me and my head on his shoulder. The steady beat of his heart and the rhythm of his breaths gave me comfort. Though I couldn't wait to see him with my eyes, in my mind I'd created a picture. While he slept, I'd gently traced his face. I'd lightly run my finger over his brow and nose, and along his defined jaw. I'd caressed his shoulders and felt the definition of his muscles. His hardness had pushed against my hips, and I knew that the top of my head fit under his chin when we stood and he held me close. I had no way of knowing if the image I'd created was accurate, but in my heart I remembered the scruffy jaw I'd detected with my touch, and piercing blue eyes.

Smiling, I remembered inviting him to sleep with me at the clinic. Though I had been nervous, I was glad I'd done it. I'd had no way of knowing it would be our last night there; however, having spent the one night in his arms made our first night here more comfortable. My thoughts drifted to that night after service, the hunger in his touch and the way his lips had claimed my body. Just the memories made me tingle. Lying back on the bed, I held my side and sighed. If only he weren't so worried about my ribs.

Courtesy of the truck ride yesterday, the injury was more aggravated then it had been. I'd tried hiding it. Shaking my head, I wondered if it was possible to hide anything from him. According to Elizabeth it wasn't allowed. The way I saw it, I wasn't lying. I was withholding information for the benefit of both of us. By the way his breathing became labored and his body hardened that night at the clinic, I wasn't the only one who wanted to make love.

It seemed as if it didn't matter if I told Jacob what I was thinking or not; he knew. Somehow he always seemed to know, sometimes even before I did. Maybe it was because we'd been together so long.

If only I could remember how long.

The sound of the rising garage door pulled me from my carnal thoughts, and I covered my cheeks. With a giggle I hoped they weren't as flushed as they felt. If they were, he would know what I'd been thinking . . . I shook my head. I didn't want that conversation. Exhaling, I willed the pink away.

When I heard the garage door lowering, I stood and made my way toward the stairs. Wearing the boot on my right foot made walking with my cast much easier. As I approached the landing, I took a deep breath and visualized the stairs. Since I'd counted them multiple times, I knew there were fifteen steps. I might not have my sight, but I was trying to be as self-sufficient as possible. I made it only to the second step from the top when I heard his voice.

"Sara?"

"I'm coming down," I called, taking one step at a time, cautious not to go too fast.

Even before I reached the bottom step, I knew he was there. When we went to service, I'd realized why I associated him with the scent of leather; it was his coat. When he wasn't wearing it, just the right amount of aroma lingered around him. When he wore it, as now, the leather scent was overpowering. That, plus the sound of his boots walking and stopping on the wood floor, prompted me to stop on the fourteenth step. If I went one more, I was afraid I'd run into him.

"Sara." His voice came from very close.

Gripping the banister, I tilted my face toward his. Smiling and hoping my cheeks had returned to their normal color, I replied, "Yes?"

"Did you hear the garage door go up?"

"Yes."

"And what did you think that meant?"

"I assumed it meant you were here."

"So you knew I was home and yet you chose to not greet me?"

What the hell?

"Answer me," he demanded, his tone now too calm. "Why weren't you waiting for me at the door?"

The thoughts I'd entertained upstairs evaporated. I knew this tone. I not only recognized it, but with everything in me, I wanted to avoid it. My heartbeat quickened and my mouth dried like the Sahara. "I was on my—"

Interrupting, he rebuked, "On your way is not there, waiting as you're supposed to be. When I return, I expect to find you waiting for me, greeting your husband."

The bubble of apprehension that had waned and waxed in my chest since I awoke nearly three weeks earlier began to grow. "At the door . . . wh . . . I'm sorry . . . I didn't know . . . *you* didn't tell me to—"

He grasped my arm, the harsh movement a stark contrast to the eerie calmness of his voice. "Do tell, Sara, are you blaming me for your forgetfulness?"

What the hell is his problem?

"I'm sorry," I pleaded. "I'm not blaming . . . I didn't remember. If you told me . . . from now on, I'll do it."

"Must I remind you of everything?"

"I'm trying to remember; I am. I'll be there from now on, at the door, when you come home."

"Perhaps you need a reminder?"

My body sagged and my knees weakened. The bubble within me grew and popped, filling my nervous system with dread. "No. I don't need a reminder. I'll remember from now on. Please give me another chance." If it hadn't been for his iron grip on my forearm, I might have fallen to the step where I stood.

If I had, I wasn't sure if it would have been because of the sudden dizziness his tone induced, the bout of trembling, or that it would've enabled me to beg. It wasn't something I was proud of considering, but to avoid his belt, at that moment, I was willing.

"Sara, go to the door."

Inhaling more pleas, I nodded. When he released my arm, I stepped down and down again. Around the steps, past the closet, I found the door between the living quarters and the garage.

He was right behind me, his voice still eerily calm. "You may stand or kneel; the choice has always been yours."

I swallowed the vile bile bubbling from my stomach. In that moment I couldn't for the life of me fathom that merely minutes ago

I had been having pleasant thoughts about this man. I also couldn't imagine kneeling.

Who does that?

I brought my feet together, straightened my neck, and said, "I'll stand, thank you."

He reached for my chin and lowered it.

"This is where you are to be when I arrive, and if you choose to stand, your head will be bowed."

"Yes, Jacob."

I didn't move from where I had been told to be, as the rustling of his coat filled the silence.

"Reach out your hands. You may take my coat and hang it in the closet under the stairs."

It was heavier than I'd expected, causing me to wobble slightly when he laid it in my arms. Inside the closet I fumbled until I found a hanger. Once his coat was secure, I closed the door. When I turned he was right in front of me, grasping my shoulders. I sucked my bottom lip between my teeth and waited for the order I didn't want to hear.

Will he tell me to go to the bathroom like last time, or our bedroom?

"Sara, we have so much happening right now. I do not want, nor do I have time, to rehash basics. You must remember."

The tears teetered as I nodded within his grip. "I'm trying."

"Trying and doing are two different things. Remember that. If you can't, the next time I won't be as lenient."

My body sagged with the rush of relief that I wasn't going to be corrected. "Thank you, Jacob. I will be waiting next time."

He took my hand and led me to the couch. Handing me a tissue, he said, "I'm going to tell you exactly why we came out here, out of the community." His calmness was gone. The voice beckoning me was my husband's, that of the man I wanted to know.

"Thank you," I said cautiously, taking the tissue.

"They figured it out."

"I don't understand."

"They know that I answered for you, when Brother Timothy was in your room."

My trembling resumed. "What . . . I don't know what that means. He said I needed to go before the Commission."

"You don't. At least not right now. I've been before them, multiple times."

"You have? In my place?"

Devotion and sadness rang in his words. "You've been through enough. I tried."

"But you told them the truth."

His grip on my hands tightened. "I told them what I thought was best."

Everything inside me screamed to ask, to question. Instead I waited.

"Do you remember the way you reacted in the hospital, before I slapped you?"

Ashamed of the memory, I nodded and softly replied, "Yes."

"That's how you were before the accident. You were upset, grabbed my keys, and rushed out. I didn't know your intentions, but the Commission decided that you were trying to leave The Light."

I shook my head frantically. "No! I wouldn't do that. I wouldn't leave you, or The Light, or Father Gabriel." The shaking of my head slowed, and I tilted it to the side. "I don't think I would."

"I want to believe that. I want to believe that it was a misunderstanding."

My head ached as I desperately searched my memories. "I don't remember anything . . ."

His large palms framed my cheeks. "Sara, I've put everything on the line for you. We must be honest with one another."

I nodded.

"Would you rather leave and go back to the dark, than be here . . . with me?"

I pulled from his grip and stood. The sudden disconnection gave me the strength I needed to think. One minute I'd fantasized about him, the next I'd feared him. Each step that took me away from him shed light on my answer. Stopping on the other side of the sofa, I took a deep breath and began, "I'm being completely honest. I don't remember anything before waking in the hospital."

"Anything?"

My head moved slowly from side to side.

"And?" he asked.

"And all I know is what's happened since." I paused. "I know that you've been with me. Not just *with* me, but I've heard you fight for me. I heard what you said to Dr. Newton. I trust that you were protecting me with Brother Timothy, and now you just said that you've testified for me." I took a deep breath. "I know that you care for me, that you want me, and you love me enough to correct me." Sighing, I made my way back to him, sat, and palmed his cheeks. His stubbly jaw abraded my hands and reminded me of the way it tantalized my breasts. "Jacob, I'll continue to apologize for not remembering, but just because I don't remember, doesn't mean I don't want to. I have no idea what I was doing that day or why I took your truck, but I promise, now, I want to be here, with you."

"Sara, *here* isn't where we should be."

My hands dropped to my lap as I tried to comprehend his meaning. *Compared to the hospital, I like here.*

"We've been temporarily banished," he explained.

Unable to think or reason, I stopped breathing. That was the word Brother Timothy had used. *Banished.* "What about your position? Are they taking it away? What about your job? Why did they do this?

What will happen to us? What about our friends? Is there anything we can do?"

He reached for my hands and held them still.

"Stop. I can't even count the number of times you just questioned."

Though I knew from his tone that I wasn't truly in trouble, I lowered my chin, ashamed that I'd suddenly forgotten all my training.

He lifted my unseeing eyes to his. "This is it," he continued to explain. "This is our punishment. No one, other than the occasional Commissioner or his wife, will be allowed to see us or speak to us for the next two weeks. No friends, no service, only isolation."

My chest pounded, and then after a moment I squeezed his hands and asked, "May I still have you? May we have each other?"

"Do you still want me?" Jacob asked.

I nodded. "I don't know why I did what I did. I don't remember taking your truck, but please, believe me, I'm sorry, and I won't do it again." I leaned toward him and rested my cheek on his chest. "From what I've learned since I've awoken, I do. I do want you. I don't understand everything that you expect out of me, but I do want you."

His embrace surrounded me. "I can't tell you how good that is to hear."

I sat back, pulling away. "Wait." The alarm was louder than my words. "Do you still want me?"

He pulled me back to his chest and chuckled. "You have no idea how badly I want you, but Sara, you have at least one broken rib."

I let the tips of my lips move upward and shrugged. "I think I gave you an option. I'm a little scared to repeat it."

He brushed my cheek. "There are some things that, while said in the privacy of our home, or personal space like a clinic bed . . . are not only acceptable, but valued."

"Valued, not heeded?"

Jacob lifted my face toward his. The tips of our noses brushed one another as he shook his head. "So much questioning . . ."

Though he'd just reprimanded me, his breathing told me that correction was not uppermost on his mind. I tilted my lips toward his, and his gentle kiss lingered.

"Heal, my dear wife. We'll get through this, and when we do, we'll have forever ahead of us."

"As long as you're with me, they can banish us for as long as they want."

"We're in this together; however, even with our banishment, I have a job to do. Tomorrow I must fly."

My breathing hitched. "Please, tell me how long you'll be gone."

"I'm not sure. I'm transporting Father Gabriel. If you have an emergency, there's a phone in the kitchen."

"I don't know who to call or how."

CHAPTER 20
Stella

Dylan and I made a deal the other morning when he took me to the house on Cortland Street. We agreed to keep our work to ourselves unless we believed it held a connection to Mindy. The problem with that deal was that after going through Dr. Howell's files, I was convinced everything had to do with Mindy's disappearance. Even the woman at Starbucks was suspicious.

I mean who writes an S like that?

Dr. Howell's information didn't point to a conspiracy, more a compilation. Each case was a piece of a larger puzzle. Unfortunately, each piece didn't necessarily belong to the same puzzle. I found myself constantly second-guessing and wondering if I was trying to make the wrong pieces fit. After all, there was probably a good reason that members of The Light were going back and forth to Canada.

Back at WCJB I worked on my research. *The Light* made for a very broad Internet search. There were literal lights, lighting stores, lighting-supply chains. Though I didn't think he realized what he'd done, Dylan's comment about a church was responsible for narrowing my search. While there were hundreds of churches with *Light* in their names, there were only a few churches named *The Light*. It just so happened that one of them was located in Detroit, Highland Heights to be exact. According to the website, The Light was a beacon against darkness and a home of healing for the lost. It was a self-sustaining place of devotion founded on fundamentalist beliefs that offered enlightenment to its members and freedom from the constraints of the dark.

Gabriel Clark had begun The Light in Detroit over fifteen years ago. The relatively short biography of the founder spoke of Gabriel Clark's personal calling to The Light and his willingness to share his journey with those in need. His picture was the stereotypical promotional picture showing a smiling, handsome man in his late forties or early fifties. His slicked-back blond hair and expensive silk suit reminded me of a television evangelist. However, neither Gabriel Clark nor The Light offered sermons through social media. To hear Father Gabriel, as he was referred to on the site, a prospective member was required to attend a visitors' assembly at one of the church's campuses or informational hubs. The website mentioned that there were campuses throughout the country, but the locator page indicated only the one in Detroit. There were no local informational hubs.

Out of curiosity I clicked the form one was required to fill out to attend a visitors' assembly. It didn't give a time or date for an assembly; instead it was more of a questionnaire, pretty straightforward at first, but as I scrolled the questions became more personal and intrusive. It went from name, address, sex, age, marital status, number of children, and religious affiliation to essay-type questions. These had unlimited space for answers that were to include the personal background, triumphs and challenges, and even employment history of prospective members and spouses. Near the bottom was a statement I'd also seen on the website that discussed the applicant's willingness to participate as a full-time committed believer.

What does that even mean?

The more I read, the more the hairs on the back of my neck came to attention. At the very bottom the form said that upon receipt, a Visitor Specialist would contact the applicant.

My thoughts went to the women I'd seen crossing the street. It was difficult to say because of how far away I'd been, but I couldn't remember anything distinguishing about them. I couldn't even remember what they were wearing. I seemed to recall slacks or maybe jeans. They hadn't been wearing handmade dresses such as I'd associate with more conservative groups or cults.

That word *cult* sent shivers down my spine. I opened a new tab and typed it in the browser. The definition I found said it was a system of religious veneration and devotion directed toward a particular figure or object.

Is that what this church is? Or am I reading too much into it? What does "full-time committed believers" mean, and why are they crossing the Canadian border daily?

I checked the website again. There was nothing to indicate that The Light was an international church, and the site said only that there were multiple locations within the United States. That was when I noticed the Outreach tab and clicked. *Preserve the Light* was at the top of the screen, with pictures of jars of jams and jellies. The blurb said that the church's homegrown, homemade jams and jellies helped support its outreach. A testimonial from a member of The Light read as follows:

"I was lost in a world of darkness, using my body to support deadly habits, when I found The Light. Today, I only use my body to create Preserve the Light, serve my husband, and follow Father Gabriel. I've never been as content and fulfilled. The Light and Father Gabriel saved me. Please purchase Preserve the Light so others may be saved." The testimonial was attributed to "Follower of The Light, Sister Abigail Miller."

Serve her husband? My skin crawled.

Well, at least this woman wasn't out selling her body anymore, and the location in Highland Heights made sense, if the ministry was about helping people who were dependent on drugs or alcohol. I wasn't sure why or if I believed there was a connection, but I wanted to learn more.

I started with Preserve the Light. Clicking on the Order Here box, I filled out my request. Ten dollars was a lot to pay for a jar of jelly, but

I reasoned that it was for a ministry. After entering my shipping information, I selected strawberry. With the weather turning colder and the
leaves changing, the fruit reminded me of summer.

The other agreement that Dylan and I had come to was that I'd stay
out of Highland Heights. Maybe it wasn't so much of an agreement as it
was him telling me to stay out. I didn't want to argue about it, but if my
work took me back there, I couldn't say no . . . or more like I wouldn't
say no. It was Bernard's informant who had led me to The Light, so I
owed it to Bernard to be sure there wasn't a connection between The
Light and the drug smuggling we were trying to uncover at the border.
The idea that there was a connection between this church and missing
or dead women came to mind. Just as quickly I dismissed it. That was
ludicrous and likely a result of my vivid imagination. Besides, nothing
about those women set off my radar. Then again, I was a ways away.

Two things were for sure. One, I was excited about my homemade
jam. I hadn't had good strawberry jam since I was a little girl. Thinking
about my grandmother's jam had my mouth watering. Two, I was going
back to Highland Heights. I wanted to find out what was going on in
that school building across the street from The Light. If it was only a jam
factory, then I'd be able to tell Bernard that the lead hadn't panned out.

That wasn't a conversation I'd relish. This investigation was taking
longer than either of us had expected, and coming up with dead ends
seemed to be my new specialty. Thank God, Foster was keeping Bernard
busy with some new stories. Nevertheless my boss was definitely getting anxious. It wasn't until I'd gotten him, maybe not on board, but
at least entertaining the compilation theory that he'd agreed to let me
keep working this angle. In order to do that, I'd had to share some of the
information I'd learned from Dr. Howell. I didn't tell him my source,
but I gave him a taste of the incidence of women dying from suspicious
causes over the last ten years in the Detroit area. When I did I watched
his wheels turn. Even the slightest possibility of a connection between
the dead and missing women and the drug smuggling made his brow

and upper lip glisten with perspiration. Bernard foamed at the mouth like a rabid dog with the need to uncover this story.

When my phone rang, I glanced at the date on the screen and my heart clenched. It'd been six weeks to the day since I'd last spoken to Mindy. I tried to suppress the lump in my throat as I answered the phone.

"Hello, Stella Montgomery."

"It's Foster."

"Hi, I obviously didn't look at the number. What can I do for you? You're saving my ass keeping Bernard busy. Otherwise he'd be chewing it every chance he had."

Eddie Foster's laugh filled my ear. "Not a problem. We all have some stories that fall into place better than others. Have you found anything lately?"

"Jelly."

"What?"

"Never mind," I said, waving my free hand. "What do you need?"

"It's not so much what I need. I have a couple questions for you."

"OK, shoot."

Foster cleared his throat. "You know we keep an eye on our own, right?"

"You're making me nervous. What are your questions?" I bit my lip.

"What do you know about real estate in Bloomfield Hills?"

"I know that some of the partners at Preston and Butler live there, and it costs more than I'll ever have."

"OK, have you ever heard of Motorists of America?"

I shook my head toward the phone, as if he could see me. "No, Foster. Is this for a story?"

"No, not really. Like I said, we keep an eye on our own."

"Hey, I love you, but jump ahead. My mind's so rattled with this case, I'm missing the point."

"Motorists of America, MOA, was a retirement endeavor set up in the late sixties for employees of the big auto companies. It was a private option for members of UAW and Teamsters. It didn't replace their union dues or retirement; it was billed to supplement it." I had no idea where he was going. "That was fifty years ago. I'll spare you the history. Let's just say it was one of the many ventures that didn't deliver. The funny thing is that I remembered it was something Mindy had mentioned, and recently I was doing a search and it came up."

"Foster?" We'd already canvassed all of Mindy's research. MOA hadn't been there, so it must have been a while ago that she'd mentioned it.

"Give me a minute."

Securing my lip once more to stop from telling him I didn't care, I nodded.

"I can give you more detail, but obviously you want the CliffsNotes. MOA declared bankruptcy in the eighties. Operations stopped, but it wasn't dissolved."

My patience was wearing thin.

"After bankruptcy a company is unable to . . ."

"Foster, I really want to care. Are you saying this isn't a story and somehow has something to do with me?"

"Jesus, Stella, listen a minute. MOA has a list of assets a mile long, valued in the millions, hell, billions. I don't know. I just got started into all of this. The part that jumped out at me, the reason I even stumbled upon this, was because of a six-bedroom home in Bloomfield Hills."

"Are you and Kim house shopping?"

"Like we could afford to live there. No, I may have been running some searches on Dylan Richards and his name popped up on a utility bill, gas, for that six-bedroom. His name was only there one month, and then it was changed, but you know how slow utility companies are? Their records last forever."

What the hell?

I shook my head. "Let me save you any further trouble. It's not *my* Dylan Richards; you've got the wrong one. Next, explain to me why in the hell you're running a search on my boyfriend."

"I suppose that's possible, that it's not him. What's his father's name?"

I bit my lower lip. "Um, Mr. Richards? We haven't really made it to the parent part of this relationship. He doesn't talk about them. Now answer my other question."

"Bernard asked me to check him out."

"Holy shit!" I covered my mouth and looked around the office. Apparently my outburst had gone unheard, or people were used to them. Not drawing attention, I lowered my voice. "Don't. He's a cop. We've only just started discussing allowing Fred to visit. Seriously, he's a detective. I promise we're good. He's good." I ran my hands down the length of my ponytail and twisted the end.

"Fred?" Foster asked.

"Never mind. Actually, this pisses me off."

"Cool your jets. Bernard comes across all corncob-up-the-ass-ish, but listen, I've worked for him for a long time. He's got good instincts and, well, he said he'd feel better if everything checked out."

I straightened my neck and shook my shoulders. After pursing my lips, I asked, "And what else did you find?"

"Stuff I'm sure you know, criminal justice at Wayne State, straight to DPD where he spent five years as a patrolman before making detective and moving straight to narcotics and homicide. That's a bit unusual, but the flags aren't red, only amber. I mean, usually people start with less prestigious assignments. Your man went to the top. Personally, he's been dating this hot investigative journalist . . ."

If Eddie weren't happily married with two kids I might have been offended, but since he was I just laughed.

"Seriously," he went on, "commendations, few complaints. The only thing that struck me as odd was the one-point-four-million-dollar home owned by MOA with his name on the gas bill. I'm diving deeper into MOA. I just wanted to ask if he had that kind of money lying around. Did a rich uncle die?"

"Foster, you've got the wrong Dylan Richards. I've been to his house. It's a nice renovated two-story in Brush Park: backyard, fence, and plenty of shelf room for Fred." I giggled. "He's my fish. I hate leaving him. He gets depressed."

Foster scoffed. "Well, Fred should be glad he doesn't live at my house. I don't know what my kids do to their goldfish, but I bet we buy a new one at least once a week. Kim said that when she enters the pet shop, all the goldfish try to hide behind the little castle."

"OK, remind me not to let your kids babysit Fred."

"Listen, Stella, I'll look into this. You're probably right, and don't say anything to Bernard. He doesn't want anyone to know he's a nice guy. I'll talk to you later."

"Hey, wait." I had an idea. "Did Bernard ever have you check on anyone for Mindy?"

"Stella . . ."

"Come on. Did he?"

"You know she wasn't dating anyone when she disappeared."

I nodded. "I know, but before that. I mean we were tight, but I was super busy when I worked for Preston and Butler. I didn't know if . . . ? Or did he ever have you investigate her?"

"I wish I could tell you yes. If I had, I would have already given it to the police. Stella, we all want her back. I wouldn't hold anything like that without sharing it."

I shrugged. "It was worth a try. Thanks, Foster. Go find Bernard some more stories and stop worrying about Dylan."

"Yes, ma'am. Bye." The line went dead.

I took a deep breath. I wasn't sure Mindy's disappearance would ever get easier, not as long as I didn't know. The thought of identifying her came back. I scrolled through my contacts until I found Tracy Howell, and I hit "Call."

"Charlotte, so nice of you to call."

I snickered. "I only do it because I love my new name. It's like I have this whole dual personality thing happening." After the first time she'd called me that, I'd learned that Charlotte was her sister. She'd recently spoken to her and it was the first name that had popped into her head.

"I was going to call you."

"You were? Is it about Min—"

"No," she interrupted. "No, this was about something else. Could I call you back tonight? Will you be free?"

"I can be. Give me a time."

"How about six?"

"Sounds good, bye." It was funny how even a glimmer of hope could make my body tingle with anticipation. I couldn't wait to find out what she had to say. I looked at the corner of my screen. Damn, it was after one and I'd forgotten all about lunch. Grabbing my purse and phone, I logged off my computer and walked toward Bernard's office, but before I reached the door I made myself stop and take a deep breath. I didn't care if he was being nice. Having Dylan investigated was definitely a violation of my privacy. Another deep breath. I walked to his door.

"Bernard, I'm heading . . ." His office was empty. So I grabbed a Post-it from his desk and wrote him a note:

Bernard, Grabbing lunch and going to stake out a church for a couple hours. If you need me, call. Stella.

~

On the corner diagonally across from The Light was a burned-out house, its driveway blocked by an overgrown tree with saplings all around. I pulled my car behind the foliage and sat. In another few weeks this wouldn't work, the leaves would be gone. As it was they were various shades of orange and red and doing a great job of hiding my gray car. Unfortunately, they also blocked my vision, seriously limiting my view of the church and totally blocking my view of the old school building. Before I'd parked, I'd driven around the old school twice. While there still wasn't any indication that it was being used, I did see an alcove that I hadn't noticed before. It faced toward Glendale Avenue, but what lay beyond was hidden inside. No matter how slow I drove, I couldn't see if there was an actual door. My curiosity was building. Since this wasn't the door I'd noticed with the chain and lock, and based on where I'd seen the women cross, it would be the only place they could have entered.

I looked for a worn path in the overgrown grass, but I didn't find one. There was a cracked sidewalk that would hide footprints. I was sure Bernard wouldn't appreciate my postponing this research until I could see tracks in the snow.

The streets weren't as empty as they'd been the last time I was here. I watched the occasional man or woman walk across the intersection, but no one went into or out of The Light. I knew Dylan would be mad if he knew I was there, but that didn't stop me. I'd driven to my apartment from WCJB and grabbed a bite to eat. There I'd developed a plan. I'd run. It didn't matter that I'd gone five miles this morning; a woman jogging along the streets would be less conspicuous than one walking, especially one with a thousand-dollar camera.

After one more look around, I eased myself from my car into the autumn air. The afternoon sun had raised the temperature considerably since my morning run, yet again I wore long tight running pants and a long-sleeved T. Putting my purse in the trunk of my car with my camera, I grabbed my keys and phone. With my phone in hand, I hit my camera app and stretched, all the while watching for anyone.

Taking a deep breath, I headed east.

While driving I'd noticed a small park about a half a block past The Light. I started running toward it. The dilapidated surface of the road required my attention as I evened my strides. The last thing I wanted was a twisted ankle during my reconnaissance mission. I slowed as I neared the gate that I presumed the women had entered. There was a rust-free chain holding it closed. I snapped a picture. I'd need to compare it to the pictures I'd taken last time, but I didn't remember the lock being there. Without getting through the fence, there was no way I could be sure there was a door in the alcove.

As I snapped the picture, I noticed the same SUV I'd seen before turn onto Second Avenue and head toward me. I moved to the side of the street, placed the phone to my ear, and continued to run. Keeping my head down, I watched as the SUV eased into the same parking lot as before. When I turned into the park, I stopped and watched through the colorful bushes. This time four men got out of the SUV. *Damn, I want my Nikon.*

Using my phone, I snapped pictures as they made their way out of the vehicle and around to a back entrance. Three of them were wearing blue jeans as before, but one was in a suit. I gasped. That was the man I'd seen earlier today on the website, Gabriel Clark.

What do they call him? Father Gabriel?

I was about to stop photographing when the men opened the door and a stream of women came out. Each one appeared to bow her head as she passed the men. They were headed toward the school.

Shit! Fuck!

I wanted to run back in that direction, but could I? The men had seen me running, and they were still in the parking lot. I watched from a distance as one of the women opened the gate and the rest entered. Then, after the gate was secure, they all disappeared into the alcove.

I knew it!!!

CHAPTER 21
Sara

Father Gabriel's strong recorded voice echoed throughout the living quarters. I walked the length of the room and tried to concentrate on his lesson. While his teachings were instructional and some of his stories made me smile, listening while sitting on the sofa wasn't working for me. Despite my best efforts, my eyes kept closing, and I was pretty sure I'd even fallen asleep more than once. It wasn't that Father Gabriel's lessons were boring or that I wasn't curious to learn more about what we believed, it was that Jacob had needed to wake earlier than normal this morning, which meant I had too. Though Jacob still didn't think I was healed enough for *all* my wifely duties, despite my current lack of vision I was able to make him coffee and breakfast each morning.

He and Brother Micah left before five o'clock this morning to retrieve Father Gabriel from the Eastern Light. Jacob had taken him to the Western Light less than a week ago. I didn't know how Father Gabriel got from the Western to the Eastern Light, where those places were, or even how far apart they were from one another. Though I was curious, I didn't ask. I knew that if I talked about these things to Elizabeth or Raquel they'd tell me that if I needed to know, Jacob would tell me. They'd also tell me that I should be happy with whatever information my husband gave, and I was. After all, if he hadn't told me where he was going and when he'd be back, I wouldn't have known when to be ready to greet him.

During this first week of banishment, he'd done other things to help me. One was finding me a clock without a covering over the hands. With it I could tell time by myself, which was especially helpful while he was away. Every step toward more independence helped me feel stronger and more like the person I believed I had been before I lost my memories.

Although Jacob told me when to expect him, his arrival was contingent on Father Gabriel. Wherever the Eastern Light was, I figured it was far away, because even though he and Brother Micah left early, they weren't scheduled to return until after six in the evening. I suspected that their goal was to have Father Gabriel back to the Northern Light in time for tonight's service.

Even if Father Gabriel made it back in time, Jacob and I still weren't allowed to attend. Not only had we missed last Sunday's, we'd be missing one more week. We'd almost completed our first week of banishment.

During our time away I'd learned more about asking and questioning. When I asked how The Light had service with Father Gabriel gone, Jacob explained that Father Gabriel could conduct service from anywhere. His image was projected on a big screen in the temple, and with the technology he could even see all the followers. Since I couldn't remember any of what he described, I was becoming increasingly anxious to see it with my own eyes. I'd had contact only with Jacob since we'd arrived at the pole barn. Though Brother Micah worked in the hangar, he never entered the living quarters. I hadn't even heard his voice; most of the time I knew he was there only because of the noises coming from the other end of the building. However, noises didn't necessarily indicate his presence; according to Jacob, other men came to load and unload supplies as well as help maintain the planes. He mentioned them as a reminder that I wasn't allowed to leave the living quarters. With our banishment, I was allowed to speak only to Jacob and the Commissioners or their wives.

I didn't care about the Commission; mostly I missed Raquel and Elizabeth. Since I'd woken from the accident, my world had seemed very small. The longer we were separated, the more I realized the important role my friends played.

The other day, after everyone left the hangar, Jacob took me out and gave me a tour. I couldn't see the planes, but I could experience them. First he took me inside the smaller plane. It had two seats for pilots, a large open area for cargo, and even multiple jump seats for extra or unexpected passengers. Because we were so far away from everything, with so many people, I understood why he needed to transport a lot of supplies; what I didn't understand was how or why he had unexpected passengers, but I didn't ask. Even though there were two pilots' seats, apparently the smaller plane could be flown solo. I figured it was the one Brother Micah used while Jacob was with me.

As soon as Jacob opened the cabin of the second jet, I knew it was different. If he flew in it often, the luxurious interior undoubtedly added to his signature scent. The furnishings in the passenger cabin were covered in the softest leather I recalled ever feeling. Walking up and down the aisle, I ran my fingers over the multiple chairs and the sleek interior. Unlike the smaller plane, this jet required two pilots. Jacob laughed when I sat in one of the cushy chairs and told him I was ready for him to take me someplace, now or later. Since the jet held ten people and usually flew only Brother Micah, Jacob, and Father Gabriel, I'd been serious. If Father Gabriel had been restricted to the smaller plane while I was in the clinic, I understood why he wanted Jacob back to work.

Even though I was essentially as trapped in the pole barn as I had been in the clinic, I wasn't in a hurry to leave. I knew this was punishment, and I shouldn't like it, but I kind of did. It gave me a chance to stop worrying about a past I couldn't remember and relearn my role as

Jacob's wife. Things were continuing to improve since the first day when I'd forgotten to greet him at the door. Thankfully our banishment was the only punishment I'd endured since the previous week. My goal was to keep it that way. As long as I kept that eerie calmness out of Jacob's voice, I was even beginning to enjoy his company.

Sometimes the wind would howl, and I'd think about the polar bears. However, knowing how big the pole barn was eased some of my worry. The living quarters were only a tiny part compared to the building as a whole. After all, the hangar had to be large enough to hold two jets, as well as all sorts of other things, like cool carts that attached to the jets and moved them in and out of the hangar. There was also a whole shop area with tools and an office area with desks and computers. When I thanked Jacob for my tour, he said I'd been out there before. Of course, I didn't remember.

Just as I finished rewinding Father Gabriel's lesson, the sound of the rising garage door startled me. After that first day, I'd gotten very good at distinguishing that sound from other clatter. I hurried to the clock, wondering if I'd slept more than I'd realized, but it was only twenty minutes after three. Jacob wasn't due back for more than three hours.

My pulse raced as I stood in dark silence, waiting for a knock. With each moment my nerves stretched and my palms moistened. With my blood pumping in my ears, I wondered what to do. I hadn't gone through the door to the garage without Jacob and suddenly wondered if it even had a lock.

The knock never came; instead I held my breath as my fear materialized and the door opened. As soon as the click of high heels upon the wood floor registered, I recognized my guest.

She wasn't alone. When she entered I'd heard two distinct sets of footsteps. Figuring the other person was either Sister Ruth or Brother Timothy I sighed with relief, knowing that they were people with whom I could speak. I was also glad that I'd restarted the lesson. If they'd entered with the recording near the end, with the way my mind was wandering, I'm sure I would've failed their round of twenty questions.

"Sister Sara," Sister Lilith finally greeted me.

"Sister Lilith," I replied.

"We heard that Brother Jacob would be gone and decided this was a good opportunity to speak to you."

"Thank you, that's very kind of you."

"Hmmm," she hummed.

Her strange reply brought the fine hairs on my arms to attention. While the unique scent of her perfume, as well as her steps, let me know she was getting closer, the citrus reminded me that I didn't smell vanilla. Sister Ruth wasn't the person still near the door. I took a chance and turned in that direction.

"Brother Timothy, welcome."

"Sister," he said.

"I see you're adapting well without sight," Sister Lilith said. "I do hope that your eyes will be better soon."

"Thank you; I'm patient for God's time."

As silence filled with the click-clack of her high heels, I envisioned her taking a white glove and evaluating my housecleaning skills. If she was, I wasn't concerned. I'd dusted, pushed a dust mop back and forth, and even washed and put away my dishes from lunch.

"Sister, we have questions and feel it's time for your answers," Brother Timothy said.

This wasn't right. Jacob had said I didn't need to go before the Commission. I struggled with my next move. If it had been only Lilith, I could've questioned her, but it wasn't. I knew from experience that I couldn't question Brother Timothy. Reaching for one of the four chairs at the table, I did my best to weigh each word. "Brother, Sister, if you'd like, we may sit, and I'll be happy to answer anything that Brother Jacob has given me permission to discuss."

Chairs moved, the screech of the legs over the floor indicating my guests' locations. Since the person on my right sat first, that was Brother Timothy. I waited until Sister Lilith was seated before I sat.

"Sara," Sister Lilith began. "While I'm pleased with your progress, I'm here on behalf of the Commission and Assembly wives."

I couldn't believe her. She'd lied about that before. Nevertheless I was careful about what I said. "Thank you for taking the time to come all the way out. I know that I'm only allowed to speak to the Commission and Commission wives. Your visit means a lot."

"This is more than a visit," Brother Timothy began. "This is officially part of your correction."

My stomach twisted.

"Sister, I'm going to get straight to the matter at hand. Do you remember when I came to your room, right after you awoke after your incident?"

I turned toward his voice. "Yes, Brother Timothy, I do."

"Do you remember me asking you questions about your incident?"

"Yes."

"Do you remember your answers?"

My pulse quickened. "Brother, I must obey my husband. I haven't received his permission to discuss this with you or anyone."

"Sara," Sister Lilith said. "Father Gabriel teaches that next to him, the Commission rules our community. Brother Timothy is one of Father Gabriel's chosen. Brother Jacob may be on the Assembly, but he does not supersede my husband."

"Sister, I've learned so much through your training. Thank you. I believe I learned that what you said is true for you. Since only Father Gabriel has the power to supersede our husbands, I must obey Jacob." Though my heart was about to leap from my chest, I sat tall, confident in my response. Turing toward Brother Timothy I added, "I'm sorry, only with my husband's permission may I answer your questions."

"Sister," he asked, his volume lowered. "Did Brother Jacob inform you that you could only speak with the Commission and their wives, or did he not?"

Shit!

"Yes, Brother, he did."

"Are you aware that I'm on the Commission and that makes Sister Lilith a Commissioner's wife?"

"Yes."

"Does it not seem that Brother Jacob then indeed gave his permission?"

My head went from side to side, swinging the low ponytail I'd secured earlier this morning across my back. "I'm sorry. I don't believe that he meant—"

"Sister." Brother Timothy slapped the table. The reverberating sound caused me to jump as it echoed throughout the living quarters. "Do you presume to know what Brother Jacob meant? Are we to understand that you've been given the gift of discernment concerning all men or only your husband?"

"No, I don't presume . . ."

"Rest assured that this will be discussed with Brother Jacob."

My breaths came fast and shallow with the realization that I was not going to win. If I didn't answer, Brother Timothy and Sister Lilith would tell of my lack of cooperation, if I did, I was disobeying Jacob. I was damned if I did and damned if I didn't.

Lilith spoke. "Sara, obeying your husband is your duty; however, so is being truthful. You told us, through Brother Jacob, that you remembered why you were in his truck. You said that you were obeying Brother Jacob. Now we've been told you don't remember. Tell me, were you lying then . . . or now?"

"I'm not lying. I wasn't."

"So it was Brother Jacob then? An Assemblyman was the one who lied?"

"N-no, that's not—"

"Brother Jacob testified before the Commission saying that you're having difficulty with your memory. That was why my wife was helping you remember your training. Tell us, Sister, are you truly having problems with your memory, or are you selectively forgetting details to justify your behavior?"

"I am . . . I'm really having trouble." I couldn't think straight. They were twisting my words. I moved my slick palms to my lap and rubbed them over my skirt.

"So if you don't remember what happened before your incident, tell us, who lied in your hospital room, you or Brother Jacob?" Brother Timothy questioned.

Shit!

"Please, please," I begged. "If we could wait for Brother Jacob, when he's home we can answer everything together." Tears streamed from my bandages.

"Sister Sara, you do remember that this isn't your home, don't you?" Sister Lilith asked.

"Brother Jacob told me that we have an apartment. We're only here for our banishment."

"That's correct. You're here as punishment for your sins. When one among us transgresses, Father Gabriel teaches swift appropriate retribution for their disobedience. Do you remember that?" she asked.

"Yes, I mean, I know that now."

"So you didn't know that before, when you drove away in Brother Jacob's truck?"

Once again my head moved from side to side. "I don't remember what I was doing, but I do know about punishment."

"Yes, Sister, I believe you do, and not solely in theory." She leaned closer. "Tell us what Brother Jacob did last Wednesday after your lapse in judgment, after you had the audacity to question Father Gabriel."

I wanted to disappear. That was supposed to be over. Jacob said it was over, but the glares I couldn't see burned my skin, expecting my response. Balling my fists in my lap, I willed my tears to stay hidden; instead they slipped from my bandages onto my charred cheeks and interrupted my words. "He . . . punished . . . me."

"Did you deserve your husband's punishment?"

I nodded.

"Sister?" Brother Timothy said.

"Yes."

"Why?" Her interrogation continued.

"Because I questioned Father Gabriel."

"Will you do that again?"

"No."

"Why?"

"Because I don't want to embarrass my husband again."

"Is that the only reason?"

I took a ragged breath. "I don't want to be punished."

"What form of punishment did Brother Jacob choose to implement, to help you reach this decision?" Brother Timothy asked.

My heavy chest heaved as I fought with myself, not wanting this conversation. "He used his belt."

"After his correction was complete, did you remember it?"

"Yes."

How could I forget?

"How?"

"I don't understand"—I hiccupped a breath—"why we're having this . . ."

"Sister, what did Brother Jacob say about the evidence he left on your skin from his correction?"

"He said . . . it was my reminder."

"Sister," Brother Timothy's deep voice echoed. "Calm yourself."

Though I nodded, calming myself wouldn't happen as long as their interrogation continued.

"Do you believe his reminder was useful?" Sister Lilith asked.

"I won't forget."

"Very good. Now this correction that you and Brother Jacob are currently enduring," Brother Timothy said, joining the cross-examination. "What will help you remember—be your reminder—not to lie to a Commissioner again?"

My breaths stuttered, as panic infiltrated my reply. "I-I didn't lie."

"What will be your reminder, Sister?"

"I-I don't know . . . memories?"

"But you said you're having difficulty remembering." Sister Lilith's condescending tone twisted my already knotted stomach.

I shook my head. "Sister, I have difficulty remembering before my accident. I recall everything since."

"Isn't that convenient?" Brother Timothy asked.

"I'm sorry. I don't believe I should say anything else." I tried unsuccessfully to fill my lungs.

"Very well," Sister Lilith said, her chair moving.

Thank Father Gabriel, they are leaving.

"Sister, stand," she demanded.

My body stilled. "What?"

"Is the ability to hear another of your medical problems, or is it only obeying?" Brother Timothy asked.

I scooted back my chair and reached for the table. With shaky knees I stood. The movement of Brother Timothy's chair let me know that we were all standing.

"As we told you, we're here on behalf of the Commission. While Father Gabriel's decree has far-reaching implications, The Light believes that retribution of sin cleanses the soul. Playing house out here alone is hardly severe enough punishment for lying to my husband."

"Sister, I didn't lie. I was confused, and this punishment was Father Gabriel's ruling."

"Yes, and we're here today to deliver your reminder, to help you not commit this sin again."

"M-my reminder? What . . . why are you . . . ?"

"Rest assured," Brother Timothy said. "I'll discuss your continued questioning with your husband."

My body trembled as I contemplated Jacob's response. I tightened my grip on the table, and then a strange sound caught my attention.

"Hair," Brother Timothy explained in a tone that reminded me of Jacob's eerie calm, "is a woman's crowning glory. The reminder you'll receive today will help you to remember to be truthful. This reminder won't only be for you, but also for your husband. Each time he sees your short hair—"

What the hell is he saying?

"—he'll remember the shame you brought to him. Sister, the entire community will see your reminder and know of your punishment."

"My hair? What do you mean?"

"Sister, expect your husband to be informed of your continued disobedience."

The next few seconds occurred in a blur. The sounds I heard, the snip and clip, suddenly made sense. It was as though my darkened world moved in slow motion; nevertheless I couldn't catch it. As I reached for my hair, Sister Lilith lifted my ponytail and cut.

"No!" I screamed, my ponytail sagging in my grip. "Why?!"

Sister Lilith's hand connected with my cheek. "That is enough questioning. You're in the presence of a Commissioner. Apparently the reminders you've been given require reapplication."

Stumbling to the table, I found that my knees no longer held my weight. I fell into the chair I'd recently vacated, still gripping my detached ponytail.

Oh my God. What did they do? What will Jacob say? Will he punish me for this?

Though their voices were close, I couldn't distinguish them with any clarity. Their phrases faded into my internal mayhem.

". . . when you think about this, remember that it was done for your own good. It seems as though Brother Jacob has more work ahead of him." *What am I going to do?* "Your willfulness needs continued correction." *Why are they doing this?* "Remember this reminder was your doing and, as always, avoiding future reminders is your choice." *My hair! Jacob!* "Prepare yourself for your husband's additional correction when he returns." *Oh, please. This can't be happening.* "As you yourself said, you are his responsibility; only he can truly correct your behavior."

Perhaps I was in shock, but I didn't respond. There was nothing I could say as their accusations and warnings swirled through the air and my mind. The meanings of their words, the shock at my loss, and the promise of impending punishment paralyzed me. The weight of it all held me captive until their footsteps disappeared behind the closing door and the garage door went up and down.

Finally freed, I moved and took a ragged breath.

When I did, my entire body revolted. Shock waves swept through me from my head to my toes. The knotting in my stomach painfully twisted, propelling the remnants of my long-ago-eaten lunch upward. With perspiration dotting my brow, I hurried toward the bathroom. Falling to my knees, I emptied the contents of my stomach into the toilet. Over and over I retched until nothing but heaves racked my body. My clammy and trembling body, as well as the reality of what had happened and would happen, pinned me to the floor.

As the fog lifted, I remembered my ponytail. Panic erupted when I realized that in my desperation I'd dropped it. "No . . . no . . ." I cried, making it shakily to my knees and desperately searching the darkness. The strands were scattered, like the shards of my heart. With painstaking determination I gathered the pieces together. Once I had them in one place, I hugged them close. The uneven tips of my hair brushed my wet cheeks as I held my detached ponytail, pulled my knees to my chest, and cried.

Time lost its meaning.

Finally I made my way to my feet and the sink. After carefully placing my hair on the vanity, I cupped water in my hands, rinsed the awful taste from my mouth, and washed my tearstained cheeks. Slowly thoughts began to surface, reminding me of my choices. Brother Timothy had said it was my choice, and so had Jacob.

What if I chose to leave?

Obviously there wasn't a lock on the door. I could leave. Tears resumed as sobs resonated from deep within. Instead of fear, sorrow overwhelmed me as my thoughts went to my husband. I recalled how he'd helped me wash my hair and the way he'd run his fingers through its length. No matter how hard I tried, I couldn't make myself reach for the hair now dangling near my cheeks. *My haircut of disgrace.* Though my trembling had stopped, my rapid pulse remained.

Did I want to leave? If I did, where would I go? Would I take Jacob's truck again? Was this why I'd taken it last time? Had it been because of fear? Had the fear been of Jacob or others? Driving wasn't an option. I couldn't see, much less drive, but I could walk . . . to where, to whom? Wouldn't I have had the same questions before? Where had I been going then?

As I remembered the polar bears I heard the distinct sound of the garage door opening. With a heavy heart I knew . . . I knew with clarity that this time it was Jacob.

Clutching the remnants of my long hair, I debated my options. Go to the door, confess my questioning of Brother Timothy, and receive punishment, or stay in the bathroom, close the door, hide, and, of course, receive punishment. As I caressed the length of hair, I knew there weren't options. Jacob might have said I had choices, even Brother

Timothy had said the choice was mine, but it wasn't. Like everything since I'd awoken, my fate would be determined by Jacob.

For the first time since Sister Lilith had taken the scissors and cut my hair, I dared to touch what remained. Placing the neatly gathered strands back on the vanity, I raised my fingers to the ends that skirted my cheeks. My empty stomach knotted as I followed them toward the back of my head. They were even shorter there than in the front. The tears and trembling I'd finally stilled bubbled, clogging my throat with an erupting sob. My sorrow wasn't as much for what I was about to receive, as for what I'd lost.

Everything was happening in slow motion, even the closing of the garage door, but finally the sound stopped. With my chin to my chest, arms tightly wrapped around my midsection, and lip secured between my teeth, I willed my feet forward, through the kitchen, around the table where I'd been uncrowned of the glory Brother Timothy had determined I no longer deserved, and toward the door. Shame from my loss left a gaping hole as I stopped exactly where Jacob had told me to be. As the knob turned, my memories went to that afternoon when he'd reminded me where to greet him: even then he'd given me a choice.

No longer strong enough to face my husband, ashamed that once again he was about to suffer embarrassment at my hands, I chose the option that less than a week ago had seemed impossible. As the door opened, I sank to my knees.

CHAPTER 22
Jacob

With the doorknob still in my hand, I heard Sara's sobs echoing throughout the dimmed room.

What the hell happened?

"Sara?" I called, flipping the light switch. The relief of being back to the Northern Light and having Father Gabriel back in time for service was gone. My wife was on the floor, her body quaking with shuddering breaths.

Reaching for her shoulders, I lifted her from the ground and stifled a gasp. What I saw was unquestionably the cause of her anguish. Her beautiful hair was cut—not cut, butchered. The sight ignited a fire inside me, detonating rage such as I hadn't known in years, not since I was a young man in the heat of a war I willingly fought but never wanted. Clenching my jaw, I made the same vow I had then.

This will not beat . . . us.

It wasn't the same vow; this time one word was different.

Sara's body trembled as my grip upon her petite frame tightened. I pulled her close, unaware of my cool leather coat. Though its temperature undoubtedly added to her shaking, all I could think about was holding her, wrapping my arms around her, and sheltering her from whoever had done this.

Who did this?

"I-I'm sorry," she muttered.

Her apology tore my heart to shreds. "Shhh, you're all right."

"No, I'm not."

Her words came out muffled against my embrace. As I cradled her in my arms, her body sagged. "You're OK; I'm here now," I tried to soothe as I carried her to the sofa. When I sat her down, she reached out and clung to me, burying her face in the crook of my neck. Her tears dampened my skin.

"Sara, let me take off my coat. It'll be all right. I don't know what happened, but I promise, it'll be all right."

She gripped me tighter. "N-no, my hair . . . it'll never be all right."

I kissed the top of her head. I'd only partially seen what had happened, but now, in the brightness of the room, I clearly saw the tattered tips of her once-long hair. Caressing her back, I waited until she took a deep breath and her grip lessened. Easing my arms out of my coat, I let it fall to the sofa. Once again I pulled her close, and asked, "Tell me what happened. You didn't do this, did you?"

Her head moved from side to side against my chest.

"Who?" I asked again.

She didn't answer as hiccups sabotaged her quest for air. I lifted her chin. "Sara, tell me." My voice was harsher than I'd intended. "Tell me who did this to you."

"They said it was my fault, my reminder of what I did." With each word she tried unsuccessfully to lower her chin. Stubbornly, with the return of my fury, I refused to loosen my hold.

They?

I knew. I knew whom she meant, but I needed to hear it from her.

"They? Who *they*? And what did you do?"

Like liquid, her body freed itself from my grasp, flowing from my lap and pooling on the floor. As she clung to my legs, her sobs returned. At first her murmurings were unintelligible, but soon I understood.

". . . said I lied, o-or you lied. They wouldn't let me wait for you. I-I tried." Her head dropped lower. "I told them I couldn't discuss it . . . y-you hadn't given me permission. I'm sorry, I know what you're going to do. I-I know I was wrong. I didn't . . . I don't . . . understand why they did this . . . I questioned . . ." She shook her head with her forehead near the floor. "You never said I could . . . I tried . . . he said I *presumed* . . . I didn't . . . I wasn't . . . but she said I needed more correction . . ." Her volume fluctuated, as did the speed of her words, some coming fast and low while others came slow and loud. With each of her phrases the muscles of my neck tightened. "I'm so sorry . . ."

When I reached again for her shoulders, she wordlessly resisted, her body going limp in her effort to remain prone.

"Sara, stop apologizing." My heart broke, shattering at her desperation. "Please, let me hold you. You don't belong on the floor."

Her face snapped up toward mine. Blotches of red covered her cheeks, neck, and chest. "I do," she declared with conviction. "I don't deserve you. You deserve a wife who isn't a disgrace. I'm an embarrass—"

"Stop now." I waited as her words floated away, replaced with more tears. Again I demanded, "Sara, stand up." Her body obeyed. "I've asked you before. No more apologies. I want names. Don't make me remind you that I should be answered the first time."

With her arms wrapped around her midsection, her entire body shuddered. Even her long skirt fluttered with movement. Finally she replied, "Brother Timothy and Sister Lilith."

I gripped the arm of the sofa. Every cell in my body desired to drive to the community and confront the cowards who'd done this in my absence. I didn't understand their problem with me, but whatever it was, it was with *me*, not Sara. Yet I couldn't drive to the community, not now, not with my shattered wife standing before me, holding herself and shivering as if the she were outside in the Alaska cold instead of inside in a warmed building. Taking a deep breath, I willed my anger away. Sara needed something different.

As I stood, Sara took a step back. Her trepidation of me twisted the proverbial knife in my heart.

"Sara, do you think you can get away from me?"

Her breathing hitched as she shook her head. The severed ends of her hair swung about her face. "No."

"Do you want to?"

Her lip disappeared between her teeth before she whispered, "No, but I'm afraid."

Watching her stand in front of me, I wondered about Brother Timothy and Sister Lilith's intent. Was it to break her, to break us, to assure my failure? If that was their intention, they'd never win. Despite it all, Sara had the strength to answer me honestly.

"You're afraid of me, your husband?"

She shook her head. "No, not of *you*, of what you're going to do."

I ran my hands up and down her arms, barely touching, yet warming my palms on the sleeves of her sweater. "What is it that I'm going to do?"

Releasing her lip, she replied, "I know I was wrong. I deserve your correction."

My hands reached for hers. "Let me hear your transgressions, and then I'll make that decision."

"But Sister Lilith told me you would, that I deserved and needed . . ."

The temperature of the room rose a degree with each mention of their names. Nevertheless I couldn't let Sara sense that anger. If correction was coming, it wasn't to be done out of anger, but out of responsibility. "Your correction isn't up to Sister Lilith or Brother Timothy; it's at my discretion. Do you want me to ask again for your transgressions?"

"No," she answered quickly. "I spoke to them without your permission, and after . . . my hair . . . I questioned . . . them both. Brother Timothy said I *presumed discernment*." She shook her head. "I didn't mean to, but he's a Commissioner, so I must have."

"Is there anything else?"

Her lip blanched as she concentrated. "I think I fell asleep during Father Gabriel's teaching. I didn't mean to," she added quickly. "It's that we woke early."

I couldn't stop the smile that crept across my face at her childlike honesty. I kissed the top of her head. "That would make four, unless you have more to add."

Her hand flinched in mine at the number four. I knew what she was thinking: four transgressions equaled twenty lashes. Releasing one hand, I led her toward the stairs. "Let's go upstairs."

She didn't fight or beg; instead her shoulders sagged and she willingly walked toward our room. As we reached the top step, Sara said, "Jacob . . ."

"Yes?"

"I understand why you're doing what you're doing. I'm not asking for leniency, but I want you to know how truly sorry I am."

The redness on her cheeks and neck had nearly faded.

"Sara, it's time to prepare."

Nodding, she sat on the bed and removed her boot. When she stood and her black-and-white-striped skirt fell to the floor, I marveled at her calm. It was as Father Gabriel taught: once she'd given her transgressions to me, they were no longer her concern. As she pulled her sweater over her head, my pretense disappeared.

My gaze roamed her beautiful body, covered only by her bra and panties. The last remaining evidence of her accident was her cast. Other than that, her flawless skin glowed under our bedroom lights. I stepped closer, wanting to brush her arms as I had her sleeves, needing to touch her.

This time she didn't step away; instead her face inclined as my chest met hers.

"Though your answer won't change my decision, I want to know"— my arms ached to hold her, yet remained still as I completed my question—"do you believe you deserve correction?"

After only a moment's hesitation, she replied, "I love and trust you. If it's your wish, I accept it. If you choose otherwise, I'll accept that too."

My arms no longer obeyed. They wrapped around her and pulled her to me. With my lips against her hair, I said, "I had no intention of punishing you." She melted into me. Lifting the tips of her hair, I continued, "This wasn't supposed to happen. It wasn't Father Gabriel's decree. You've had enough reminding for one day. My dearest wife, I don't think you need any more. Do you?"

Moving her head from side to side against my chest, she said, "Thank you. I'm still very sorry."

As I lifted her chin, my body ached for her. "No more apologies. You were wronged; you didn't do anything wrong."

"But—"

I brushed my lips against hers to stop her rebuttal. However, instead of stilling her words, the connection served as a release. The desire I'd kept corralled for too long raged like a wildfire. Its flames consumed any remaining semblance of willpower. My grasp moved to the back of her neck. Only briefly did I think about the long blonde locks that were no longer there. They didn't matter. My only thought, my only need, was to get closer to Sara, to feel her warmth beneath me, to take what God and Father Gabriel had given to me. To please her in the way I'd never done.

Moans filled our room as she pressed her body toward mine and began undoing the buttons of my shirt.

Though I ached at the confinement of my jeans, I wouldn't hurt her any more, not today, not after all she'd been through. "Sara, what about your ribs?"

Sliding my shirt over my shoulders, she reached for the hem of the thermal beneath. "Please, Jacob." Once she'd stripped my chest, her petite hands roamed my shoulders, arms, and torso, seeing what her eyes couldn't.

I unfastened her bra and gently pulled it away, freeing her small breasts. As I palmed one of them, her nipple beaded, and I decided their size was perfect. Holding her hips tightly against me, I bent down and sucked the hardened nipple. Her whimpers encouraged me as she wove her fingers through my hair.

It was as she reached for the buckle of my belt that I regained a small bit of control. Stopping her hands, I said, "Sara."

"Please let me unbuckle it. I want to associate your belt with more than pain."

Fuck!

I released her hands and watched as she unlatched it, pulled it from the loops, and dropped it to the floor. Her smile melted my heart while at the same time sending more blood to my already engorged erection. It wasn't until she released the button and zipper of my jeans that I sprung from the confines of my boxer shorts.

"Oh, Jacob," she purred as she grasped my width and ran her hand along my length. My heartbeat soared when she dropped to her knees.

"God, you're amazing," I remarked, "but I want you to stand." Reaching for her hands, I helped her up. As she stood, our lips collided and our tongues danced. "Trust me, I'd love that, but I need to be inside of you. It's been so long; I don't think I could hold back."

Her grin was the trigger to my explosion. I'd never make it in her sexy mouth. Taking her hand, I led her to the bed and removed my boots. In record time I littered the floor with my clothes.

"Now," I said with a smirk as I turned toward Sara.

Her chest rose and fell in anticipation as she scooted back against the pillows.

Magical sounds escaped her lips as I looped my fingers in the waistband of her panties and slowly lowered them down her legs and over her cast. Beginning at her exposed ankle, I tenderly kissed the insides of her legs, alternating between them, each touch of my lips higher than the one before. Though her skin was covered in goose bumps and her muscles tightened, she willingly opened herself, allowing me full access.

"Oh, oh," she panted, her hands clenching the sheets as my tongue lapped her essence.

With each taste, a war raged within me. My hardening erection demanded what my mouth was enjoying. Sara's bucking hips and sexy moans encouraged my every move, prompting my tongue to delve deeper. Though I suspected she wasn't a virgin, I'd also spent enough time around other men to know that I was large, larger than most, and I didn't want to hurt her. She'd be able to handle my girth better after she'd released. Lapping and sucking, I continued tormenting her body until her muscles tensed and she called out my name.

"Oh, God, Jacob, that . . . that . . ."

Slowly, I worked my way up her beautiful body until she was completely surrounded.

Reaching for my face, she pulled my lips to hers and dove inside.

While our tongues intertwined, I positioned myself, ready to claim my wife. "If I'm too heavy, we can do what you . . ."

"Please, take me," she breathlessly interrupted. "I need you inside of me."

It wasn't a request she needed to make twice. Back and forth, I moved as she shifted her hips. Once I was completely buried, I stilled and gazed down at my wife. She was so damn beautiful. In the light of our first time, I didn't see her hair. I saw the contented smile on the face of the woman who was completely mine. I'd already claimed her mind; her answer when I'd asked if she deserved to be corrected told me that. Now I also had her body.

"What's the matter?" she asked, her hands holding my shoulders.

"Nothing." I kissed her grin. "I'm just watching the loveliest woman in the world and thinking how damn lucky I am."

Her cheeks flushed, and I began to shift my hips. Our movements and rhythms occurred in sync. While one gave the other took, and then we'd switch, always giving more. My lips teased her nipples, kissed her lips, and moved everywhere in between.

Father Gabriel had given me this woman, my wife. Though I'd resisted, with our bodies united I couldn't ignore the overwhelming emotion she evoked. The passion of our fervent desire filled our room. When she once again detonated, her legs stiffened, sounds escaped her lips, and her body hugged mine from within. The spasms pushed me over the edge: one final thrust and with a guttural groan I collapsed, our bodies still connected.

With reckless disregard for the possibilities our futures held, I kissed my wife and whispered, "I love you."

Her demure grin returned. "I love you too. It's just . . ." She didn't finish her sentence.

"What?"

She shook her head. "I'm embarrassed."

Easing out, I lay on my side, pulled her close, and spooned with her, her back against my front. Holding her in my arms, I peppered the top of her head with kisses. "You can always tell me anything. Why are you embarrassed?"

She shrugged in my embrace. "Maybe I'm more ashamed."

"You've piqued my curiosity."

Her neck craned to brush her lips to mine. "I just can't believe I couldn't remember that. I mean, it was like, wow." Her hands came up to cover her face. "See, I'm blushing."

My chest vibrated with soft laughter. She may have been blushing, but while her confession stoked my ego, the proximity of her soft, naked body had me considering a second round. Part of me was on its way to recovery at that very second. It was the scent of her shampoo, the flowery aroma, that brought our most recent problem back to my mind. I rolled her to her back and kissed her nose. Playing with the ends of her hair, I smiled, hoping she could hear it in my voice. "It's cute."

She exhaled and pursed her lips.

"It is!" I exclaimed.

"No, it's not. I'm ugly. I know you like my hair." She burrowed her face into my chest. "*Liked.*"

I brushed her cheek. "I like your hair. I love you, no matter what your hair looks like."

"But I'm ugly."

I caressed her arm, her warmth combining with mine. "Sara Adams, you could never be ugly. Even if you were bald, you're the most gorgeous woman in the world. And by the way, you're not allowed to argue with me. If I say you're beautiful, you're beautiful."

"I don't even remember what color it is."

I laughed. "It's the most beautiful color of corn silk and sunshine."

Her neck straightened. "So it is blonde?"

I drew her face to mine. With our noses touching, I nodded. "It is."

She cuddled closer. "Thank you."

Inhaling the combined scent of flowers and lovemaking, I sighed, "No, Sara, thank you." And then I remembered the time of night and how I'd found her. "Have you eaten? Are you hungry?"

She pulled away. "Oh, I'm sorry. I'm not, but I'll make you . . ."

I hugged her tight. "I'm not hungry. Like I've told you before, you're mine, all mine, and you're my responsibility. I wanted to be sure you're all right."

Her fingers splayed on my chest before she traced the edge of my jaw. "I wasn't, but now I am." Another kiss. I kissed her forehead.

"One more thing about tonight." I had to tell her this. I didn't want to wait.

"Yes?"

"When I got home, and again at the couch . . ." I took a deep breath and lifted her face to mine. "I know I gave you the option the other day, but Sara Adams, you're the wife of an Assemblyman. Don't kneel. You don't belong on the ground. I'm perfectly content with your words and the bowing of your head." It had killed me seeing her grovel. "Do you understand?"

"Yes." She paused. "I'm just wondering if there could ever be any exceptions. I mean, earlier, you didn't let me finish . . ."

Laughter bubbled from my throat. "I suppose there can always be exceptions. Get some sleep. It's been a long day."

"Good night, Jacob."

CHAPTER 23
Sara

I nervously waited for Jacob's return. He'd left earlier than normal this morning for Assembly. He hadn't mentioned Brother Timothy or Sister Lilith, and I couldn't ask, but the subject hung in the air like a thick cloud. When I washed my hair this morning, I'd gotten a better idea of how much was left. It was longer in the front, hanging just past my chin, and shorter in back. She'd cut it right at my ponytail tie.

Though I should've been listening to Father Gabriel's teachings, my mind was too much of a whirlwind to concentrate. Before Jacob left he told me that Brother Micah would be in the hangar today, as would others. Apparently they'd picked up supplies while at the Eastern Light, and they needed to be unloaded and driven back to the community. When I asked how they transported supplies, since the larger plane was mostly that soft luxurious cabin, he'd said that under the cabin was a large cargo area accessible from the outside.

Admittedly, it'd taken me a while, but I was getting the hang of asking, not questioning.

I'd recently heard a lesson about the sin of being prideful. It reminded me of Elizabeth's comment, and I decided it was one of my areas that needed work. Raquel had once said she needed to work on her patience. So it must be all right to have areas that needed improvement, as long as you recognized them. However, instead of working on it, this morning I was relishing in it. I wasn't prideful for myself; I was prideful for my husband, the important work he did for Father Gabriel and on the Assembly, and mostly his discernment. I'd been ready to accept his correction last night, conceding my transgressions and accepting his judgment. When he'd led me upstairs I knew what was coming, or I thought I did. I said more than one silent prayer that he'd show leniency. Despite the fact that the thought of twenty lashes seemed incomprehensible, once I confessed, there was a peace in knowing it was no longer in my hands. That didn't mean that I expected what happened. Never in a million years could I have foreseen his contrary reaction.

My face flushed as I thought about last night. It wasn't as if it had been our first time making love, but to me it had felt that way. How I could ever have forgotten Jacob's mastery in bed was beyond me. I'd been right when I predicted that he conquered unapologetically and bestowed unsparingly. Maybe it hadn't been a prediction, but a memory. Either way my body ached—in the best way—with my reminders of last night. Unlike other reminders that I wanted to avoid, the ones I currently experienced could recur every day and I wouldn't complain. I knew that making love didn't change our dynamic, but in a way it did. As I made his breakfast and prepared his coffee, I'd realized how much I wanted to please him. Especially if he still supported me with the way I looked. Maybe it wasn't prideful that I felt, but blessed.

While I debated, sounds echoed from the hangar. I knew Jacob had told me about Brother Micah and the others so that I wouldn't panic at every noise. Of course it also helped when he mentioned that Brother Timothy would be at Assembly and Sister Lilith couldn't drive out of the community alone. Though that made me feel better about me, I still worried about him. I doubted he would let their actions go without some kind of confrontation.

I bit my lip wondering if Jacob, an Assemblyman, could confront Brother Timothy, a Commissioner. And what would happen if he did?

As the garage door rose, I hurried to the clock. It was almost ten thirty. Assembly would be over. Hoping this was Jacob, I went to my spot near the door. Briefly I recalled my husband's words from the night before about kneeling. I wasn't sure how he did it, but despite my obvious transgressions and his supreme power over my life, he made me feel loved and worthy. I no longer had lingering feelings of resentment about waiting for him to enter. I was happy to do it.

The door opened and my breath hitched. Instead of only Jacob, there were multiple voices. Lowering my chin, I waited.

"Sara," Jacob said, placing his coat in my arms. "Dr. Newton is here with me. We have a surprise." He kissed my cheek.

I nodded. "Dr. Newton."

"Sister Sara."

Cautiously I walked toward the closet carrying Jacob's and Dr. Newton's coats. My mind was a blur of questions. Was this about my eyes? Jacob had changed the bandages this morning, but could the bandages be ready to be permanently removed?

As I began to juggle their coats, a hand touched my shoulder. I spun toward it, immediately recognizing the touch as well as a faint scent of honeysuckle. "I-I thought . . ."

Raquel hugged my shoulders. "Let me help you with those coats."

I nodded, the sound of Jacob's and Dr. Newton's voices reminding me that we were limited in what we could say.

She took one of the coats from my hand and we both reached for hangers. Quietly she whispered, "I don't know everything, but Brother Jacob got a special dispensation from the Commission and Father Gabriel. Since I work with Dr. Newton, they let me come." She squeezed my hand. "I've missed you."

The lump in my throat made it hard to speak. "I've missed you too," I whispered. I hadn't realized just how much until that moment.

"Sara," Jacob called, "it's time to do this."

"All right," I replied, allowing Raquel to lead me to one of the kitchen chairs.

"Sister Raquel," Dr. Newton said, "turn off the lights and close the drapes. We need to progress slowly."

Jacob reached for my hand, and his voice came as if he was kneeling near my chair. "Dear God and Father Gabriel, I pray that you've seen fit to heal my wife's sight."

"Amen," came from all.

I bit my lip, amazed given how fast my heart was beating that it stayed contained within my chest. Like Jacob's actions last night, this caught me off guard. I'd had no idea this was coming. If I had, I'd have spent my entire morning imagining what I hoped to see. Squeezing Jacob's hand, I confessed, "I'm scared."

"We'll survive no matter what happens today. You've done well for the last three weeks. If you don't have sight, we'll learn how to go on."

I nodded. He was right, as usual. That didn't mean I wanted to learn to cope. I wanted to see him, to gaze into the piercing blue eyes I remembered, to see their approval and admiration.

"Sister Raquel," Dr. Newton said, "hand me the scissors, so I may remove these bandages."

"No!" I blurted without thinking. Jacob unwound them. He didn't cut them.

"Sara?"

Suddenly trembling, I pulled toward Jacob. "I-I'm sorry. I'm sorry, Dr. Newton." I sat straight. "It's the scissors. I'm sorry. I do want the bandages off. I didn't mean . . ."

Raquel touched my knee. "It's all right. We understand. Let's get these bandages off, and then I'm going to help you with your hair."

She is?

I took a deep breath and nodded again. "I'm ready."

"Keep your eyes closed," Dr. Newton said.

I nodded. The snip and clip of the scissors echoed through the pole barn like nails on a chalkboard, yet I remained still. The tightening of my grip on Jacob's hand and my clenched teeth were the only indicators of my apprehension. While Dr. Newton cut the bandages from around my head, Raquel removed them. Though we changed them daily, my heart trepidatiously soared as I thought that they would not need to be replaced, but at the same time I feared it wouldn't matter.

"Sister Sara, tell me about your headaches."

"I haven't had any for a while. A little yesterday, but I think it was stress."

Jacob squeezed my hand reassuringly.

"That's a good sign regarding your optic nerve," Dr. Newton said. "My biggest concern has always been the flash from the explosion. However, it's been four weeks since your accident. If they're going to heal, they'll be healed by now."

I nodded.

"OK, Sister, this is it. Slowly open your eyes."

I took a deep breath and exhaled. Fluttering my lids, I gasped.

I saw light!

I squeezed Jacob's hand and blinked a few more times. The room was dim, very dim. I knew what I wanted to see. Turning my head, I took in the man who'd been by my side throughout my memory. With his forehead on my leg, his closed-eyed profile made him look as if he were praying.

Tears escaped as my smile grew.

I can see! I see my husband.

As I beheld the dark, wavy hair that covered his ears, my heart stilled. The jaw and chin I'd traced in the middle of the night were also covered with the same dark hair, only unlike the longer waves on his head, it was trimmed close to his face. I saw his closed eyes and high cheekbones. He was bent forward, silently waiting for my response. His light shirt—the color difficult to distinguish in the darkened room— stretched across the broad shoulders that I'd caressed. On his shirt were darker stripes that crisscrossed over the material. The darkness of my skirt contrasted with his skin. As I reached for his hair, my heart over-flowed with emotion, as I saw what I could recall only feeling.

"Jacob, I can see." My voice was barely a whisper.

Dr. Newton and Raquel sighed. I wasn't ready to look at them. I needed to fully see the man kneeling at my feet. My cheeks rose as his handsome face turned my way. Moisture glistened in his eyes—his dark-brown eyes.

My elation evaporated. I squeezed my eyes shut, trying to hide my disappointment.

"Sara, what happened? Are you in pain?"

I willed myself to listen, to hear the man I loved.

He didn't have piercing blue eyes!

Shaking my head, I inhaled and exhaled. "No, I'm just emotional."

A lovely dark-haired woman with light-olive skin, probably in her late twenties, hugged me. Her white shiny smile drew me in. Her round cheeks had just the right amount of pink, and her blue eyes sparkled with compassion. "Of course you are. This is a miracle. Praise God. Praise Father Gabriel."

I nodded, noticing how her hair was secured at the nape of her neck in a low bun. Staring at her slender frame, I recalled how she'd helped me at the hospital, getting me in and out of bed. The turtleneck sweater she wore under her scrubs accentuated her long neck. I reached for the necklace Jacob had placed around my neck, seeing the same cross on her. On her feet she had warm boots, and I wondered if she wore running shoes in the clinic. Her footsteps had always sounded differ-ent from Jacob's or Lilith's. I took her hands in mine. "Raquel, I didn't remember what you looked like. You're so pretty."

She smiled and lowered her chin. "Thank you, so are you."

Touching my hair, I said, "Not anymore."

She turned to Jacob, who was now standing. I craned my neck upward, seeing how tall he truly was.

I'd hoped that my sight would reveal the answers I'd been missing, allowing the pieces of the puzzle to fall into place, but it didn't. Instead of its shining light on my life, everything was suddenly more foreign. When Jacob nodded at Raquel, I started to ask what they were planning, but stopped myself.

"Honey," Raquel said, "when Brother Jacob told me what happened, I offered to help."

I shook my head. "I don't think anyone can help."

"It really is cute. It just needs to be evened up a bit."

Jacob squeezed my shoulder. "I told you it was going to be all right, and I said it was cute. Need I remind you that I'm always right?"

I could tell by his voice he was joking; nevertheless my cheeks flushed as I lowered my chin and said, "No, I believe you."

"Good, Dr. Newton and I'll go out to the hangar for a little bit and let you two ladies do the beauty parlor thing. Then I need to return Dr. Newton and Raquel to the community."

My pulse quickened at the idea of being alone, especially now that the Commission meeting was surely done. Before I could say anything, Dr. Newton spoke, and I turned his way.

With my eyes down, I noticed both of the men's shoes. Jacob wore boots, work boots with a hard sole. Those were the boots I'd heard pace my hospital room as well as walk the wooden floors of the living quarters. Dr. Newton wore shoes that too had a hard sole, and slacks as opposed to Jacob's jeans. Dr. Newton was older and shorter than Jacob and had gray in his thin hair. He was rather nondescript—neither handsome nor homely.

"Sister Sara, is anything blurry?" he asked.

"No."

Raquel opened the curtains. No wonder they did such a good job keeping the sun out, there wasn't any, not really. I looked to the clock, the one with the hands I could feel. It was nearly noon, yet it looked like dusk through the windows. "It's so dark," I commented.

"That's what happens in the dark season," Jacob replied, as he turned on lights. "It won't start getting lighter, well, until . . . February."

I shook my head.

Shouldn't some of this be familiar? February? What month is it?

"Sister, let me look closer at your eyes."

Dr. Newton shone a bright light directly into them. He then asked me to read a few things at various distances. Though I was thrilled everything was working, the strange sense of wrongness I'd had when I first awoke was back.

When Raquel and I were alone, I asked, "What month is it?"

"It's November, but December is coming fast." She squeezed my hand. "I'm so excited that you'll be home soon. There's so much happening with the holidays around the corner."

I stood.

"Where are you going?" she asked.

"To find a mirror."

"Oh, no." She giggled. *I really have missed her.* "Not yet. Let me work a little bit, then you can."

I scrunched my nose. "Is it that bad? Come on, be honest."

She squared her shoulders, and her petite frame stood tall. "You know I'm always honest, brutally, even, and I agree with Brother Jacob, it's cute. You'll probably start a whole new trend."

I sat back in the chair. "Oh, I'm sure. Can I be the one to cut Sister Lilith's?" I quickly covered my lips with the tips of my fingers as my eyes opened wide.

Shit! I was so overwhelmed, I wasn't filtering.

Raquel came close and whispered, "Only if I'm the one who gets to hold her down."

We both stifled our laughter.

When she first brought out the scissors, I had to remind myself that this was my friend and we had Jacob's approval. Ignoring the sounds, I concentrated on my breathing. Soon Raquel had me forgetting about the scissors. She clipped and chatted, talked and snipped. Every now and then she stood back and assessed. The pieces of hair that fell to the ground were short, an inch here and half an inch there. Seeing them reminded me of my ponytail. I'd looked for it this morning, on the vanity where I'd left it, but it was gone. I was sure Jacob had thought he was helping me, and I didn't say anything, but I missed it.

While she worked, Raquel spoke about the other Assembly wives. There were twelve of us altogether. I couldn't keep up with all the names. One named Deborah was expecting a baby very soon. I was confident that I'd be able to spot her in the crowd. Another named Esther had recently had her second. Apparently she was very tired, especially with her time away from her job coming to an end. I learned that the Assembly wives didn't sit together only at service, but that twice a week, during prayer meetings, we met separately with the Commission wives for study. Even the word *Commission* made me bristle.

"Raquel, what do you know about what happened today, with Jacob I mean? How'd he get you here?"

She shrugged. "I really don't know. Benjamin was the one who told me I could come. I didn't know about what'd happened, umm . . . with your hair . . . until Brother Jacob told me during the drive here."

I bit my lip. "I'm afraid he'll get in trouble if he pursues this, and I'm also afraid they'll come back."

She was looking at me and shaking her head.

My hand went to my hair. "Is it worse?"

"No!" Her worried expression morphed to one of glee. "Not at all. It really is cute. I remember this style, longer in front than in back. It fits your face very well."

"Well, thank you for fixing it, but I want it to grow back."

"It will."

After a quick glance toward the door, I whispered, "You remember the dark?"

She nodded.

"What's it . . . is it . . . ?" I sagged my shoulders. "I don't remember. I wish I did. I wish I remembered anything."

"It may all come back. I know I work with Dr. Newton, but I don't know that much about memory things. I know what I've been taught."

I contemplated the dark. It seemed like such a scary place.

Why would I take Jacob's keys? Why would I want to leave people like Raquel?

"There!" she proclaimed. Removing the towel from my shoulders and looking to the floor, she said, "Oh, Sara, I'm sorry. We should have put towels on the ground. I've made a mess."

I stood and brushed the hair from my lap. "Don't worry about it. I'll get it cleaned up. First I want to see."

With a tight-lipped smile, Raquel looked as if she were about to burst. "I want you to, but I think we should wait—"

"Please, don't say for Jacob. I want to see my own reflection." I might have sounded like a three-year-old, but I wanted to see.

"I tell you what. Where's the broom? Let's get this cleaned, and if he's not back, you can slip into the bathroom."

I liked her. She didn't tell me I was willful or prideful. She'd even offered to hold Lilith down while I cut her hair. I wrapped her in my arms for a quick hug. "Thank you, Raquel. I'll miss you during the next week. I can't wait to get back to the community."

"Good. We all want you back."

As we were putting the broom and dustpan away, the door to the garage opened. Deciding to err on the side of caution, I forgot about the mirror and hurried toward the door.

Despite his unfamiliar eyes, his smile melted me. In the eyes I didn't remember I saw love and adoration that filled me with warmth like a flame to a candle.

Tenderly Jacob brushed my cheek and lifted the hair near my face. As he let it fall, his grin grew. "I like it. Turn around."

I did. When our eyes met again he reached for my hand.

"Have you seen it?"

"No, I was waiting for you."

Out of the corner of my eye, I caught Raquel's change in expression and had to consciously keep from rolling my eyes.

"Then let's go." Jacob tugged my hand. "Close your eyes," he commanded, as we neared the bathroom.

I did as he said, and he led me to the vanity. The warmth of his body behind me filled me with strength. With his hands on my hips, he told me to open my eyes. There in the mirror were two strangers. I opened my eyes wider, watching the woman in the mirror do the same. When I lifted my hair, so did she. Jacob's description of its color had been accurate, corn silk and sunshine—very blonde. Raquel was also right: the way the hair framed my cheeks worked with my oval face. I tilted my head from side to side. Though I hadn't seen it before, my hair was now all even with layers toward the back. Soon the anxiety left my eyes, mellowing them, leaving behind a baby-blue sheen of contentment. Directly behind and above me in the mirror was Jacob watching my every move.

When I finally shrugged, I lifted a corner of my mouth in a half smile. "I guess it's all right."

Raquel squealed from the doorway and clapped her hands. I hadn't realized she was standing there.

"Sara." In one word he reprimanded me. "All right?" he asked, repeating my words.

Lowering my chin, I raised my eyes and met his gaze in the reflection. "No, it's better than *all right*. It's cute."

His smile blossomed. "That's better."

While I retrieved everyone's coats, Jacob said, "Sara, you'll need your coat too."

My lips snapped shut, holding back the questions that threatened to come forth. Finally I said, "All right."

I hadn't noticed it before—because I hadn't been able to see—but the truck had a backseat. Raquel and I sat there while Jacob drove and

Dr. Newton rode in front. For most of the ride, Jacob and Dr. Newton discussed things and people with names I didn't recognize. Getting to the community wasn't as easy as it had sounded. There were three different rows of fences with gates. The inside one was more of a wall. Codes were needed to open each gate. The whole setup seemed pretty elaborate for polar bears. With each new barrier I felt unfamiliarity and uneasiness.

No matter what, I was ready to be back inside the fences and walls; obviously it was much safer in there than out where we were. I stared at the unfamiliar buildings as we drove into the community.

When we arrived at the clinic, Raquel gave me a hug before getting out. "One week, I can't wait."

"Thank you for this," I said, pinching my hair with my gloved hands.

"You'll start a trend; I'm almost certain."

I knew that wouldn't happen, but it made me smile.

I wanted to move to the front, but instead I bit my lip and waited. It didn't take long until Jacob gave me permission. I understood how Raquel, or anyone, could have problems with patience. Waiting for permission to do things that seemed natural seemed, well, unnatural. Once my seat belt was fastened, I couldn't get enough of what was outside the windows. There were people of all ages and skin colors coming and going, some other vehicles, and many buildings. It truly was a community. Despite the cold, there wasn't a lot of snow.

"Does it help to see? Is it coming back?" Jacob asked.

"Yes, it helps to see, but no, it's not coming back."

He laid his hand on my leg, just as he'd done the first day he drove us out to the pole barn. I placed mine on top of his, seeing the difference in size for the first time. As our fingers intertwined, he replied, "That makes sense." Glancing my way and then back to the road, his brow furrowed. "I think I was hoping . . ."

"I'm sorry. So was I."

His hand squeezed mine. "But you can see. That's the most important thing."

"I disagree. If that's wrong, you can punish me, but my sight isn't the most important thing to me."

I saw the surprise in his expression. "You do? It's not?" With a hint of amusement in his tone, he continued, "Well, you've gone this far, please continue. What is the most important part, to you?"

Shit! I hadn't thought that offer through.

Forcing a smile and pretending I hadn't just volunteered for punishment, I replied, "The part where you didn't leave me alone in the pole barn. That's the most important thing to me. Thank you."

The corner of his mouth went up. "I hope you like Sister Ruth."

"Oh, I do!"

"Good, because she'll be with you whenever I need to fly. Tomorrow I have a short trip to Fairbanks for supplies."

Though the road was still rough, my ribs were much better than they'd been a week before. I sighed and leaned back against the seat.

"What is it?"

I pursed my lips before revealing a grin. "I don't think I'll be able to sleep through any more of Father Gabriel's lessons."

"Is that what you've been doing?" Though he'd made his tone serious, now that I could see the gleam in his brown eyes, I knew he was teasing.

"Not intentionally. I only remember doing it that one time, that I've already told you about."

"Sister Ruth will keep you honest."

"I'm already honest."

He lifted our gloved hands to his lips. "I liked seeing you with Raquel. It reminds me of how it was before . . ."

"Thank you for doing whatever you did to get permission for her to come out. I feel a lot better about everything than I did yesterday."

"That's my job."

I lifted his hand and brushed it against my cheek. "You're very good at it."

CHAPTER 24
Stella

I giggled as Dylan teased my neck, gently pulling back my long hair and kissing that spot that sent goose bumps up and down my arms and legs.

"You don't play fair," I said, through laughter and chills. "What if I had work to do at home?" The truth was that I wanted this break as much as he did.

"You work too much; besides, I never claimed to play fair."

I did work too much, not that it'd done me any good as of late. I'd spent the majority of my spare time in the last week home alone, devoted to my quest. Turning toward Dylan, I kissed his soft lips. "I'm glad you talked me out of work tonight, but you're a cop—aren't you supposed to be fair and be all about the rules?"

His kisses dipped lower. "I'll never be fair when it comes to you. If I have to play dirty to get you to spend time with me, I'll do it every time, and as for rules, I never took you as much of a rule person."

I reached for his face and pulled his stunning blue gaze to mine. "You're right. I don't do the rule thing, not very well, at least. Tell me, though"—I grinned—"if you made rules, would breaking them be fun?"

His sexy bedroom expression morphed into a bright smile. "You're something else. In the mood of hot, popular women's fiction, sure, I'm willing, but in real life . . . hell, no. I'm not into that, and besides, I wouldn't try to change your sexier-than-shit rebellious ways. I can only think of one rule that might make me change my mind."

My shoulders slumped. This was a subject I was tired of debating. "I can't help where my job takes me."

He sat up with his stubbly jaw set and the muscles in his cheeks clenching. "I don't know how to emphasize this any other way. Do not go to Highland Heights. If I have to fucking go talk to Barney, I will."

I closed my eyes and shook my head.

This wasn't some pissing contest. It was my life and my decisions. Besides, Bernard didn't even know I'd been in Highland Heights the week before. I didn't want to get his hopes up. Not that I'd learned anything definitive. When I couldn't run back down Second Avenue, because of the men and the SUV, I'd gone around the block, looping around the old school. From an empty lot I had a view of the back of the old school building. In an area covered on both sides by the building, there was a greenhouse. It wasn't big; nonetheless there were about a half-dozen women in it, moving around. If I were to take everything at face value, I'd say that the greenhouse allowed The Light to grow the produce for its Preserve the Light preserves. Then I'd say that in that old school building, the women were making preserves. If I logically took it one more step, I'd say The Light's cars crossed the border daily to deliver jellies and jams.

What I'd spent the majority of last week deciding was if everything was truly that logical. Was I paranoid by nature, or was my gut telling me that it was a cover for something else?

Since my greenhouse discovery over a week before, I'd furthered my research. That didn't mean I'd advanced my knowledge on The Light. Information on the church was limited at best, yet I couldn't shake the feeling that things weren't as they appeared.

Maybe everything made too much sense?

Dylan stood, bringing me back to the present, and ran his hand through his dark-blond hair. "Tell me that you haven't been back to

Highland Heights, not since I took you there. Come on, Stella. Please tell me that you're not that dumb."

The fine hairs on the back of my neck stood as I inhaled, sat, and pulled the sheet around my breasts. "Seriously, you're calling me dumb?"

"You know I don't think you're dumb, but if you go back there . . ."

"This conversation went from fun to shit faster than I ever imagined."

His chest expanded and contracted as his volume rose. "And the shit's going to hit the fan if I learn you've gone back there. Your safety isn't debatable."

What had Bernard said about shit hitting the fan? He said that when the shit hit the fan, it wasn't time to turn away. It meant the source of the manure was close and something was growing. Though it might stink, whatever it was, it was going to be big. He'd said that it was time to put on my shitkickers and plow through, to believe in myself . . .

Believe in myself.

I took a deep breath. "If this doesn't pertain to Mindy, we can't discuss it, remember?"

"A while back, you asked about DPD and HHPD working together. I'm not giving you particulars, but HHPD has been monitoring their residents. For the last . . . I don't know how many years . . . they've been working on this big initiative. They're watching populations, trying to get to know people and help. The thing is that women have been disappearing."

My eyes opened wide. "Shit! Do they have statistics? What . . . ?"

"Stop it. Stop asking. Fuck! I shouldn't." He exhaled. "I'm not talking everyone, not women like Mindy, not professional, educated women. I'm talking about runaways, drug addicts, and prostitutes. Not all of them," he added, and took a deep breath, and paced the width of his room. "You really can't call it disappearing when it's a runaway. It's difficult because they're a transient population." He took another breath. "Some of them end up in the morgue, where you've been called. It's the others—they evaporate into thin air. Of course, it doesn't have to indicate foul play. One of the most viable theories is what's happening"—he pointed—"out the window."

I glanced at his bedroom window and into the darkness beyond the panes of glass. Now that we were officially in autumn, the early part of October, the days were getting shorter. It would get worse when the time changed. With standard time we'd fall back an hour. "I'm not seeing anything," I said, "except for your reflection, if you stand there."

He sighed. "It's Michigan. The leaves are changing and it's getting cold. You've lived around here long enough to know that winters can be brutal."

"Yes?"

"If you were homeless or a runaway, would you want to live here through the winter?"

"Hmm," I acknowledged, "I've never thought of it that way."

"Say that HHPD was in contact with a few of these women or even one of them, and the next time they stop to check on her, she's missing. Who's to say she didn't hitch a ride to a better climate?"

I nodded. "Why are you telling me this? I thought this was out of our range of sharing."

"Because I'm a cop—hell, I'm a detective—and Highland Heights scares the shit out of me. There's no reason for you to be there. Yes, it's high crime and there are bodies showing up . . ."

"Bodies? More? Have there been new ones?"

Dylan knelt on the bed and crawled toward me, his movements graceful and defined. Though I wasn't sure I'd ever tire of watching him without a shirt—all the working out, the CrossFit or whatever he and his police buddies did religiously, certainly yielded results—I suddenly had the sensation of being prey. Even so, I fought the urge to reach out and touch the definition in his bicep. Before he had the chance to say anything, I leaned forward and kissed his lips. "I get it. You're protective. I like it. I also have a job to do, not to mention a promise to keep." I was losing my battle of wills as his kisses returned me to the horizontal position. "Dylan, you didn't answer me."

"Shhh." He fanned my hair over the pillow and touched my lips. "I've said more than I should. Stop asking questions. I love your inquisitive nature, but it makes me nervous. Some people aren't as forgiving."

Though Dylan's actions were monopolizing my thoughts, my gut told me that there was something more in Highland Heights. I wasn't sure I could ever stop asking questions. And what people? Did Dylan know what was happening? And was that why he was trying to protect me?

It was then that I remembered Foster's call. "Dylan?"

He laughed. "See, you can't follow instructions worth shit."

I shrugged. "Fine, I won't ask you what I wanted to ask." I kissed his cheek. "By the way, it had nothing to do with Highland Heights, Mindy, or bodies. It's actually kind of funny, but never mind."

"Oh, no, now I'm curious."

I reached for the waistband of his shorts. Tugging at the elastic, with a grin I said, "I suppose it can wait."

His chest inflated before he blew out a deep breath. "Yeah, I think something else just came up."

～

Walking from Dylan's bathroom, I made my way to his dresser and opened the top drawer. I couldn't believe I'd caved and brought clothes over to his house. I hadn't brought many, but even I admitted it was nice, better than showing up to work in the same clothes as the day before. Admittedly, with the food tablets, Fred was doing better on his own than he used to do. I'd put an old clock radio near his bowl, and twice a day, for two hours at a time, he had the pleasure of listening to music. I realized that a little music didn't put me in the running for fish owner of the year, but the way I saw it, it was all about meeting his needs. He was a fish. He needed food and water, and a little interaction.

What was better than R&B?

Dressed for the day, I secured my hair in a low side braid that lay on my shoulder and made my way to the kitchen. Though I wanted to see the sexy guy with the jeans hanging low on his hips, it was the aroma of bacon that propelled me down the stairs.

Stopping in the doorway, I stared. Standing at the stove, still shirtless with his dark-blond hair all bedhead sexy, was Dylan. Not only was he handsomer than hell, he was making magic in a frying pan. Sneaking up behind him, I wrapped my arms around his waist, and whispered, "Aren't you afraid of bacon grease?"

He planted a kiss on my lips. "Don't you remember who you're talking to? I'm not afraid of anything."

I was about to remind him of his lecture regarding Highland Heights, when I was distracted by a row of bacon strips neatly arranged on a paper towel near the stove. I picked up a crispy piece, put it in my mouth, and bit off the end. Ambrosia exploded in my mouth. "How do you do that? When I fry bacon it's either black and sets off the fire alarm or is limp and gross."

Dylan's eyes twinkled. "Yeah, no one likes limp."

I slapped his shoulder. "Hey, have you seen my phone?"

"Yes, it's plugged in over there. It's been ready to self-destruct for the last hour. Why do you think I keep inviting you to my house? I'd rather avoid the fire alarm." He shrugged. "Though, I admit, it was nice to meet your neighbors when the firemen evacuated your floor."

I contemplated slapping him again, but opted for shaking my head as I turned in the direction he'd pointed. "It wasn't that bad," I contended. "If you would've opened the window like I said, we could've avoided the entire fireman thing."

"Sorry, I was busy putting out the flames."

There had not been flames! But instead of correcting him, I swiped the screen of my phone to three text messages.

The first one was from Bernard. It simply had my name with a question mark. The second was from Tracy.

```
Tracy Howell: CHARLOTTE, ARE YOU FREE?
CAN YOU MEET ME FOR LUNCH? TEXT ME, AND
WE'LL SET A TIME.
```

I'd wondered what had happened to her. The last time we met, she'd told me she might have a new angle and when she knew more, she'd let me know. All that she'd said was that it might shed some light on a recurring injury. I hadn't heard from her since.

Sitting at Dylan's breakfast bar, I remembered what I'd wanted to ask him the night before; however, instead of jumping into real estate that I knew he couldn't afford, I asked, "Do you need any help?"

"No, we don't have time for fires."

"Very funny. Fine. Have I told you about my parents?"

"A little," he said with his attention more on the food. "Do you want an egg?"

"Sure." I looked down at the third message.

```
Dina Rosemont: STELLA, IT'S DINA. WE'VE
BEEN GETTING A FEW CALLS FROM OUR FLYERS.
I'VE CONTACTED DPD, BUT IF YOU HAVE A
MINUTE, CAN YOU CALL ME? I'D LIKE TO
DISCUSS YOUR THOUGHTS ABOUT THIS WOMAN
WHO'S CALLED TWICE.
```

"Stella?"

I looked up. "I'm sorry. What?"

"How do you want it?"

I moved my head back and forth. "Want what?"

He inhaled and exhaled. "Sex. Do you want it on the table or the floor? Maybe the counter?" He held up the spatula. "I've been thinking about our conversation last night, and I'm ready if you want to break my rules."

"You're hilarious." My tone wasn't amused.

"Your egg . . . scrambled, fried?"

"Oh, I don't care. No matter how you make it, it'll be better than the breakfast bar I usually eat."

"What about your parents?" he asked. "I know they live in Chicago. You went to visit them a month or so ago."

I had. After spending time with the Rosemonts, I'd wanted to hug my mom and dad. "Where are yours?" I asked.

He turned, his face suddenly solemn. "Umm. I'm sorry. I guess I planned on telling you this . . ."

I put my phone down and walked toward him. "What is it? I'm sorry. Is it bad?"

He shook his head as his shoulders moved up and down. "My parents died in a robbery gone bad. Same old adage: wrong place, wrong time. I was a senior in high school and they were on a business trip." His glistening eyes drew me toward the blue. "That may be why I'm the way I am about you and Highland Heights. I don't think I could take another . . ." He turned toward the sizzling pan on the stove.

I rubbed his back, not knowing what to say.

After he'd flipped the egg, he turned back and kissed my cheek. "You're trying to distract me from my cooking, aren't you? You're secretly into firemen more than cops and didn't know how to break it to me."

I stepped behind him, wrapped my arms around his waist, and put my cheek against his shoulder. "I'm sorry. I shouldn't have just blurted that out. Do you have other family?"

"No siblings, I had grandparents. My mom's parents stepped in after . . . well, since I was already eighteen, it was more of a formality.

They're both gone now: grandfather by cancer and grandmother, six months later, by a broken heart. See, there's nothing good in that story. I guess that's why I haven't said anything."

I feigned a smile. "So no rich uncle?"

He spun toward me. "Why would you even say that?"

I shook my head. "It's nothing. I just . . . in a couple of months it'll be our first Christmas together"—I shrugged—"unless you get rid of me before then because of my cooking."

He reached for a plate and plopped a fried egg in the center. "No need for two cooks in the kitchen. I've been doing this as long as I remember. Cooking was something I enjoyed doing with my mom, and after . . . it reminded me of her."

I swallowed my sorrow. "With everything . . . I guess more because of Mindy . . . I want to spend time with my parents at Christmas. I was wondering if you'd be willing to come with me to Chicago."

He walked our plates to the breakfast bar. "I usually work the holidays. That way the people who actually have families can have the time off. Besides, I look forward to that check: it's overtime—time and a half plus holiday pay."

"You've been with DPD long enough, you can get the time off, can't you? Please see if you can get it off. My folks will love you. My mom talks way too much, especially after a few glasses of wine, and my dad is great, a little quiet until you get to know him. We just can't tell him you're a Tigers fan. He's really into baseball, and the Cubs have always been his team." I tried lightening the mood. "However, I'm warning you right now, watch out for my little sister. She's recently gone through a divorce." I tightened my smile and moved my shoulders. "And I'll be honest: I don't think there's a male who's safe within fifty feet of her, but don't worry, I promise to run interference."

Dylan winked as he took a bite of his toast. "Wait, before you run interference, let me know, can she cook?"

"Yep, I taught her everything she knows."

"Hmm, so her ex was the one who filed, right?"

I shook my head. It was good to see his smile. My phone buzzed and I swiped the screen. Exhaling, I said, "That's number two from His Majesty, Bernard."

"Even a royal summons can't keep you from your breakfast."

Carefully I stacked the egg and bacon on one half of the toast and put the other half on top. "Look. I've got this! I'm an eat-on-the-run expert." Kissing his cheek, I said, "Please think about asking for the time off."

He slipped his fingers in the belt loops of my slacks and pulled me close. "Promise me, no Highland Heights."

All I could see was blue, the same eyes that only minutes ago had been sad. "I'll do my best."

"Don't forget," he said with another sexy wink, "I have my spatula, and I'm willing to use it."

"Maybe you could use one from my kitchen. It's less likely to be in the dishwasher."

He grinned as I picked up my egg-and-bacon sandwich and grabbed a napkin. On my way to WCJB, I planned to call Bernard. However, sitting in my car, instead of thinking about my boss, my thoughts went to Dylan. Maybe it was time to take the next step. I was ready to let Fred visit.

As I drove I decided that Foster obviously had the wrong Dylan Richards. The one I'd just left had no rich uncle, had no family to speak of, and was willing to work Christmas for the extra money. It didn't take an investigative journalist to know he couldn't afford a $1.4 million home in a rich neighborhood.

After finishing my breakfast sandwich, I checked the clock. Since Dina Rosemont lived near San Francisco and it was three hours earlier there, her call would need to wait. As I waited to access the interstate in a slow-moving line of traffic, I pecked a text message to Tracy.

Stella: LUNCH SOUNDS GREAT UNLESS I'M
CALLED AWAY. TELL ME WHEN AND WHERE.

And then one to Bernard.

Stella: I'M ON MY WAY, ABOUT THIRTY
MINUTES OUT.

My phone immediately buzzed.

Bernard: MEET ME AT THE COFFEE SHOP.
USUAL TABLE.

Shit!

My stomach twisted. No doubt he was pissed about my lack of progress. My continual dead ends were beginning to wear on me, and I was a hell of a lot more patient than he. I'd gotten my job based on results. In the last seven weeks I'd produced exactly nothing. I knew Bernard had faith in me, but faith wouldn't keep me employed.

My lack of progress sure wasn't for lack of trying. Since the afternoon I'd run near The Light, I'd spent most of my free time doing research, and not only at work. I'd spent hours alone in my apartment surfing the Net. After continually coming up empty on The Light, three nights ago I'd found something. It wasn't about The Light, but it was interesting.

I was on one of those searches where I clicked site after site, following bread crumbs that kept me moving forward yet never seeming to reach a destination. I was about to call it a night when I poured one last glass of wine and stumbled across a blog post with an interesting thread of comments.

The original post was dated from over five years earlier, and buried deep in the Internet. It was written by a woman who claimed her daughter and son-in-law had been kidnapped by a cult. Though they'd disappeared, with the help of an investigator she'd located them. Once she did, she'd contacted the local police. Her daughter refused to speak to her, or anyone, but her son-in-law had sent a message saying that they were happy and willingly living within the community. Without probable cause, the local police refused to do any more. The woman took her concerns to the federal level, but without proof of wrongdoing, the authorities' hands were tied. Her post asked for help understanding cults and asked why a young woman who had always had a good relationship with her family would suddenly turn her back on them.

Maybe it was the wine, but the post made me sad, and, of course, reminded me of Mindy. Though this woman's situation was difficult, at least she knew her daughter was alive. The Rosemonts didn't have that luxury. The last sentence warned people to recognize that even in this day and age, cults still existed.

Hours passed, and I found myself enthralled by the comment thread. The ones immediately following HeartbrokenMother372's post were sympathetic to her plight. I continued reading, hoping that I'd learn if she'd ever gotten her daughter back. Unfortunately, I never saw anything else from HeartbrokenMother372, but the more I read, the more I wanted to know. With each comment I found myself questioning my belief and understanding of cults. There were more than a few posts that discounted their existence given modern technology, especially within the United States, stating the difficulty of being truly isolated in this day and age. I wondered if these people had ever heard of Waco.

With my bottle of wine about gone, I continued to read. Though none of the information I gleaned was referenced, I knew from experience that obscure sources often shed the most light. One man posted about his personal experience with living near what people in his community considered a cult. He called them a sect. He didn't give the location of his town, city, or state, but he mentioned something about skiing. He also said that in all the years he'd lived there, he'd never seen any of the women or children who lived in the sect and had seen only a few of the men. Nevertheless he estimated that hundreds of people lived in the encampment. He claimed that the general consensus was that as long as the people in the sect didn't bother the townspeople, the townspeople wouldn't bother them.

As I scrolled I found posts referencing a group of people with whom I was familiar. After all, I'd lived in Michigan for many years and recognized the term *Amish*. It wasn't uncommon in a rural area, especially south and east of where I lived now, down into Indiana, Ohio, and Pennsylvania, to drive over a hill and meet up with a horse and buggy. To me the Amish were always good, moral people who simply shunned technology. Though I couldn't imagine not driving a car or having my cell phone with me at all times, I accepted them for who they were and had never considered them a cult, but the comments made me think.

The definition I'd seen earlier had said that a cult was a system of religious veneration and devotion directed toward a particular figure or object. I was relatively certain the Amish believed similarly to most Judeo-Christian groups.

Could that mean that cults didn't need to have nonconventional beliefs? Could they truly exist in the open, where most outsiders turned a blind eye?

The comment that I hadn't been able to shake was from a woman who claimed that for over a year she had been an unwilling member of a cult. The date on her post was from only one year earlier, and her online name was MistiLace92.

Everything else I'd read thus far had been from outsiders looking in. Even the original post was from a mother whose daughter had willingly gone to live with a group. This was different and made the hairs on the back of my neck stand at attention. I read the comment.

I don't know what to do. I'm scared and need help. I just found this thread. I'm hoping someone will see this and know what to do. No one believes me, but I swear it's true.

I lost over a year of my life to a cult. I'm afraid if I name them, they'll hurt me. I just want people to know that this is real and it can happen to anyone.

During the year I was held captive, I watched people come willingly into this community. I wasn't one of them, though I thought I was. Let me explain. One day I woke up and I was someone else, someone everyone knew, a follower of this group and of a man. I couldn't remember anything prior to my waking. For some reason my mind played tricks on me. I was obviously the one with the issues. Everyone else knew me.

They told me I was married. I had no proof otherwise. My husband was abusive, yet I had no option but to be obedient. His behavior was accepted by everyone around me. It was the way the entire community lived. We all had jobs and requirements. I still don't know exactly what I did; I helped to package things. I worked on an assembly line, and all I saw were plain boxes going into bigger plain boxes. Ten hours a day I did that. I wasn't alone; everyone did something. The thing that's hard to explain was that we all did it willingly. We weren't paid, but we had food and shelter and friends. I accepted my life, until one day, when I was instructed to tell a new follower that she wasn't new, that she belonged with us that I began to see. My husband told me it was our leader's will and an honor to do his work. That was when my questions came back.

I wasn't the woman they said I was. They'd done the same thing to me.

I know that if they find me, they'll kill me. I just know it. Leaving wasn't an option. There were select chosen members who decided the fate of others. I didn't know them well, but if they considered me a threat, I'm sure I'd be eliminated—banished.

As soon as I got away, I told the police my story. They said I was crazy.

Before I disappeared, I had a drug problem. The police said that what I described was impossible. They said I'd hallucinated, and if I pursued my claims, they'd have me institutionalized.

Help! I want to tell my story. Someone please
help me.

I wanted to comment, in hopes MistiLace92 would respond.
Unfortunately, the comment thread had been closed.

As soon as I got to WCJB the next day, I contacted a friend with an
affinity for everything computers. It took him all of fifteen minutes to
track down the IP address for MistiLace92's post. It originated from a
public library in Columbia Falls, Montana. I called the Columbia Falls
Police Department. It transferred me to three different people. Finally I
was informed that there weren't records of a Misti or anyone else filing
a report with such claims. I sent the comment and IP information to
their e-mail address; minutes later I received a response claiming the IP
address was incorrect. My friend swore it wasn't.

I asked if there could possibly be a cult nearby. They told me no. A
search for Misti Lace came up empty for that area; however, I found a
Misti Lacey on the national registry of missing persons. Unfortunately,
Misti Lacey's only living relative, her mother, was now deceased. I'd hit
another dead end.

I wasn't sure if my interest in MistiLace92 was connected to my
interest in Mindy, but whatever the reason, for the previous few nights,
her story had haunted my dreams.

As I drove toward the coffee shop I still wondered: if MistiLace92
was really Misti Lacey, why was she still on the registry of missing persons? Her post had been made over a year ago.

Shouldn't she be found?

CHAPTER 25
Sara

As I lay on my side, wrapped in Jacob's embrace with his bare chest against my back, the skin-to-skin contact seemed right, yet I couldn't shake the unfamiliarity of his stare. With our legs slightly bent, I caressed his arms and wondered about the blue eyes from my dreams. Maybe that was all they had been, a dream. I sighed and nuzzled my cheek against the pillow.

"You've been quiet since we came back from the community. Do you have something you want to say?"

"I don't think so."

"Are you sure?"

Closing my eyes, in the dark of the bedroom, forced the tear teetering on my lid to fall to the pillow below. Shaking my head, I said, "No, Jacob. I'm not sure of anything."

We'd just made love and I was crying, not exactly what a husband wanted from his wife. There hadn't been anything wrong with the sex—it was fine, just different from the previous night.

Now that I could see, everything was different.

Jacob pulled me closer, and his breath skirted across my hair. "Whether you remember it, or you've recently relearned it, tell me what Father Gabriel says about a wife's thoughts."

I exhaled. "Just like everything else, they belong to you, but," I added, "I'm not keeping anything from you. I really don't know how to say what I'm thinking. Honestly, I'm not even sure what I'm thinking." As more tears silently fell to the pillow, I tried to still my shudders, not wanting Jacob to know I was crying. When he didn't respond, I swallowed and went on. "I wanted to remember your face. Why can't I remember? Will I ever have a past?"

He kissed the top of my head. "We all have a past. This morning was your past, so was the day before and the one before that. If further back never comes, a year from now, this will be our past."

A closed-lip smile came as I nodded.

"A past is as long or as short as we want to make it. When we came here to follow Father Gabriel, we chose to leave our lives in the dark behind."

When his hold loosened, I rolled toward him. "I don't want to go back to the dark. I just want to know, to have the memories. Is it wrong to want that?"

"To want it?" he repeated. "No. To question the reason it was taken from you, yes."

I sighed. "That means that I can't ask about it."

Jacob leaned over me, his chest flattening my breasts. With our proximity in the darkened room, I could only make out his form, his shoulders, arms, and the silhouette of his hair against some distant faint light. There were no details. Hearing his familiar voice, without seeing his unfamiliar eyes, eased my anxiety. He smoothed the hair away from my face and kissed my nose. "We both follow Father Gabriel. You aren't the only one who must obey the rules. I can't question why you lost those memories any more than you can question me. All I can do is hold tight to the memories I have of us, for both of us. Even though you don't remember my face, I remember yours." He traced under my eyes, wiping away the remnants of tears. "I remember your beautiful blue eyes, the way they open with amazement at new discoveries and the way they flutter as you come apart beneath me." He was back to stroking my hair. "I remember the first time we made love and every time since.

"I remember the first time I saw you, the first time I heard your voice, and"—he brushed his lips against mine—"the first time I kissed you." He scoffed, "It wasn't supposed to happen, but I couldn't resist. I knew you were mine from the first time I saw you, even if you didn't."

His memories gave me a sliver of my past. "I didn't?"

"No, not then. You were dating someone else."

"What? That was before we were here, right?"

"Yes, it was before everything."

He sighed and laid his head back on his pillow. I was afraid he'd stop talking, yet more scared to ask him to continue. Thankfully, he didn't stop, but when he resumed speaking, his voice had a faraway tone, as if he was seeing it all again.

"You were laughing, and I thought you were one of the prettiest women I'd ever seen. You have a great laugh." He reached for my hand and intertwined our fingers. "I know this crash course in remembering how to be an Assemblyman's wife hasn't given you many opportunities for laughter. That's why I want your memories to come back. Sometimes it seems like we're back at the beginning. I want to be beyond that . . ." He was back up with his elbow beside me and his head on his hand. Looking down at me, he continued, "To where you laugh instead of cry."

"I'm sorry."

He touched my lips. "To where you're not constantly apologizing."

I kissed his finger. "I'd like that too, but you have to admit, this hasn't been easy. I mean my eyes, leg, and ribs. I've just gotten my sight back. We've been banished, and my hair is gone."

"I do." He exhaled. "I admit that it's been a rough few weeks, but we can see the light at the end of the tunnel."

"The Light?" I asked with a smirk.

"Yes. See? It's something everyone wants."

"I do see that, and I understand that we're here, on the biggest campus, as part of the chosen." I ran my palm over his handsome cheek. "And at one time, I chose to be here with you. Though I don't remember that, I wanted it, and I still do. I want The Light." I shook my head. "I'm sure that as we go forward there'll be times when I mess up and you'll correct me, but when I do, I'm asking you to understand that it's not intentional. Today, driving off the campus made me sad. I want to go back. This pole barn and the hangar might not be the dark, but for the life of me, I don't think I was driving away in your truck. I can't imagine wanting to leave you or Father Gabriel. I mean, first off, you said we're on the edge of the circumpolar north. Second, Father Gabriel travels by plane." My volume rose. "Third, there are polar bears. None of that makes it even seem possible to drive away, and if it were, it wouldn't be something I'd be willing to do alone."

"Once our banishment is over and Father Gabriel reintroduces us to followers, the accident is over. Just like any other correction, it's gone, as if it never happened."

"Reintroduces us? Do you mean like in front of everyone?"

"Yes."

I groaned and buried my head in his hard chest.

"Don't make me tell you again about your hair and how proud I am to have you at my side." His tone was somewhere between tender and stern.

"I think maybe I could wear a scarf."

"Around your neck to stay warm."

"A hat," I tried.

"Sara."

Yes, I was pushing this too far. "Fine, whatever you say. Jacob?"

"Do not suggest another head covering."

I shook my head. "I'm not. I wanted to thank you for arranging to have Raquel here today and Sister Ruth tomorrow."

"I'm confident that Brother Timothy and Sister Lilith won't try anything else, but Brother Daniel suggested that Sister Ruth come out, and I thought it would make you more comfortable."

"Why are you confident they won't do anything else?"

"Sara." His tone wasn't joking.

"I'm sorry." *Shit! Now I'm apologizing.* "I know you said Brother Daniel is our overseer, but he's on the Commission. I'm afraid that all the Commissioners are like Brother Timothy."

"They're not." He lay back and pulled me to his shoulder. As I cuddled close with the knee in the cast on his thigh, I listened as he talked about Brother Daniel and Sister Ruth. Apparently when we first arrived I hadn't been as good a cook as I was now—*I didn't know I was*—and Sister Ruth had spent a lot of time with me, teaching me. "It's pretty obvious she's a great cook," he added.

I laughed. "I knew it. From the way she hugged me at the hospital, I knew she was a bigger woman."

"Did you hear that?"

I lifted my head; all I'd heard was his voice reverberating from his chest with the steady beat of his heart. "No, I didn't hear anything."

"I did," he said, lifting me and pulling my cast across him. "It was your laugh."

"Jacob?"

"I believe you mentioned something—an alternative—at the clinic."

Oh, wow!

I laughed again. Holding on to his chest, I moved my knees to either side of his torso. With my breasts hanging above him, he leaned forward and captured a suddenly hardened nipple between his lips. As he sucked, noises came from my throat and my insides came back to life.

Gazing up at me, he brushed my cheek. "Sara, I'd like this to bring back your memories, but if all I get out of it is that magical laugh, I'll take it."

Placing my hands on his shoulders, I rose to my knees, and asked, "Is that all you're getting out of this?"

With my hips trapped in his strong grip, he grinned and replied, "No, I'm getting more; I also want those sexy moans of yours." A mere shift of his arms and I was up and then down.

"Oh, God," I whimpered as we came together for the second time in one night. I'd definitely be tender tomorrow; however, as his rippled torso flexed under my palms and his neck craned with pleasure, tomorrow wasn't one of my concerns.

Though I was on top, I held no illusion of control. Jacob's large hands choreographed, directing my speed and position. I was merely along for the ride, but oh, what a ride. He knew exactly how to manipulate, taking me to the brink and backing away. On and on I rode until finally my world imploded. My body, no longer mine, fell slack against his. When our foreheads came together he pulled my hips toward his, animalistic need radiating so strongly through his grasp that I wondered if I'd have marks in the morning. Before I could give it a second thought, a deep guttural growl came from his chest and his lips curled to a smile just before they captured mine. Compared to the desire he'd just shown, his kiss was tender. He released my hips and hugged my shoulders.

Once our breathing settled, still lying on top of him, I asked, "May I ask you something?"

"You may ask . . ."

"But you may not answer," I quipped, mocking his usual response. My behind stung with the swat of his hand.

"You're too smart for your own good. Ask before I use more than my hand."

"I guess it isn't really a question. It's just that I wanted to say I loved hearing your memories, like our first kiss, the first time we saw one another, and the first time we . . . did this. Thank you for sharing."

"Thank you for making those memories with me."

~

I couldn't have been more wrong, thinking Brother Daniel would be like Brother Timothy. The moment Jacob met him and Sister Ruth at the door, I knew they were different. Even when Brother Timothy had come to my room right after I woke, I'd sensed Jacob's unease. With our overseer my husband was as comfortable as he was when the two of us were alone.

After greeting Jacob, Sister Ruth came straight to me, framed my face with her cool, pudgy hands, and looked me right in the eye. The faint scent of vanilla surrounded her. "Sara, I want you to know that I've prayed every day for your sight. Thank Father Gabriel that you've been healed." Her smile stretched her cheeks. "And, my dear, Sister Raquel has done quite the job: you're absolutely lovely. I know Brother Jacob knows how blessed he is." She winked. "But I'm going to remind him, just for good measure." She whispered the last part as she surrounded me in her hug.

I looked to Brother Daniel, a tall, older man with graying hair, and said, "Thank you, Brother and Sister, for coming out. Jacob shared that it was your idea. Thank you for helping me feel better."

"Sister," Brother Daniel said in a deep, commanding voice, "on behalf of the Commission and Father Gabriel, while it will take a while for your hair to grow, once your banishment is complete, the incident will be behind both of you." He reached for my hand. "That is what Father Gabriel teaches. Never doubt his word."

My head moved from side to side. "I never would, Brother. I willingly accept his decree, and I'm anxious to return to the community."

He smiled from me to Jacob. "Sister, that's good to hear." Looking to Jacob, he said, "Call once you land. I'll come back and get Ruth."

"I will, Brother. The plane is ready. I should be able to leave soon."

Brother Daniel clapped Jacob's shoulder and turned to Sister Ruth. I had no doubt they had the same type of relationship that I shared with Jacob, yet I wondered how long they'd been married, because the adoration in both of their gazes was tangible. "Ruth, remember, if necessary, you have my permission to use the phone."

"Thank you, Daniel." She squeezed my hand. "We'll be so busy, nothing will bother us."

I liked her confidence, and wondered what she had planned.

"Brother Jacob," she said, "we had to park outside. In the back of Daniel's SUV are some bags. If you'd be so kind as to bring those in for us, I believe your lovely wife will have a dinner fit for a king when you return."

The way his eyes grew at that possibility made me smile.

"I'd be happy to get whatever you need to make that happen."

It was true that so far we'd eaten only already prepared meals. With my lack of sight, my *great cooking skills* had been limited to warming things and to preparing cereal, toast, coffee, and sandwiches. This morning I'd ventured to eggs and bacon.

After a few minutes the men were gone, and I was putting the contents of Sister Ruth's bags on the kitchen table. Salmon wrapped in white paper, sweet potatoes, onions, peppers, apples, the ingredients kept coming, and not one of them was from a box or packet.

"Sister," I sighed as I looked at everything, "Jacob told me that you taught me how to do this once. I admit I don't remember. I'm excited to receive a refresher course."

She patted my hand. "We made notes the first time. I believe they're in the kitchen of your apartment. Hopefully, that can help you, but you know that you can always ask me. With Daniel's permission, I'd love to spend more time with you."

I lowered my chin. "I'm sorry if I embarrassed the Assembly and Commission wives."

She lifted my chin. "Sara, I'd never be ashamed of you. I accept the Commission's decision and Father Gabriel's decree, but the strong, intelligent young woman I know would never willfully leave The Light nor her husband. I remember the first time I saw you and Brother Jacob. The love that you two shared hasn't disappeared. I know that. Brother Daniel and I've been married for over thirty years. The way you look at Brother Jacob and the way he looks at you, your love is still there. Isn't it?"

"It is," I admitted. "I don't know if it's as obvious as what I noticed between you and Brother Daniel, but it's there. I love my husband."

Her inviting smile filled me with the sense of a mother or grandmother. "Now," she said, "let's get started. You have a lot of cooking to do."

I bit my lip. "I really don't . . ."

"Stop. When I first came to your room after your accident, you didn't remember Father Gabriel. Do you know who he is now?"

I nodded. "I do."

"If I asked you to recite our declaration of faith, could you?"

I took a breath and stood tall. "I could. 'We the followers . . .'"

She winked. "I know it; you don't need to recite it. I'm proud of you. In another week you'll be making your husband's meals just like you used to."

The day flew by as we chopped, sliced, peeled, and created. The entire time we talked like old friends. When I put the apple pie in the oven, I blew out a breath. "If you hadn't told me otherwise, I'd swear I'd never done that before."

Sitting at the table with a cup of coffee, Sister Ruth said, "I'm sure you remember that not all meals will be this elaborate. When I was your age and still worked, I used my Crock-Pot much more often."

I hadn't thought about my job. Brushing the flour off the counter, I turned, and asked, "What do I do?"

"Oh, Sara, you really don't remember?"

I moved my head back and forth. "Sister, everything really is gone."

"You work in the chemistry lab with Brother Benjamin and Brother Raphael."

I widened my eyes. "I do?" Scrunching my nose, I asked, "You don't know what I do there, do you?"

"No, my dear, Assembly wives have more distinguished jobs than the average follower. Obviously most of them, men and women, work in the processing plant. It takes a lot of manpower to produce Father Gabriel's product."

I nodded. "Does his product have something to do with chemistry?"

"Yes, Brothers Raphael and Benjamin perfect the formulas. To be honest, I don't know how it all works. You probably know more than I do, since you work with them."

I moved to the table and sat. "And the followers produce the . . . ?"

She patted my hand. "Medications—pharmaceuticals. Father Gabriel delivers medication to those in need all over the world. It's a wonderful ministry that spreads The Light to those who can't afford it or areas where health care is limited."

"That's great."

"It is. We've been with Father Gabriel since The Light began. Even early on he knew this vision of his would come to fruition. It's not up to us to question how it all works. We do our part to make it happen. Truly, we're blessed to be part of this ministry. Now, of course, in case you've forgotten, the particulars of his vision can't be discussed with all the followers. There's a reason we're part of the chosen."

I nodded, thankful that she'd come and helped me remember so much. My mind wandered to my job, and I worried about Brothers Raphael and Benjamin. I hoped they'd be as patient with me as Raquel, Sister Ruth, and Jacob. "Sister? If I have difficulties at my job, would Brother Raphael or Benjamin . . . correct me?"

"Of course, they're men—it's their right." Losing her grip on the warm mug, she patted my hand. "However, only our husbands have the right to deliver the correction you're concerned about. But rest assured, if they believe it's necessary, they'll tell Brother Jacob."

I'm sure they will.

~

The remaining days of our banishment passed without incident. Sister Ruth visited two more times, always leaving me more confident than she'd found me. I actually made edible meals and continued to study Father Gabriel's teachings. By the time Jacob came back from Assembly on the final Wednesday morning of our banishment, I thought I was ready to be back in the community. However, when he announced that Father Gabriel wanted us at service that night, my stomach knotted; I swallowed as my expression undoubtedly gave away my trepidation.

"Sara." The one word was delivered as both a warning and a reprimand, one I'd learned to discern, having heard it a thousand times in the past month.

"I want to ask about the scarf again, but I won't."

"Good."

"I just thought that our banishment didn't end until tomorrow. Today isn't two weeks. Tomorrow will be."

His brows lowered and his more familiar eyes narrowed. "You've done so well. I don't want to correct you before service or make that a Wednesday-night habit, but if you question even one more time, I will."

I shook my head. "Thank you for your reminder. I won't."

"After service we won't be coming back here. We'll be going back to our apartment. So today while I'm working, you'll need to pack our things. I'll bring the suitcases in from the garage."

"Yes, Jacob."

"Also, dinner will need to be done and cleaned up before we leave. We want to leave the living quarters as we found them."

Nodding, I slowly turned, taking in the living quarters, and sighed. I'd studied Father Gabriel's word on the comfortable sofa in the living room, gazed out the large windows at the wall of trees, and relearned how to cook in the small kitchen. I turned toward the stairs and mentally traveled upward to the room where I'd rediscovered my husband.

"Do you have any questions?"

I grinned toward my husband. "No, I was just thinking that this place will be my past."

Jacob's lips curled upward and his brown eyes sparkled. "Yes, it will."

That evening, with my hand tightly encased in Jacob's, we entered the temple. Though I saw all the people in the foyer, Jacob led me down a hallway and up a staircase. I didn't know where we were going, though I was relatively sure we hadn't gone this way two weeks before. My palms moistened with each step as we approached double wooden doors.

I bit my lip to keep from asking about our destination; however, as we neared, I had a good idea. When Jacob knocked on the large door, he whispered, "Remember what I said. Do not embarrass me. This is almost over."

I didn't have the chance to verbally answer, so I nodded. The lecture I'd received for most of the truck ride into the community suddenly made sense. Taking a deep breath, I worked to keep my chin even.

"Enter, Brother," came from the other side of the door.

When Jacob opened the door, I inhaled and began my own monologue. Instead of telling myself to keep my head up and wear my short hair proudly, as Jacob had done, my internal lecture was much simpler.

Don't faint!

The table we stood before held five men. Though I didn't remember having seen him, I was confident the man in the middle with slicked-back blond hair and a very nice gray suit was Father Gabriel. I recognized only one of the other men, Brother Daniel. When our eyes met, he smiled and nodded. Based on expressions, I deciphered that the man on my far left was Brother Timothy.

"Father Gabriel, thank you for your correction. Sister Sara and I are ready to reenter The Light, with your blessing."

I bowed my head as Jacob spoke. Once he was done, I looked up.

"Yes, Brother Jacob and Sister Sara." *I was right. I'd know his voice anywhere.* "I'm pleased to have you back where you belong. Sister Sara, is there anything you'd like to say to me or the Commission?"

Oh, my!

Apparently, I didn't swear even internally in his presence.

Straightening my shoulders, I concentrated on Jacob's hand over mine, as it'd been the day I awakened. "Father Gabriel, Brothers of the Commission, I deeply apologize for my behavior, thank you for your correction, and I look forward to being back in The Light."

Father Gabriel smiled and stood. Looking from side to side, he asked, "If any on the Commission has issue with our brother or sister's return to the Assembly, speak now."

As silence fell, I held my breath, summoning all the self-control I could muster to keep my eyes on Father Gabriel and away from Brother Timothy. Just as we all grew confident in the silence, it ended.

"Father," Brother Timothy said.

Jacob tightened his grip.

"Yes, Brother."

"I don't have an issue; however, before reintroductions, I'd like to hear Sister Sara's answer to one question."

Father Gabriel sat. "Go ahead, Brother."

Brother Timothy stood. "Sister, what is the purpose of your new hairstyle?"

I tilted my head down, ever so slightly, gathered my poise, and spoke clearly. "Father Gabriel and Brothers of the Commission, my hair was cut as a reminder of my correction. As I wait for it to grow, I'll continue to remember my transgression. Thank you for my correction and my reminder."

Jacob's grip relaxed and I took a breath. He approved.

"Brother and Sister," Father Gabriel said, seemingly also content with my answer. "Please go to the vestibule. I'll be down after prayer. You'll enter the stage after the Commission. Once I reintroduce you, you may go to your usual seats."

"Thank you, Father," Jacob replied.

"Thank you," I added.

After we'd left the room, I walked silently, wondering why Jacob hadn't told me where we were going. It wasn't until we were in a small area that must have been the vestibule that Jacob brushed my cheek and whispered, "I couldn't tell you. Remember me saying that I also had requirements? You were perfect."

"Thank you," I whispered. "Although I'm still embarrassed about my hair, I promise I won't show it."

"You're the wife of an Assemblyman. Never forget that."

Moments later, following Father Gabriel and the Commissioners, we stepped onto the stage. While we waited to be reintroduced, I scanned the crowd, looking for Raquel and Sister Ruth. I found Sister Ruth first; her smile shone toward us. As my gaze went behind her, I gasped.

Though Jacob's stare silenced me, I couldn't believe my eyes. The two rows behind the Commission wives held eleven women and one empty chair. I immediately recognized Raquel on one side of the seat I knew was mine and on the other side was a beautiful redhead who I surmised was Elizabeth.

The reason I'd gasped was the Assembly wives' hair. Every one of them had a cut similar to mine.

I had indeed started a trend.

CHAPTER 26
Stella

I spotted Bernard as soon as I entered the coffee shop. This wasn't Starbucks or anything that tried to duplicate the modern-day successful chain. This restaurant had been sitting on this corner in Midtown for over fifty years, and if I were to guess, the Formica tables and plastic-covered seats had been here on opening day. That didn't stop the patrons. The place was always busy. The bar with the swivel seats bolted to the floor was filled to capacity as I made my way toward the back and eased myself into the red vinyl booth. The overpowering aroma of grease hung in the air like a cloud, and grew stronger as I neared Bernard's partially eaten plate of eggs, bacon, and potatoes. I didn't know how he could eat that every morning and stay fit.

His dark eyes lifted to me as he paused between bites, wiped his mouth on a napkin, and said, "I ordered you a coffee. Do you want food?"

"No, I've eaten."

"Do those cardboard bars count as eating?"

My stomach was in knots. "Is this my last meal?"

"I sure as hell hope not, but I need more answers than I've gotten in the last"—he dropped his fork to the plate, the clank echoing above the din of patrons—"since Mindy went missing. I think that's the problem."

I steeled my shoulders and lowered my voice. "You think it's a problem that my best friend is missing? Or you think that because my best friend has dropped off the face of the earth, I'm no longer able to do my job?"

The waitress placed a cup of coffee in front of me, but hearing my tone, backed away before asking if I wanted anything to eat. Bernard's beady eyes watched me over his coffee mug. When he didn't respond I sighed and fell back against the seat, forcing the air from the vinyl with a whoosh.

Finally he spoke. "Stella, give me something. What's going on in that pretty little head of yours?"

I pressed my lips together at his sexist comment. Did he ask Foster what was going on in that handsome head of his?

Instead of divulging all, I replied, "I've been following leads. It's just that they've been coming up empty."

"You told me about the women, no pattern, just women in this area turning up dead. I've done some research, and you may be onto something."

My eyes widened. "What have you learned?"

"The incidence of female homicides, as well as the potential for women to end up missing, is statistically higher per capita here, not only in Detroit, but in this general region, than in any other place in the country. Yet with all the stats that people spout, this one is rarely mentioned." He leaned forward. "My gut tells me that it's because of what you called the nonpattern. If the women were all tied together by one race or any common factor, it would send up red flags."

I nodded. "Why isn't it enough that they're all women?"

"We need more."

"I followed your informant's lead in Highland Heights. I don't know what the building is used for, the one that holds the address of the registrations for the cars that cross the border. It looks abandoned to me; however, I don't think it is."

"Why?"

"While I was watching, an SUV pulled up and some men got out. They walked between the buildings." I shook my head. "They didn't stay long. So when they pulled away, I followed them to another part of Highland Heights. They all got out at a church and went in. I've been back and I've seen the same SUV there again."

"Why haven't you told me any of this?"

"Because I don't have a connection from the church to drugs crossing the border. As a matter of fact, I think the reason they're going in and out of Canada is because of preserves." I nodded toward the little rectangular packets stacked in a silver bin at the edge of the table.

"You think they're transporting jams and jellies?"

I shrugged. "I found the church on the Internet. It doesn't have much information, but what little it does have says that they sell homemade preserves to support their ministry."

"In Highland Heights? Why would a church in that part of town be selling preserves? I wouldn't think there'd be a big market for anything homemade, other than meth."

I released my lip. "I know. I've told myself the same thing. It's kind of weird. I've been back a few times. I've seen men in cars and women walking from the church to what seems like an abandoned school. I think that they make the preserves in the school. And maybe there isn't a market here; that's why they're going to Canada."

"Who owns the old school? Does the church?"

Shit!

"I don't know. That's one way I didn't take this."

"Look that direction. Find the money trail."

I nodded. "So you're not taking me off of this?"

"Not yet, but you need to keep me informed."

"I know you believe my thinking is off because of Mindy, but I recently learned that HHPD has been trying to keep tabs—in a good way—on their transient populations, primarily females. This has been going on for a while, yet no one talks about it, maybe because they lose them. What I mean is runaways and prostitutes go missing."

"I'm not sure that's newsworthy."

I scrunched my nose. "Who knows, I could be trying to pull too many things together? I'm trying to connect all of it, and most likely none of it is connected."

"I've found that money talks," he said between bites. "I'm talking following the money trail, not paying someone off. See if you can come up with any connections under the surface since on the surface things aren't materializing."

"I will. May I ask you something?"

Bernard took a long drink of coffee. "Of course, but if it's classified, well, I may have to kill you."

I grinned. "I'll take my chances. This isn't specific, but what do you think about cults?"

"Cults?" His brows disappeared beneath his dark salt-and-pepper hair. I didn't know why he didn't wear it like this on the air. The way he greased it back for television made him look more like a used car salesman. This style was actually becoming. "I think," he said, "it's a derogatory term associated with deviant or unusual beliefs."

"What if it isn't, or they aren't? I mean, what if they aren't all like Waco or Jim Jones? What if they exist right in front of us?"

"Are we talking brainwashing, kidnapping, sexual abuse, and mass suicide?"

I shook my head. "I don't know. I don't think so. I don't have any proof of anything. Probably too many nights with wine and my computer."

Bernard grinned. "You'd better be careful. My wife killed her motherboard that way."

"That's why my glasses are stemless."

"I'm glad to know you're being cautious."

I shrugged. "They're bigger too."

"I don't know if you're barking up the wrong tree or not. It seems like you're trying to pull too many things together. Concentrate on the money trail and get back to me."

I looked at my coffee. I hadn't even touched it. "Thanks for not firing me."

"Stop worrying. I'm not firing you, but I am setting a deadline. If you don't have a story for me in by the end of the month, you're moving on to something else."

"Got it, boss."

~

Instead of going straight to WCJB, I did what I'd led Dylan to believe I wouldn't. I drove back to Highland Heights. I didn't plan to get out of my car. I just wanted to drive around and get a feel for the property I'd be researching. In front of the old school was a large **FOR SALE** sign. I recognized the realty company immediately: Entermann's Realty, a client of Preston and Butler. I'd done some work on a case in which a woman sued Entermann's because she'd tripped and fallen on property owned by the company. My job was to discredit the claimant. It wasn't difficult; she was one of those litigious people with multiple cases pending. Apparently she'd been successful in more than a few of her endeavors, because without record of employment she was financially solvent. Following her from her meeting with the attorneys, I found her walking around the deck of her twenty-five-foot boat docked at the river. It was a beautiful Hydra-Sports with two motors and a lower cabin. It wasn't the boat that interested Preston and Butler—it was the lack of the walking stick or neck brace she'd sported merely an hour earlier.

As I drove back to the building I'd watched weeks before, I longed for an open-and-shut case like that one. Externally the building hadn't changed. It still appeared abandoned and the one beside it that looked like an old firehouse did too; nevertheless I wondered what the men did between the buildings. Though I drove slowly, the way the passage between the buildings was shaded meant I couldn't see anything but light at the other end. I drove around the block again and parked at the far end of the building, away from the street. I wanted to get my Nikon out of my trunk, but hearing Dylan's words, I opted for fast, and turned on the camera app on my phone. I stepped out of my car and tried to shut the door softly. Once I had, I shook my head. No one was there. I was just being ridiculous.

Birds squawked above my head as I moved toward the building. My low-heeled shoes weren't especially good for walking through the taller grass, but I chose that direction to avoid the obvious path of the sidewalk. Approaching the gap from the rear, I peered around the corner. Closer to this end were two doors directly across from one another, one to each building. Taking a deep breath, I stepped into the passage. The closer I came to the doors, the more audible voices became. I pressed my body against the rough brick and listened, trying to decide which building the sounds were coming from. Just as I determined it was the one that wasn't the old firehouse, the sound of tires on the loose gravel in front of the buildings made my heart race.

With only the nose of a black SUV visible, I hurried in the other direction, out the passage, and toward my car. Once inside, I let out the breath and hit the "Lock" button. Before I could convince myself that it was Dylan's fault I was so jumpy, a big dark hand knocked once on my window.

I recognized the man immediately: his picture was on my computer. He was the driver of the SUV I'd seen on my first stakeout. Of course, from behind the tinted glass I hadn't gotten the full experience of his girth. His waist was higher than the bottom of my window, and he bent forward. His not-so-welcoming face was at the glass as I eased my window down a little bit.

"Yes?" I asked.

"Lady, you lost?"

"I may be," I lied. "I'm supposed to take pictures of some real estate for my company. Do you know if these buildings are for sale?"

"Not to my knowledge. I suggest you get yourself out of here, and tell your boss if he sends you here again, you better have a gun."

I nodded. "Thank you," I mumbled, rolling my window up and backing away. I may not have taken a full breath until I was back on Woodward Avenue.

~

I was so lost in the money trail of the buildings that until my phone buzzed, I'd forgotten about my lunch with Tracy.

> Tracy Howell: CHARLOTTE, I'M SORRY. INSTEAD OF LUNCH, CAN WE DO DRINKS, SAY FIVE? I'M WORKING THROUGH LUNCH AND WILL DEFINITELY NEED ONE BY THEN.

Shit!

> Stella: YES! I'M KIND OF BURIED AT WORK TOO. SEE YOU AT FIVE . . . JUMBO'S?

> Tracy Howell: I'LL BE THERE.

I turned back to the computer screen and rubbed my temples. Since I'd been back to WCJB I hadn't left my cubicle or even stood up. The pages of chicken scratch I'd accumulated wouldn't make much sense to anyone but me, and even I wasn't sure what it all meant.

The school that I suspected was the preserves processing center was indeed owned by Entermann's Realty. According to everything I could find, it was officially empty, out of commission, and had been since Highland Heights Public Schools closed the doors in the midnineties due to decreased enrollment. I wondered if anyone was even aware that it was being used.

Entermann's had purchased it two years earlier from a bankrupt developer. The developer, Uriel Harris, had snatched up numerous rundown and vacant properties over a ten-year span. His plan had been renovation, all hinging on tax breaks and grants. Though the tax breaks had been approved, the revenue base continued to drop. That was when Entermann's stepped in and bought it for pennies on the dollar.

Before Harris, HBA Corporation made a bid on the property. It's one of the largest builders of hospitals in the country. I understood that the size of the building meant it would have made a good hospital, and the area needed health care; nevertheless HBA was outbid by Wilkens Industries. Fifteen years earlier, Wilkens had paid $5 million for the property, purchasing it from Highland Heights.

What I found interesting was that the old firehouse and the large building beside it had at one time also been owned by Highland Heights. The money trail for the firehouse was different, but currently it was owned by Wilkens Industries. The building housing The Light was owned by The Light, a not-for-profit, paid in full, having been given to the ministry by Marcel Clarkson, a wealthy benefactor.

I made a note to research Marcel Clarkson and tried another route. I called a friend at Preston and Butler.

"Jenn?" I asked, hearing her voice on the other end of the line. She and I'd hung out after work on more than a few occasions. Her choice in men always lent itself to some late nights filled with plenty of beer and pep talk. I hadn't seen her in a while, not since leaving the firm, but I hoped we were still close. "It's Stella Montgomery."

"Hey, Stella, what's up? How are you doing?"

"I'm good. I've been working a story, and I was wondering if you could help a friend out?"

"I'm not sure," she replied. "But I'll give it a try. What do you need?"

"I'm following a trail on some property. I keep seeing Entermann's Realty coming up. I remembered that the realty firm was a client of Preston and Butler. Would it be possible to send me a list of all the properties they currently own?"

"Jeez, I'm not sure."

"Jenn, I totally get it, but if you could, you'd save me a ton of time, and I can't tell you how depressing this has been. I keep coming up empty on all counts."

"Stella, for all those times you sat and listened to me bitch about Jimmy, I'll give you this. Can you give me a day or two to get it all together? Then I'll e-mail it to you."

I bit my lip. "How is that scumbag?"

She laughed. "You always did have a way with words. I actually kicked his lazy ass to the curb."

"Good for you!"

"Yeah, you convinced me I didn't need a man around. We need to hang out sometime."

"We do. I'd love to catch up. Guess what?"

"What?"

I smiled. "I'm kind of dating someone."

"No way! Single-for-life Stella . . . we do need to catch up. Just tell me he's not like Jimmy."

"So far no, and he's employed."

"Sounds like a winner. I'll get that list together as soon as I can and send it to your e-mail."

"Thank you!"

I hung up and tried a search for Wilkens Industries. Founded in the early nineties by the original CEO, Marcel Clarkson . . . *ding ding* . . . it served as an umbrella for a few defined subsidiaries. In 2000 Clarkson stepped down due to medical reasons and was replaced by Matthew Lee. He was still the CEO. Under Lee's supervision Wilkens Industries had grown exponentially. The board of directors read like a who's who of nobodies. With last names like Smith, Johnson, and Jones and first names like Robert, Steve, and John, I couldn't have found the individuals unless I'd entered a board meeting and asked for their Social Security numbers. Being as Wilkens was a privately owned company, accessing its payroll records would take some time. Though it was private, I was able to access tax information through IRS records. Currently the net worth of Wilkens Industries was listed near $55 million, with a plethora of diverse investments and subsidiaries, one of which was Entermann's Realty. *Ding.*

Interesting.

As the clock neared four fifteen, I closed my search and sent a text to Dylan.

Stella: I'M MEETING A FRIEND FOR DRINKS. I'LL CALL WHEN I GET HOME.

Dylan: IF YOUR FRIEND IS A FIREMAN, WE NEED TO TALK BEFORE THEN.

I grinned.

Stella: YOU'RE THE ONLY PUBLIC SERVANT I PLAN ON TALKING TO. MY FRIEND'S FEMALE.

Dylan: GOOD TO HEAR.

"That's the best smile I've seen on your face all day."

I looked up at Foster. "I haven't had a lot to smile about."

"Still coming up empty?"

"I just feel like I search for days and all I do is go in circles." I shook my head and stood. Oh, my back didn't appreciate sitting at a computer all day, but after my scare in Highland Heights, I wasn't in the mood for surveillance either. "Hey, I meant to tell you. I spoke to Dylan. Whatever you found isn't connected to him. His parents are deceased, and he doesn't have a rich uncle."

He nodded. "I haven't had a chance to follow up. I know you don't want me to, but I probably will anyway, just to keep Bernard happy."

I shrugged. "Fine, have at it. You're wasting your time. I'd rather have you help me figure out how Uriel Harris is connected to Wilkens Industries."

"Uriel Harris, the developer?"

"Yeah. He owned some property I'm looking into."

"He owned a lot of property, paid way too much for it, and lost his shirt."

"That's what I saw. His loss was definitely Entermann's gain."

"Are you looking into Entermann's holdings or their tax write-offs? They purchase shit property all over the city so they can take the loss. It's not uncommon, but they're one of the best."

I nodded. "That makes sense. I was wondering why they owned so many dilapidated buildings. I hope to get the full list of their holdings soon."

Foster smiled. "I'll be glad to take a look when you do. Sometimes two sets of eyes are better than one."

"Thanks," I said, grabbing my purse and phone. "I need to run."

"It was good to see the smile."

I grinned as I made my way to the elevator.

This time as I walked into Jumbo's, Tracy was waiting for me. She had a short glass of a dark drink. It looked like Coke, but judging by the way her face scrunched as she sipped, I suspected it contained something stronger. "Hi," I said, sitting down. "Bad day at the morgue?"

She huffed, blowing her bangs in the air. "Is there ever a good day at the morgue?"

CHAPTER 27
Sara

Despite everyone's best efforts to the contrary, my past continued to begin the day I awoke in the clinic, nearly four months ago. My cast was gone and my body healed. It was my mind that couldn't remember. Over time my closest friends, Raquel and Elizabeth, shared secrets from our past, and Jacob continued to remind me of forgotten memories. Each story or statement helped me reconstruct a time I couldn't recall and gave me glimpses into my former self.

Since the end of our banishment and our return to The Light, the community, and our lives, when I was with Jacob, whether in public or in private, my movements no longer required conscious effort—they belonged to him. While my mind continued its struggle, my body willingly submitted. With a touch, a glance, or one word, his expectations were made clear. Though some small part of me resisted, the sensible part of me wanted to be the best wife an Assemblyman could have. After all the support from the unified Assembly wives, as well as the way Father Gabriel had welcomed us back to the congregation, I understood that Jacob and I truly were part of the chosen. The idea that I'd somehow almost jeopardized it made my heart hurt.

After we first returned to the community, I had problems. Often I'd awake in the middle of the night chilled to the bone, my heart racing, engulfed in darkness. The terrors of my nightmares included dragons with foul breath and razor-sharp teeth as well as a faceless man scream-ing *stop* in the darkness. Once awake I'd fall victim to an overwhelming sense of remorse—guilt over what I'd almost taken away from not only Jacob, but myself. When I felt that way, I was careful not to wake my husband. I'd usually move from his embrace, cling to the far edge of the bed, and muffle my tears with my pillow.

I knew Father Gabriel's teachings; I studied hard. According to him, once a correction was complete, the transgressor was freed from the responsibility of the sin. It was done, as if it'd never happened. Yet I didn't feel free.

One night as I clung to the far side of the bed and my body shud-dered with muffled cries, Jacob's warmth came behind me. I froze, com-pletely unable to move and fearful that he'd be upset. Instead, his arms once again surrounded me and he asked, "What is it?"

I'd been crying too long; my words didn't form. All I could do was shake my head.

Gently he rolled me toward him, and in the darkness he asked me two things: "Who are you?" and "Who am I?"

I tilted my head to the side, pondering his unusual questions. With stuttering breaths I replied, "I'm Sara Adams and you're my husband, Jacob Adams."

He tenderly wiped my cheek with his thumb, and brought our noses together. Whispering softly, he said, "That's all that's important. Go to sleep."

Though it seemed too simplistic, he was right. Concentrating solely on us, I curled into his warmth and laid my head on his chest. With the sound of his steady heartbeat against my ear, I drifted to sleep. When I awoke the next morning, I remembered not having been able to answer him the first time and my overwhelming sense of guilt and loneliness. I expected a reprimand, more questions about what had happened, or a lecture on how all my thoughts were his. He didn't mention it.

The next time the dragon's hiss woke me, instead of rolling away, I cuddled close and remembered his questions. As his even breaths flowed across the top of my head, I reminded myself of who I was and who he was. Before long I drifted back to sleep. In time the dragons faded away.

Although I knew I should talk to Jacob about my nightmares and guilt over the accident, my courage to do so waned with each passing day. After all, if I'd followed Father Gabriel's teachings, I would've told Jacob immediately. I knew the penalty for disobeying; I'd experienced it more than once.

It wasn't until I had multiple consecutive nights of uninterrupted sleep, while we were alone in our apartment, that Jacob asked me again about what had happened. He led me to the sofa and calmly demanded answers.

"Sara, I've been waiting for you to tell me this on your own. Obviously you haven't. I'm not sure why, but I want answers. Tell me why you were crying during the night."

I took a deep breath, wanting to be truthful, but equally fearful of his reaction. "It started as nightmares. I think." I tried to explain. "That's what woke me, but then I believe it was my guilt." My chest heaved. "I still can't believe I risked everything here, you and our friends, by taking your truck. I don't understand why I'd do that. I don't think I would, but obviously I did." A tear fell from the corner of my eye.

He lifted my chin. The way he stared stripped me bare. His soft brown eyes sought not only me, but my honesty. I didn't look away, nor did I want to. Captive in his grasp, I needed him to see my sincerity. Holding my breath, I waited for his gaze to narrow and his voice to lose emotion.

"What does Father Gabriel say about correction?" His eyes still searched, while his tone remained full of emotion.

I exhaled. "I know. I do. I know we were banished and now we're back. I know it should be gone." Unable to move my chin, I lowered my eyes and slid my lip between my teeth. I'd confessed and now all I could do was await the punishment I deserved for doubting Father Gabriel's teaching.

"Sara, it's not that it *should be. It is.*"

I nodded, and my body trembled. "I do believe it, but I just don't know . . ."

He lifted my balled hands and opened my fists, finger by finger, until he could kiss my palms. Then, with his thumb, he gently freed my lip. "Why are you so tense?"

"Because I know Father Gabriel's word, but I must not be living it. If I were, I wouldn't have those thoughts, a-and I don't know what you're going to do."

"What do you think I should do?"

My heart sank as the dinner we'd just eaten churned in my stomach. I hated when he asked me. Those simple questions turned the responsibility back to me. I didn't want it. It was his. Again I tried to lower my chin, but to no avail. I sighed and added to my transgressions. "I've also kept something from you. I didn't tell you that this was going on for a few weeks."

His grip on my chin tensed.

"I didn't want you to worry," I added hastily.

"Have you felt this way lately? Have you awakened in the middle of the night upset without telling me?"

I shook my head. "Not since the night you asked me who we were. Well, only once, and when I did, I did what you said: I reminded myself of us and stayed close to you. Since then, nothing."

Jacob exhaled. "Sara Adams, what does that tell you?"

"That I should be punished for not telling you sooner?"

His hands slipped to my arms, moving up and down with a ghostly soft touch. "It does say that you should have told me sooner, but no, this isn't about correction. It's about learning. Thoughts come and go; it's dwelling on them that's detrimental. The way you let them go is to release them to me. If I punished you for your thoughts, why would you share them with me?"

I hadn't thought of it that way.

"The accident," he went on, "is over, and now that you've shared your sense of guilt, it's over. I want all of you"—he caressed my cheek—"even if it's a part that hurts and makes you cry. Give it to me. Once it's mine I won't let it hurt you anymore, and no more apologizing for what's in the past. Remember, it's as if it never happened."

Nodding, I fell against his chest. Even though in my mind our history was short, as his arms wrapped around my shoulders, I knew I was where I was meant to be. My earlier feelings of doubt no longer existed.

As we made our way through the temple, when Jacob slowed or stopped to speak to other followers, I'd slow or stop with him. As we arrived at the room where the Commission and Assembly wives met for prayer, he reached for my hand, and I peered up through my lashes. When my light-blue eyes met his, my heart swelled at his silent message. I might not remember the beginning of our life together, but we'd found our way back. In the crowded hallway, his brown eyes, the slight upward turn of his lips, and the squeeze of his hand said more than words. The shimmer of suede in his eyes and partial smile told me that he loved me, while the grasp on my hand warned me to think before I spoke. I didn't need the warning because I had no intention or desire to receive his correction.

Though I'd relearned Father Gabriel's lessons well and knew my place, my continual area of downfall was my inquisitiveness. No matter how hard I tried, there were times when my mouth spoke before my brain could tell it to stop.

Eleven of the women gathering in the room I'd entered were my sisters, equal sisters under Father Gabriel. All the Assembly wives had made a significant sacrifice for me when they cut their hair. Truthfully, it had also been a show of support for Jacob. Without their husbands' consent, it never would've happened. As I glanced about, I was glad that all our hair was growing. Most of us could at least gather it at the backs of our heads, but nevertheless I'd never forget their gift. As we gathered together, we showed affection with a hug, squeeze of the hand, or warm greeting. Although the Commission wives hadn't cut their hair, they'd also welcomed me back without reservation, even Sister Lilith.

Father Gabriel taught to forgive and forget. That was what Jacob said I should do with Brother Timothy and Sister Lilith. While I'd forgiven, forgetting wasn't as easy. Not only did I remember, I also wondered why they hadn't been punished for the way they'd treated me. After all, Jacob had said it wasn't their place. The night I voiced that question aloud, to my husband, gave a prime example of my mind not controlling my tongue. As soon as I had asked my question, it hung in the air like a cloud, and I immediately knew it was wrong.

"Sara?" Jacob said, using his emotionless tone and narrowed gaze. "Who are you that you can question Father Gabriel's decisions?"

In the past he'd told me not to kneel; an Assemblyman's wife shouldn't be on the ground. The first time he'd mentioned kneeling, the idea had seemed incomprehensible. Yet four months later, when his voice and eyes reprimanded, I had an almost irresistible urge to fall to my knees. It wasn't that I wanted to beg for mercy; mercy was at his discretion. It was that his simple cues filled me with an overpowering sense of shame as I realized that I'd failed him once again. Instead of kneeling I respectfully bowed my head and, through veiled eyes, apologized: "I'm sorry. You're right; I don't have the right to question Father Gabriel's decisions."

Thankfully, that night I received only the tone and the gaze. Though Jacob was probably more lenient and patient than many of the other husbands, since I'd awoken I'd received correction by Jacob's belt a total of three times. Never, other than when I first awoke, had he struck me with his hand, and never had he willfully harmed me. He made it clear that it was as he'd explained: discipline, not abuse, and even though each time my transgressions outnumbered one, he never gave me more than five lashes. That was more than enough to help me remember to try harder.

As everyone sat for prayer, I noticed Deborah, one of the Assembly wives, wince. It wasn't obvious; however, since we'd all experienced it firsthand, we were proficient at catching the subtle signs of correction. Each time, we'd offer support, while reminding our sister, as Raquel had reminded me after my first correction—in my new memory or new past, as I liked to think of it—to thank God and Father Gabriel for a husband who loved enough to correct. Yet as Deborah settled into her chair, I knew my thinking was wrong and I needed to confess it again to Jacob. Instead of telling her to be thankful, I wanted to tell her to talk to one of the Commission wives, and I wondered why they didn't notice.

As I watched my Assembly sister, my gut told me that things were different for Deborah than for most of us. Not only had she recently given birth to a beautiful son, she'd gone back to her job and worked six hours a day at the clinic with Raquel. Sister Esther mentioned once in confidence how difficult it was to leave her baby and return to work; however, there wasn't an option to do otherwise. It was Father Gabriel's rule that all babies be under his word in day care by five weeks of age. What bothered me about Deborah was that even while she was pregnant, she was often corrected. Brother Abraham not only used his belt, but often her cheek or eye was bruised. More times than I could count there'd been visual evidence.

It wasn't up to women to question Brother Abraham's reasoning, but after the short time I remembered having known Deborah, I found it difficult to believe that she was that disobedient. Honestly, she was quiet and sweet, and now that her son, Philip, was here, she was tired. Once in a while in service, I'd watch Brother Abraham. Truth be told, not only was I concerned for Deborah, but he also scared me. Though I knew Jacob would never allow another man to touch me, I wasn't comfortable around Brother Abraham. If my instincts were correct, Deborah felt the same. As others comforted her and reminded her to pray, she said the right words. Still, there was something missing.

After prayer meeting Elizabeth, Raquel, and I walked down a corridor toward our husbands. As we did, I rubbed the tips of my fingers together, wondering if I'd ever get used to the strange sensation. Once a month, all followers pressed the pads of their fingers onto a special prayer sponge. Symbolically it removed our individuality, making us all equal parts of Father Gabriel's family. Though we were chosen, our behavior was an example to the other followers. It didn't hurt. It just felt odd.

As we were on our way to the Assembly room, a female follower with long blonde hair secured in a braid approached. Though something about her caught my attention, I couldn't remember having seen her before. Then again, as an Assembly wife I was rather isolated.

"Sister Elizabeth," the blonde said.

Elizabeth nodded toward Raquel and me as she greeted the woman. "Sister Mary, so nice to see you." Since Elizabeth and Brother Luke worked with new followers, she seemed to know almost everyone. It wasn't uncommon for female followers to come to her with questions. Though I wasn't a *new* follower, I understood the appeal of having women to help you understand.

Not wanting to intrude, Raquel and I stepped back. Elizabeth reached for Sister Mary's hand and spoke softly as Sister Mary nodded. I watched as Elizabeth's red hair fell in soft curls near her shoulders, veiling her lips and keeping their conversation private.

"She's so good at what she does," Raquel whispered.

I nodded. "Have you ever seen her before—Sister Mary?"

"Yes, in the clinic."

My eyes widened. "In the clinic? Was she sick?"

"No, it was just . . . when she first arrived. You know . . . to make sure she's healthy and didn't have any illnesses from the dark."

"Oh, yes, that makes sense." I watched as Mary bit her lower lip and smiled. "I don't know why, but she looks familiar."

Raquel laughed. "I know why."

"You do?"

"Yes, don't you see it?"

I scanned Mary one last time as she wiped a tear and nodded to Elizabeth. "Not really, but I must admit, I admire her hair."

Raquel tapped my arm. "She looks like you, even her hair."

I pouted. "Was it really that long?"

"It was, and it will be again. I've enjoyed the shorter cut. It was a fun change."

Before I could respond, Elizabeth was back, and we made our way toward the Assembly room.

All the Assemblymen lived in the same building in similar apartments. The only differences were the color and placement of the furniture, not that there were many options. Space within the community was limited, but we had what we needed. No one questioned. After all, even Father Gabriel lived as we did. According to Elizabeth our apartments were bigger than those of the regular followers. Her and Brother Luke's jobs meant they often visited followers in their homes. As an Assemblyman's wife, I too was supposed to help with the wives of followers under Jacob's direction. So far I'd met with them only in the temple. But going to them and helping them understand Father Gabriel's word was a responsibility I was honored to perform again, and one of the reasons I'd studied so diligently.

When we arrived back at the apartment building, Brother Benjamin asked Brother Luke and Jacob to come to his apartment. The way they looked at one another, I assumed they wanted to discuss something from their meeting. Whatever it was, we wouldn't be told the details, especially if it was something they believed needed to be discussed in private. Before they left, Jacob said to the others, "With your permission, the ladies may wait together in our apartment."

I bit my lip and waited: there was something I wanted to discuss too. As part of the chosen, we had to be careful what we did or said in public.

Brothers Luke and Benjamin agreed.

"Come on in," I said, as my two best friends entered my apartment. "Would you like something to drink?"

Raquel chatted about something as I made coffee and contemplated bringing up the question of Deborah. If it had been only Raquel, I wouldn't have hesitated, but sometimes Elizabeth was more rigid with the rules.

"Elizabeth?"

She looked up from the sofa as I handed her a cup. "Thanks."

"What's up? You look far away." I looked to Raquel, who shrugged.

"Nothing," Elizabeth said. "I'll talk to Luke about it."

"Do you always tell him everything the women tell you? Like whatever you were talking to Sister Mary about?"

She nodded. "I have to." Her striking green eyes scanned from Raquel to me. "I mean, we work together. For example, if Sister Mary were to tell me something that her husband needs to know, then Luke would be the one to do that." She shrugged. "It's up to Luke, really."

"But if she talks to you in confidence?" I asked.

Elizabeth's head moved back and forth. "Sara, you know that there can't be any secrets or confidence or whatever you choose to call it between a wife and husband."

I nodded. "What if all marriages weren't like ours?"

"What do you mean?" Raquel asked.

I sat on the other end of the sofa from Elizabeth, pulled my knees to my chest, and tucked my skirt around my legs. "I mean, what if some husbands take the whole discipline thing too far?" I exhaled. "OK, I'm just going to say it. I'm worried about Deborah."

Raquel nodded while Elizabeth's lips formed a straight line of disapproval.

"Why," I pointedly asked my friend, "Elizabeth, is it bad for me to be concerned?"

"Concern is your right, but you need to give it to Brother Jacob and pray about it. Not gossip about it."

I blew on my coffee, helping it cool. "First, I'm not gossiping. If I were, I'd be telling you something you didn't know. You know what I'm saying. And, second, I have given it to Jacob."

"You have?" she asked, surprised.

"Yes, and it's still happening."

Raquel became uncharacteristically quiet.

"Raquel?" I asked. "Deborah works with you. Do you think my concerns are unfounded?"

She shook her head, and then, looking to Elizabeth, she said, "I've done the same as Sara."

"And what did Brother Benjamin say?"

"He said to pray and support Deborah."

I placed my cup on the table and flung my body back to the sofa. "I don't think she's happy, not like us. I mean, I get that Jacob is the head of our household. I even accept his correction, but I also know he loves me, and I love him."

Elizabeth and Raquel shared some strange secret smile.

"What?" I asked.

Raquel patted my knee. "Nothing. We're just happy to hear you say that."

I scrunched my nose. "Isn't it obvious? I mean it is with you and Brother Benjamin and you and Brother Luke." I smiled at Raquel. "Even when Brother Benjamin mentions you at the lab, his eyes go all adoring."

Raquel's cheeks blushed as she looked down.

"It is obvious," Elizabeth said with a smile. "It's also nice to hear."

"But that's just it," I pursued. "It isn't obvious between Deborah and Brother Abraham. I mean, have you watched them together? I think she's afraid of him, and I don't see the adoration or love, from either of them."

"Sara!" Elizabeth said, "You can worry and talk about Deborah, but you can't presume to talk about Brother Abraham."

I exhaled, unable or unwilling to hold my tongue, even if it meant my own correction. "We're wives of Assemblymen. Are we just going to sit back and wait until Deborah isn't at the clinic as a nurse, but as a patient?"

Raquel sighed. "It's already happened."

"What?!" I asked, while simultaneously Elizabeth exclaimed, "Raquel!"

"Elizabeth, you heard Sara. She's here, fully. She needs to know."

I tilted my head. "What do you mean, I'm here . . . fully?"

"I mean, you're back, like a hundred and ten percent. As you were recovering from your accident, we didn't want to burden you."

"I don't understand. Why can't we help her before it's too late?"

"Because," Elizabeth began, "Brother Abraham is also an Assemblyman. If he were a follower, like Brother Adam, it would be different."

"Who's Brother Adam?" Raquel and I asked in unison.

Elizabeth shook her head. "Forget I said that."

My mind spun. "Is Brother Adam the husband of the woman who spoke to you, Mary?"

"It's not something I can discuss." Her green eyes shot toward me. "Forget I mentioned it."

"Wait, so let's say hypothetically"—I paused. When she didn't respond, I went on—"a female follower comes up to you and tells you in confidence that she has a problem with her husband. I'm just going to say it. He's abusive. Then do you tell Brother Luke and let it go from there?"

"Hypothetically," Elizabeth said, "yes."

"So with Deborah, if she said something to her overseer's wife, could that Commissioner's wife tell her husband, and then could he talk to Brother Abraham?"

"Theoretically," Raquel said, "but guess who's Brother Abraham's overseer."

I had four choices: Brothers Raphael, Daniel, Noah, or Timothy. I knew Brother Daniel wouldn't turn a blind eye, and I worked with Brother Raphael. He'd always been kind to me. I didn't know much about Brother Noah, other than Jacob said he worked with the finances of The Light. When new followers came to The Light they sold all their possessions from the dark and donated the money to help buy supplies. That left me one option: Brother Timothy. "Either Brother Noah or Timothy. I'm going to guess . . ."

Raquel nodded. "Without Brother Timothy's consent, the concerns, even if they're voiced by Deborah and Sister Lilith took them to her husband, can't be taken to Father Gabriel. Nothing can be done." She looked at Elizabeth and then back to me. "It's better if you don't say any more. It was brought up about a year ago, and you probably don't remember . . ."

I shook my head.

"After that was when she was a patient. It didn't do her any good. It made it worse."

Horrified, I turned toward Elizabeth. "Is that what happens to people like Mary if you tell Luke?"

"Hypothetically?" she asked.

I nodded.

"Sometimes, but usually not. Followers respect the opinion and advice of Assemblymen. Luke carries a lot of weight. He can usually help the situation."

"But just like Jacob helps Brother Daniel with the followers he oversees, doesn't Brother Abraham help Brother Timothy?"

They both nodded.

"So if a follower is unfortunate enough to be assigned to that chain of command . . . ?"

Elizabeth nodded. "Then they still have Luke and me. We just have to be sure to follow the rules, but we still can do our best to help."

I took a drink of my coffee. "Wow, Elizabeth, I didn't realize how difficult your job was. I'm never complaining about the lab again."

Raquel laughed. "Hey, you complained about working with my husband?"

"No," I said, smiling. "I actually like working with him and Brother Raphael. They've been very patient, and so has Dinah. She's been great."

They both nodded. "She's one of us. We stick together."

I sighed. "I wish we could help Deborah. I still worry."

CHAPTER 28
Stella

I handed Foster the list of properties Jenn, from Preston and Butler, had e-mailed to my personal address last night. "I've only glanced through it, but it seems like a lot of property. I always assumed that realty firms arranged the sale of property from the owner to the new buyer. I wasn't aware that the firm would own so much itself."

Foster shrugged. "They do both. It really depends on the size of the company. While Entermann's began as a broker, looking at this list, now I'd call them an investment company."

"Did you know that Entermann's falls under a list of subsidiaries of Wilkens Industries?"

"I thought you were talking the other day about Uriel Harris and his connection with Wilkens Industries?"

"I was. Here, let me see this list." I took the list and circled the property on Glendale, the old school. "This property is currently owned by Entermann's, but before that it was owned by Harris, and before that Wilkens Industries. Since Wilkens owns Entermann's, well, I'm seeing a circle, but why?"

"It's only a complete circle if Harris is connected."

"That's what I want to know. I've been trying to find current information on Uriel Harris. In the day, he was all over, buying property, but then all his holdings were sold. He took a big loss and disappeared." I shook my head. "I don't mean literally. There's no record of his death. What I mean is that I can't find him. His last known address was 12560 Kingsway Trace, Bloomfield Hills." As soon as I said the address, my heart clenched, and I looked up at Foster. "Tell me that isn't same address as the MOA house you told me about."

"Shit, it isn't, but it's damn close."

I shook my head, my braid skimming across my back. "See, this is what I mean. Circles, that's all I'm getting is circles."

"Have you accessed Harris's taxes?"

"I did up until he sold everything. For the last two years there's nothing. No personal or corporate. Nothing."

"Stella?" Foster asked, looking at the list of properties. "Did you just say 12560 Kingsway Trace?"

I nodded, looking down at where Foster's finger was on the list. "Entermann's owns that too?" I asked in disbelief.

"According to this list."

Remembering a recent conversation with Dina Rosemont, I asked, "What do you know about a private airstrip off of Woodward Avenue and Eastways Road?"

"Not much, but that's up in Bloomfield Hills. There are lots of wealthy people, so a private airstrip wouldn't surprise me. Why?"

"I promised a friend I'd go check it out. I think while I'm up there I might check out this house on Kingsway Trace."

"Well," Foster said, "be smart and take I-75. Woodward would get you there, but I recommend you avoid Highland Heights."

Why hadn't I thought of that? Woodward goes straight from Highland Heights to Bloomfield Hills.

I rolled my eyes. "Have you been talking to Dylan?"

"Me? No. Why?"

I shook my head. "Nothing. I'll call after I have a look around. While I'm up there, do you want me to check out the MOA house?"

"No. You have enough things going on with this story. You don't need another. Besides, there's no reason to think it's connected."

"You're right. I'm overly suspicious of everything. It's the whole compilation theory."

"Compilation?" he asked.

"Like everything is a piece of something bigger. I think I'm trying to fit everything together when they don't fit."

Foster's voice softened. "I just picked up a story about a teacher at East Grove. A mother claims she saw inappropriate pictures on her daughter's phone. If you'd like to take that, I'll take this over. I can tell it's wearing on you."

"Thanks, but I don't want to give it up. I feel like I'm so close. I just need one break."

"OK, the offer stands."

I smiled at my friend as I gathered my things.

Driving on I-75 to Bloomfield Hills, I remembered my conversation with Dina Rosemont and how impressed I'd been with her strength and determination. She had said she would never give up her search, and from the sound of her voice I believed her. We both knew the statistics weren't in Mindy's favor and got worse the longer she stayed missing. I shook my head, thinking how it had been over two months. I didn't know if the story I was researching would help her or help us learn about her, but my gut told me it would. That was why I couldn't hand it over to Foster. Even so, Bernard had given me only until the end of October. That was less than three weeks. I needed to learn something, soon.

Dina told me that she'd received a phone call from a woman who had seen one of the flyers she'd hung. The woman wouldn't give her name, but said that as a mother she needed to call. Apparently the caller lived near Woodward Avenue and Eastways Road, and there was a wooded area near her home where her children liked to play. A private airstrip was located there too.

The caller admitted that a twelve- and thirteen-year-old weren't the most reliable witnesses, and though she didn't want them personally involved, she felt compelled to share what they had told her. Even before the caller heard about Mindy on the news, her children had told her a story about a man carrying a woman from a truck to a plane. The woman calling admitted that because her children had been known to be imaginative, she hadn't paid much attention to their story. She'd figured there could be any number of good reasons why they thought they'd seen what they described. However, once Mindy's picture appeared on TV, her children brought up the story again. Even then, they only told the story; they didn't mention the connection. It wasn't until they were out one day and saw one of the flyers that her thirteen-year-old daughter pointed at Mindy's picture and specifically said, "Mom, that's the lady who couldn't walk, so they carried her on the plane."

My heart stopped as I asked what they'd meant by *couldn't walk*. Dina said she'd asked too. The woman hadn't known. After they hung up, the woman had asked her children and called Dina back. Her children told her the woman had been sleeping.

Dina said she'd called the detective in charge of the investigation, and he'd said he'd look into it, but she wanted me to know. I'd looked up private airstrips, but the ones I'd found weren't in the area the woman had indicated. That was the main reason I was driving north on I-75.

Exiting the interstate, I made my way into Bloomfield Hills. As I drove around the beautiful area, I thought about Foster's suggestion that Dylan could afford a home here. Honestly, it was too bad that he and I together couldn't afford one. Though I wasn't ready for full-time cohabitation, as I drove the curvy roads around the majestic homes I found myself imagining the interiors with a very nice shelf for Fred's bowl.

The last known address of Uriel Harris wasn't one of the big homes lining the hilly streets. The address took me instead to a large solid gate.

Shrugging, I parked my car, walked up to a box beside the gate, and pushed the button.

A man's voice came from the box. "May I help you?"

"I'm looking for Uriel Harris."

"You have the wrong address."

I knew I didn't. "Maybe I have his old address. Can you tell me how long you've lived here?"

"This is private property. I suggest you leave."

Well, that was rude.

"Thank you for your time," I said as I released the button.

Going back to my car, I grabbed my Nikon and walked the perimeter along the front wrought-iron fence. It didn't seem to matter where I tried—I couldn't see the house, or even get past the trees to take a picture. Though most leaves were gone, this property was lined with rows of pine trees, creating a living wall beyond the fence. Not only couldn't I see the house, I couldn't even get a feel for the size of the property. Still I snapped a few pictures here and there.

I hoped that once I downloaded the photographs, I would be able to enlarge them and make out more than I could see in person. When I reached the end of the front fence, I saw that the angle of the side fence indicated that the property was wider in the back. As I took a few more pictures, I decided I should get the schematic of the property from the assessor, but first I'd try Google Earth.

It wasn't until I got back into my car that I noticed the security cameras at the gate. Sighing, I fought the urge to wave. Well, I couldn't see them, but apparently they could see me.

Next I spent an hour driving in circles. If there was an airstrip off Woodward Avenue and Eastways Road, I couldn't find it. I couldn't even find the access road. Maybe I did, but instead of an accessible street it was another one of the gated private driveways like the address on Kingsway Trace. The more I drove the more frustrated I became.

Dead ends, I was so damn sick of dead ends!

While I was on my way back to WCJB, lamenting my progress, my phone rang. Dylan's name appeared on the screen in my car. I hit the green image and said, "Hello."

"Stella?"

His voice sounded different. Maybe something had happened at work. "Hey, is everything all right? You don't usually call during the day."

"Where are you?"

Shit!

I'd been so frustrated with the dead ends I'd forgotten to take the interstate and was on Woodward Avenue, approaching Highland Heights. "Why? I'm on my way back from checking out a lead."

Wanting to be able to honestly answer that I wasn't in Highland Heights, I turned east toward the interstate, just north of the city limits.

"I just had . . . never mind."

I wasn't used to hearing Dylan anything less than confident.

"Did something happen?" I asked.

"No, I was just wondering if you could do dinner tonight?" His tone lightened. "Or do you have drinks with that hot fireman again?"

I laughed. "Dinner would be great, but I need to be home tonight. I have things to do on my computer."

"You work too much."

"It doesn't have to be all work. You could stay?"

"Only if you let me take you out to eat."

"Sounds good. I'll go home after work and you can come over. We can go out after that."

"See you tonight."

∾

After dinner, while I downloaded my pictures, Dylan sat on my sofa. His legs were up on the ottoman as he watched TV. Looking at him, I wondered if this was what it was like when two people were together long enough to be comfortable. I'd never really dated anyone long enough to move into that stage. Maybe it was finding out about his parents, but since that morning a few days ago, I'd found myself thinking about him a lot more.

Once I had my pictures from the day on my computer, I entered the address of the house I'd visited. Google Earth wouldn't show me the exact dimensions of the property, but I was curious what was beyond that gate. The house was huge—no wonder it was valued at more than $7 million. There were a pool and tennis courts. Beyond the tennis courts were multiple smaller buildings, and then behind that, away from the road, closer to Eastways, was what I'd been searching for. There was an airstrip.

"Holy shit!" I gasped.

"What?" Dylan asked, coming up behind me.

I shook my head. "I really don't know." I pointed at the screen. "See this?"

His hands tightened their grasp on my shoulders as his face came up beside mine. When I turned toward him, I saw the muscle in his jaw flex.

"It's an airstrip," I explained when he didn't speak.

"Are you looking to do some flying?" he asked, from behind clenched teeth.

"No. See, Dina Rosemont called me about a phone call she received from someone who saw her flyer. She said that the caller told her a story about seeing a woman matching Mindy's description being carried onto a plane."

Dylan spun my chair around until our noses touched. "She needs to tell that to DPD, not you. You have too much going on. I'm worried about you."

I kissed him. "I'm worried about you too. Did you ask about getting time at Christmas? And don't worry, she did call DPD. Have you heard about it?"

"No, I'm not directly involved with her case." He shrugged. "You don't want me to be."

"You're right. You're homicide. I'd rather her case not make it to you."

"So was that where you were today, following that lead?"

I nodded, though I had been there for my story too. Our agreement was to discuss only Mindy-related work information. Turning back to the screen, I answered, "Yes, I couldn't find it."

"Well, I guess that's why it's *private*. Did some lady really say she thought she saw Mindy getting on a plane?"

I shook my head. "She said her children saw a woman, not getting on a plane—being carried onto it. It's the first news that gives me hope. I mean it scares me, but at least maybe there's a chance that she's still alive. Now I want to learn who owns this property." I shrugged. "I know who owns it. I want to know who's living there. I guess I didn't realize the airstrip was on it."

"What do you mean you know who owns it?"

I put my finger on his lips. "We're getting into non-Mindy stuff."

"Stella, please stop. You're too smart for your own good."

I brushed his lips to mine. "I love your support, but if I'm so smart, why is none of this making sense? Foster offered to take the story and put a fresh set of eyes on it." I sighed.

"Do that!"

"You know I can't. I mean, yes, I was at this property for Mindy, but I'm so close to something—something big—that I can feel it."

"Quit WCJB. We could use you at DPD. You're really that good."

"Oh, I don't know if we should work together. I get the feeling our styles match better in private."

Dylan took my hand. "No more computer, pictures, or Google Earth searches. Let's work on that private compatibility."

CHAPTER 29
Stella

"Stella," Dr. Howell said, "I need you to meet me at the medical center—right away."

I blinked awake at the sound of her anxious voice. "What is it?" I focused on the clock near my bed; it wasn't even three in the morning.

"I'd rather show you. Can you be here, in the ICU, in half an hour?"

This time of morning there wouldn't be much traffic, but that was still cutting it close. "I can be there in less than an hour. I'll hurry."

"OK, and please don't tell *anyone* where you're going."

I looked to my right, saw Dylan with a pillow pulled over his head, and replied, "If it's that important, I won't."

"Believe me, it is."

"OK. I'll see you as soon as I can. Bye."

The line went dead. Dylan rolled, his eyes blinking in the red glow from the bedside clock. "Jesus, Stella, do you ever get to sleep through the night?"

I leaned down and kissed his lips. "Go back to sleep. You can lock up before you leave. I need to run."

He huffed, rolled back under his pillow, and muttered, "Shit, I'd argue, but I've got a lot happening today. Besides, you wouldn't listen anyway."

I hurried to the bathroom and made myself presentable, as presentable as one wants to be this early in the morning. Less than ten minutes later, dressed in jeans and ready to go, I made my way back to Dylan. "I'm sorry this woke you. I'll leave a key for you on the table by the door so you can lock up." I bent down to kiss his cheek. His inviting scent combined with his radiating warmth pulled me closer. The outside temperature had dipped the last few nights, making Dylan and my bed a much more compelling option than Tracy and an ICU. Just as I was about to kiss him good-bye, he wrapped his arms around me and pulled me closer.

With a raspy morning voice, he asked, "A key? You're giving me a key?"

I shrugged in his embrace. "You have to be able to lock up."

Burying his stubbly face in the nape of my neck, he mumbled, "I'll give it back tonight."

It took every ounce of my willpower not to climb back into my bed. "Or you could hold on to it, and then if Fred ever needs something, and I can't be here, you could swing by."

"I could do that. The little guy and I really bonded. Did you see how excited he was last Sunday to watch the Lions game with me?"

I laughed. "Yes, you two were something else. Call me later?"

"Or since I have a key . . ."

"I"—I hesitated—"will see you later." I kissed his cheek and went to find my warmer coat.

Since that night over a week ago when Dylan had stayed at my place, he'd done it more. I'd thought about giving him a key before now. After all, I had one to his place, though I'd been reluctant to accept it. He'd convinced me to take it at the same time he'd convinced me to leave clothes. I guess they kind of went together; however, I'd never used his key. Maybe I hadn't felt comfortable being at his place without him. While I waited for my car to warm, my cold cheeks rose; I was comfortable leaving him alone at my place. As I exhaled, faint crystals of ice hung suspended in the cool morning air. My empty stomach clenched at the realization: as I'd said good-bye to the sexy man in my bed, I'd almost told him that I loved him.

When the hell did that happen?

Last week when I'd told my mom, on the phone, that I'd invited him to Christmas with us, you would've thought I'd told her that one of my stories was being considered for a Pulitzer. She was beyond elated that I was in a steady relationship. With two daughters, she was champing at the bit for grandchildren. Currently all she had was Fred. I'd felt bad when I let her know that he wouldn't be making it for Christmas. Fish and carsickness made for a messy bowl.

I shook my head at the possibility. Maybe at twenty-nine years old I was ready to look at a future with someone. I'd never thought it would be with someone like Dylan, a detective, and someone others considered a hard-ass. However, when we were together, I didn't see him the way others did.

The Saturday before he and Fred bonded over football, had started a little rocky. For some reason he wasn't happy about my strawberry jam. I'd walked into the kitchen and found him staring at the jar. When I asked him what was going on, he explained it was an allergy. I promised I wouldn't use it when he was near, but I would eat it. It was delicious.

Later that day we went to Dearborn for the Apple Harvest Festival. Though my research was finally falling into place and I wanted to keep working, Dylan persuaded me to take a day away from everything. I smiled at the memory; I had enjoyed the outing. The day was one of those unseasonably warm autumn days, a gift from the prewinter gods. With a warm breeze and a clear blue sky, we walked hand in hand around the festival, talking, laughing, and enjoying candied apples. As evening came, we sat on a blanket with another one wrapped about our shoulders, drinking spiked apple cider and listening to live music. While Dylan drove back to my place, I dozed off and on. For the first time ever, I experienced a complete sense of security and contentedness.

Later I told myself that it wasn't all about Dylan; it was also about the progress I'd made on the money trail surrounding the buildings around The Light. Doing as Bernard suggested, I'd finally connected some dots. Though I'd done it all without revisiting Highland Heights, I planned to go back as soon as the first snow fell. I wanted proof that the abandoned building was in use. Footprints behind the locked fence would be that evidence, and with the way my teeth currently chattered, I'd be getting those soon.

My most exciting connection I'd made, the one I'd yet to share with anyone, was about Marcel Clarkson, the benefactor who'd donated the building that currently housed The Light. Marcel was also the original CEO of Wilkens Industries. He'd begun that private company in 1972 and had one son, Garrison Clarkson. My moment of discovery came when I realized that prior to 1990 Gabriel Clark, the founder of The Light, didn't exist, and after 1990, Garrison Clarkson ceased to exist. The paper trail on Garrison's demise was fuzzy at best. There was a small hospital notice listing Garrison Clarkson as deceased; however, I couldn't verify that with state death records. The only other mention of Garrison was in a 1998 interview with Marcel in which he mentioned the loss of his son.

Though The Light's website gave little information on Gabriel Clark, other than that he claimed to have risen from the ashes of darkness, assuming I was right and he truly was Garrison Clarkson, that couldn't have been further from the truth. Garrison had grown up in a stately older mansion in Angell, one of the most expensive neighborhoods in Ann Arbor, Michigan. He came from old money, earned off the backs of autoworkers. His father, Marcel, had begun Wilkens Industries and diversified the family fortune during the stock market boom, increasing its worth exponentially. Garrison had attended the University of Michigan, followed in his father's footsteps, and climbed to the top. Then in the late 1980s the markets crashed and, according to undisclosed insiders, a family feud ensued. That was about the time Garrison disappeared and Gabriel Clark was created.

If I'd connected the right dots, Garrison Clarkson became Gabriel Clark, a divine preacher and prophet of God.

The early 1990s was the boom of self-discovery. Men and women faced with financial devastation flocked to self-help and motivational seminars. From what I'd pieced together from archived media blurbs, Father Gabriel, as he branded himself based on the archangel, rose to the top. Perhaps ordained, or perhaps recognizing the financial potential, Gabriel traveled about the country conducting free seminars for thousands of participants. Each seminar encouraged *only the participants interested in personal success* to purchase his materials. According to the IRS, in 1992 sales from his books, manuals, and videotapes topped $10 million.

Near the turn of the century, the same time that Marcel became ill, Gabriel stepped away from the traveling circuit and settled down with The Light. By that time he had a ring of three trusted advisors who were named as members of his advisory commission. Their names were listed on the original application for tax-exempt status: Michael Jones, Raphael Williams, and Uriel Harrison—interestingly, all archangels.

If Uriel Harrison was Uriel Harris, the developer, my circle was complete.

Without evidence, I assumed the feud between Marcel and his son had ended before Marcel Clarkson's death, because in 2001 Gabriel Clark's and Marcel Clarkston's combined net worth was transferred to The Light. On paper, Garrison Clarkson or Gabriel Clark, was penniless.

My theory was that Father Gabriel was still connected to Wilkens Industries, the entity that also owned Entermann's Realty. It was still a leap, and I was working on the particulars; however, if I was correct, Father Gabriel didn't live in a run-down church building in Highland Heights. He lived in the mansion in Bloomfield Hills, the one with the landing strip. He also wasn't penniless, but based on flight plans, flew in a multi-million-dollar plane.

His having the old school building under his control guaranteed its abandoned appearance, and he also had control of the two buildings with the passage between, and the perfect cover for production of anything he wanted.

If I took my theory to the next logical step, and the witnesses' mother was also correct, there was a connection between The Light and the missing women. I wasn't convinced it also included the dead women. Perhaps that was me trying to incorporate too much, but I knew that at the very least I had something for Bernard, and that story alone could get him entry to the old school building on Glendale. If the only thing that was being done inside its walls was the making of delicious preserves, then we had a missing-persons story, possible tax fraud of a not-for-profit, and tax evasion of Gabriel Clark/Garrison Clarkson. If instead there was a connection to the drug story I'd originally begun researching, then Bernard Cooper would hit pay dirt. With a week and a half to spare on Bernard's deadline, this story that had taken me months had the potential to give him national exposure.

Since the pieces were just now falling into place, I hadn't shared them, but I'd saved everything on my laptop. Each day I also e-mailed the zip files to myself, knowing that in the case of fire or burglary, they'd at least exist in cyberspace. As one last precaution, I backed everything up on a hard drive that stayed hidden in my underwear drawer. Though it seemed excessive, I knew this was big. For that reason I purposely didn't have any information on my work computer. I feared the server wasn't secure.

The rush of it all made me almost giddy. I made my way through the medical center in search of Tracy. I found her sitting in the waiting area with her knee bobbing up and down. As soon as our eyes met, she got up and hurried in my direction. My elation evaporated at the lines around her eyes and her furrowed brow.

"Tracy, what is it? Is someone you know . . . ?"

That didn't make sense. She wouldn't call me.

"No," she said, taking my hand and leading me through a pair of double doors. "I have a good friend who's an emergency room doctor. We went to med school together." Her voice was a low whisper. "We were talking a few weeks ago about unusual cases; I mentioned some of the things we'd discussed. Then last night she called me." As we moved along the quiet corridor, she looked about nervously. "I promised her that you wouldn't use her name. HIPAA violations are seriously frowned upon, but when she told me about the woman's fingertips, I came to see. That's when I called you." We stopped at a private room where beeps came from behind the door. Tracy squeezed my hand and whispered excitedly, "Wait until you see this!"

My heart raced as we approached the woman in the bed. She was connected to multiple tubes and equipment. Her right cheek was swollen and purple and her eyes were closed. Tracy reached for the unconscious woman's hand and turned it palm upward. Her fingertips were white, the skin freshly burned.

I gasped. "Has she spoken? Does anyone know what happened?"

Tracy shook her head. "No, she was found near Woodward Avenue and Richton Street, running and stumbling with no coat or shoes. A motorist picked her up and brought her here. The man said that she was barely conscious when he found her, but by the time he arrived, she was passed out."

"Did she say anything to him? Have the police been called?"

"I don't know any more from the man who brought her here. Even what I've told you is classified. DPD came when she first arrived, but nothing can be done without her statement."

I scanned her from head to toe: only her upper chest, head, and arms were visible. "Other injuries?"

Tracy nodded. "Again, I haven't been told much. We need to get out of here before someone finds us. That's why I wanted you to come now, before the morning commotion."

"We passed the nurses' station," I reminded her.

"I have a few friends. Officially we've never been here."

I touched the woman's arm and thought about the victims in Tracy's morgue. Thankfully, despite what she'd been through, this woman was warm.

"Let's get out of here," Tracy said. "As long as you promise her anonymity, my friend who was the attending doctor last night said she'd talk with you."

I agreed.

A few minutes later we were seated in the hospital's cafeteria, nursing cups of hot coffee and talking with Dr. Jennings, a young woman of Asian descent, with tired eyes and pulled-back hair.

"I can't go on record," she began.

I shook my head. "You won't. I promise. Thank you for speaking to me."

She nodded toward Tracy. "She told me what you've been trying to do. As soon as I saw the fingertips, I remembered Tracy's stories. That's why I called."

"Did the patient say anything?"

"No, she's been unconscious since she arrived. Not only is she injured, but she was suffering from hypothermia. I think it was near twenty degrees last night."

I took a deep breath. "What about the Good Samaritan who brought her in? Did she say anything to him?"

Dr. Jennings shook her head. "He said she was incoherent, all she talked about was a light." Dr. Jennings rubbed her temples. "The poor man said he kept telling her not to go toward it. I think he was afraid she might die right there in his car."

My entire body trembled. I needed to speak with this woman or even the man who had saved her. *A light* had to be *The Light*, it just had to be. This would be the connection to the dead women.

Dr. Jennings agreed that I could wait for the woman to regain consciousness, and if that happened before her identity was learned and her family or the police stepped in with an order prohibiting visitors, I could talk to her.

I waited impatiently, wishing I'd brought my laptop to record my observations and nursing my third cup of coffee. Without food, my stomach continued to twist, creating knots upon knots. Perhaps that was why I startled when one of the nurses from the ICU tapped my shoulder. "Miss Montgomery?"

"Oh! Yes, is the patient awake?"

"No, ma'am, not yet; however, there's a call for you at the nurses' station."

I straightened my shoulders. "For me?"

"Yes, ma'am. He asked that I get you."

I nodded. "OK"—I stood—"thank you."

As I followed the larger woman in dark-blue scrubs, my mind searched for who could possibly be calling me at the hospital. It wasn't yet seven in the morning, and I hadn't even told Bernard or Foster where I was.

"Hello?" I asked tentatively.

"Stella Montgomery?"

My forehead furrowed. "Yes?"

"My name's Paul. I'm the man who found the woman last night on Woodward. I have a few minutes before work if you'd like to get my statement."

My tired mind came to life. "Yes, Paul. Thank you, I'd love to do that. Thank you so much for helping her and talking to me. Can I get your last name, and where I can meet you?"

"I'd rather do this off the record, so no last name. But I want to help that lady. I work at a dry cleaner on Grand Boulevard in New Center. Martin's. Can you meet me there?"

My body tingled with excitement. "Yes, I understand. I won't use your name. I'll be there in less than half an hour."

"It's kind of busy this time of day, but there's a flat lot two blocks away behind Market on State Street."

Behind Market on State, I made a mental note.

"Thank you, Paul, I'll be right there."

It was probably all the coffee and the lack of food, but my grip tightened on my steering wheel as I approached Market. It wasn't a street, but a big building filled with different establishments. It had another name, but people who were familiar with the area called it the Market. Over the years, locals shortened that to just Market. Turning off the main street, I turned onto State. In this area of town it was more of an alleyway than a street. The flat lot had an attendant.

Rolling down my window, I asked, "May I park here?"

"Five bucks for an hour, thirty for all day," the man said, handing me a ticket.

As I put the ticket on the dashboard, the screen in my car lit, indicating a new text message. Out of habit, I hit the button for my car to speak.

```
Text message from Tracy Howell: I SPOKE
WITH PAUL SWIVEL, THE MAN WHO FOUND THE
WOMAN LAST NIGHT. HE SAID HE'D THINK
ABOUT GIVING YOU A STATEMENT. I'LL KEEP
YOU POSTED.
```

As I looked back up at the attendant, the large black man suddenly seemed vaguely familiar.

There was a sharp pain in my neck and my world went black.

CHAPTER 30
Bernard

I sent another text message to Stella; that made four. She'd never refused to answer me before. I knew I'd been a hard-ass about the deadline, but there were other stories out there that she could research. She said it wasn't because of Mindy that she continued to pursue these leads, but I knew in my gut it was. I also knew that if she could connect the dots—if there were dots to connect—it'd be one hell of a story. That's why I'd given her so much time. It wasn't as if I had to answer to anyone. She worked for me. I worked for the station, but WCJB wouldn't question my allocation of hours.

I picked up the desk phone and called Foster. "Have you heard from Stella today?"

"No, she's probably checking out one of her leads. She's been getting excited about things coming together."

"Has she told you any of it?" I asked.

"Some. I know she was checking out properties owned by Entermann's Realty. There was something about a private landing strip in Bloomfield Hills. That's all she's shared."

"I wish she'd text me back."

"Bernard, she's not Mindy. She's smart and has a good gut. Besides, she's got Richards looking out for her. Give her some space. She'll text back."

I rubbed my temples. He was probably right. Mindy's disappearance had us all on edge. "Hey, speaking of Richards, what did you learn about him?"

"Nothing that we don't already know. There was that one quirky thing about a utility bill on some mansion, but none of it checked out. Stella told me his parents were deceased. That checked out. Everything else was pretty boring."

I shook my head. "Fine. If you hear from her, let me know."

"Sure thing."

Meetings, calls, and general business ensued. It was nearing five in the evening when Foster knocked on my door.

"I'm heading out. I never heard from Stella, have you?"

Shit!

"No, hang on a second. Let me call her again." I'd already called three times and had no idea the number of text messages I'd sent. Just like the other three times, the call went straight to voice mail. I shook my head.

"What about—?" Foster asked.

"Richards? I've got his number here someplace."

Foster placed a Post-it note on my desk. "I'll admit it, the Mindy thing has me worried too. Stella's a smart girl. I'm sure everything is fine. I'd just like to know."

Nodding, I dialed the number on the Post-it note. Richards answered on the third ring.

"Richards."

"This is Bernard Cooper. I was wondering if you've spoken to Stella today."

"This morning, why?"

"When this morning?"

"Why? Where did you send her?" Richards's volume rose.

"What are you talking about? I didn't send her anywhere." My eyes met Foster's.

"Sure you did," Dylan Richards replied. "She got a call early this morning. I don't know, like three o'clock or something. Hell, I don't remember. I went back to sleep."

My heartbeat quickened. "What the hell are you talking about? I didn't call her at three in the morning."

"Well, fuck, someone did. She took off."

I shook my head. "And you have no idea where she went?"

"Listen," Richards said, modulating his voice. "Tell me she said something about wherever she went once she got to the station."

"That's just it. She never came to WCJB. I haven't been able to reach her all day."

"How about her apartment?"

I shook my head. "What about it?"

"Maybe she went back there and fell asleep. It was early when she left."

I took a deep breath, my eyes still fixed on Foster's. "Foster's with me. We'll meet you there."

"OK, shit. I have a key. I can be there in forty minutes."

"Richards, I'm calling DPD to meet us." My chest clenched at my next sentence. "In case it's a crime . . ." I couldn't say it.

"Fine, I won't go in, but I'm knocking the shit out of that damn door. This better be some big fuck-up, or else . . ."

My neck straightened. "Or else what?"

"You know where you've been sending her. Don't you give a fuck about her safety?"

"Richards, shut the hell up. We'll be there with DPD in forty minutes."

"I am DPD. I'll have someone with me."

～

One week later—still nothing. The evening at Stella's apartment had come up empty. I might not have liked Dylan Richards, but the man was a basket case. Between the DPD officers who'd accompanied him and ours, we'd had a shit-ton of officers there. He kept it together better than most would in his situation with his girlfriend missing, but once the crowds thinned he did little to hide the frustration and desperation on his face. I'd talked to him almost every day since.

DPD taped off her apartment and searched it thoroughly. Her laptop was missing. I'd seen it with her sometimes while she worked. All we could assume was that she took it with her that morning. Richards said he didn't know. He'd fallen back asleep after she'd left. No flash drives or backup hard drives were found.

The DPD forensics team was able to get her MAC address from her router. With that the team searched for her computer. All it would take to find it, would be for it to be turned on and connected to Wi-Fi. It hadn't been since the night before she disappeared.

Foster gained access to her personal and work e-mails as well as her search history on her computer at WCJB. The search history confirmed her research into Entermann's Realty and Wilkens Industries. She'd searched Google Earth, but specifics couldn't be found. When Foster went back in time he found her preliminary research into the property on Glendale Avenue in Highland Heights. It was what had prompted her to dig into Entermann's Realty. Foster said he'd seen a list of their holdings, yet it wasn't in her e-mail. We could only presume she'd deleted the e-mail to protect her source. Of course her e-mail trash was empty. One of the oldest and usually most reliable ways to back up information is to e-mail it to yourself. There was no evidence that Stella had done that.

The only other source of information was her phone. A call had been placed to her at 2:48 a.m. the morning of her disappearance. It had come from the assistant forensic pathologist at the Wayne County Medical Examiner's private cell number. Dr. Tracy Howell claimed she and Stella had become friends and admitted to calling her and asking Stella to meet her at the medical center to see a patient. Unfortunately, the patient she mentioned had never been identified and was now in the Wayne County Morgue. There was an ongoing internal investigation at the medical center, but primary information indicated the patient had suffered a severe allergic reaction to pain medication. Anaphylactic shock had occurred before treatment could commence, and resulted in death.

No calls or text messages had been sent from Stella's phone the day of her disappearance. Calls from Richards, Foster, me, and Tracy Howell had been received but never answered. Some of us had left voice mails. Text messages had been received from Dr. Howell, Richards, and me. There was absolutely nothing else.

Her car had been found the day after her disappearance in a flat lot in New Center. The crime lab dusted it—nothing. Unfortunately, Stella had chosen one of the few lots in the New Center area without video or even picture surveillance.

Each day was worse than the one before. Two women working for WCJB were officially missing. Vanished from sight. Disappeared into thin air. While speculations ran wild, for those of us who knew them, it was devastating.

CHAPTER 31

Sara

One morning in June, Dinah and I met Raquel and Elizabeth in the coffee shop before work. Since the Assemblymen needed to be at Assembly early, the night before at prayer Raquel had mentioned that we should start our day with friends. To my delight our husbands had agreed to this unusual impromptu outing. Standing at a tall table, I stirred cream into my coffee and half listened as the other wives chatted about nothing in particular. When something was said about *the dark*, my ears perked up.

I leaned over the table and spoke quietly. "I know I shouldn't, but I wish I remembered. I think it's cool that you do."

"I don't remember either," Dinah said. "I think I blocked it out."

Elizabeth sighed, her green eyes moist.

I reached out and touched her hand. "What's the matter?"

She looked up. "Nothing."

Raquel hugged Elizabeth. "Maybe we should go somewhere a little more private?"

Standing taller than her already tall height, Elizabeth swallowed and nodded.

"We'll see you later," Raquel said as she led Elizabeth away.

I turned to Dinah. "What was that? I've never seen Elizabeth that way."

Dinah leaned close. "I feel so dumb. I wasn't even thinking."

My eyes silently questioned.

"She's not allowed to talk about it, but she did open up once in prayer meeting. You must not remember."

"I don't, but if she said it in front of me once, would it be wrong if you shared?"

She wrinkled her nose. "I don't think so, but not here. Let's head over to the lab. Brothers Raphael and Benjamin will be at their meeting for a while."

Scooping up our cups, we moved out of the shop and toward the lab.

Once we were there, she exhaled. "Elizabeth loves Father Gabriel, The Light, and Brother Luke. She'll be the first to tell you that she has no regrets about coming to The Light, but once a year, around the time of her birthday, she gets sad."

I shook my head. "We don't celebrate birthdays." It was something I'd learned early on with Sister Lilith.

Dinah's lips formed a straight line. "That doesn't mean they don't happen."

I nodded. "OK, but why is she sad?"

"In the dark she has a sister, a twin sister. From what she said, they decided to follow Father Gabriel together, but after they did, her sister changed her mind. Elizabeth doesn't begrudge her sister that right. After all, we're all here because we want to be, but according to her, she never got the chance to say good-bye. Being twins and all, they were very close. She said she knows that the dark isn't death, but after Brother Luke told her that her sister changed her mind, Elizabeth felt a loss, as if her sister died. Like all of us, Elizabeth was ready to give up everyone and everything from the dark. She just didn't expect to give up her sister. It bothers her the most around her birthday." Dinah shrugged. "*Their* birthday."

"Wow, poor Elizabeth."

"Please don't mention it to her. Of course, we were all glad we could help, but Brother Luke didn't approve of her sharing. As you know, Elizabeth is usually the poster child of obedience. Being corrected for her plea for help reminds her not to bring it up again."

Reminders!

I nodded. "Thanks for telling me."

~

There wasn't much extra space within the walls of the community, but on the north end there were a few acres of woods with paths. When I first awoke from my accident it was the beginning of the dark season; now we were into full light. Though it never got warm at the Northern Light, it was considerably warmer near the end of June than it had been in November.

"Hurry up," Jacob teased as he ran ahead.

"I am," I said with a laugh as my feet pounded the hard dirt and my lungs filled with fresh air.

Lately Jacob had been required to be gone more, including for overnights. However, since the weather had warmed, whenever he was home, we tried to run together, either early in the morning, before our days began, or later, before dinner. The first time he'd mentioned running was the first time I remembered the memory I'd shared with Elizabeth six months earlier. Though Jacob said we'd done it regularly before, the first run since I'd awoken had been when the frigid temperatures finally broke in April. Two months later we were still running together.

Reaching the end of the woods, we came to the small grassy area just before the innermost wall. With the sky bright above, Jacob reached for my hand, and brought us to a stop. Looking out to the wall, I thought about running a longer distance. Not leaving, just having more room.

"I'd ask if we could go to the hangar and run where we had more space, but . . ."

"You'd rather not be eaten by polar bears?" he asked with a grin.

"Yes, that's a big deterrent."

"But," he teased, "just think how fast you'd run."

Smiling, I leaned into his embrace.

Now that I was no longer in what he'd called a crash course of remembering, I loved the way he was when it was just the two of us. His wit and humor made me laugh. That didn't mean he didn't correct me; it meant it wasn't often necessary.

As chosen, we had the responsibility of setting examples for the followers; thus in public we didn't show affection. However, running, especially in the early morning, allowed us more freedom. Despite being outside, we were alone. I rose up on the tips of my running shoes and kissed his cheek. "You know, I love this."

His features softened. "I know you do. So do I."

I sighed. "It's strange, but it's one of the few things I think I remember."

He kissed the top of my head and played with my still-short pony-tail. "Who knows, maybe more will come back."

With my hand still in his, we began walking and I confessed, "I'm not trying to be selfish, but I miss you when you're gone. I wish you didn't have to leave so often."

"You know that I . . ." He'd mentioned that he'd been given more responsibility but couldn't tell me more.

I nodded. "I know you can't say and I'm not asking. But I've been wondering about something else."

"You have? That inquisitive, intelligent mind of yours scares me. Sometimes you're too smart for your own good."

I didn't say more; instead I pushed my lower lip out playfully.

Jacob kissed my pout. With sparkling eyes he said, "Go on. What have you been wondering?"

"Before my accident, did we ever talk about children?"

Jacob's feet stopped. When I looked up, his face was ashen as if all the blood had drained from his cheeks. "We did," he finally admitted.

"We did?"

"We decided that we weren't ready." He began walking again.

"*We* did, or *you* did?"

"Sara, even though that is questioning, it was a decision we made together."

I sighed. "Then I'd like to ask to revisit *our* decision."

He kissed my cheek. Releasing my hand, with a smirk, he lengthened his stride, and called over his shoulder, "If we hurry home, we could practice." He shrugged. "I'd want to be sure we had it right first."

Though I shook my head, I couldn't stop the smile that pushed my cheeks higher. I was confident we had it right, but there was always room for practice. In no time we were running side by side, back through the woods, while long beams of light shone down, and back to the community on our way home. As our strides took us closer to our apartment, I thought about the babies at the day care. I'd been going there lately to meet with a female follower. Often I'd hold and rock one of the babies as she did the same and we talked. At first the small humans had seemed foreign, but now I found myself excited to go there. Their soft skin and sweet smell woke something inside me. Maybe it was like it was for Jacob with me. I wanted to love someone so much that I took full responsibility for them, like he had me.

As Jacob helped me out of my running clothes, I contemplated the birth control medication that I took every morning. The idea of *not* taking it seemed more and more appealing. I'd probably receive correction for making that decision without Jacob's permission, but I knew my husband. Once he found out we had a baby coming, he wouldn't stay upset; he couldn't.

Once we were both completely naked, Jacob captured me in his arms and pulled me close. Though our skin was warm and slick from our run and the temperature wasn't cool, as my breasts flattened against his chest, goose bumps peppered my flesh and my nipples beaded. The scent of desire mixed with his normal leather and musk created an intoxicating concoction. Inhaling, I inclined my face toward his and chuckled. "You know I need to be at the lab by nine and you need to be at Assembly."

"An advantage of living in the community is that our commute time is minimal."

I shook my head. He was right. We both could walk to our destinations in less than five minutes.

Loosening his embrace, Jacob tugged my hand. With a sly grin and his sexy, raspy voice, he said, "I think we both need to shower."

"I thought you promised me a practice session?"

"I'm all for killing two birds with one stone."

As Jacob turned on the rain of warm water, the muscles in his arms, back, and tight, bare rear flexed, causing my insides to liquefy at the magnificent man in front of me. Only fleetingly did I recall the showers after my accident. At that time my husband's touch had been gentle but aloof, and he'd obviously been fearful of hurting me. No longer was he tentative—in any way. I was his to have and claim whenever he desired. Yet when he did, it was always with complete reverence, always confirming that I was willing and ready for him. He needn't have worried; just the sound of his raspy voice and the way his eyes shimmered with lust had me ready. I couldn't recall ever having had an issue with being willing either.

That didn't mean I wanted to forgo foreplay.

Under the warm spray, I leaned my head back as moans escaped my lips. With my breasts willingly exposed to his masterful inclinations, I ran my fingers through his dark hair and pulled his mouth closer. His stubbly cheeks created the perfect abrasion as a fever burned within me, making the water sizzle as it fell upon our hot skin. The sensations he produced as his tongue and lips teased my hardened nipples sent pulsations throughout my body. In time his ministrations turned to nips as he cupped my behind and pulled me tightly against him, capturing his hardness against my stomach.

No longer just ready, my body ached with need as my insides tensed to a painful pitch. "Please," I begged.

A resonating growl filled the shower as his fingers probed, no doubt learning just how ready I was.

One finger, in and out, and then two . . .

I tasted his salty skin as my tongue and lips kissed and sucked his bristly neck. My grip on his broad shoulders tightened as my body mindlessly moved to his touch. When my breathing quickened and I was ready to quake in his grasp, his strong arms lifted me, pinning me to the wet tile. As he continued his erotic assault, eliciting my pleasure, pushing me toward the edge, my legs tightened around his waist. Just before I fell to ecstasy, his fingers disappeared, and we came together.

"O-oh, God, Jacob," I moaned. My core clenched as I adjusted to accommodate his size. The delicious stretch filled me, electrifying every nerve in my body. From my fingers to my toes, sparks ignited.

"You feel so good," Jacob said. "I'll never get enough of being inside of you."

"It's where I want you," I purred.

His lips captured mine, swallowing my words and sounds. Our tongues danced to the song our bodies sang. He created the rhythm, but the melody came from both of us. The combination of his resonating hiss, my whimpers of desire, and the slap of skin against skin filled the shower with the indistinguishable sound of two people moving in sync and lost in one another. Up and down we moved, until the sparks he'd ignited detonated.

As I teetered once again on the edge, my breath stuttered and my legs tightened.

He didn't stop. He knew my body better than I did. He knew the signs that I was close. Nipping my breast, he commanded, "Come on, Sara, come for me."

Fireworks, volcanoes, and stars falling from the sky paled in comparison to the explosion.

I cried out as every cell inside me discharged, leaving me shattered, held together only by his arms. Holding tight, I clung to his neck as wave after wave rippled through me, instigating uncontrollable spasms. Another thrust and I opened my eyes in time to watch his handsome face go from strain to utter bliss. Seconds later Jacob's eyes met mine and I smiled.

Seeing him like this let me know just how much influence I had over my husband. He was in charge of our lives, but I held power too. With a sly grin, I admitted, "I may not be able to stand."

His smile grew. "I've got you."

Exhaling, I said, "I think you'll have to let me go. I'm not exactly ready for work."

"Oh, don't worry." He kissed my forehead. "I'll help you with that too."

My kisses trailed from his shoulder to his chest as he lowered my feet to the floor. "How did I get such a helpful husband?"

"Lucky, I guess," Jacob said with a smirk as he reached for my shampoo.

I felt my cheeks rise, loving his expression and the tone of his voice. I didn't know—and couldn't ask—about things on the Assembly or with his flying, but I knew that lately he'd seemed stressed. It wasn't anything he'd said, more what he hadn't. The only thing he'd shared was that Xavier, the pilot who came to the Northern Light, had been ill and until there was a replacement, there was more work for him and Brother Micah.

Though I wanted to help, without being disobedient and questioning all I could do was help him relax. Running was one way, but

I witnessed his expression of pure bliss only after we'd come together as one. Even if I hadn't loved every second of making love to my husband—and I did—I'd willingly have given myself to see that.

As he massaged shampoo into my hair, the scent of flowers replaced the musk, and the warm water continued to rain.

"Do you think I could ever go away with you? So we wouldn't need to be apart," I asked.

Behind me Jacob tensed. I spun around, putting my small hands on his chest. "I'm sorry if I shouldn't have said that."

One side of his lips turned upward. "Don't be sorry for wanting to be with me. I love having you with me."

I exhaled and turned back around. "I know I have my job, and it couldn't be done without permission, but if I could, I'd love that too."

"No matter where we are, I love you." He kissed my neck.

As I craned my neck toward his lips, my heart was full. We kissed. "I love you too."

CHAPTER 32
Jacob

The small airstrip nestled in an unassuming valley of the Rocky Mountains was near Whitefish, Montana, as the crow flies. To drive from Whitefish to the Western Light required off-road vehicles. Accessing the Western Light's campus by land was almost as difficult as driving to the Northern Light, in Alaska. That was Father Gabriel's plan—keep them remote.

Passing the challenges Father Gabriel and the Commission had put before me, I'd finally earned the right to learn the specifics regarding the unique calling and activities of the Western Light. Not its fellowship or religious activities; those mirrored ours, as did the Eastern Light's. To the unsuspecting tourist or resident of the nearby ski towns, the Western Light was nothing more than a group of religious zealots who kept to themselves. Those people had no idea of the billion-dollar operation happening in their midst.

The Light's tax-exempt status, as well as the freedoms afforded by separation of church and state, kept all of The Light's campuses a mystery to outsiders. Father Gabriel might have stated in the beginning that God had given him visions of The Light's current greatness; however, even as an Assemblyman, I wondered if he had ever fathomed its current magnitude.

The Northern Light was the brightest, the most profitable. However, this campus, the Western Light, was doing better than many Fortune 500 companies, a fact most would disbelieve based solely on its outward appearance. The Western Light's deceptive facade was even more important than ours. Though driving to the Western Light was difficult, flyovers were much more common in Montana than Alaska.

While our community concentrated on the production of product, the Western Light had a twofold goal. Primarily it packaged and distributed the pharmaceuticals. Its second goal was production of Preserve the Light preserves. Most of the females of the Western Light worked around the clock—literally, in shifts—producing and canning preserves. The jams and jellies were made from local berries, grown in the community. The Western Light followers who weren't part of the chosen worked tirelessly in the gardens, the greenhouses, and the preserve plant, producing and canning. If they weren't working there, they were in the packaging plant, preparing the pharmaceuticals for distribution.

Production of the preserves never stopped. To the outside world it was the acceptable source of income for The Light. To those who were chosen to understand, Preserve the Light was the cover for the illegal distribution of pharmaceuticals created at the Northern Light.

Members of the Western Light's Assembly and Commission organized all the logistics. Father Gabriel had chosen the location of this campus perfectly, as Canada made the perfect market for low-cost medications. With Brothers Raphael and Benjamin's research, the pills and capsules created by the followers of the Northern Light were indistinguishable from those produced by mainstream pharmaceutical giants. Since Father Gabriel's followers worked not for worldly goods or money, but to maintain their standing in the community, production costs were minimal. The followers believed they were making the medications to help others.

They were, just not the *others* they thought.

When I first entered The Light, it was through the smallest campus, the Eastern Light, in Detroit. At that time I was led to assume that the production and sale of illegal drugs was the focus. Over the last three years I'd learned that illegal drugs were present, but only as the smallest piece of The Light's revenue pie. The crack and meth produced and sold through the Eastern Light were more of a diversion—Father Gabriel's backup plan. If the time ever came when the operation was discovered, each campus had enough paraphernalia to give the perception of a large illegal drug network. The investigation would satisfy the FBI and ICE, Immigration and Customs Enforcement. Though they would boast the closing down of a large illegal drug organization, in reality they would have stopped only the tertiary source of income.

Even the preserves made more profit.

Until my recent promotion, I hadn't known the breadth and scope of the entire operation, governed by Father Gabriel, on three campuses, with twelve Commissioners—four at each campus—and thirty-six Assemblymen—twelve at each campus. The hundreds of non-chosen followers were completely unaware.

Being Father Gabriel's pilot offered me access that others didn't enjoy. I had the pleasure of flying to Father Gabriel's mansion outside Detroit, though I was never invited up to the big house; I'd seen the telecasts that gave the appearance of mundane surroundings while knowing they were recorded in the large luxurious mansion. Keeping those secrets had been some of my first tests. Passing those first tests undoubtedly aided my rise to the chosen.

Sharing my knowledge wouldn't benefit anyone. It would result not only in my banishment, but also in the banishment of whomever I told, including other members of the chosen. I wouldn't nor could I risk that. Micah and I were the only followers at the Northern Light who saw things away from that campus.

Each challenge presented to me was a test or a stepping stone. The only way to access the knowledge of the inner workings of The Light was to succeed. With the addition of a wife, I hadn't only passed one of the final tests, I'd become vulnerable. That vulnerability made me less of a threat, less likely to breach The Light's trust.

That vulnerability was one of the reasons Sara's desire to have children could never be fulfilled. I couldn't increase my susceptibility. There was already too much at stake.

Over the past three years, each decision I'd made and each action had worked together to gain Father Gabriel's confidence. It also helped that Xavier had recently become ill. Since his replacement wasn't trusted enough to ship product, Father Gabriel decided that I was.

Finally I'd been entrusted to deliver a full order of pharmaceuticals. While I finished the transaction, from the depths of my jean pocket, my cell phone buzzed. Though the men before me were capable of appearing as nondescript as any member of The Light, they were undoubtedly professionals. Father Gabriel didn't use run-of-the-mill traffickers in his organization. This well-oiled machine required over-the-top devotion as well as top-notch performance. Kinks in the system were eliminated with the utmost proficiency. Without a doubt my phone could wait. I'd come too far to appear as anything other than completely devoted. I couldn't risk becoming an eliminated kink.

Under the cover of the hangar, my plane sat emptied of merchandise and fully refueled.

"Brother Jacob," said Brother Michael, the leader of this small party, offering his hand.

Though I was larger physically than Brother Michael, he'd been on the Commission of The Light from the beginning, and the aura of power and control that surrounded him was equaled only by that of Father Gabriel. He was one of the four founding fathers. While everyone within The Light was given a biblical name, only the founders had been given the names of archangels. According to Father Gabriel that was because, like the archangels, these three men and he were with God, welcomed into His holy of holies and His private sanctuary. Brother

Raphael at the Northern Light and Brother Uriel at the Eastern were also among the founders.

Brother Michael's power didn't come only from his aura; the two large men on either side of him helped to maintain his standing. They obviously were more than members of the unloading crew. As Brother Michael and I discussed the transaction, his bodyguards made no attempt to conceal the weapons strapped to their sides. If I were to guess, each had at least one more gun strapped to the inside of his ankle. I knew I would, if I could, but delivering the pharmaceuticals unarmed was one of Father Gabriel's requirements. He said it was a show of faith to our brothers.

Even if I could, I wouldn't have argued. This was Father Gabriel's show and they were his rules.

We shook. "Brother Michael, I'll be sure to inform Father Gabriel that you inspected the shipment personally."

"Yes, do that, and let him know I'm pleased." Michael tilted his head toward the big guy on his right. "Brother Reuben has something for Father Gabriel."

I looked in his direction, my gaze scanning his large muscular frame. Whatever he had for Father Gabriel wasn't a payment. Actual money never changed hands. Untraceable overseas accounts kept people like Brother Noah at the Northern Light extremely busy. The billion-dollar operation had the whole checks-and-balances accountability thing happening. It involved accountants from all three campuses. That was the one part of the business I'd yet to learn. As far as Father Gabriel and The Light were concerned, money handling wasn't my thing, nor was accounting. I was first and foremost a pilot.

Brother Reuben reached inside his jacket, suspiciously close to his gun, and paused. The dramatization was for effect. I was the new kid in this assignment and no doubt was being tested at every turn. I nodded with a cocky grin, letting him know I didn't fall for his ploy, all the while praying he wouldn't shoot me before I made it back to Sara. Finally he removed an envelope from his jacket and handed it to me. The outside simply read *Father*.

"Thank you, Brother Reuben," I said as I took the envelope and turned back to Brother Michael. "Brother, is there anything else you'd like me to pass along to Father Gabriel?"

"No, everything appears in order." He stepped forward and patted my shoulder, sharing a grin of amusement at my reaction to Brother Reuben's show. "I believe this will work well. Father Gabriel's judgment has not been proven wrong yet. I'm sure we'll be seeing more of each other."

"Thank you, Brother, I'm honored to have been chosen."

"As you should. You've reached an honorable level within The Light in a short time. Keeping our chosen with us and productive is our goal. To that end, my brother, have you seen the forecast? It's been changing by the hour. Perhaps it would be better if you chose to stay here until tomorrow. Northern Light is a far journey."

I smiled respectfully, hoping the new vibration of my phone would continue to go unnoticed. "Thank you. My flight plan has me landing at Lone Hawk for the night. I won't be heading back to the Northern Light until morning." I wasn't sure if his invitation was another test, but my flight plans were set and clear. Even with a small plane, it was best to have records of arrivals and departures. Lone Hawk was one of my favorite airports, privately owned with few questions asked. Even so, I'd never land my plane there with a full load of product. Once I landed, I planned to buy supplies. I wasn't looking for anything to draw attention, only normal living-type stuff, things to make my stop believable. Besides, it didn't make sense to fly back to the Northern Light in an empty plane.

I checked my watch.

Yes, right on schedule.

"Very well, Brother, safe travels."

Once I completed my preflight checklist and was in the air, I checked my phone. It hadn't vibrated since I'd spoken with Brother

Michael, and due to the recording device in the plane, I wouldn't be able to return a call until I landed at Lone Hawk. Above all, I didn't want to risk anyone from the Western Light questioning my ethics.

When the screen came to life my pulse quickened. I'd missed one call from Brother Benjamin's phone and five from a burner phone.

Shit!

After the incident with Brother Timothy and Sister Lilith, I'd set up an emergency chain of communication. The long and short of it was that I was simply gone from the Northern Light too much. Even if Father Gabriel believed that the entire episode with Brother Timothy and Sister Lilith had added to Sara's eventual success, I refused to allow anything like that to blindside me again. While having a wife increased my risks, with this system, I increased my odds. It was a gamble, but I believed Sister Raquel would help, if necessary.

According to the screen, it was time to cash in the chips.

Once I had the Cessna secured on Lone Hawk's tarmac, I searched for the manager, Jerry. He was a quiet man, friendly in an unobtrusive sort of way. I made my way back to a small apartment area near the back of the hangar. I didn't know if he lived there all the time, or just when he was working. Either way, I was happy when he answered my knock.

"Jacob, I saw your approved arrival on the CBP e-mail. Welcome back to the big city of Whitefish."

"Thanks, Jerry. I have some business in town and was hoping you had that truck here I could borrow. I'll bring it back in the morning, promise."

"No. Sorry. That piece of shit has seen better days." His furrowed his weathered brow. "But I'll tell you what, my old lady's Chevy Tahoe is sitting out back. She ain't going nowhere tonight. Besides, I've got my new truck if she needs a ride. You're welcome to take the Tahoe into Whitefish."

"Thanks, Jerry. I owe you."

"Next time you're here, you can bring me some of that Preserve the Light jelly. The old lady goes nuts for that stuff."

"I'll do my best," I promised, taking the keys he handed me and heading toward the beat-up Tahoe.

If Raquel had used that burner phone, it meant only one thing: trouble, serious trouble. As we'd agreed, I could answer a burner only with a burner.

Before checking into the cheap hotel, I stopped at a gas station and purchased two burners. Something in my gut told me one wouldn't be enough. Once in the hotel room, I plugged them both in and recalled the telephone number I'd hoped I'd never need to call. I waited for the ringing to stop. Once it did, I asked, "Raquel?"

"Brother Jacob, tell me she went with you."

"What are you talking about?"

Her voice changed to a low whisper. "Sara. Benjamin said you asked the Commission about her going with you on some of your flights. Please tell me that you did it, you took her without permission, and she's with you."

I had asked the Commission, but I sure as hell wouldn't bring her on one of these trips. The last thing I wanted was to have my wife around Michael's goons. I took a deep breath. "Raquel, I left her in our apartment. She was in the kitchen cleaning up after breakfast." I tried to hide the trepidation. "She couldn't have come. I didn't have the Commission's permission, and besides, she was scheduled to work in the lab today."

"I know. Benjamin was the one who contacted me and asked if I knew why she didn't show up at the lab."

No longer content to sit, I paced the confines of the ratty hotel room. "That doesn't make sense." I searched for answers. "Was she ill? Have you checked in on her?"

"I went to your apartment. When she didn't answer, I used my key. She wasn't there."

"And you're sure this doesn't have anything to do with Brother Timothy or Sister Lilith? God help me!" I wasn't even trying to hide my distress any longer.

"I really don't think it does. At least nothing approved by the Commission."

"Why?"

"Because Benjamin said it wasn't mentioned during Assembly. He didn't know until he got to the lab. Then when I couldn't find her, he took me out to the pole barn." She muffled a cry. "I prayed, but sh-she wasn't there. Oh, Brother, I'm so scared."

My left hand held a fist of hair as I tried to think. "Talk to me, Raquel. Tell me what you're thinking. Because right now, all I can think is I need to get in the damn plane and confront Timothy and Lilith, the Commission, hell, even Father Gabriel. If Timothy came up with another reason to have her banished, a reason to get at me . . ."

"Brother Jacob, what if *they* didn't do it? What if it had nothing to do with Brother Timothy?"

Her words reverberated in my head. "What do you mean?"

Raquel took a deep breath. "I should have said something. I just knew she wanted—"

"Tell me!" My desperation sounded foreign, even to my own ears.

"I know Benjamin will punish me when he learns I didn't say anything." She swallowed, suddenly sounding more composed. "And he'd be right too. I should have told him, but . . . Sara's my friend. I didn't say anything because I didn't want to get her in trouble with you or the Commission and because I understand her desire for children."

I couldn't make sense of her words. "What are you saying?" My voice echoed against the dingy white walls.

"A little over a week ago, she and I were talking. She told me that the two of you were discussing children."

I nodded. "We were. She said she wanted one, but I'm not ready, not with my new responsibilities." *Among other things that I can't explain.* "What does that have to do with anything?"

"Sara said she hoped you'd change your mind if she became pregnant." Raquel paused. "She confided in me that she stopped taking her birth control. She didn't tell you . . ."

Her words trailed away as I doubled over, holding my stomach.

I was going to fucking throw up.

"When? How long ago?" My questions were barely audible over the mayhem in my head.

She'd stopped taking her birth control. It wasn't just birth control. It was the drug that specifically suppressed her episodic memory while allowing new memories to form. It was the unique creation of The Light and the foundation of why she believed she was Sara while having no recollection of being Stella Montgomery.

"Over three weeks now."

My heart fell to my feet and tears blurred my vision. "Oh, God, do you think? Did she say anything to make you think she remembered?" I couldn't even say it: I couldn't say *her life before me, before us*.

I hadn't wanted a wife. I'd avoided it, but from the first time I saw her, before she was brought to the Northern Light, before Abraham and Newton hurt her, before I lied to her, I fell in love with her. I fought it with all my might. That day in the cold, her injuries were supposed to be worse, but I couldn't let him keep going. I had to stop him. And then when I arrived at the hospital and her neck was bruised, I knew that Newton had hurt her more, and I refused to leave her again. I couldn't.

Raquel was speaking. ". . . didn't, not that I picked up on at the time. Now I'm not sure. And there's one other thing."

I nodded, trying to quiet the voices in my head, trying to still the chaos. "What?"

"When we went to the hangar this afternoon, Brother Micah said that Xavier's replacement, Thomas, had recently left."

"What are you saying?"

"Well, he's been in the community, unlike Xavier. I've seen him a few times."

I couldn't speak. Sara wouldn't risk punishment by speaking to a man she didn't know. She surely wouldn't leave the community with a man. My head moved dismissively from side to side. No, she wouldn't do that. She was just talking about children, about wanting us to be a family.

God, I was really going to be sick.

Sara had said she loved me. That was the last thing I'd heard her say. "Raquel, are you saying Thomas may have taken my wife?"

"Technically, yes, but I'm wondering if it wasn't an abduction." Silence filled the room. Finally she continued, "Brother Jacob, I'm afraid Sara may have gotten her memory back, or at least some of it, enough to confirm that she wasn't Sara. Benjamin and I haven't said anything to anyone. We know what Sara's leaving will do to you with the Commission. They've already met today. Tomorrow Benjamin said he'd have to say something if Sara wasn't back. But when he does, Benjamin said he'd remind the Commission that you requested permission to take her.

"Do you think you can find her and bring her back?" Hope came back to her voice. "If you do, you can tell everyone that you took her. They won't know she left."

"Find her . . . ?"

My entire fucking world was gone, exploded, imploded. Years of work and sacrifice threatened, hell, most likely ruined. And while that should have been my focus, it wasn't, not really. All I could think about was Sara. If she'd remembered, if she'd figured it out, then she undoubtedly thought I was responsible and knew I'd lied—that we'd all lied. "Raquel, if she remembers . . . she won't want to see me."

"I remember."

I didn't know what to say.

"I've known for a long time," she continued. "When my memories returned, Benjamin told me the truth and I chose to stay. That's what I was praying would happen with Sara. Brother Jacob, Sara loves you."

"Sara, Raquel. *Sara* loves me. If you're right, if she remembers, then I'm not looking for Sara. I need to find Stella, and I suspect Stella hates me."

"Think about it. I remember the Eastern Light. What will happen if The Light finds her first?"

A cold chill ran through my body. "If you remember, then you know what will happen."

Raquel cleared her throat. "Brother Jacob, I'm completely out of line and I'll pray about it, I will. If you choose to tell Benjamin, I won't deny it, and I'll accept whatever punishment he deems necessary. But I'm breaking the rules by asking you to question everything, no, I'm begging you . . . please, go to Detroit and bring Sara home."

"How?" I asked. "How did you know she's from Detroit?"

"Because that's where I came from—the Eastern Light. Isn't that where we all come from?"

I took a deep breath. "If I make it back to Northern Light with Sara, we never had this conversation. If I don't, we never did. No matter what, it *never* occurred. You know what would happen if the Commission learned that you withheld information from them."

"I can't lie to Benjamin. I trust him."

I nodded. "That's between you and your husband. I'll pray too. Destroy the phone you used. I hope we see you again."

"Me too. Godspeed, Brother Jacob."

The line went dead, and seconds later the phone that I'd been holding in a death grip struck the wall and, leaving a dent in the plaster, shattered to pieces. Picking up the largest piece, I pulled out the battery and the small SIM card. Then I dropped the remaining parts and, using the heel of my boot, smashed them to bits. With each stomp I contemplated my next move.

I was so fucking close to finishing this, to reaching the end. Three long years. But . . . now . . .

I knew without a doubt where she'd try to go, whom she'd try to reach.

Nearly a year ago when I'd seen her in Dearborn outside Detroit, she'd been with *him*. She had been so happy, smiling and holding his hand. They had been walking through a sidewalk festival and laughing. I remembered the look I'd seen in her eyes. It took months before I saw a smile even close to the one she'd given to him. She'd trusted him.

Fuck!

Even if I did reach her before The Light found her, she wouldn't trust me. If The Light got to her first, there wouldn't be a question of what they'd do. My question was about Dylan Richards.

What would he do? Would he do it again? Would he do what he'd done last October? If she contacted him first, would he willingly hand over his girlfriend in exchange for his pathetic existence? Would he once again deliver Sara to The Light?

Once a dirty cop, always a dirty cop.

I knew that.

What I didn't know anymore was what kind I was.

Taking a deep breath, I recalled the number I'd memorized and stored away. I steadied my hand as I fired up the other burner phone and dialed. Running my fingers through my hair, I listened to the rings.

Special Agent Adler, my handler, answered on the fifth one. "Agent McAlister?"

"Yes, sir," I answered through gritted teeth.

"Fuck! We haven't heard from you in over two years. Tell me you're calling because you've got the evidence. Tell me to get the bureau ready, that you're ready for the raid. Tell me you've got what we need to bring Gabriel Clark down."

"Special Agent, we have a problem."

UNTIL . . .

Away from the Dark

Book Two of The Light series

ACKNOWLEDGMENTS

Thank you to everyone who believed in me: to my husband, children, parents, and friends. Without your support and love I would never have brought this new story to life. Thank you also to my readers. You have turned my world upside down and I will be forever grateful.

Thank you to my agent, Danielle. Your faith in my work has given me the courage to enter new challenging arenas. I would never have taken this leap if it were not for you.

ABOUT THE AUTHOR

Photo © 2015 Erin Hession Photography

Aleatha Romig is a *New York Times* and *USA Today* bestselling author whose work includes the twisty, darkly romantic series Consequences (which has graced more than half a million e-readers), Tales from the Dark Side, and Infidelity. Aleatha was born, raised, and educated in Indiana, where she reared three children of her own. She lives with her husband just south of Indianapolis.